ALANA KAY

SHADOW
OF DEATH

—RADIANT LEGACY BOOK TWO—

ISBN: 979-8-9912918-8-0 (Ebook edition)
ISBN: 979-8-9912918-9-7 (Paperback edition)

Library of Congress Control Number: 2025923295

First edition 2025

The story, all names, characters, and incidents portrayed in this production are fictitious. No identification with actual persons (living or deceased), places, buildings, and products is intended or should be inferred.

Cover by Miblart
Edited by EJL Editing

Published by Fate Unbound Publishing LLC
Los Angeles, CA

Visit the author's website at www.alanakayauthor.com for content details.

For everyone who shipped the loser in an early 2000s love triangle. I promise not to hurt you (like that).

SHADOW OF DEATH

RADIANT LEGACY BOOK TWO

ONE

Unspoken rule of the Fringes #8:
Adapt or die.

CELINE

My stilettos hammer the pavement in punishing, clipped snicks—darts burying their points in the wrong target. I can only hope they absorb the impact of my sprint through the musty Vegas streets without breaking to pieces.

He says he's your husband.

Imani's voice echoes in my head, the words bouncing around and knocking into each other like beads dumped on a tile floor. I can't hear anything over my loud pants, racing heart, and the screaming in my mind.

I flex my wings in case I need to fly—subtlety be damned. There's no reason to hide who I am if I'm about to die. It's never been my ambition to go out in a blaze of glory. I'm not some idiotic warrior with more testosterone than brains, but I have no intention of going quietly either.

A neon sign bathes my bare legs in a magenta glow as I jump over a piece of unidentifiable plastic garbage.

He says he's your husband.

It must be a trick. My father wouldn't have involved *him*. This is a ploy to throw me off balance and rock me emotionally. Dad's minions know they'll have an easier time cutting off my head if they score a hit to my heart first. It's already bruised to hell and humiliated after that ugly scene in the club. *Gods, what a monumentally terrible night.*

The flapping of wings grows louder, drowning out my thoughts. The impostor is gaining on me. *Shit.* Pushing harder, I sprint around a corner, gripping the rough concrete wall to help me make the turn without skidding out.

I left my keys at the Naked Fang in my hurry to get away from Ciprian the Liar and Alistair the Slut Shamer, but I can't let that stop me. I'll hot-wire my bike and ride so far away they'll never find me. Better to start over again than be back under Dad's tyrannical rule. It would be better to die than to go home. And I am not fucking ready to die.

Air caresses my bare back, a cool threat against my flushed skin.

A thud follows. Too close for comfort. *Faster, dammit.* Legs burning, I push myself harder. It's a mistake. My left heel snaps, the crack louder in the narrow alley than a gunshot.

Fuck. Fuck. My bike is too far. I've got to fight.

Spinning, I raise my fists—

No. It can't be . . .

I freeze. Every muscle in my body locks as I get my first glimpse of Malach in more than six years.

Tall, chiseled like someone carved him from marble, his hair falls in gentle waves around his ears. It's longer than I've ever seen it. Darker than the last time I saw him too—closer to brown than blond. His green eyes rake me from head to toe, cool and assessing.

He says he's your husband.

My heart throbs because it's a lie. Malach isn't mine. He never was. That dream, fantasy—whatever the fuck it was—didn't last long enough to become reality. How—no, why is he chasing me through the streets of the supernatural Fringes of Las Vegas?

"You have no business here," I tell him, using the language of our shared echelon. *Nish thatsha,* I think bitterly. Such a small, proud group—bound by our radiant words. Never again. Not for me. Even if my only good memories from home are staring back at me from his piercing emerald eyes.

Malach holds my gaze mercilessly. I stare back. I won't be the first to look away.

"Your business is our business, my truth," he says. "For as long as we both draw breath."

I blink in surprise. He said that in heavily accented English. But Malach hates learning languages. He always has. How and when did he add one from a foreign realm to his repertoire? None of this adds up.

Heavy footsteps pound as Luca careens around the corner; his pupils are stretched into horizontal slits. My heart flips. There's murder in his yellow eyes, but Malach can't die. I won't allow it. I open my mouth to tell Luca to stop or Malach to run. Something. Anything to fix this. But my head is spinning.

Breathlessly, I watch in slow motion as Luca's fist slams into Malach's left eye. An eye squeezed so tightly shut that the skin at the corner crinkles like the folds of an accordion.

He knows. About Luca's basilisk. *How does he know?*

They collide, trading dirty, brutal blows as they grapple in the street. Luca knees Malach in the gut, trying to catch his eyelid and peel it open. "Is this guy your ex or something?" he demands, landing a crushing blow to Malach's throat.

I wince at the bite of suspicion in his tone. Luca's trust in me is rattled, and I can't blame him. Malach showed up and claimed to be my husband. If the situation were reversed, I would be losing my shit.

My breath catches, inhales tripping over exhales until neither action brings me oxygen or relief. This is bad. Horrible. Completely out of my control. If I could wake up tomorrow and forget all about this terrible night, I would.

"Stop fighting," I gasp. Biting my lip, I use the pain to ground myself. "I need a minute. Please."

They ignore me.

Malach lands a heavy punch on Luca's forehead. Luca retaliates by driving an elbow into his ribs. I frown and hobble toward them, putting my weight on the balls of my feet to avoid my stupid, broken heel.

"Stop," I snap, sounding more like myself. They still don't listen.

Shoving bodily between them, I grab Malach's fist in one hand and cover Luca's murder eyes with the other, accidentally poking his right eye since I can't look directly at it.

"Fuck, Celine," Luca grunts.

"I'm sorry," I mutter. "But you weren't listening."

Malach unclenches his fist. His fingers graze my palm and send sparks shooting along my nerves as he attempts to hold my hand with his eyes closed. I squint at his stubborn, chiseled profile, lit by the fluorescent streetlight, and clear my throat. "Since you can speak English so well, why don't you tell Luca you aren't really my husband?"

"Why would I do that when the expressions on his face and yours were everything I hoped for?" Malach grins around his split lip, and I want to punch the dimple in his chin. I settle for shoving him instead.

"Because it isn't true," I remind him. "We never got married."

Malach frowns. "And our betrothal vows meant nothing to you?"

I grit my teeth. He knows I can't lie about this. This is his bull-headed way of backing me into a corner. "You're over-simplifying something more complicated than most of this realm's economies," I sputter. "We were kids, Malach. I wanted to make Mom happy, and I trusted you."

His eyelids flutter until he's staring carefully at the ground, his gaze fixed on my broken heel. "And have I ever betrayed that trust? Even for a moment?" There's hurt in the question. It echoes in my chest.

I shift my weight, wishing Luca weren't here to hear this. "I didn't leave because I didn't trust you," I admit.

Malach nods, satisfied with himself for pulling that truth out of me, then sighs. "I know why you left, my truth."

"Then you know I won't return," I whisper. "Why are you here, Malach?"

Luca stands rigidly at my side, tension radiating off him in cold, angry waves. Malach isn't moving either, but I can't sense even a glimmer of how he feels. When did he become so stoic? The silence stretches between us until I'm desperate for anything to break it.

"I'm here because I made a mistake," he says gravely.

My wings quiver, and the itch returns violently to the middle of my back where it's impossible to reach. Every instinct screams that whatever Malach says next, I'm not going to like it.

"Explain," I grunt.

He sighs. "You've been visited by other angels?"

"Yeah, Dad found me." I narrow my eyes. "He's been sending assassins. And orphans. Honestly, it's been a strange few weeks."

Malach glances at the night sky—carefully avoiding Luca—then meets my gaze, his green eyes glittering from the combination of street and starlight. "Your father did not send assassins or orphans." He clears his throat; the first sign of nervousness I've seen from him. "I brought the children to spare them from their fate. I knew you would help them."

"Wait. Slow down," I interrupt. "You dropped the orphans here? What about the killers? The ones who attacked Alistair and Luca—they were here to assassinate me."

Malach lifts his chin stubbornly. I'm immediately dragged back in time to our teen years, when that same mulish tilt used to set me off at least once a week.

"I acted as I saw fit," he says.

My wings smoke, wisps curling around the three of us as my anger grows. *Not now, dammit.* I flap my hand to clear the cloud building in front of my face.

Luca takes a step back, dropping his shirt from his bloody nose as he eyes my wings. "Deep breaths, baby," he warns.

Ignoring him, I get in Malach's face and jab my finger into his chest. "What did you do?" I demand. The itch is so bad, I'm pretty sure I'll regret even asking him the question.

"If they want to stand at your side, they must prove themselves worthy of the position," Malach grunts, crossing his arms over his chest.

I hold up my hand to stop him, a horrible suspicion taking shape in my mind. "Are you telling me you sent a dozen angels to attack Alistair and Luca as some kind of test?"

"Not a test: judgment," Malach says, his lips twitching. "Which they all failed except for the demon. He alone is worthy."

I see red as what's left of my patience vanishes and my wings erupt in sparks and flames. A headache pounds at the base of my skull.

How many betrayals will I be forced to swallow tonight?

Of all the people for Malach to judge and find worthy, he picks Ciprian? It's too outrageous to be real. I must be dreaming. Any second now, I'm going to wake up and realize this whole fucked-up sequence of events was a nightmare.

"Can I kill him, baby?" Luca asks, his voice vibrating with rage.

I'm so mad that I consider it, only shaking my head once terror douses the fire in my wings. They switch to knives and droop, the bladed edges scraping against the dirty pavement.

"Explain better," I insist, shuddering from the emotional whiplash as my mind races. "How did you find me?"

"Find you?" Malach runs his fingers through his hair, his pearl-colored wings fluttering. "I've always known you were here. That unregistered gateway off realm? I made sure you found it. I've come back over the years to make sure you were safe, but things have changed, Celine. Your father—"

"Is trying to kill me," I interrupt, wrapping my arms around myself and glancing in both directions. "I know that already."

Malach arranging the gateway, though . . . That's new information.

I think back, but my memories of that day are fogged by grief and fear. I remember stumbling away from my father's estate, vision blurry with tears, my heart screaming in agony. At the time, finding the gateway unguarded, with the tracking technology switched off, seemed like fate—a lucky break after a lifetime of cruelty.

Did Malach help me leave him?

He stares down at me, green eyes swimming with gods know what. "The guardians you killed here were under my command, Celine. They volunteered as a training exercise, knowing the risk. S'lach didn't know where you were until yesterday." I flinch at hearing my father's name spoken aloud, and Malach hangs his head. "He planted a spy within my legion who evaded my security measures."

The things Malach is telling me are the poisoned cherry on top of a toxic night.

I stumble away from him, forgetting my broken heel as my head spins. "Let me get this straight," I say. "You're telling me my dad wasn't after me before, but he is now?"

Malach nods, his face too grimly earnest to belong to a liar. I can tell even without using my magic. My heart sinks, then sputters irregularly in my chest.

"Hey," Luca says, lacing his fingers with mine and squeezing. "There's clearly a lot for you two to . . . catch up on, but we're not safe here. Those *guardians* are still in the street, and Alistair told everyone in the club that Ciprian is not only part of the enclave, but an *heir.* Casanell could be sending a team after us as we speak, baby. This is messy. We need to clean up and lie low."

Malach frowns at Luca, then nods, pursing his lips to whistle. A fluttering ribbon of gold magic leaves his mouth, hazy and smoke-like in the dim alley. It swirls in the air, gracefully looping twice before darting around the corner.

"What the fuck was that?" Luca demands.

"Still a showoff," I grumble.

Malach spreads his arms. "If a man cannot use his talents to impress his betrothed here, we should choose another realm to reside."

"I hate this." Luca tugs his hand free from mine and shoves hair out of his eyes angrily. "Did he kill his own men? Most of them were only knocked out."

I shake my head. "It's a clean-up trick. Malach's a glorified housekeeper."

"Mess is distasteful." Malach glances at Luca's lip piercing deliberately, and I shoot him a warning look. If he thinks he's off the hook for trying to have Luca and Alistair killed, he's lost his godsdamned mind. I'm going to kick his ass for that. Then I'll let Luca kick it again once I'm done.

I tense at the sound of shuffling, only relaxing somewhat as the remaining guardians stumble toward us, their eyes cast down. Their motivation for that—whether to avoid Luca's death stare or the curve of my ass—is anyone's best guess, but they resemble scolded puppies. Given who their boss is, their idiotic refusal to look at me in lingerie while attacking Luca makes perfect sense.

I can't believe Malach has been checking in on me. It's been six years since I fled the celestial realm and left him behind. *Why can't he cut me loose and move on?* My younger self screams with rage, hating that idea, and I tell her to shut up. She doesn't get it. She has no idea the things we've had to do to survive.

"Go back to the base," Malach orders the guardians in the common tongue. "I will return with my wife to her home." *Wait, what?*

"Stop calling me that," I snap, too distracted by the title at first to realize the bigger issue: his declaration that he's coming home with me.

I should put a stop to this. I should send him away. I should—

"I will not stop," Malach interrupts my train of thought, obstinate to a fault, even now, on turf where he couldn't be more out of place if he tried. "And you won't ask it of me unless you intend to formally rescind your vows."

Fuck me; I forgot. About his sincerity. How the simplest of words from him always sounded like promises. Time made my memories hazy, and now they're rushing in—sharper than ever—to hack through my defenses.

My stomach leaps to my throat, then dives. Physically, I'm standing in an alley, balancing on a broken heel. Mentally, I'm free-falling off a cliff and plunging into ice water, only to be dragged away by a current I'm not strong enough to escape. Emotionally . . . Fuck, I can't even go there.

So I retreat, kicking myself for my cowardice even as I back away on my wobbly, busted stiletto. Damn shoe—I feel just like it —ornamental and a godsdamned liability.

"I am here to prove that I, too, am worthy to stand at your side." Malach's eyes beg me to understand. "I seek your judgment, Celine, and yours alone."

I want to stop him. It's all I can do not to cover my ears. Doesn't he know his whispered words are tearing me to pieces?

My skin pebbles, and my wings wrap around me protectively as I resign myself to the inevitable pain that having Malach in my life again will bring. Because he won't stay. And I won't go back.

He looks away, and a flicker of intuition brings my itch roaring back to life. "There's more, isn't there?" I whisper. "You still haven't explained the kids."

"I will tell you once we're safe," Malach murmurs, glancing at Luca while avoiding eye contact. "As your shifter said, we're exposed."

Sighing, I lead them back to the Fang, my heel dragging through grime until it's as dirty as the other broken things in this alley. My mind races, each thought worse than the last: Malach is here. Ciprian is a fraud. Alistair is cruel. Luca is angry. And I don't have a clue how I'm going to bring order to this mess.

TWO

MALACH

Celine walks in front of me, her gait uneven. My eyes devour her, greedy for her attention after years without it. I would sooner gouge them from their sockets than look at another, yet I've led a monster to her door.

Not the monsters she invites to her bed, although I will undoubtedly have to get used to them, but the one who created her. The being who excised the full extent of his own twisted soul on those he should have died before hurting.

Killing Celine's mother was the catalyst for S'lach. With Valenara dead and Celine gone without a trace—I made sure of that—S'lach turned his darkness on the realm. Fools that we were, we let him dig in. Now there's no one left to speak against him, no one who can manage it but her. My truth. My Celine.

She's strong, powerful to the depths of her soul, and the only person who can stand in his way.

I would do anything to change that.

Celine's wings are bladed. Moonlight reflects off the metallic feathers, each as biting as a freshly sharpened axe.

A muscle in my jaw ticks. She tries to appear cool and controlled, but her wings tell the truth. She's upset. Stressed. My head aches, a tangled blur of desperate thoughts in half a dozen languages jockeying for position.

Her show of vulnerability destroys me.

Celine shouldn't have to bear another moment of her father's presence, yet that's exactly what I must ask her to do. For our people; not only the *thatsha* . . . but all seven *nish*.

As her betrothed, I want to shield her from S'lach and the pain of her past, but I swore vows on her word and mine. I must tell her the truth.

She will hate me for it. And I will deserve it.

"You're staring, Malach," Celine says, not bothering to turn around.

Blood rushes to my cheeks, and I'm grateful for the dark. "Can you blame me for fixing my gaze on your beauty when ugliness presses in from all sides?"

The basilisk snorts, an uncouth sound he should try to avoid.

"Luca," Celine warns.

"What?" He shoots me an angry look, as if it's my fault he got scolded. "It was corny."

I smile at him, enjoying his obvious jealousy, then replay his words and frown. "Corny?" I ask. "How can my compliment be compared to mere starch?"

"Corn is a vegetable, dude."

"I believe you're mistaken," I say kindly. "My research indicated that corn was a starch consumed by many Earth-dwelling cultures."

"Your research was wrong," Luca snaps, wiping a drop of blood away from his nostril. "I'm not a fucking scientist, but I know for a fact it's a vegetable. It grows on stalks."

"It's a starchy vegetable." Celine sighs. "Both of you shut up about it. Please. We have more important things to worry about."

"Of course," I soothe her. "But in the interest of my continued erudition, perhaps you could explain . . . I remain unsure how my remark can be seen as food-related."

Celine groans. "It's slang. He's saying it wasn't original. Think . . . umm, banal or something."

"Ah, that word I understand." I glare at Luca and imagine plunging my sword into his belly. "He sought to insult me."

Luca scoffs. "Where did you learn English that you picked up banal and skipped right over corny? William Shakespeare's greatest hits?"

"I don't think they call books greatest hits," Celine mutters.

"I can't take your word for that, baby." Luca nudges her with his shoulder, carefully avoiding her jagged wing. "Anika says you aren't smart."

"That's not fair!" Celine's lips fall open in outrage. "To Anika, no one is smart."

As they tease each other, strains of music and muffled voices spill into the alley. A door opens with a high-pitched whine. Someone laughs loudly. We're approaching the Naked Fang. After lurking outside their workplace for weeks, the sounds are easy to recognize.

I've never been inside, though.

My stomach flips. I ignore it, taking the opportunity to observe Luca. His mouth and mind keep up with Celine while his eyes scan our surroundings as if someone might jump out and snap his neck at any moment.

I hum under my breath, satisfied. My training is working.

As we approach the back entrance of the club, Celine levels me with a serious look. "Stay here. I'm grabbing my bag and keys, and then I'll be right out. Also, stow the wings. I don't want to have to explain . . ." She waves her hand at me as if I'm a problem she doesn't have the words to describe.

Gritting my teeth, I absorb my wings. Her frustration with me stings. "Anything you need," I tell her.

I'm sincere, but my words trouble Celine. She pushes through the door stiffly, leaving me behind. Again.

I'm here to win her back, yet it seems my truth has no interest in being won.

By the time Celine unlocks her apartment, my nerves are buzzing. Riding on the back of her bike was almost as exhilarating as flying. The humming engine, her warm curves pressed against mine . . . I never wanted it to end.

"Get comfortable, baby. I'll make a snack." Luca hangs his car keys on the hook as Celine stows her helmet. His pet name for her sets my teeth on edge. It's infantilizing. Celine is powerful, not a toddler stumbling over her own feet.

Celine glances between us as if she's weighing the odds of us coming to blows while she changes clothes, then nods and heads down the hall. The bedroom door closes behind her.

Luca studies me until the hairs on the back of my neck stand at attention. "Should I worry about vengeance?" I ask, returning his gaze steadily, determined to remain calm.

"She's been through a lot—"

"You think I don't know that?" I hiss, losing my temper even though I vowed to myself I wouldn't. He speaks of her with such familiarity; it makes my insides churn. All the time I've lost with her has been his gain, and he's grinding my face in the sacrifice.

"I don't have a fucking clue what you know, but tonight was bad. She's hurting. She'll hide it; she always does. If you stomp on her feelings, though, I'll have no choice but to—"

"Kill me?" I scoff. "How *corny*."

"That doesn't work for that," Luca mutters, yanking on the door of the coolant box. *Refrigerator, fool.* "If you're done cutting me off . . ."

I nod stiffly.

"Until I know whether your death would hurt her, you're safe from me. I won't do anything to cause Celine pain."

"She won't thank you for interfering." I cock my head as I study him. His knuckles are bone-white from his unforgiving grip on the refrigerator handle. With the other hand, he methodically removes an assortment of jars and boxes from inside and places them on the counter.

"I don't need her thanks, asshole." Luca slams the appliance door, and the contents rattle noisily. A strand of brown hair falls in his face, and he shoves it back. "I need her to be safe. And as happy as I can make her."

I grind my teeth. Luca speaks as though his place by her side is guaranteed. Where does he get his confidence? "You didn't pass my judgment," I remind him.

"I'm standing here, aren't I?" He grins, but there's no friendliness or humor in the expression. "Your goons can't say the same."

"Celine helped you." I cross my arms and wait for him to show the proper amount of shame for that weakness.

Luca only shrugs, smearing something bright yellow and pungent on a crusty piece of bread. "That's the part that's pissing you off, isn't it? Even sprinting in six-inch heels, she had my back without question. Would she do the same for you?"

My wings burst free, knocking one of his glass jars off the

counter. His hand darts out—faster than lightning—catching it before it hits the floor and returning it to the counter.

"We made vows," I snarl.

"Words mean nothing," Luca hisses. "I've watched out for her for years."

My fingers curl. "You know nothing of our words. Our traditions are sacred."

"We'll see, won't we?" He places meat and cheese between the bread, then returns to the refrigerator, his head disappearing inside. "Do you want a glass of wine, baby?"

"Red, please." My head whips around at the sound of her voice. Silently, I curse myself for allowing the basilisk to infuriate me. He wants to erode her trust in me. I can't allow that to happen.

"Okay, Malach," Celine murmurs. I shudder with pleasure at the sound of my name on her lips. "Tell me what's going on—don't leave anything out."

I glance at Luca, but he's focused on the plate in front of him.

"If you're sure you're ready . . ."

"Don't insult me." *Never, my truth.*

"S'lach has risen in power. He controls the *nish thatsha* with an iron fist, and through them, the entire realm. None stand against him. They fear—"

"His word." Celine scrapes a hand over her face and begins to pace. "How did the other leaders let this happen? He was powerful when I left, but plenty of the other *thatsha* hate him."

"He silenced some. The others didn't notice until his web was too tight to escape. He's become fixated with balance, enacting a birth application mandate over the lower echelons. Any angels born without permission are terminated."

"The orphans?" Her brown eyes swim with emotion.

I nod. "Many in the lower *nish* hide their offspring, but he has them hunted. The parents are punished, and the children . . . Many of them go missing as well."

"So, you take them first?" Celine raises her eyebrows.

"I tried to help as many as I could. S'lach must have been watching me more closely than I thought. I'm a wanted fugitive now."

A headache prods at the base of my skull. I ignore it.

"What about the plague that killed Anika's parents?" Luca asks me, handing Celine a wine glass filled to the brim and nudging the plate closer to her.

"It started as a simple sickness, nothing the healers couldn't handle, but S'lach forbade the *salum* from treating patients in the lower echelons. Thousands died in the name of—"

"Balance," Celine breathes. "He always was obsessed with things being exactly how he thought they should be. Control is everything to him."

"He cannot control you."

I mean it as a compliment, an acknowledgment of her strength, but her brown eyes flash with rage. "And I've paid for it a thousand times over." She gulps the wine, consuming half the glass at once. "I know why you're here, Malach."

"For you, my truth."

"Maybe," she whispers. "But the timing, your calculated scheming; it's too exact. You want me to go back. I won't do it."

My stomach flips. I glance away from her and focus on the counter. There's a single crumb on the surface. Luca wiped it down after making the food, but this piece escaped him, hiding among the faux stone patterns.

A million responses come to mind. I hold them all in. Instead of speaking, I incline my head in acceptance, feeling both awkward and anxious in her space. Our separation has made us strangers. The lone crumb and I are the same—the only two things out of place in Celine's home.

"You're disappointed in me," she says. "I see it on your face."

"Never," I insist, sweeping the crumb into the trash and facing her again. "No matter how much I burn to bring our people justice, you are my priority. You always have been."

Celine breaks our eye contact this time and examines her plate. "That's not easier to hear," she says. My insides tremble as her wingtips drag against the tile.

"Things will look better in the morning," Luca says, putting his hand on her shoulder.

Celine huffs a laugh, but it's angry and strained, a wire pulled too tight. "Do you believe that?"

"Sure." He smiles softly. "Because you'll be well-rested and we'll have coffee."

She tries to return his smile. Her lips twist instead. Celine covers her eyes, but not before I see how glassy and bloodshot they are. Luca pulls her into his chest. Jealousy burns inside me.

Celine clears her throat and drops her hand from her face. "I'll show you to the spare room, Malach."

"I know where it is," I admit.

"Right." She shakes her head. "Of course you do, because you broke into my apartment and made a huge mess. How could I forget? Once I've had some sleep, we're going to talk more about that. You painted my fucking walls, Malach—that's over the line."

I hide a smile, relieved to see her angry instead of sad. "It worked, didn't it?"

"And knocking on the front door wasn't an option?"

"Anonymity ran its course, but it was the optimal move at the time."

She gestures for me to follow her into the small guest room, stiffening as she looks at the strange bed-like contraption. The covers are neatly tucked, and it smells strongly of demon. An unzipped suitcase sits open in the corner.

"I'll get clean sheets." Celine brushes past me and marches down the hall.

Luca glances through the door. His eyes land on the suitcase, and he bites his lip. "She's bruised."

"I see that," I admit, keeping my tone neutral. "I'll tread lightly."

He takes in my thick leather boots, raises his eyebrows, then trails his dangerous gaze up my body before shaking his head. "Something tells me that'll be tough for you."

He leaves before I can tell him to keep his opinions to himself. I've not found him worthy of my Celine yet. Until I do, this uneasy truce between us is the best I can do.

THREE

UNSPOKEN RULE OF THE FRINGES #65:
PAIN IS A BITE THAT NEVER ENDS. INTERRUPT IT BEFORE
IT CHEWS YOU UP AND SPITS YOU OUT.

ALISTAIR

Moving from shadow to shadow, I search the streets, my fangs throbbing.

The hum of a nearby generator drowns out the muffled bass from one of the more popular Fringe bars. A rat the size of a loaf of bread skitters behind a dented trash bin plastered with fading flyers for shows that long ago lost any hope of catching my attention.

The only thing I care about right now is finding Ciprian Casanell—nightmare demon, enclave heir, and lying son of a bitch. I used to think our interests aligned. Now I just want to make him pay.

He's ruined everything. For me—for both of us, really—but fuck him and fuck how his involvement toppled everything I built with Celine.

Luca alone may survive the fallout from tonight, slithering clear of the rubble in the way of snakes. I know better than to expect his help; his loyalty lies with her. He won't risk the cold now that he's known her heat. I can't blame him for it.

My anger burns, but it isn't all reserved for Ciprian.

The things I said to Celine were unforgivable. The pathetic vitriol of a vampire so used to rejection that I cut her where I knew it would hurt most, desperate to wound her before she could wound me.

I want to blame it all on bloodlust, but that would be the coward's way out.

I learned to lash out long before I had fangs. No one ever noticed how hurt I was if I hurt them first. As a child, it was understandable. As an adult, I have no excuse.

Stopping for a beat, I listen to the Vegas night. The crackling hum of streetlights. The uneven footsteps of a drunk shuffling home. Then a grunt, a thud, a curse. I move toward the fight, upping my pace when I smell blood.

I'd recognize it anywhere. It's the same blood that saved my life. The blood that runs through Ciprian Casanell's veins.

I snarl as my eyes confirm what my ears and nose already know: he's under attack.

My arrival startles the three ragged shifters beating the shit out of him. They scatter.

I let them go, listening until their footsteps fade.

Ciprian's face is covered with blood to the point that I barely recognize him. He's curled in on himself, trying to protect his stomach. One arm is tilted at an unnatural angle. His breaths are slow and erratic, and I smell the sickly sweet bite of liquor beneath the coppery tang of his blood.

My fury cools. Moments ago, I wanted to see him brought low. Now, I just feel wired.

His face flashes through my mind—free of bruises and

swelling—as I remember the way he looked outside the club, begging me to let him explain.

I turned him down and told everyone in the Naked Fang who he was.

Why would his father blow his cover? Dimitri Casanell is hated on the Fringes—for good reason. Putting his own son in danger, though . . . What could his motive be? As for Ciprian, he had plenty of ammunition to bring us in. Why didn't he?

All the lies, his deception. I thought I knew why he did it, but so many of Ciprian's choices don't align with the enclave's methods.

Maybe he deserved this, maybe he didn't, but I need to hear his side to be sure. Not having all the information is eating me alive.

Ciprian stirs, twitching twice before going still.

I shift my weight as a hot breeze ruffles my hair.

These streets appear empty, but we aren't the only supernaturals on the prowl. I could leave him here and let the gods decide whether he lives or dies . . . except that doesn't feel right.

When an angel drove a sword through my gut, Ciprian fought to keep me alive. The memory cuts me deep enough to scar, the phantom taste of my blood mixed with his on my tongue as he desperately tried to replace what I'd lost.

I can't leave him this way. Gritting my teeth to ignore the lure of his blood, I slip his shattered phone into my pocket and hoist him over my shoulders.

Ciprian groans, the sound pitifully weak, and his ribs shift in an unnatural way.

He may not live through this beating even with my help. I find myself hoping he does. I have questions to ask him, and dead demons don't talk.

Ciprian survives the night, his breathing labored. His obsidian eyes, swollen and bruised, crack open as dawn breaks, and a mix of feelings rush through me. He looks terrible.

"A-Ali?" he gasps.

"Only my friends are allowed to call me that," I hiss, a muscle in my cheek ticking. "I have a witch's healing potion I can give you, but only if you answer my questions."

Even through the bruising around his eyes, I see him become cagey.

"I can't promise to answer everything," he wheezes. "There are people whose trust matters more to me than my life."

"Lucky for them," I seethe, the sting of his trickery slicing me again.

He sags against the couch, the skin at the corner of his eyes pulled tight by the swelling. But he doesn't beg for the potion.

The air conditioning blows a cool, synthetic breeze from the overhead vent. The faint hum is deafening compared to the silence of our standoff.

In the end, my curiosity trumps his stubbornness.

"Start at the beginning," I say. "Why did you come to the Fringes?"

Ciprian sighs. The noise is wetter than it should be. *Is he bleeding internally?* The cloying, primal smell of blood is so thick in the air of my living room it's impossible to tell. I lean forward and take another whiff. My fangs graze my lower lip, and the scraping sensation snaps me away from the urge to steal a taste.

If he dies, all my efforts will be for nothing.

"Roscoe"—he coughs—"was one of my father's guards. His favorite."

I stiffen. That's worse than we thought. Roscoe's death was unavoidable, but none of us had any idea he was that connected. "You were sent to find out what happened to him?"

Ciprian nods, and I frown. Why would Dimitri Casanell send

his son into the Fringes alone for a missing guard? It's reckless and dangerous.

A wry look eclipses the pain on Ciprian's face before it fades to a grimace. "Our family dynamic is"—another raspy cough—"pretty fucked-up."

In that, I can empathize. I'm an only child, but if Mum had been fortunate enough to have another before she was turned, she would have liked them more. I'm sure of that.

"Not the favorite son?" I taunt him, but Ciprian isn't bothered by my jab.

"Depends on w-who you ask." He shifts on my couch, then goes rigid, holding his breath until I'm waiting anxiously for his next gasp. When it finally comes, it sounds less like a stream of oxygen and more like water being sucked down a storm drain.

My palms prickle, and I'm moving before I make the conscious decision. I shoot down the hall, retrieve the healing potion from the locked box in my bathroom, and return before I can change my mind.

Favorite son or not, if Ciprian Casanell dies on my couch, I'll be held responsible. I'm not performing a kindness for a traitor; I'm saving my own skin.

Unstoppering the vial, I curse his shaking hands and bat them away. Once the glass touches his lips, I pour the liquid into his mouth. He chokes. Bubbles—stained a streaky pink from his blood—run down his chin, but he manages to swallow most of the tonic.

"Thanks," he wheezes.

"I'm not doing it for you," I snap. "I need to know what's going on so I can protect her."

"That's cold, Ali." Some of the pain leaves Ciprian's body, and he raises one pale eyebrow as he meets my eyes. "I didn't tell Dad what happened to Roscoe. I planned to take Celine's secret to the grave; I just didn't expect to find myself climbing in this soon."

That surprises me, but I don't show it. Instead, I search his face for any signs of deception. I'm not a lie detector like Celine, but I'm typically good at judging intent—at least I was until I met Ciprian.

"Why would you conceal it?" I ask.

He scoffs. The sound is raspy, but it's livelier than his previous death rattles. "Really? Why would I protect Celine from the bullshit consequences of killing an asshole? You're smarter than that, dude."

"Please," I drawl, rolling my eyes. "You think I believe you severed a lifetime of allegiance over one kiss? How do you expect me to swallow that?"

Ciprian sighs, his thick eyelashes fluttering against his bruised skin. When he looks at me again, there's steel in his bottomless black stare. "I can be loyal to both."

"No," I hiss. "That's where you're wrong, Casanell. Here in the Fringes, we know the consequences of split loyalty. If you can't make the choice, we'll make it for you."

Anger swirls in my belly, although my bloodlust has settled to a manageable level.

Anyone dumb enough to bring their executioner to bed with them deserves what they get, and my angel is far from dumb. She won't forgive him for hiding his identity.

"If that's how you feel, why didn't you let those guys finish the job?"

There's no self-pity or curiosity in Ciprian's question. It's more like he's delivering a prompt—a barbed, poisonous harpoon meant to penetrate my subconscious and rot my brain from the inside out.

I shove to my feet. "You have until sundown to leave my apartment. If you're still here then, I'll be happy to fetch my shovel and bury you."

Ciprian nods, his shoulders dipping with . . . relief? I can't tell.

I don't trust my ability to read him anymore—the duplicitous enclave heir who thought he could fit in on the Fringes, and nearly succeeded.

I leave him on the couch and go to my room, satisfied he's not likely to die or get up any time soon. My entire apartment reeks of blood. And Celine's scent on my pillow is almost gone. I stop in front of the vent and let cold air blow directly on my face.

Everything's wrong, but if I can clear my senses, maybe I'll be able to see the best way forward.

I believe Ciprian's story. It lines up with what his father's man said outside the Fang, and his infatuation with Celine would be hard to fake.

His truth comes too late, though. We'll never be able to trust him again.

Bridges burned around here never get rebuilt—that's the way it is. The sooner Ciprian accepts that, the more likely he is to escape the Fringes with his life.

FOUR

UNSPOKEN RULE OF THE FRINGES #12:
TIMING IS EVERYTHING
KNOW WHEN TO RUN AND WHEN TO FIGHT.

CELINE

Emotions suck. Caught in the middle of the storm, I lay in my bed, feeling like someone tied me to a stake so the wind could peel the skin from my bones.

I'm strong, but I'm not strong enough to let this go.

I don't even know how.

My apartment feels crowded and empty at the same time. Alistair, Ciprian . . . I don't want them here, but every time I think about the fact that they're gone, I want to cry. Both hurt me in different ways, but Malach's revelations must be my priority.

Father will come for me. The attacks we went through before weren't even assassination attempts; they were Malach's stupid testosterone-fueled schemes to test his competition.

He shouldn't have bothered. They showed their true colors,

eventually. Only Luca put his money where his mouth was . . . and only the gods know if that will last.

I roll my head to the side. His handsome face is slack with sleep except for the furrow in his forehead. How long will Luca stick around under the weight of Dad's wrath? He could leave or be taken from me at any time.

His features blur, and my tears fall silently. Tomorrow, I'll put on a brave face and come up with a plan, but tonight, I let myself cry.

For Ciprian, who made me laugh, fed on my deepest fears, and hid his truth from me.

For Alistair, who made me feel like the only person in every room but saw me as an object all along.

And for Malach, the boy who knew all my secrets. He's become a man I don't recognize.

Father's angry face flashes through my mind, pink and mottled with rage. The vein on his temple pulses as he screams, a jagged lightning bolt of boiling blood.

Now that he knows where I am, he won't rest until I'm gone.

I couldn't beat him before; what makes me think I have what it takes now? Independence? This life I've created? They mean everything to me but are laughable in the face of his power. Puny, insignificant. Naïve even. Deep down, S'lach and I both know I'm destined to be gobbled up and spat out by life. Just like Mom.

Mostly, I cry for the little girl who was never strong enough. I can only pray that the woman she's become has what it takes to defeat a monster.

Crying is cathartic, but it's hell on the eyes.

I wince at my reflection as I brush my teeth and wash my face, applying a dab of witch cream to the puffy skin around my eyes. If Ciprian were here—*no, don't think about him.*

He's not my friend; he's enclave. And I told him I killed Roscoe.

They could come for me at any time.

With this many variables, I only know two things for sure: one, now is not the time for romance; and two, I've got to get back in fighting shape.

Even though Malach's goons weren't trying to hurt *me*, my stance with the sword felt unfamiliar. And my run with Luca a few weeks ago proved I'm not at the top of my game. Dancing has made me strong and agile, but I need to harden up. It's been years since I took a punch. That's got to change.

Luca stumbles into the bathroom. He yawns and kisses my neck, then drops his underwear and steps into the shower. I glance at his sculpted ass in the mirror and mentally smack myself. No more distractions, no matter how delicious.

"Do you know how to contact the owners of the Mouth of Hell?" I ask.

Luca pokes his head around the curtain, and I meet his narrowed hazel eyes in the mirror.

"Why?" he asks, his voice suspicious.

"Someone needs to tell them their beer is subpar," I deadpan, propping my hip on the lip of the sink then rolling my eyes. "Because I want to fight. Why else?"

His head disappears behind the curtain again, and he sighs so loudly I hear it over the running water.

"Do you have something to say, Luca?"

The quiet is getting to me. He took Malach's arrival in stride . . . hasn't mentioned Alistair once . . . and reacted to Ciprian's identity reveal as if it was the least interesting thing he's ever heard. At first, I thought he was trying to give me space to process my feelings without adding his own to the mix. Now I'm not sure.

"I don't know the owners of the Mouth of Hell." Luca finally answers my original question. I wait for him to say something else, but the silence is thick.

That's it. Storming through the steam, I brew a cup of coffee, pour it into a silver, insulated tumbler, then stomp back to the bathroom. I shove the tumbler into the shower, avoiding the pounding spray, and wait until he takes it from my hand.

"Thanks," Luca grunts, "but you forgot to detach the strings, baby."

"Don't fuck with me," I snap. "I need you caffeinated."

"Why?"

"Because you're tiptoeing around me like I'm fragile or tyrannical, and I don't know which is worse. Knock it off or I'm going to overreact."

Luca snorts a laugh. "Okay, we can talk."

"Good." I pat the side of my head and wince when my hand comes away damp. "The steam is ruining my hair—I'll wait for you in the bedroom."

I get dressed, yanking on some stretchy clothes to work out in, and pile my hair on top of my head in a high, tight ponytail. It'll give me a headache if I leave it this way all day, but it's perfect for what I have in mind. By the time Luca strolls into the bedroom with a towel slung low around his hips, I'm more than ready to have this out.

He puts the tumbler down on my bedside table and eyes me warily. "You look like you want to fight."

"And you look like you're scared of that," I retort, getting straight to the point. If Luca is afraid to be honest with me . . . We can call it now. A fun, sexy romp and nothing more.

"I won't let you push me away, Celine." Luca plants his hands on his hips, and a bead of water runs down the side of his neck. "I want to give you everything you want, but I won't be your opponent."

"I want you to say what you're thinking," I say. "Alistair and Ciprian do the calculating, but you—"

"Are too stupid to be strategic?"

"I don't think you're stupid," I insist, sinking down on the bed. "But I do count on you to tell it to me straight. Whenever you go silent, I get worried."

He raises his eyebrows. "You want to know everything I'm thinking? About the last twenty-four hours?"

"Yes," I say. "I need your opinions; I'm sick of mine."

"Okay, baby, remember that you asked for this." Luca begins to pace. "First, I think you should talk to Alistair. Give him a chance to apologize."

I grit my teeth. "What else?"

"We also need to hear Ciprian out. You and Ali exploded on him at the Fang, which was understandable and also dumb. He knows about Roscoe, and now we're in the dark about where he stands."

My shoulders sag. "It was an ugly fight."

He glances at me, and his face softens. "It *was* an ugly fight, but they're both gone . . ." Luca snaps his fingers. "Just like that. Then, some dude from your past shows up with all the answers, calls himself your husband, and manages to worm his way into your spare room? I don't like it, Celine."

I blink as he rakes his fingers through his wet hair. Dammit, I asked for this, but I hate it. Even hearing him say Ciprian and Alistair's names out loud is upsetting.

Shooting to my feet, I block his path with my body. "Stop," I whisper. "I changed my mind. I don't want to talk about either of them."

Luca grabs my shoulders, his grip painfully gentle. "You've got to, baby. Pretending last night didn't happen—shit, that the last few weeks didn't happen—that's not healthy. You're hurt, and that's okay. Anyone would be."

"Do you want to hear me say I'm an idiot?" I whisper, a telltale burn searing the back of my nose. "I couldn't even tell Ciprian was a phony."

"That sounds like someone else talking." Luca's voice is too soft and understanding. I have to look away. "Alistair was mad because he fell for it too, baby. He exploded. There's no excusing it, but you can't take what he said to heart."

I pull free of his hold and wrap my arms around myself. "I've known who I am all along," I insist. "Alistair is the one who couldn't handle what he saw when he got a closer look."

Hissing, Luca yanks me fully into his arms. His hug is tight, and I know I'll feel it long after he lets go. "I don't think that's true," he murmurs, his breath tickling the skin below my ear. "Can you let him make it up to you if he tries?"

I consider that, and my wings twitch as annoyance overtakes my hurt. "Do you see him beating down my door?" I demand. "Alistair knows where I live."

"The sun is out," Luca says calmly.

"He has my phone number, smartass."

"Don't forget, I'm on your side."

"Doesn't sound that way," I grumble, knowing full well I'm being petty.

Luca isn't bothered. He rolls his eyes and kisses me, his tongue slipping through the seam of my lips. I kiss him back, wishing—not for the first time in my life—that my emotions weren't rigid. I feel everything too hard. It makes forgiveness difficult and forgetting impossible.

I dodged Luca's question earlier, but the truth is I don't know how to let Alistair make it up to me. Not when his hateful words and angry red eyes are burned in my brain and playing on repeat.

Determined to put it out of my mind, I slide my fingers under

Luca's towel and—someone knocks. Luca groans and glowers at the door. His hazel eyes flicker yellow, and I wonder if he's trying to turn Malach to stone through the flimsy wooden barrier.

"What?" I ask, trying to keep the frustration out of my voice.

"I require nourishment and am unable to identify the items in your food closet."

A shiver runs down my spine. I don't know if it's Luca's hard dick in my hand, Malach sounding all grown up, or the fact that he almost certainly wrecked my carefully organized pantry.

I uncurl my fingers reluctantly and reach for the door, but Luca reels me back in, licking into my mouth with another heated kiss. "To hold me over," he says, "while you babysit your hubby."

I groan. "Not you too."

"It's funny because of your reaction, but . . ." Luca winces. "I don't want to be your guy on the side. If you decide to get rid of me, be gentle, baby."

I gape at him, surprised to hear him voice insecurity and gutted by the thought of not having him with me. I already lost the others; I can't lose Luca too.

"Group relationships are common in the celestial realm," Malach says through the door. "But you must prove yourself to me or I won't consider your submission."

"Submission? The fuck?" Luca brushes past me and yanks the door open. "If you're waiting for me to submit, you'll be waiting a long fucking time, motherfucker."

Malach peers at me, ignoring Luca entirely. "He's fond of that expletive, isn't he?"

"Explain the submission part," I say, my lips twitching as I hold in a giggle.

"His submission: a formal declaration and intent to bind himself to you."

The laugh bubbles out of me before I can stop it. "Application, Malach. You want him to apply, not submit."

"If you say so," Malach mutters, leveling Luca with an appraising stare.

Luca rumbles low in his throat as he looks at me. "I'm not doing that shit either. What Celine and I have is between us, and I've made my intent crystal clear." He focuses back on Malach. "Where she goes, I go. I will want her forever, and you can judge that however you want."

"I'll consider that your application," Malach says. "Now, about the food closet."

"It's a pantry," I correct him automatically, an idea taking shape. "I'll help you find something you'll like on one condition: stop me from getting past you."

As soon as the words leave my mouth, I charge, pushing Luca to the side and feinting right and left as I face off against Malach. My hallway is narrow, and he's about twice my width. I can pretend I'm going around him all I want, but the only way past my childhood sweetheart is straight through him.

I rock to my left, pretend to be off balance, then kick Malach in the gut with my full strength. He skids backward . . . a whole foot. That same kick would have sent anyone else flying.

Letting someone win is a foreign concept in both the Fringes and our home realm. Malach would consider it shameful to throw this fight, which means I'll have to beat him fair and square. The challenge gives me a rush of energy I've been missing for years.

He reaches for me, and I rock back, losing a few inches of hard-earned ground. It's smart to dodge, though. If I let him get those tree limbs he calls arms around me, I'll have to destroy my apartment to get loose.

"You're out of practice, my truth," Malach observes. His voice is pragmatic, and I punch him in the side as payback. I may not be as strong or practiced at sparring as I used to be, but I'm a lot more flexible than I was before.

I glance to Malach's right side, then spring the other way.

Planting one foot on the wall and the other between his ear and shoulder, I shove him, creating enough room to get by.

The only thing standing between me and victory is five simple steps.

I only make it three.

Malach snakes his arm around my waist and tries to toss me back, but I latch on to his forearm and take him with me. We collide with the drywall, Malach planting his feet just in time to keep us from going through it.

He pins me there, using the entire length of his body to hold me in place.

A ripple of awareness runs through me. My blood runs hot, and a telltale burn stirs low in my abdomen. Malach gasps—no, that's me. Absently, I hear my breath coming in loud, ragged pants. *Good gods.* My reaction to him is mortifying. I can only hope he thinks I'm winded.

"You can yield at any point," Malach says. "Your skills arc still there. You'll be back in fighting shape in no time, my truth."

There's something about the gravelly way he assures me I'm not permanently pathetic that makes me furious. Suddenly, the most important thing in the universe is proving to Malach that I'm still the best fighter he knows.

I grind my ass against his crotch, a move I've never once thought about using in combat with him before, then drive my elbow into his gut. He freezes against me, and I spin, shoving him into the opposite wall before darting into the living room.

When I turn around to celebrate my victory, the words dry up on my tongue.

Malach hasn't moved an inch away from the wall. One hand supports a painting we must have dislodged during our scuffle. The other is fisted at his side. And his eyes . . . they burn. Pure, vivid green. He rakes them over me hungrily. It's as unfamiliar and dangerous as grinding my ass against him.

This is uncharted territory for us, and judging by his slack-jawed expression, Malach is as stunned by his body's reaction as I am by mine.

"I'll find you some food anyway," I say, clearing my throat to banish the breathlessness. "Let me show you my organizational system so you don't mess it up."

Malach grumbles in the language of his specific *thatsha* blood-line. I used to understand it, but I've been gone too long to pick out the individual words.

Heart pounding, I show him the pantry and let him taste my assorted cereals until he finds one he likes. He chooses a bright blue box of sugary corn flakes, the sickeningly sweet ones that Ciprian snuck into my last grocery order. I wince.

Grabbing a loaf of wheat bread for myself, I toss a couple of slices in the toaster and do my best not to think about the two-faced demon. Luca wants answers, and I guess I do too, but not yet. I'm not sure I can stomach an explanation until everything else settles down.

"Baby, you need to hear this." Luca's voice pulls me out of my thoughts as he enters the kitchen. He's chewing on his lip ring, fingers clenched around his phone.

My heart leaps to my throat. "What now?" I ask, slumping against the counter. Gods above, I'd rather get slapped in the face once an hour than keep fielding constant surprises.

"I talked to Alistair." Luca runs the fingers of his free hand through his damp hair. "He can get you in touch with the owners of the Mouth of Hell . . ."

"That's good news," I say, ignoring the slight pang of embarrassment from having to ask Alistair for help. When Luca's tension doesn't ease, I freeze. "That's not all, is it?"

Luca shakes his head slowly and sighs. "Ciprian was attacked last night."

FIVE

UNSPOKEN RULE OF THE FRINGES #111:
SUPERNATURALS CAN LIE, YOUR REFLECTION CAN'T.

LUCA

Celine wipes her face of all expression, and my heart sinks.

She's taking this hard. Will she ask about him? Should I make her? The belligerent avoidance is stressful, and I'm not sure how to handle it.

"Is he alive?" Malach asks what she refuses to voice.

He's shoveling cereal from his bowl like it's going to run away if he takes a breath. I scratch my chin. Is the himbo angel eating Frosted Flakes? I had him pegged as a Wheaties or plain oatmeal guy . . . maybe porridge, whatever that is.

Remembering his question, I nod. "Alistair ran the attackers off, but Ciprian is in bad shape."

"Alistair rescued him?" Celine scoffs and angrily bites off a hunk of plain toast. "After the way he lost his shit at the club, I would expect him to be doing the beating."

"He was mad," I remind her, running my fingers through my

hair and wincing when they catch in a tangle. "Alistair gave him a healing potion and told him to be gone by dark."

"If he was in bad enough shape to need a healing potion, can he do that?" Celine drops her half-eaten toast, fury sparking in her brown eyes. I can't tell who she's more pissed at: Ali for telling him to get lost or Ciprian for getting jumped in the first place.

"My magic found the demon worthy," Malach says.

We both glare at him, but he doesn't flinch, ignoring us and shoveling a massive bite of cereal into his mouth. The silence in the kitchen is interrupted only by his nonstop crunching. Fuck me. Is that bowl bottomless?

"Anyway," I hiss. "What do you want to do, baby?"

Celine shrugs. "See if Alistair can set up a meeting for me at the Mouth of Hell. I think there's a fight scheduled for later this week. I could try out if they want."

Internally, I groan. She's going to pretend I never mentioned Ciprian or the attack. I'm not sure if I should push her to talk about it or lay off.

As for the fight club, I get why she wants to train. If my dad decided to have me whacked, I would do the same, and the Mouth of Hell is about as organized as supernatural fighting gets around here. It's also dangerous as fuck. Celine could get hurt.

Although watching her grapple with Malach was eye-opening. And hot. I've never seen her move like that, all controlled strikes and sensual violence. Her dirty move may have surprised Malach, but it turned me on.

My blood only returned to more useful parts of my body during my tense conversation with Ali. He spat every word at me. The calmer I was, the angrier he became. Between him and Celine, I'm not sure who's trying harder to avoid addressing the obvious.

Thankfully, my basilisk is lying low. If Alistair had taken that tone with me another time, it could have gotten messy.

"I'll look into it," I tell Celine. "Is there any yogurt left?"

Her head of bright red hair disappears inside the fridge, then pops back out. She slides a cup of peach yogurt across the counter, and I smile and thank her.

"Malach." I force myself to say his name without using a tone. He looks up, pinning me in place with his intense stare. "Do you have any reason to believe Celine's dad will attack soon?"

He considers the question, his square jaw working rhythmically as he chews and swallows. "No. I suspect S'lach will wait until he believes he cannot fail."

"That's—well, it's fucked-up," I say. "But it's also good news for us. Do I need to order weapons?"

I don't know how to do that, but I'm confident I could figure it out. A few pistols would be easy to find, except gunshots are the opposite of covert, and we've already made enough noise by killing Roscoe outside the Fang. The last thing we need is to give the enclave another excuse to punish us.

"I will provide the steel," Malach says, chasing the final soggy flake around the milk in his bowl, then triumphantly shoving it into his mouth.

I shake my head, remembering how many blades his henchmen had. We've killed a few of Malach's crew. It stands to reason he's holding on to some swords without owners.

My basilisk lifts its head warily, sensing rising tension in the room.

It's all coming from Celine.

"Could you teach me how to sword fight, baby?" I ask, hoping to coax a smile from her. "I've always wanted to try fencing."

"She won't be able to sink to your level." Malach's Adam's apple bobs as he slurps a spoonful of milk.

Celine frowns. "Malach, that's rude."

"It's no indictment of his ability as a student," he argues.

"Rather, a criticism of your teaching skills. You lack the patience to instruct a beginner."

I choke on a laugh as Celine sputters angrily. "You're talking a lot of shit for someone who's been lurking in dark corners trying to murder his rivals."

Malach climbs calmly to his feet. "I told you; it was judgment —do you doubt the truth of my words?"

She presses her lips together, then shakes her head.

His face softens. "If you continue to consider your lovers rivals, you'll force them to fulfill that destiny." Malach calmly collects his bowl—bone dry, without a flake in sight—and crosses to the sink to wash it.

I glance at Celine. Hands clenched, her wings are smoking. She pushes away from the kitchen counter and heads down the hall.

I wince as her bedroom door slams.

Malach glances up from the sink, and I study his profile. He doesn't seem upset, but I don't know his tells yet. He could be the most stoic guy in the universe for all I know. Just because Celine can't hide her emotions to save her life doesn't mean other angels have the same issue.

"The venom will consume her if she invites it in," he says quietly.

I raise my eyebrows, and his shoulders sag. The massive, pearly wings droop until the ends graze the kitchen tile.

"S'lach is toxic. Especially for her," he murmurs. "He drove her from her home, from any chance of happiness with me. I don't begrudge her for building a life here, but she must excise the wound before it can fester."

I blink, tempted to press him for more. While I know everything about Celine's present, Malach is part of her past. He can give me a clearer picture of the woman I love . . .

"I've known her for years," I say. "But she's only recently

mentioned him to me at all. Those memories . . . she's kept them buried for a long time."

Something unknown flickers in Malach's eyes. "She's strong. I must believe it's not too late." *It can't be.* He leaves that last part unspoken, but I hear it anyway.

He leaves me alone in the kitchen, and I take the opportunity to think. If Malach is right and Celine's avoidance is destroying her, I'll have to make her face her demons—even if she hates me for it.

"Stay with Luca at the bar and keep your wings tucked," Celine says for the tenth time, climbing into my passenger seat and giving Malach no choice but to wedge himself in my compact backseat.

He does it without complaining, tilting his head at an awkward angle to avoid banging the roof. "I will remain with your shifter. Stop fretting," he grumbles.

"I don't fret." Celine tosses me a disbelieving look, and I focus on the road so she doesn't see the smile I'm fighting. Fretting isn't the word I would have used, but damn if it doesn't fit.

"Malach," she says, glancing at him in the rearview mirror. "You know what I do for work, right?" Oh boy. It's smart of her to clear the air, but if he says one rude thing to her . . .

"You use your body to sell a fantasy."

"Yeah?" Celine asks, her tone wary. "What do you mean by that exactly?"

Silently I curse Alistair for feeding her worry with his bullshit. If he shows up here tonight, I may knock those sparkling white fangs loose on principle alone.

"You allow your patrons to imagine a reality in which they

might be allowed to touch you." He sniffs. "You are generous to allow them to pretend. It's charity work on your part."

I chuckle, low key obsessed with Malach's definition of stripping. "Couldn't have said it better myself."

Celine shifts in the passenger seat, and from the corner of my eye, I watch her press her flushed cheek against the window. I squeeze her knee and turn the air conditioner on.

We'll get through this one day at a time. Together.

Our shift at the Fang starts normal, a standard weekday afternoon. Not dead, but certainly not busy. I'm fine with that. An easy day at work is exactly what we need.

As ordered, Malach camps out at the bar with me. Most people hunch or sprawl when they sit on a barstool, but not Malach. He perches like someone shoved one end of a flagpole up his ass and drove the other into the concrete floor.

"Yo," I huff, rapping my knuckles on the counter in front of him. "Do you know how to slouch?"

"Of course." He sits up even straighter, and I wonder briefly if he traded his spine for a yardstick. "Am I drawing unwanted attention?"

Malach glances around, looking so concerned I feel bad for the guy. Yes, he did try to have me killed, but he did it for Celine. In a twisted way, I get it. My basilisk rattles. It doesn't think we should forgive the new angel.

"You're fine. Try to sit less . . ." I scratch my chin, trying to figure out the right word. ". . . militantly. You're giving super soldier, even without your wings."

He considers that, his green eyes searching my face, then nods.

After glancing around, he drops his elbows to the bar and goes rag-doll limp.

I blink at the change. Malach transformed from killer-for-hire to the saddest man in the world. If I put a glass of whiskey on the rocks in his hand, it will be the perfect look.

I scoop some ice and pull one of the top-shelf liquors down. Malach is far from home; the least I can do is show the guy how good the booze is here. I pour him a few fingers and press the glass into his hand. "This is for sipping," I warn him. "And when a tall, black-haired vampire shows up later, don't even think about mentioning—"

"Mentioning what?" Alistair appears directly beside Malach, and I swallow a curse. There's a pink tinge to his blue eyes that isn't usually there. From the heavy dark circles he's rocking, I know he didn't spend the afternoon sleeping.

"Nothing," I mutter. "Blood Tide?"

"Cut the bullshit, Luca. I need to see her."

"Her next set is in fifteen."

Alistair's low growl makes the hairs on my arms stand on end.

I sigh and look him dead in the face. "I won't make her talk to you until she's ready. She's dealing with a lot, and, frankly, you royally fucked up. Give her time, Ali."

He hangs his head, shoulders drooping pathetically. I glance at Malach's similar pose and shake my head. They're different sides of the same coin. While Malach is all golden, shiny excellence, Alistair is the kind of trouble you beg for until the moment it kills you.

With clientele hooting and hollering under the neon lights all around us, there's not much I can do to comfort him. But I lean across the bar and put my hand on his shoulder anyway, grazing my thumb over his neck.

Alistair meets my gaze, and the devastation on his face is brutal. "Don't think I forgot what you were saying when I arrived," he says.

I snort a laugh and drop my hand. "It's not important right now." I see Celine approaching and lower my voice. "Just know that if you ever want her back, you can't kill him." I tilt my head toward Malach.

Alistair gives the burly angel a ferocious once-over, confusion erasing some of his sadness. "Why would I bother killing him?"

"Storage room. Now," Celine interrupts before I can answer. "You get five minutes, Alistair, then I have to take my clothes off for a bunch of people who aren't you."

Ali surges to his feet. He stares at Celine like a roaring flame scopes out a pile of dry brush. She stares back at him blankly—as if he's nothing—and I wince. Celine looking at me that way is my worst nightmare. If Alistair is smart, he won't push her, but his control is slipping.

"Angel, please," he begs.

Celine pivots, leaving without a word. Alistair's hands curl to fists at his side.

"You better go," I say gently. "And tread lightly while you're at it."

The look he tosses at me is red-rimmed and desperate. "What choice do I have?"

None. Alistair is out of options, and I'm not going to help him. If he wants to make things right with Celine, he's going to have to figure it out himself. For all our sakes, I hope he does.

SIX

ALISTAIR

The lights hurt my eyes. The raucous cheers make me homicidal. And Celine's swaying ass as she storms away from me casts everything my thoughtless words have cost me into sharp relief.

Celine opens the door to the storage room, and I follow her inside, inhaling deeply.

If I try hard enough, I can still see us in here all those weeks ago when my fingers mapped her curves for the first time. Her eyes were locked on mine and glazed with pleasure. Tonight, she looks right through me. Like we were nothing.

"Angel," I breathe. "Please allow me to apologize."

"Go for it," she says, her words crisp.

My heart skips a beat, and I reach for her, only to run into a briskly delivered stiff-arm.

"But . . . I-I thought," I sputter, my hope turning to dust even as my throat burns.

"Thought what?" Celine snaps. "That one flimsy apology would erase what you said?"

She gestures to her metallic, shimmery lingerie, then jerks her thumb at the closed door. "Out there, under those lights, on that stage, I work. I like to dance. It makes me feel powerful, and you've proven you can't handle that. You can apologize all you want, Alistair, but unless you can convince me you didn't mean what you said—and we both know you did—then we've got nothing left to talk about."

I capture her hand and bring it to my lips, kissing her knuckles. "No," I whisper, defeat churning low in my belly. "I didn't mean a single godsdamned word—I was angry."

"We have that in common," she says.

What can I say to make it better? No words are right. I swallow them all—it's what I should have done last night—and marinate in my misery.

My fingers ache to drag Celine into my arms. I want to make her so wild for me she forgets every stupid thing I've ever said. How many orgasms would it take to make her forget?

She stares at me, chin rigid, chest heaving as the bass rattles the closed door. I've never felt this far away from her. I won't win her back tonight, but if she thinks I'm giving up . . .

"The owner of the Mouth of Hell is willing to meet with you tomorrow before the fight," I say. "She didn't reveal any details, but I poked around anyway. You'll have to fight someone she thinks you can't beat. If you succeed, you'll be added to the rotation."

"Thanks. I'll be there," she says.

Celine's eyes spark with excitement, none of it focused on me. I look past her shoulders, hoping her wings will give me a better idea of what she's feeling. They aren't there.

A flicker of hope runs through me. "Where are your wings?" I ask. If she's hiding them from me, she doesn't want them to give her away.

The excitement in her eyes dims, and she levels me with a flat stare. "They didn't go with my outfit." She spins to leave, and my fingers twitch. With her hand on the doorknob, Celine freezes. "There won't be any more attempts on your life. If you stay away from me, you're safe to go on as you were before you got dragged into this mess."

No! Absolutely fucking not. Stay away from my angel? Only if I'm dead.

I reach for her because I can't hold off any longer.

My fingers curl around nothing but air; she's already gone. My mind races as I replay what she said. If Celine thinks I'm no longer in danger . . . I've missed something important.

She wasn't interested in explaining, but I know a hazel-eyed killer who will.

"He's her what?" I snarl.

"You heard me, Ali." Luca tosses me an unimpressed look. "You picked an ideal fucking time to be a stupid, jealous fuck—you know that?"

Heat ripples off the alley pavement even though the sun abandoned the Fringes hours ago. The air is thick with spilled beer and my growing anger.

"We could kill him," I suggest, glancing at the door of the Fang. "It would be easy."

"Sure," Luca drags the syllable out, glaring at me as if I'm chewing on his last nerve. "That's a great fucking plan . . . if the goal is to make sure Celine never speaks to either of us again. Tell me what happened to Ciprian."

"He was gone by sunset, like I told him to be." I cross my

arms, my helpless fury growing as I imagine the hulking angel in Celine's apartment whispering vows or some other bullshit from their past in her ear. I hate it.

"Do you think he's okay?" Luca asks.

I narrow my eyes. "Who cares?"

"Well, fuck . . . Me, I guess." Luca's lip ring winks in the dim glow of the streetlight and the Fang's neon sign. "And you're not as blasé as you act. You wouldn't be this mad if you didn't care."

"Don't tell me how I feel." I poke his chest, and he slaps my hand down.

"Uh-uh. No way. You don't get to snap at me, Ali. I'm mad at you—you aren't allowed to be mad at me. Not when you're the one who decided to be a dickhead and leave me alone in a tiny apartment with two angels dead set on pretending everything is fine when it isn't." He tosses his arms wide. "You should feel the tension; it's so thick you could choke on it. And Celine's in her stone-cold, can't-be-fucked with anything mood. It's stressing me—"

I grip the back of his neck and shut him up by slamming my lips to his.

I would kill to be there—doesn't he know that? I didn't plan to freak out and drive her away. Our kiss is furious, dripping with heat. I nibble on his full bottom lip, scraping my fangs over the delicate skin.

"None of that." Luca pulls his lip free from my teeth.

"I'm sorry," I grunt, pressing my body against his and nipping at his lips again until he kisses me back.

"Shut up," he hisses, switching our positions until I'm the one with my back to the graffiti-covered concrete wall. "Fix it, Ali. Do you hear me?"

I nod, kissing down his neck, then drop my forehead against his shoulder. "I'll figure it out; I swear. She's not ready yet."

"Godsdammit, I already told you that!"

"I won't give up, Luca."

"You better not." He threads his fingers through my tangled hair and jerks my head up, sealing our lips again. My desire roars to life as his hard cock rubs against mine, and my fangs throb in my gums.

Luca still wants this; he hasn't turned on me.

I cling to that realization, using it to soothe my panic. If I can earn Celine's forgiveness, we can have what I envisioned before Casanell showed up and angels started falling from the sky.

"I've got to get back inside," Luca whispers. "I have an angel to babysit and drinks to serve."

"Don't go," I beg, wincing at how needy I sound.

Luca pulls away, raises his chin slightly, and meets my eyes. "Ali . . . She's my priority, you know that, right?"

I nod, stepping back as a chill runs through my veins. The outsider. Always alone. Why am I surprised? "Of course," I say calmly, trying to recover the stoicism I'm known for. "You better not do anything to jeopardize your place in that apartment."

"I won't."

Luca kisses me again, but this time is different. The press of his lips is soft. Is he trying to cheer me up? When he drags his lips away from mine, I see the rush of blood in his cheeks. I wasn't imagining it: Luca Saratelli was trying to comfort me, and he's embarrassed by it. He shouldn't be. It's the only good thing that's happened to me since that enclave asshole called Ciprian by his full name.

"Thanks," I rasp, licking my bottom lip to get one last taste of him. "Be at the venue at sunset tomorrow. I'll make the introduc-tion . . . And Luca, if she's serious about fighting there, she has to win. I can't get her a spot otherwise."

He sighs. "She's more than serious about it; she's an army of one preparing for war. Gods help anyone who stands in her way."

He disappears into the Fang, but his words linger with me long after he's gone.

I never want Celine to feel alone. My temper landed us here, allowing a shiny, stacked angel to swoop in and claim her attention at the exact moment our fragile unit fractured.

Self-loathing mixes with my determination, and I groan.

I smell his blood before I see him.

"Risking death already?" I mutter. "Life at the enclave must be grim."

"I'm leaving town, but I'll be back," Ciprian says, stopping ten feet from me, his face bathed in shadow. "I want to make it clear again before I go that your secrets are safe with me."

I scoff. "Which ones?"

"All of them."

Examining my hand, I feign disinterest. "Run along then, back to your daddy."

"Fuck you, Alistair." Ciprian steps into the light. His pale face is mottled with bruises. Every inhale floods my nose with the smell of dried blood. "Are you so prejudiced that you would hold my parents against me? That's not a popular mentality here on the Fringes."

I roll my eyes. "That mentality only applies to non-enclave heirs."

"Well"—Ciprian laughs, the sound dripping with bitterness—"if you need an enclave heir in your corner, you know how to find one."

"Thanks for the warning, but I prefer my former allies stab me in the face, not lie to it."

Ciprian sighs and sways, catching the wall with his hand to stay upright. "Cool. You can hate me all you want, Alistair. We both know my blood is the only reason you're standing here."

He backs away, swallowed by the night before I can tell him that's exactly why I'm furious.

SEVEN

UNSPOKEN RULE OF THE FRINGES #38:
FLASH TOO MUCH MUSCLE, AND SOMEONE WILL TEST IT.

CELINE

"If you keep walking like there's a piano strapped to your back, we won't make it there by sundown." I toss a disgruntled look at Luca as he ambles along behind me, making our two-block walk seem endless.

He yawns. "You woke me up after four hours of sleep and made me run for miles. I'm exhausted, baby."

I scrub my hand over my face. He's right, but without training I won't be able to defeat my dad. And with Luca glued to my side, he needs to be ready too.

The four hours we slept weren't enough, but I'm too wired to be sleepy. Experience tells me I can survive months this way before I crash. Luca will adjust.

"I appreciate you running with me," I tell him.

"Scary," he mutters. "You're about to say something awful, aren't you?"

"We'll be doing that run every morning."

"Like that." Luca sighs and jogs reluctantly to my side. He drapes his arm over my shoulder. "Are you ready for the fight? We can call it off if you want more time."

"I'm ready for whatever they toss at me."

I smile brightly at him even while caterpillars explore my stomach lining. The nerves are a good sign. They mean I'm locked in. Fighters should respect their opponents enough to feel a rush of anticipation before a match.

As dusk falls, the Mouth of Hell appears the same as any other warehouse. Far off the Strip and deep in the heart of the Fringes, the setting sun casts the graffiti—colorful, magic-infused witch wards meant to repel humans—in honey-tinged gold. Beautiful, but gone too soon. The sun dips behind a building, returning the wall to its normal, shadow-gray pallor.

"Do you think Malach will burn the apartment down while we're gone?"

I glance over my shoulder, then peer up at the darkening sky. "I'm more worried he's sneaking around watching us. He was weirdly chill when I told him he had to stay behind."

"Agreeing to avoid a lie?" Luca chuckles. "That's not a bad evasive maneuver."

I grind to a halt. "I'm not an obstacle course."

Luca presses a kiss to my temple. "No, you're more complicated than that."

I want to argue, but I can't. Not unless I want to get slapped by my own magic. "I'm going to win this fight, Luca," I say instead.

"I know, baby." He groans. "I'm just praying my basilisk doesn't lose it if you take a hit."

A pleased warmth settles over me.

Luca's basilisk is protective and deadly. I like that a lot.

When I sense Alistair coming, the caterpillars in my stomach transform into butterflies. *He thinks you're a slut, Celine. Get over him.* No matter how many times I deliver the lecture to myself, it won't stick.

"Angel," he whispers, his voice a molten purr that rolls over me like hot wax.

I dip my chin to acknowledge him, pleased when I manage not to shudder.

"Luca." Alistair looks him over hungrily.

Luca rubs his thumb over my stiff shoulder, laughter in his voice as he glances between us. "Hey, Ali."

I want to smack the smirk off his face. This isn't funny. It's maddening. I'm mad, dammit, and maybe a little crazed too. "Great," I say sarcastically. "We all know each other's names. Can we get this show on the road?"

"Certainly." Alistair raps his knuckles on the rusty metal door of the warehouse.

Rocking on the balls of my feet, I hammer out my battle plan.

When the door swings open, I find myself face-to-face with a tree of a woman. Easily six feet tall, she's all sharp angles, sleek muscles, and lean, barbed energy. A gnarly scar cuts through her left eyebrow, past the corner of her eye, and bisects her cheek. A claw mark, maybe? It's hard to tell what made the scar, but the jagged, raised white line does its job: this woman radiates danger from every pore.

We study each other silently. I think I like her.

"Come in," she says, her voice a sensual rasp.

I walk into the familiar venue and blink as the harsh fluorescent lights reveal the practical side of the supernatural fight club. Bottles clink as workers stock the bar. A handful of witches circle the pallet towers, casting stasis charms on the rickety platforms. That explains why the stacks never tip over, but I'm a little disappointed that the ramshackle vibe is more for aesthetic than anything else.

Suspended high off the ground, the cage in the middle of the warehouse hasn't changed since the last time I was here. A man sweeps the floor while several others test the strength of the walls by tossing bricks at them. The heavy projectiles bounce right off, the cage walls crackling with lime-green magic as they absorb the hits. When one of the bricks ricochets and smacks a sweeping worker, he curses and throws his broom, making the others laugh.

"The tryouts will begin once they finish checking the cage."

I nod at the tall woman and survey the rest of the room. To the side of the cage, a handful of people are stretching and wrapping their hands. My eyebrows shoot up. For some reason, I thought this was a solo audition, but apparently, I'm not the only one in the running for a slot.

"Resker," Alistair snaps. "Do you expect Celine to defeat all these fighters? That's ridiculous."

I grind my teeth, annoyed by his interruption. I asked him to connect me with the owners of the Mouth of Hell, not hold my hand and pick fights on my behalf. He's over involving himself, something he promised me he wouldn't do.

Ignoring him, Resker winks at me. "Something tells me your champion doesn't need coddling, Alistair."

"I don't," I assure her. "I want to get back in top form. While I'm not as good as I used to be, I have a lot of . . . training. And I'm an expert at putting on a show."

"Of that I have no doubt." Resker shoots Alistair a smug look, then gestures for us to follow her to the ring.

"Don't embarrass me," I hiss at Alistair, including Luca in my glare to be safe. He hasn't said a word, but you can't be too careful with the two of them. We may be standing in a boring warehouse now, but fighting will shift the energy, and I don't need any more enemies.

We follow Resker to the cage, and I mentally adapt my strategy based on the new information. If this is a last one standing competition, I'll be at a disadvantage. Instead of toying with my opponent and illustrating my showmanship in the process, I'll need to fight efficiently.

Resker glances at her watch and waves her hand at one of the guys testing the cage walls. He grabs a lever on the edge of the octagon and lowers a steep, narrow staircase.

"If you're fighting for real, you'll enter from the top trapdoor, the tunnels, or one of the spelled pathways, but for this audition, you'll go up the boring way." Resker winks at me, obvious interest in her eyes. I consider setting her up with Imani, then remember I'm here to crack heads, not matchmake.

"Got it," I say. "What are the rules?"

"No killing. Other than that—impress me, angel."

I flinch at her use of Alistair's nickname, and he freezes at my side. My skin prickles. I glance to my right and swallow a curse.

Gone are Alistair's crystal-blue eyes. They've been replaced with crimson slits. He's fully vamping out, fangs bared menacingly at Resker. I ignore how the raw possessiveness in his expression makes me burn and bump him with my hip. "Snap out of it," I whisper.

"Yes. Unless, of course, you want to work that aggression off in the ring," Resker coos. There's an undercurrent of cruelty as she speaks to him. I'm not sure how Alistair knows her, but there's a sinister rivalry boiling beneath the surface. Another secret it would have been nice to know about in advance—like his disdain for strippers.

"Five minutes, Resk," a big, beefy man shouts from the floor of the ring, his misshapen face disappearing from the trapdoor above the stairs.

"Wonderful." Resker claps her hands, her conniving expression nowhere in sight. "I'll leave you to get ready, Celine. I can't wait to see what you bring to the table. I have high hopes."

"Me too," I mutter, doing my best to shake off my trepidation.

She walks away, and I focus on loosening my joints and

stretching my arms and legs. Adrenaline from the fight will take me a long way, but it won't give me the win by itself. I'll have to stay calm, strategic, and brutal, which means I can't waste focus worrying about what Alistair is doing with those fangs.

"You good?" I grunt, not bothering to look at him. He's paying attention; I can feel his eyes on me.

"I'm fine," he barks.

"Don't fuck this up for me, Alistair. Your temper—"

"Is under control. I apologize."

I nod, not pushing him harder. If he says he's fine, that's good enough for me. Just because I no longer want him in my bed—*liar*—doesn't mean I think he would betray me.

Unfortunately, there are miles of ground between trust and its opposite. That gray area is where we all live, breathe, and eventually die. Finding the limits of your tolerance is key to forming any kind of alliance on the Fringes.

"Luca?" I ask, bending to stretch my right calf.

"I'm great, baby." He cracks his palm against my ass, and my fingers curl around his throat before I realize what I'm doing.

"Great reflexes," he wheezes, winking at me. "You've got this."

"Celine and Dominic—you're up." Resker's voice echoes off the concrete walls of the warehouse.

I kiss Luca hard, then release his throat to crack my knuckles. After a measured inhale, I walk to the narrow staircase and climb. My wings are stowed, but I have a few situations I might bring them out for. The element of surprise is worth its weight in gold.

I'm two steps from the top when the staircase shudders. I've got company, and something tells me Dominic is a brick house. Good for him and better for me. The big ones always fall harder.

"Nice ass." His voice sounds like a godsdamned landslide, but it's the amusement in it that sets my teeth on edge. *Whatever.* He's free to underestimate me all the way to the morgue. We'll see if he's still laughing when I make him gargle his own blood.

"Thanks," I say breezily, reaching the top of the stairs and winking at him.

He pops out of the trapdoor, his shoulders grazing the edges as he squeezes himself through. Good grief. He's bigger than big. Less brick house and more brick hotel. Adding to the visual, Dominic is also the most rectangular person I've ever seen—his body might as well be made from a pile of cinder blocks.

If he manages to get me on the ground, I'll be toast. But I'm hoping a man of his size has spent most of his life relying on intimidation to discourage others from challenging him.

Dominic checks me out too, but his stare is less assessment and more interest, like he's window-shopping for something he wants to own but can't afford. I can work with that. Stretching my arms over my head, I arch my back so he can get a better look at my cleavage.

He licks his lips.

Internally, I vomit. Externally, I toss him a shy smile. "Be gentle," I whisper, doing my best to set him up for a humbling he won't forget.

"Sure, sweetie." His grin is wide and eager, and I catch a glimpse of blunted fangs. Some kind of shifter? Or maybe a vampire. Either way, I plan to stay away from those teeth.

"Fighters ready?" Resker pops her head out of a tube on the right side of the cage, magic flickering around her face as she penetrates the protection barrier.

I nod. Dominic grunts. The bell rings.

Dropping into a standard fighting stance, I distribute my weight and rock on the balls of my feet. We circle each other a few times, then Dominic laughs and stands up straight.

"You know what? You're hot as hell. I'll give you one free shot, darlin'."

I smile, then pout. "If you're sure."

He nods and taps his chin invitingly. I squat and spring

forward, zipping through the air and driving my fist into his forehead with all the strength at my disposal. The crack of the punch is as loud as a gunshot.

Dominic's pupils surge, black overwhelming the medium brown. His right eye spasms, its pupil shrinking to a pinprick before his eyelids flutter closed. The breath leaves his lips in a single puff, and he falls—slowly, like a sawed-off tree. Dominic collides with the cage floor with enough force to rattle the walls.

I step closer, examine his body to make sure he's out cold, and glance at Resker. "His pupils went wonky there for a second," I say. "Might have a brain bleed."

Resker laughs, throwing her head back as the rich, cruel cackle bounces off the walls. "A brain bleed? He's lucky if his brain isn't soup after that hit." She snaps her fingers, and two burly guys enter the ring to drag him out.

I shrug, flexing the fingers of my right hand. My knuckles hurt like a bitch, but I was careful. I don't think they're broken. Nothing an ice pack can't fix.

"Next," Resker shouts.

I eye the trapdoor with wary curiosity. I can't keep up the one-hit wonder act. It's good for making a statement, but there are better ways to put on a show. A woman pops through the hatch and bumps her knuckles against mine. Her grin is as wide as the Grand Canyon. There's a gap between her front teeth, almost big enough to fit another tooth. The look works for her.

"Nice hit," she says. "It was all I could do not to shout timber when he went down." When she speaks, there's a whistling lilt to the words. It's charming. "Kind of ironic if you think about it. Humans think unicorn pigs are extinct, but that one will wish he is when he wakes up."

"Thanks." I smile.

"Ready, ladies?" There's a veiled eagerness in Resker's question that snags my interest. She's excited to see us fight—which immediately puts me on guard. My opponent may not be massive, but she's here for a reason. On the Fringes, it's far more likely to be schadenfreude than masochism. *Thanks, Imani, for that word of the day.*

"Ready," I say, deciding to hold back until I'm sure what her moves are.

"Let's do it."

The bell rings, and I dodge on instinct alone as a glob of white goop flies by my face and hits the wall behind me with a malevolent hiss. I have no idea what the fuck that was, but I know for a fact I don't want that shit on my face.

My opponent starts to . . . Weave isn't the right word, and she's not bobbing either. Shit, she's skittering around the cage, her feet nothing but a blur. When she drops to all fours and picks up the pace, I steel my nerves and stop moving. I can't match her speed, and if I keep trying, she'll wear me out.

Another glob of white paste flies at me. I dodge, but the next one grazes my bare arm, and I hiss in pain. Gods. It's fresh lava, acid eating away at my tissue until nothing but bone remains.

"She's an arachne shifter, baby," Luca shouts. "Don't look at the web; it's a trick." There's a grunt from below the cage, but I've already heard him loud and clear. Maybe my arm is rotting away, maybe it isn't. If I take my eyes off her, I'm fucked.

Gritting my teeth, I lower my head and charge.

Her arms and legs shift and multiply, and when she runs up the side of the cage, I jump, grabbing her by the base of one spiny foot and throwing her on the floor. The end of her leg is razor sharp and covered in tiny barbs. It tears through my skin and muscle, blood oozing between my fingers and making it hard to get a good grip.

The second we hit the mat, I grab her throat with my left hand. Her human head disappears, turning into a horrific spider face. Gone are the cute, gapped teeth. In their place are massive, wriggling fangs as big as my forearms.

Only an inch from my bare skin, I watch them and grimace.

It's time to end this fight—she is terrifying. Tightening my grip, I press on her throat, then roar in pain when one of her legs pierces my side. Hot agony—there's nothing to blunt the pain. My fingers slip, and I give up using my free hand to hold her legs down and use it to grab her neck too.

Desperate, I squeeze harder. Her eyes—round, black, and shiny as marbles—roll back in her gruesome head. She lets out a pained squeak, digs two more legs into my sides, then taps the floor of the cage with another.

"That's a tap out. Celine wins." Resker's voice reaches me faintly, and I release my hold and roll to the side. I'm a pincushion, and I can only hope those legs weren't poisonous. Thankfully, the last two punctures don't seem as deep as the first.

"You're awesome," I wheeze, flopping my head to the side so I can see her.

Clothes hanging in tatters on her trunk, she smiles back at me. "No, you're awesome. I'm Lyss. Lyss Venmara."

"Celine," I sputter, lifting two bloody fingers to my mouth. "What do you call those crazy fangs?"

"Chelicerae." She frowns. "Most people call them mandibles, but that's stupid. I'm not a fucking ant." Good thing I asked, because that's exactly what I would have called them. Why does my lack of scientific knowledge keep biting me in the ass?

Resker's blurry face appears above us, her eyes glittering with excitement. "You're both in. Now get out of my cage so we can mop up the blood. The others will keep fighting, but I want you two rested and ready for your first fights next week. Welcome to the Mouth of Hell, ladies."

EIGHT

TRADITIONAL *NISH THATSHA* BETROTHAL VOW:
THE MAGIC IN MY HEART—MY MOST CHERISHED GIFT—
WILL ALWAYS COME SECOND TO YOU.

MALACH

The locks slide free one by one while I sit rigidly on the couch. They're bickering, and Celine's voice is tight with . . . pain? My control snaps, and I surge to my feet as the door swings open. Her shirt is soaked with blood, and the thick, shapeless fabric tied around her waist does a terrible job of hiding it.

"You're hurt," I say.

"She is." Luca nods at me, the yellowish tint to his eyes telling me this argument has been going on for a while. I knew I should have followed them.

"I'm fine—*fuck*." Celine careens to one side, her body jolting in pain because she lied to me. "I mean, I will be fine," she corrects herself sullenly.

"You're right. You'll be fine once Alistair gets here with the potion." Luca wraps his arm around her waist, supporting her weight and ignoring her annoyed grimace.

"I already told you, no potions," she snarls. "I don't want Alistair here, and I don't want to owe him for anything else. My ledger is already dripping red where he's concerned thanks to Malach's murder attempt."

"Judgment," I mutter. "It was judgment."

"It was fucked." She glares at me, her skin paler than usual with two pink streaks slashing across her cheeks, before setting her sights on Luca. "Since you've decided to interfere with my decisions, you can help me clean the blood off."

"You can't dance tonight, baby—"

"Don't tell me what to do."

"Unless . . ." Luca draws the word out obnoxiously. "You take Alistair's magic potion."

"He could be trying to poison me."

Luca rolls his eyes. "Yeah right. He'd rather walk naked down the Strip at high-fucking-noon. Go get in the shower and quit being stubborn."

My eyebrows shoot up when her lips curl. Is she enjoying riling him up? Determined not to be left out again, I follow them down the hall, through the bedroom that smells strongly of my wife, and into the bathroom.

Celine notices me, and her brown eyes narrow. "What do you think you're doing?"

"Ascertaining the full extent of your injuries, as I vowed to always do."

Celine sags and stumbles. I reach for her, but Luca is already there, grumbling under his breath, with a wild look in his eyes. "You've lost a lot of blood, baby. Stop arguing with Malach and get in the fucking shower before I lose my fucking mind."

"You're bossy," she says, slurring her words. Her eyes, glassier now, focus on me with difficulty. "And you—using our betrothal vows to get your way. That's shady."

"Malach, help me," Luca says. "I don't like this. She should be healing by now. I need to see what we're dealing with."

Fingers trembling, I reach for the hem of her shirt and carefully pull it off, forbidding my eyes from wandering.

Celine's head lolls to the side and falls against Luca's chest. Her hair, like burnished silken flame, grazes my forearm. It's the most intimate position I've ever been in with her. It's ruined as soon as I catch sight of the deep gouges below her ribs.

"What weapon did this?" I demand, looking to Luca for answers.

"Spider legs, three of them," he grunts, flipping the water in the shower on. "Hold her up, would you?"

I nod, sliding my arms under Celine's to support her weight. She nuzzles my neck, but she's mostly unconscious. I sigh. I hate her wounds but understand her need to fight. If Celine hopes to stand against her father personally or on behalf of our people, she must be at her strongest.

Luca helps her step under the spray and begins to carefully clean blood from the punctures, oblivious to the water soaking his clothes. "You didn't ask if she won," he says to me. "With injuries like these, she might have gotten her ass kicked. Aren't you curious whether she earned the spot or not?"

I frown at him. Foolish statements such as this make me question whether he's worthy of her. "She wouldn't accept a loss," I say slowly. Perhaps that will make it easier for him to understand. "Not due to three simple wounds."

Luca shrugs. "You're right; she won. Her first official fight is next week."

I nod, satisfied and unsurprised to be proven correct. "I'll put together a rotation of drills to ensure she's ready."

"She's going to be spread too thin." Luca groans, and a strand of sodden hair falls in front of his eyes. "Working at the club is already physically demanding, with late hours. If she adds training, when will she rest?"

His concern is valid, but it's new for me to hear it spoken aloud.

In the celestial realm, rest is rarely prioritized. Productivity, yes. Efficiency, doubly so. Order must be maintained, and it's the responsibility of each echelon to divide its responsibilities accordingly. But rest? In my entire life, I've never heard anyone champion its importance.

I wonder how Celine feels hearing Luca guard her energy so fiercely. Is it nice? Threatening? With her eyelids heavy and her breathing slow, I'm not sure she even hears us.

Luca whips his head up at the sound of muffled pounding. "If you've got her, I'll go let Alistair in." The thumps get louder, and he curses. "Hopefully, before he breaks down the door."

I nod. Holding Celine with one hand, I use the other to pick up the scrap of fabric Luca set aside. Slowly, I wash the blood from her ribs, careful not to disrupt the wounds themselves.

This is the first time we've been alone in years. The lost time scores me to the bone. The day Celine fled, she took my heart, my word, and every fragment of my loyalty with her. I've been half an angel ever since.

The bathroom door flies open and crashes against the wall. Alistair surges into the room, nostrils flared, his black hair hanging wildly around his neck. Uncivilized. He grips a glass vial in his hand so tightly I worry he'll break it before it can be used to help her.

Celine jolts, her eyelashes fluttering as she tries to assess the obvious threat.

"Fuck, dude. Take it down a few dozen notches," Luca snaps.

Alistair snarls and focuses his blood-red eyes on me. "Give her to me."

Before I can remove his head from his body, Luca shoves him. "Knock it off, Ali. I'm not playing. If you want to get banned from her place for the next century, keep being an idiot. But if you're trying to make things right, give her the damn medicine."

The red in his eyes melts to faded blue. He nods and pours the potion into Celine's mouth with shaking fingers. I tilt her head back until the pale skin of her throat bobs as she swallows.

"How quickly before it—damn." Luca whistles and points at her side, where the deepest of the gouges is already knitting itself back together.

"I got the strongest one I had," Alistair says.

"Was that necessary?" Luca raises his eyebrows. "You know what? Don't mention that to her at all, Ali—it'll piss her off."

"You washed the blood away," Alistair says, his lips curling into a pout as he rakes his eyes down Celine's skin.

Luca chuckles and shakes his head. "You'll get plenty of opportunities to convince her to let you lick it off after her other fights. Get lost before she comes to."

Alistair growls low in his throat and yanks Luca into him, fisting his hands in his waterlogged T-shirt. He kisses him angrily, then darts from the room too quick for my eyes to track the movement.

The front door slams a heartbeat later.

Luca rolls his eyes and strips his wet shirt off. "Don't drip on her bedroom carpet," he tells me. "She hates that."

"Luca," Celine whispers, her lips moving against my chest. I can't resist tightening my hold. He'll take her from me. I know it, but I'm not ready to give her up. I'll never be ready.

"Yeah, baby?" Luca hurries to the edge of the shower but doesn't attempt to remove her from my arms.

"I'm dancing tonight," she whispers. "If you don't wake me up in time, I'll be pissed."

He shakes his head, then glances at me. "Can you take her to bed? I'm going to clean up this mess."

I nod, noticing the streaks of blood the water didn't wash away, as well as the puddles from wet clothes.

"My pants are soaked," Celine says, pawing weakly at the skintight material.

Clenching my jaw, I pull them down for her, keeping my eyes on her face. I've imagined her this way hundreds of times, cradled against my heart where she belongs.

Tenderly, I lay her on the bed, pleased that her wounds have closed. Pale pink circles are all that remain of the gouges. I pull the blanket to her chin, fold it around her, and check the foot of the bed to make sure the covers are securely tucked. I don't want her to be disrupted by a draft, although the acrid heat here is brutal.

I lift my head when she calls my name, surprised to see her eyes fixed on my face. "I won today, but it was too close. You'll have to push me hard to get me back where I need to be. We'll be lucky to survive one wave of Dad's assassins if I can't—"

"Shh," I say. Grabbing her hand, I pull it off the covers and hook our thumbs together, the rest of our fingers flaring in opposite directions. Wings—locked, made whole by two hands joining. It's an older *thatsha* custom, but I want her to know I'm serious. "I swear, my truth, that I'll prepare you to face him, but you cannot get stronger if you refuse to rest."

Celine tilts her head, a small smile on her lips as she looks at our joined hands. "You've changed, haven't you?"

I nod, although I don't believe it. Can someone change when their purpose never falters? Since the first time I laid eyes on her, as a chubby boy with rounded cheeks and stubby wings, I've known she was my destiny. That was the moment I changed. Now, I simply adapt to fit her needs.

"Celine, you cannot leave me behind again," I say firmly. "Let me be by your side. Not knowing . . ." Anxiety consumed me.

She searches my face before nodding, her eyes softening. "I understand." She yawns. "For the record, I'm not hiding you, Malach, I just don't want to draw more attention to the situation than I have to. Angels aren't common in the Fringes."

"I can keep my wings tucked," I say reluctantly.

Her eyelashes flutter.

"Sleep now," I whisper. "I will ensure the shifter wakes you."

"Not sure how you plan to do that." Luca emerges from the bathroom with only a towel wrapped around his waist. "Do you even know how to read a clock?"

He slides under the covers, poking the screen of his cell phone methodically as he tucks himself into Celine's side. I grit my teeth and barely stop myself from informing him that I can tell time in at least ten different ways—no clock needed.

"I set an alarm," he whispers, kissing Celine's temple.

She nods, her breathing evening out as she relaxes in his arms.

I leave the room before I ask to stay.

NINE

ENCLAVE EDICT #94:
WE DO NOT INTERFERE. WE ENDURE.

CIPRIAN

There are bad chefs all over the universe—busy cooking up bland food, stringy vegetables, and putrid, suspicious seafood dishes. The only reason they get away with it is that we've all got to eat, and some of us aren't fans of sweating over a hot stove.

No culinary crime is worse, though, than burned steak. Blackened and charred, tough as leather—it's appealing to absolutely no one.

And that's how I feel inside.

While slinking around the compound, no fewer than ten people spot me and take off in the opposite direction. One demon even bangs his shin on the fountain in his hurry. It's almost funny, but I can't manage to laugh. Too much effort; too little reward—kind of like cooking.

I'm beginning to think I either smell of burned meat, or my mood is so obvious they're scared to cross me.

Yelling at Dad hasn't helped . . . any of the three times I've tried it. Even though I was crystal fucking clear, he only blinked at me as if he couldn't understand a word I said. It made me feel about six inches tall—which was exactly what he wanted.

Dad possesses the uncanny ability to ignore every concrete thing I say and latch on to the only loose thread, yanking on it until he convinces himself my entire argument is unraveling. It's his specialty, and a hell of a way to avoid stumbling over personal accountability.

I grit my teeth and deepen my stretch, the ache in my ribs blooming as they expand to let in air.

Bees drone around the hedge maze, and the smell of fresh-cut grass sticks to the back of my throat. I've been coming to the heart of the maze to rehab from my beating. The training grounds in the courtyard are too public—I'd rather lick my wounds in private —but the silence is tearing me to shreds.

I came here to be alone. Loneliness is eating me alive.

If Sheena were here . . . I sigh. She isn't. And I have no business feeling sorry for myself when my best friend is going through only the gods know what.

"Pull it together," I mutter to myself. Just because I tried and failed to fit in on the Fringes doesn't mean I'll never belong anywhere. It's only a setback. One day when I close my eyes, I won't see red hair, redder eyes, and Luca's grin.

Unfortunately, that day isn't today.

Heart racing, I stumble down the hall, following excited whispers to the surveillance room. Gods bless my bestie. Sheena must have known I needed her, because she's back and causing even more drama than usual.

My eyes find her in the crowded room. Short, wide-eyed, and

pale as a fucking ghost. My lips stretch into a grin. "Give it to us straight, Sheena," I drawl. "Any more urges to join the dark side?"

She squeaks and flies across the room, slamming into me with the force of a much larger woman. My healing ribs throb from the impact, but I hug her tightly, anyway.

The room is packed with people, from the tech squad to all the usual suspects.

And everyone has an opinion.

As we discuss the best way forward, I play the unbothered, flippant jokester everyone expects me to be. Despite my over-the-top delivery, it heals something in me to see Sheena thoughtfully consider my advice.

We leave her alone to talk things over with Idris. So far, having the fae join the enclave hasn't been as bad as I feared, but I haven't been around much either.

As soon as I'm out of Sheena's sight, I rub my ribs.

"You could have told her about the ass-kicking," Callum says. "She wouldn't have been rough with you."

I glance at him and shake my head. After weeks of stumbling around the enclave like the walking dead, my brother's face has returned to model perfection. Clearly, he's fed his incubus.

"Damn, you didn't waste any time, did you?" I ask, waggling my eyebrows.

"Watch it," he hisses.

I roll my eyes. Callum is touchy these days. And delusional. Sheena tells me way more than I want to know about their sex life.

"She's okay, though?" I ask, changing the subject.

"She's here"—he sighs—"and she's alive. Anything else we'll figure out. Together."

I clap him on the shoulder. "I'm glad she's back."

"She could use a distraction," Gideon says, his dimpled grin making an appearance for the first time in days.

I gasp and clutch my chest. "Is that all I am to you? A distraction?"

"Fuck off, squirt." Gideon grabs my shoulders like we're eight and ten again and jostles me playfully, making it painfully obvious that he's holding back. "Come by our room in a few hours. We'll clear out so you two can talk."

Callum nods shortly, and I'm torn between thanking Gideon for being thoughtful and telling him I'll see my best friend whenever I please—their permission be damned. In the end, I settle for a smile and leave. I know how hard the last few weeks have been for them.

Wandering aimlessly, it's no surprise to me when I end up in the shifter wing, shuffling into the Therion's apartment like a tired little boy who just got lectured about fear again. The air smells of cookies, and I follow the buttery-chocolate haze to the kitchen with a sigh.

This was inevitable.

I need mom advice, and Sarah has always been better at giving it than my actual mother. She may be a powerful omni shifter and a key part of the reason this enclave is as strong as it is, but she's also one of the few supernaturals within these stone walls who leads with her heart.

Sarah sits at the kitchen table eating a chocolate chip cookie, a dog-eared paperback in her hand. On the cover, a woman arches dramatically against a shirtless dude with long hair, the top of her dress half undone.

"Good book?" I ask.

Sarah jumps, then looks at me, her mouth curving into a warm smile. "All my boys are home," she says. "Everything feels pretty good right now."

I open my mouth to tease her about the book, make a joke, anything, but my throat has a knot in it. The damn thing bobs, and I struggle to swallow around it. When my fingers spasm at my side, I stare down at them, frustrated.

Sarah pushes to her feet, rounds the table, and wraps her arms around me. I sag into her hug. I'm a kid again, running to the shifter wing for comfort.

"Everything sucks," I mutter. She tightens her hold, one hand cradling the back of my head. "I had something, Sarah. For once —or the start of something at least—and Dad couldn't stand it, so he took it from me."

"You can't control his actions, sweetie," she murmurs, leading me to the table. "You can only control how you react to them." I sit down—in the same chair I used to hoist myself into when I needed my scraped knees bandaged—and watch as she pours me a glass of milk, then pushes the plate of cookies toward me.

"But there's nothing I can do," I tell her. "I'm not Ciprian to them anymore. I'm Ciprian *Casanell*, and that name isn't opening any doors on the Fringes."

Sarah tilts her head. "Would you want it to?"

I open my mouth and close it. Do I wish my last name made things easier? I'm not sure, but neutrality would be nice.

"The performance . . ." I throw my hands up, then let them fall as exhaustion crashes over me. "I'm fucking tired."

"Ciprian"—Sarah grabs my hand, squeezing gently. I look up and meet her warm brown eyes. "Have you tried being yourself?"

For a moment, with the smell of sugar and home all around us and no one to judge or criticize, I let myself imagine what she's suggesting. Can I be myself? Drop the act . . . open myself up to the possibility that they hate not only my last name but who I actually am?

It's exhilarating and terrifying. It's also impossible.

"It won't matter," I say, my heart sinking. "Their minds are made up. It won't change things for them, so why bother?"

"Because it might change everything for you." Sarah pushes away from the table and pats my hair as she scoops up the tattered paperback. "Take the time you need to think it over, sweetie, but remember: the Ciprian Casanell I know is creative and brave. The edge of other people's comfort zones is where he thrives. You can't expect anyone else to see that unless you show them."

She leaves me alone in the kitchen to think. It's exactly what I need, and I stuff my face with cookies until my stomach hurts. It's the best I've felt in weeks.

TEN

UNSPOKEN RULE OF THE FRINGES #14:
IF YOU ACT LIKE A GOD, SOMEONE WILL FIND OUT IF YOU
BLEED LIKE A MORTAL.

CELINE

The week before the fight is the longest and shortest of my life. Mentally I'm ready, but physically—

"You're not focused." Malach knocks me flat. Again. Air leaves my lungs faster than a tire exploding on the freeway.

"I'm plenty focused," I argue, sucking in the sweat-tinged oxygen of the gym.

Night Shift is a no-humans-allowed training facility. You won't find any Zumba classes, but lots of the better-off supernaturals on the Fringes train here. It's pricey. Too pricey. Luca signed me up for two months without telling me, paying cash and claiming I'd get evicted if I kept attacking Malach at home.

He's not wrong. The last thing I want to do is disrupt my living space. Scratch that. The last thing I want is to be murdered by my dad. The second-to-last thing I want to do is lose my first fight at the Mouth of Hell. And the third-to-last thing I want to do is break my apartment.

"You're not seizing creative openings," Malach says, offering me a hand up.

Still gasping for air, I yank him down hard instead. He twists before impact—barely—and lands with a thud on the mat beside me.

"Fuck you," I wheeze. "How's that for creative?"

"An expletive? That's not creative at all."

I groan and close my eyes, breathing in the subtle coating of disinfectant that always lingers in the gym. There's no one else sparring right now . . . and that's become a pattern. They always happen to be leaving when Malach and I arrive. Something tells me Luca paid extra for that.

Since the staff at the front desk are tight-lipped, I have no way to confirm my suspicions. Luca refuses to discuss it, which tells me everything I need to know while also serving as a sneaky way to avoid directly tipping off my magic. Clever bastard.

There are two days left until I climb into the elevated cage again.

My opponent remains a mystery. Hopefully, my first match will be someone more like Dominic, the thought-to-be-extinct pig shifter, and less like Lyss. The arachne shifter is . . . well, she's a monster. While I wouldn't mind getting a beer with her, I'm in no hurry to have her sharp-ass legs poking holes in me again.

"Overthinking won't help, my truth."

I roll my bottom lip between my teeth to bite back my retort. "I know," I admit. At my side on the mat, Malach radiates heat. It's a small comfort—at least I can still make him work up a sweat. I wish it weren't so distracting.

The thing about Malach I had almost forgotten is his pragmatic bluntness. He doesn't say things to get a rise out of me; he says them because he thinks they need to be said. And while he teases me sometimes, he's never trying to piss me off.

It's the difference between him and most Fringes supernaturals—that instinctive urge to prod, rile, and agitate. Some call it killer instinct; I think it's more about testing limits: knowing how far you can push someone before they snap.

"I'm trying not to think at all," I say.

Malach grunts. "The middle ground is the better place to make your stand."

I yawn and nudge his shoulder with mine. "Do you think this even matters? If he wants me dead, which we know he does, he won't give up."

Dad's burning eyes flash through my mind along with the familiar aura of rage that hovers around him. Sometimes dormant, it could activate over the slightest thing. There's something in him that can't be pacified, an evil that never fully goes away.

Back in the box. Put it back in the box, Celine.

"Don't talk that way," Malach says, rolling onto his side to face me. I feel his stare as intensely as if he were touching me. "You won't give up either."

"You're right," I whisper. "Because I can't."

It takes effort to peel my sore body off the mat, but I'm less winded by our training than I was at the start of the week. Even still, Malach is back on his feet before I am—proof that I'm not at the top of my game.

"We should work on your magic deflection strategies."

I chuckle. "Dodge—that's pretty much the whole strategy."

He frowns. "You're not without magic."

"Yeah, but it would cause a scene. Making more enemies is the last thing we need. Especially if the enclave decides to come for me . . ."

Malach's cheek twitches, and I shake my head. He may be grown up, but his tells are the same.

"Spit it out," I drawl. "I'm not accepting half-truths in my inner circle right now."

"That's ironic," Malach mutters.

"What's that supposed to mean?" I plant my hands on my hips and stare at his face. From the dimple in his chin to his messy curls, he looks more god-like than angelic. It's not fair.

"This enclave," he says. "You fear its judgment yet persist in lying to yourself about the demon. As you said, you only have time to face your real enemies. He will not turn you in. You pretend it's a concern when you know it isn't."

"You're way too confident for someone who hasn't even met the guy," I hiss. "Ciprian is an expert at hiding his intentions. He ran circles around the rest of us, and we never even realized. The enclave may not care if we break petty laws, but killing a guard? If he tells his father, they'll come for me."

Malach cocks his head. "I judged his intent—"

"Leave it alone. He's a liar." I raise my fists and drop into a fighting stance. "I don't want to talk about it anymore. We're wasting time. Time we don't have."

"As this clearly upsets you, this is the last thing I'll say—"

"It doesn't—"

"Yes, it does. I only ask you to consider why you're this angry with him. Is it because he withheld the full truth or because you weren't smart enough to catch him doing it?"

I attack, hitting him with a flurry of punches.

Malach doesn't have my strength, but he's plenty strong on his own, strong enough that I don't feel bad throwing haymakers his way, especially after that comment. He thinks this is about wounded pride? That's bullshit.

Ciprian lied to me. Entered my home under false pretenses, tricked me into incriminating myself in a murder, and now he's holding it over my head. It's classic psychological warfare. Malach is naïve.

His radiant judgment isn't foolproof. It measures intent in any given moment, much like my truth. It can't be tricked, but it can miss things, especially if the situation is complex. And Ciprian is the perfect example of why overlooking one critical detail can be catastrophic.

The moon rises on fight night like a ghoulish celestial voyeur. Pure white and perfectly round, it fixes its steely gaze on me as I navigate the crowded streets on my bike.

If I win tonight—which I have every intention of doing—I'll walk away with a nice chunk of cash and an even nicer confidence boost. Putting myself in the path of an angry man's fists by choice is a hell of a lot more palatable than my lived alternative.

Luca and Malach are driving over in Luca's car. I asked for this solo ride to clear my head, and it *was* working—until the moon decided to poke her nose in my business.

Sliding my bike into the tight space between two souped-up cars that scream, *'Come to bed with me. I'll be sure to leave you disappointed,'* I remove my helmet and freeze.

Alistair is here. I can't see him, but I can sense him. Call it intuition or something more supernatural—he's as impossible to miss as the big-ass moon.

"Not now," I say, each word clipped. "I need to focus. Keep your distance."

I probably look insane talking to the empty street, but I sense him backing off, sinking deeper into the shadows. My shoulder blades itch, my wings demanding I set them free. I ignore them and stride into the Mouth of Hell, turning down the dark hallway Resker told me to use.

It ends at a tall metal door, littered with dents and faded stickers. I rap on it firmly, then wait. Footsteps echo behind the door—seven of them, to be exact—before a sliding window slots open. The sticker on top of it, perfectly aligned to disguise the panel, reads "Freaks Fuck Better" and depicts an orgy that's surprisingly graphic for a collection of stick figures.

I raise one eyebrow at the face in the window. This guy is the human personification of store-brand cornflakes, and I wouldn't be surprised if I forget what he looks like as soon as he's out of my sight.

"You're here," he grunts, sounding almost surprised.

I bite my tongue and barely resist the urge to drive my fist through the peephole and give him a more interesting canvas to work with. "Obviously," I say, managing to keep the worst of my attitude out of my voice.

The orgy sticker flashes me again as the panel snaps shut, then the door opens with a horrific high-pitched whine. I cringe. Have they never heard of WD-40? They could at least slather some coconut oil on the hinges or something.

Magic scrapes my skin as I enter the room. It's crowded with fighters. Some big, some small, and some familiar. Most are stretching or sparring. A few are chatting quietly among themselves, but most are engaging in pre-fight rituals, earbuds firmly in place.

The guy from the peephole is nowhere in sight. Or maybe he's here, and I already forgot his face. I shrug, flinching as Lyss appears in front of me faster than should be possible. Her face I remember . . . both of them.

"We've got our own lockers," she chirps. "Do you want me to show you?"

"Yeah, thanks." I do my best to reconcile the way she practically skips across the room now with the sideways skitter from our audition fight. "Have they announced the matchups?"

"Yep." Lyss points at the wall by the row of lockers, where a whiteboard hangs haphazardly against the gray concrete. About two dozen names are scrawled across it, but the handwriting is so sloppy I can't make anything out from here. "I was hoping for a rematch," she says. "But I won't get one tonight."

There's disappointment in her voice, but no animosity. I guess if I'd been the one to tap out, I might want another crack at the person who put me on my back too. As it stands, I'll be perfectly happy if I never face Lyss and her roving chelicerae again.

"Who did you get?" I ask, keeping the focus on her fight instead of asking about mine. I desperately want to, but I don't want to come across anxious.

"Dominic." She grins, then thrums her fingers against the red locker we've stopped in front of. The top one is labeled Lyss, and the bottom one Celine, which is a wild choice since the arachne shifter is at least six inches shorter than me. I'll have to bend over to get into mine—not that I care. I won't be leaving anything valuable in there. That's an invitation to get fucked with.

"You've got—"

"New blood, over here," Resker shouts, cutting Lyss off. She squeals with excitement and loops her arm through mine, practically towing me to Resker.

In addition to Lyss and me, Dominic and one other man make their way over. Dominic, who seems as big and blockish as ever, winks at me. "Hell of a hit, baby girl."

I smile. "Call me baby girl one more time, and you can experience it again. Free of charge." I'm glad he's being a good sport about the knockout, but I have no intention of letting anyone here see me as a hunk of meat.

"Ooooh, I like it," Dominic says, holding his hands out, palms up.

A smaller man stands at his side—everyone is small next to Dominic—watching our conversation with heavily lidded eyes.

My skin prickles. Something tells me if we draw each other's number tonight, he won't fall for a quick shot like Dominic did.

"Shut up and listen," Resker barks. Her hair is pulled back into a severe, slicked-back bun, which might make her give off ballerina vibes if there weren't half a dozen spikes sticking out of it. It suits her. She's basically a supernatural cactus.

"I hope you've put some thought into your fighter names," she says, checking the sleek black watch on her wrist, "because I'm going to need them in two minutes."

Dominic blanches, going whiter than he did when I knocked him on his ass. For some reason I take pity on him. "Go with something on theme with what you are."

He grunts, then grins, knocking his shoulder into mine in a move that's supposed to be friendly but nearly knocks me flat. "Thanks."

"Okay, time's up," Resker says. "Let's hear them." She looks first at Dominic, her lips twitching. "Something tells me this will be good."

"Hell yeah." He flexes one enormous arm and kisses the bulging muscle. "You can call me Tusker."

Resker's eyes dip closed. "Only if you absolutely insist. What about you, Lyss?"

"Well, I thought about Silka or Widowmaker, maybe even Chelicerae—for educational purposes, you know?"

"Less process more decision, please." Resker sighs.

"The Recluse," Lyss says proudly.

I give her a thumbs-up. It's a strong name, and she's got the skills to back it up.

Resker writes it down, then looks at the silent guy expectantly.

"Thorn," he hisses in a voice that sounds like glass scraping against ice. I blink a few times. He's a creepy guy. As for the name, it's simple, and there's nothing overtly embarrassing about it. Until I see him fight, I'm reserving judgment.

Resker turns to me last, assessing me with the same greedy eagerness from before. "What about you, angel?"

I'm expecting the nickname, but it still sets my teeth on edge. Now that Alistair has shown it gets to him, I expect her to use it at every opportunity. She's carved out a solid place for herself in the Fringes, which tells me she knows how to use every piece of leverage she can get her hands on. I shouldn't forget that.

"Verity," I say, holding her stare with a "don't fuck with me" look of my own. "You can call me Verity."

"Okay, Verity—you'll be fighting Thorn, and you're up first."

ELEVEN

LUCA

Nerves buzzing, I shove through the crowd until Malach and I are inches from the cage. Close enough to see and hear anything Celine gets hit with.

Don't kill anyone, I beg my basilisk. It's rattling inside my chest at a low frequency. Not pissed yet, but on guard, and eager to see Celine fight.

It enjoyed watching her beat the spider, although it also wanted to turn the arachne shifter to stone and keep her as a souvenir. I squashed that idea, knowing good and godsdamned well Celine doesn't want a massive, half-shifted spider made of rock in her apartment.

"The fight is crowded," Malach says, his green eyes rolling over the stacks before stopping on the cage. "She will win, Luca."

I nod, not sure if he's trying to convince me or himself.

Alistair materializes at my side—a six-foot-four battering ram with murder in his eyes. He shoves two guys flat and takes their spot. They protest loudly, but their angry shouts die off as soon as they spot his narrowed ruby eyes.

"I see you're calm," I mutter sarcastically without bothering to raise my voice. He'll hear me no matter how loud the crowd gets.

"Perfectly at ease," he says.

I nudge him with my shoulder and shake my head. He's as stiff as Roscoe . . . *after* I killed him. Nothing about that says "at ease" to me. And the look he's giving Malach would make most people piss their pants.

I suck in a breath for patience, and a fresh wave of sweat and beer hits my nose.

"Did you bring healing potions?" I ask, reminding him of our earlier conversation about precautions. Celine doesn't know, and if nothing goes wrong, she won't have to. But these fights are dangerous. If things go south, we'll need a fast-acting way to patch her up.

I feel pressure in my pocket as Alistair slides his hand into my jeans, then pulls it out, leaving the weight of a vial behind. "It's the best," he assures me.

"If she asks," I remind him, "then no, the fuck it isn't."

Alistair clenches his teeth, fangs peeking over his bottom lip. "She's too stubborn. Why won't she accept my help?"

I put my hand on his shoulder. "She's entitled to her pride, Ali. For some of us, it's all we've got."

"Celine has far more going for her than pride," he hisses. "As do you."

The bell ringing saves me from having to come up with a response. An excited rumble runs through the crowd as the emcee appears in the cage through a cloud of smoke. Stretching his arms wide, he shows off his colorful tattoo sleeves to the rabid supernaturals packed shoulder to shoulder in the warehouse.

"Welcome to the Mouth of Hell," he booms. "We have a special treat for you tonight: four new fighters ready to test their mettle and whet your appetite for blood."

"Four?" I raise my eyebrows, surprised that many were added to the roster.

"Resker loves her games," Alistair mutters. I barely hear him over the approving screams of the spectators. The row behind us lurches forward, and Malach, Alistair, and I have to plant our weight to keep from getting bowled over.

"Rowdy," I say. "I've never felt so much anticipation on fight night before."

"They can sense it," Malach says. "They want to be entertained."

An ominous chill runs down my spine. His words aren't prophetic—I don't think he has magic like that—but they are spooky. "You're creeping me out, dude."

"My apologies." Malach's lips curl, and Alistair shoots me an unimpressed look.

"Already making nice with your new roommate?" he asks, his voice dripping with bitterness. "He tried to have you killed, and had me run through, I might add."

I massage my temples. "Yeah, yeah, everyone here is a murderous dick. Can we forget about it for now? We're here to support Celine."

"Indeed."

"Judgment, not murder," Malach mutters.

Despite myself, I grin. Then the announcer calls for Thorn and Verity to enter the cage, and I tense. From opposite sides of the elevated octagon, Celine and some guy I've never seen before enter through rounded gates. Once they're through, faint bands of magic quiver and wall the openings off.

Dressed in all black, Celine's tight sports bra and spandex shorts are molded to her curves like a second skin. If I weren't so worried about her, I'd be drooling. She rocks on the balls of her feet; her full mouth is pressed into a tight line.

Her hair is braided to the scalp to prevent anyone from grabbing it. In normal fighting, hair pulling wouldn't be allowed, but this is the Fringes. If you're dumb enough to have your hair swinging around, you deserve what you get.

With a fresh buzz cut, Thorn clearly got the memo. Otherwise, he's difficult to read. Of average height and weight, he's still and watchful, completely ignoring the crowd as he stares Celine down.

I can't tell what kind of supernatural he is. He looks completely human, so maybe a witch? The only notable thing about him is his ears. The tops are discolored, a mottled pink and white. Maybe a birthmark or tattoo? It's nothing I've seen before.

"What do you think?" I ask Alistair.

Celine bumps knuckles with Thorn, and they circle each other.

When Thorn charges her, I flinch.

"He's fae," Ali says. "The ears. They're not pointed because the tips have been cut off."

"What the fuck?" I snarl as Celine narrowly dodges a brutal uppercut.

Thorn's fist grazes her cheek, leaving a bloody gash in its wake. Superficial. I know that. But seeing him go for her face pisses me off. He put so much force into the blow that he's off balance. Celine sees the opening and delivers a swift kick to his gut.

"Yes, baby," I mutter, too scared to shout and steal her focus even though the crowd is deafening.

The kick sends Thorn backward, but he doesn't lose his footing. I frown. With Celine's strength, he probably has at least one cracked rib. How can he stand there as if he feels nothing?

"I don't like this." I shift my weight, my hands balling and releasing as I watch the fight.

"Relax," Malach says. His green eyes dart my way before focusing back on Celine. "She can handle him. You must remain calm."

I've almost managed to convince myself he's right when Thorn hurls a jagged burst of red energy over Celine like a net. Her head drops back, her mouth opening in a silent scream.

Celine is in pain. Terrible pain. My fingers spasm, and a low rattle escapes my chest as the familiar icy chill sinks into my eyes. My basilisk has had enough. As far as it's concerned, everyone here needs to die.

"Hold it together," Alistair hisses. "She's got this. *Fuck*—your eyes. Look down!"

Hands shaking violently, I stare at my feet. *Calm down. Calm down. Calm the fuck down,* I beg. It doesn't work. I'd rather kill the first person to accidentally make eye contact with me than miss the fight. I can still hear everything, and my brain is filling in the blanks with worst-case scenarios.

Pain stabs my gums as my fangs descend, coating my taste buds with bitter venom. I grab Ali's arm. "Tell me what's happening," I beg.

"They're keeping their distance. Circling—wait, he's charging! Move, angel!" Alistair shouts. The crowd gasps with delight.

"What?" I squeeze his arm brutally, my fingers spasming as I fight the urge to shift.

"She let her wings out and used them to dodge. Get a hold of yourself; you need to see this. She's incredible." There's reverence in Alistair's voice. I can't believe I'm missing this.

"Come on," I beg my basilisk to stop fighting me. It listens, probably only because it wants to see too, and the cloudy, cold mist in my eyes retreats.

Whipping my head up, I take in everything I missed.

An airborne Celine hovers above Thorn near the top of the cage. She's using the vantage point to watch for an opening. I've never seen her fly before, and gods, she takes my breath away. Ferocious, deadly. I'm gone for her.

"Creative," Malach whispers fiercely. "Be creative, my truth."

Thorn stares up at Celine, and the slight widening of his eyes is the only sign he's surprised. He hurls another bolt of red magic at her. She doesn't try to dodge, gritting her teeth as the magic hits her shoulder. Then her wings smoke.

"Smart." I squeeze Ali's arm. "She's letting him get a few hits in so she can get mad."

Another bolt of magic grazes the tip of her right wing. A heartbeat later, it bursts into flames—each feather burning bright orange.

Screams, gasps, and cheers erupt around us as the crowd loses it, turning into a feral mob as Celine catches fire. Frenzied, they press forward. It's all the three of us can do to keep from being shoved under the cage and trampled.

I snarl at the people behind me, but they're being pushed too.

"Back up," Alistair shouts. There's a mesmerizing quality to his voice that I've never heard before, and the hairs on my arm stand on end. Like zombies, the row of men behind us steps back as one, buying us some breathing room. Their eyes are glazed.

"What did you—"

"Compulsion," Alistair snaps. "It won't hold forever, but it should buy us some time."

I nod and drag my attention back to the fight.

Face flushed with anger; Celine snaps her flaming wings together. The move sends her hurtling to the floor of the cage—body aimed like a spear. Thorn dodges her fists and feet but forgets about her wings. Spread fully, they bathe him in fire from the tip of his head to his knees.

His clothes light up until he's a walking candle, and the crowd roars.

"Shit," I mutter. Celine didn't break any rules, but if Thorn panics, he won't survive this. And I know Celine didn't come here to kill anyone.

Luckily, he doesn't panic. Instead, he drops to the floor, rolling until the cloud of thick, gray smoke makes it hard to see what's happening.

He's saved himself from burning to death, but Celine doesn't waste the opening.

Through the haze, I see her kick him in the head—once, twice —only stopping when his head lolls to the side. With her foot in the air, she watches Thorn with a hard stare, then blinks rapidly, as if she's coming out of a trance.

Celine drops to her knees beside the fae and uses her bare hands to smother the last of the flames on his pants leg. Her wings droop, and their fire goes out suddenly. Pure white, the feathers are delicate and untouched. If it weren't for the burning in my throat and Thorn's charred clothes, it would be easy to think they were never on fire to begin with.

The bell rings and signals the end of the fight.

Celine stands on wobbly legs.

The emcee is talking. I see his lips moving, but I can't hear anything over the possessive roaring in my ears. He lifts Celine's clenched fist high, and I realize the sound in my head is real—the audience is that loud.

They're obsessed with her. Absolutely wild about my girl. With soot on her cheek, half a dozen magical burns on her arms, and raw determination carved into her face, she's never looked so dangerous. Or so hot. She looks like mine.

Celine leaves the cage through the same tunnel she entered from, and I shoulder my way through the crowd. I don't know where I'm going—all I know is that I need to find her. Now.

TWELVE

UNSPOKEN RULE OF THE FRINGES #299:
DESIRE IS CONTROL.

CELINE

I stumble down the squat tunnel connecting the cage to the locker room with shaking hands. The sting on my palms from putting the fire out keeps me grounded. Barely.

I nearly cooked Thorn. And as soon as my flames transferred from my wings to his clothes, I could have cooked myself too. Gods, I never meant for it to go that far, but beating him fair and square feels amazing.

His magic attacks hurt. Lightning replacing the blood in my veins, they seared my nerves and raised the stakes. In the cage, I wasn't Verity competing in an underground supernatural match; I was Celine fighting for my life.

A dull glow illuminates the bottom of the tunnel, and I can't tell if it's another charm or a basic strip light. Either way, it gives me enough light to navigate the tunnel. The exit is only a few steps ahead, bright and—blocked by a shadowy figure.

I freeze and raise my trembling fists.

"It's just me," Lyss says. "Are you okay?"

I wince. There's a new wariness in her voice. I don't want her to fear me . . . but maybe it's for the best. I'm not exactly doing a great job protecting the friends I already have. I miss hanging out with Imani. I miss getting drinks with Brandy, Ada, and the girls. Keeping them at arm's length is necessary, but I didn't expect it to be this hard.

I nod, not trusting my voice yet. The prickling pain from Thorn's magic is still running through my body. From the weave of the sweaty socks hugging my feet to the light at the end of the tunnel—I'm hyper-aware of every sensation.

"Good," Lyss says, walking toward me slowly. She stops in front of me, about halfway through the tunnel. "I'm going to scoot around you if that's okay."

That's when I realize I'm blocking her way; fists raised like a maniac. I drop them and clear my throat. "Of course. Sorry, I . . . Good luck, Lyss."

The signature gap-toothed grin stretches across her face. "That's The Recluse to you." She lifts my right fist and bumps it against her own.

"Knock him dead," I say, digging deep for a smile. "Or at least unconscious."

Lyss squares her shoulders and raises her chin, and I see the spider staring back at me. "On it," she says.

Sagging against the curved wall of the tunnel, I let her pass, watching until the emcee calls her name and she steps through the magic film disguising the tunnel's opening.

A muffled argument echoes from the other end of the tunnel.

I whip my head around and squint, wishing I had stronger night vision, or a godsdamned flashlight or something. If I'm about to get jumped in a glorified tube, I'd rather see whose ass I'm beating.

Another shadow blocks the opening, broad shoulders eclipsing the light.

For a heartbeat, the shadow doesn't move, then it explodes into action, shooting toward me with determined strides.

"I will fuck—" I suck in a breath when the shadow reaches me, and I recognize Luca's familiar chiseled jaw.

"Perfect," he growls. "Fuck me raw. Fuck me sideways. Fuck me up. Whatever the fuck you want, baby." Then his lips are on mine, harsh, demanding, crazed. I grab his hair roughly, desperate for him to match the heat roaring through my veins.

His tongue tangles ferociously with mine, but his hands on my face are gentle. "You were great," he groans.

"Shh," I demand. "We can talk about the fight later. Touch me. Now."

Luca doesn't argue. He devours my neck, scattering hungry kisses beneath my ear before bringing the lobe into his mouth and biting it. There's a pulse between my legs, demanding to be satisfied as the adrenaline from the fight turns to arousal with one scrape of his teeth.

I grunt, shuddering with pleasure, then shove my hand down the front of Luca's pants. His cock is hard, the skin warm and smooth. I roll my thumb over the pierced tip and grin as he jerks against my fingers.

Luca's breathing is loud in the enclosed space. Touching him makes my desire shoot from a simmer to a rolling boil, and before I realize it, I've pinned him to the side of the tunnel.

His hands skate down my ribs. Grazing my bare skin, they send little explosions of pleasure through me. After the pain of Thorn's magic, it's the perfect contrast.

Luca drops to his knees.

There's so little room in here that the position drives me against the opposite wall, his face at my waist. He rolls my spandex pants down and breathes me in, eyes flashing yellow in the gloom of the tunnel.

Then, he buries his tongue inside me. No teasing licks, no easing in—Luca fucks me with his tongue like he wants to devour me. There's something about seeing him on his knees for me in a tunnel, with fighters on one end and a crowd on the other, that drives me crazy.

I rock my hips against his face, the telltale buzz of my orgasm building.

We don't have long. The fight between Lyss and Dominic could end at any time, although the muted thuds and grunts echoing through the tunnel tell me neither has tapped out yet.

Luca's eyes dart right and left, then up at me. He winks, pulling his tongue out of my pussy and using it to lash my clit instead. I writhe against his face, not sure if I want to get away or get closer.

His grip on my thighs tightens. I could break it, but why would I want to? All I want right now is for this moment to last. The pleasure. Being held by someone I trust. It's too good. He's too good. How did the friend who watched my back for years become the guy who eats me out until I drip down his chin like an ice cream cone left in the sun?

As if Luca can hear my thoughts, I feel his grin between my legs a second before he uses his thumbs to spread me wide.

Don't come. Don't fucking come, I order myself. I don't want this to end, so I hold back.

My chest heaves as I frantically take in a new lungful of oxygen. The air smells of sweat and sex and that perfect masculine scent that is Luca Saratelli. When he runs his lip ring over my clit, I know I won't be able to hold back much longer.

Ten more seconds. Give it ten more seconds. I lock eyes with him and focus on my countdown. Three-two-one—a wave of pleasure crashes over me. For a breathless moment, I hover outside my body. Time isn't real. There's only Luca.

When I return to myself, the sounds of the fight and my own panting are the first things I notice. On his knees, Luca's calloused grip on my hips is the only thing keeping me upright.

It's the perfect reminder of why I'm fighting. Because this life is worth living—every chaotic, disruptive moment of it.

"Luca," I gasp. My legs wobble as I try to stand on my own.

He surges to his feet, ducking his head to avoid grazing the ceiling and wiping the back of his hand across his grinning mouth. "Delicious."

I face the wall, arching my back so he'll get the message: I want him more than my next breath. This entire building could collapse around us, but if I don't feel his pierced cock splitting me open soon, I'll be the one knocking it down.

Luca runs his hand over my ass and moans.

I grind against him. "Hurry up," I whisper. "We don't have much longer."

A collective shout comes from the direction of the fight. The audience is disappointed in something. I'm running through the possibilities when Luca thrusts all the way inside me. The aching stretch is exactly what I need, and I bite my lip to keep quiet.

He doesn't waste time or try to tease either of us. Each thrust is deep and fast, hitting a spot inside me that makes my legs shake. When my arms give out, I let them, dropping my cheek against the cool, rough wall as Luca fucks me without mercy.

His fingers dig into my hips, hard enough to bruise.

I smile, hoping I'll see all ten fingers outlined on my skin once I get home. I hope they don't heal fast. I hope I'm out of concealer. I hope I have to take the stage at the Fang tomorrow night with his handprints all over me, and everyone sees how badly he wants me.

His skin slaps against mine, impossibly loud in the cramped space.

Luca, my Luca, the guy who's patient to a fault but hunted me down to fuck me in a dark tunnel because he couldn't wait a second longer. My pussy flutters around his cock as my heart skips a beat. He's everything to me. Why have I wasted so much time pretending I could ever let him go? *I can't live without him. I don't even want to.*

"Luca," I gasp, my heart beating too fast.

"Yeah, baby?"

"I love you," I blurt. His rhythm stutters, and I rush ahead. "And I'm not saying it because your dick is amazing or because I might die soon, or because you said it to me first and I feel guilty for not saying it back. I'm saying it because I don't ever want to spend another day without you, and I want everyone to know you're mine."

"Yes!" He groans against my ear; his chest pressed to my back. "Say it again while you strangle my cock."

"I love you, Luca," I repeat, sobbing the words against the wall.

His hand comes down on my ass cheek. The crack echoes through the tunnel as he thrusts into me one final time and stiffens, groaning in my ear. "I love you too, baby."

Another orgasm rolls through me. This one is smaller, but it's more than my exhausted body can take. My muscles turn to jelly, and if it weren't for Luca fixing my clothes and helping me get moving, I would still be lying here in a pile of limbs when Lyss comes back.

"If the fight doesn't end soon, they'll call it," Luca says. His raspy voice sends another convulsion through me. On cue, the bell rings, motivating me to move faster.

We step into the brightly lit locker room hand in hand. It's not as crowded as it was earlier. A lot of the fighters left to watch the earlier bouts from the private balcony Resker gave us a code to access. Thorn is nowhere in sight.

Not crowded doesn't mean empty, and I see every sly smirk tossed my way. One guy winks at me and opens his mouth, only to close it again after glancing over my shoulder.

I narrow my eyes, annoyed that Luca is the one he's scared of.

He should be scared of me.

I'm the one who won a brutal fight, and I'm no less deadly to him because he finds me hot. For fuck's sake, I lit someone on fire.

Tits turn men into fools.

"You can beat him up next time, baby," Luca says, his breath tickling my neck.

"Fingers crossed." I return the idiot's wink. He blanches and goes back to wrapping his hands. "How did you get in here?" I ask Luca as I tug the heavy metal door open.

"Threats." He shrugs, ignoring my sharp look.

The door swings shut behind us with another horrific whine, and I find myself face-to-face with the oddest standoff I've ever seen.

Alistair leans against the wall, ankles crossed, in a pose that's too deliberate to be casual, and Malach stands rigidly across from him, his beefy arms crossed. The tension between them crackles, and I slump, exhaustion getting the better of me.

"Are you hurt?" Malach asks. His green eyes scan me for injuries.

I shake my head and force a small smile. Alistair says nothing, but his gaze is hot and thorough as it sweeps me from head to toe.

"Do you want to watch the rest of the fights?" Luca asks me, running his thumb over the top of my hand.

"No." I squeeze his fingers and shift my weight, wincing as I feel the coating of sweat, magical residue, and cum on my skin.

"I've had enough of the cage for one night." All I want is to get home and scrub myself clean.

Without a word, they fall in around me: Luca on my right, Alistair on my left, and Malach behind me. I shake my head. I fought a powerful fae and won, but they think I need bodyguards to make it through a crowd?

My lips twitch. It's ridiculous. Absurd. Why do I love it so much?

THIRTEEN

ENCLAVE EDICT #2408:
SINCE OUR PREVIOUS EDICTS CONTINUE TO BE
OVERLOOKED, LET THIS ONE SERVE AS A REMINDER:
YOU'RE STILL FORBIDDEN FROM USING
MAGIC IN FRONT OF HUMANS.

CIPRIAN

She is a force. Unstoppable.

I want her to look at me like she did that night in the bathroom, with her fingers in my hair and her lips dragging against mine, as desire chased the fear from her eyes.

I want her forgiveness.

The wall around Celine is bigger than ever, but I can scale it. I'm stubborn, and with Sheena taking a trip for her own safety, I've got nothing but time.

Back in Vegas, Operation Win Celine Over has my full attention.

Maybe I shouldn't have wrapped a nightmare around myself and snuck into the locker room of the Mouth of Hell. And sure, it might not have been the best idea in the world to listen to Luca and Celine fuck in that creepy ass tunnel. I stopped myself from watching barely, but damn did I want to sneak a peek.

They're both stupid hot. I thought it the first night I saw them in the Naked Fang, and it's even more true now. But they think I'm scum. I need a chance to explain why I hid my identity.

My gut tells me Luca will be the easiest to convince. His basilisk is cold and unforgiving, but the man is pragmatic—more similar to a demon than most of the shifters I know.

Leaving the venue, I tug my nightmare around myself and send magic out in a scatter pattern—not trying to latch on to anyone's mind. This type of illusion is looser and far easier to break, but it uses less energy and works fine unless someone is already on guard.

Fingers grip my throat.

My spine slams into the warehouse wall.

I force myself to relax, walling off the memory of the last time I was attacked in the Fringes. Because this isn't random . . . I know this furious vampire.

Which brings me to the second hardest part of my plan: getting Alistair to forgive me. From my current lack of oxygen, he's still holding a grudge, and if I've learned anything about him in the weeks we spent together, it's that he isn't the type to hand out clean slates.

Ignoring the pressure on my throat, I let him strangle me while I do some mental math.

Alistair hates me, but he saved my life and gave me an expensive potion. The odds of him killing me are low, even with how mad he obviously is. Black dots crowd my vision, and I go deliberately limp against the wall.

Hissing, Alistair releases me and glares. "Why are you following us, wrapped in magic like a coward? Haven't you done enough?"

I ignore the dig. Ali knows perfectly well that, for all my faults, I'm not a coward. He's just trying to piss me off. "I wanted to say hi." I shrug. "I've decided to stay in town for a while."

"Why?" he snarls.

I wink at him. "The temperate climate?"

"Don't be cute."

"You think I'm cute?" I raise my eyebrows. "I knew it!"

Alistair turns on a dime and disappears into the shadows. I smile. This is step one of as many steps as it fucking takes to get them to trust me again. I'll make it happen; I'm determined.

When Celine orders her groceries, I bribe the delivery guy and carry them to her door myself. She takes the bags from me, and I keep myself disguised, only dropping the magic on my face to wink at her as she closes the door. Her eyes widen, but I put my nightmare back in place and walk away, whistling under my breath.

At the club, I cling to the stage and pretend to be a pencil-shaped man with a nose like a beak. I tip her recklessly with crisp hundred-dollar bills, placing them on the stage in a symmetrical stack, not a wrinkle in sight. They're new and in mint condition. When she smiles at me warmly, I let the nightmare flicker until she frowns. *I knew she would love them.*

At her next fight, I arrive early, feeding my magical core by consuming the trickles of fear the fighters give off as they enter the warehouse.

On the floor beneath the cage, the noise is deafening. Money changes hands, and the biting smell of violence coats the air. Part sweat, part blood, with a dash of magic—it's primal enough to make my heart race.

These fights are far from legal, but I understand why they're popular.

Beneath the adrenaline, there's a layer of raw authenticity that supernaturals living among humans must hide to blend in. In the cage, the veneer rubs off, and the fighters are celebrated for who they are.

It's appealing, but from the number of broken bones, burned skin, and loose teeth I've seen here, I have no interest in finding out how I would stack up. I prefer to watch.

Celine—I mean *Verity*—is fighting a wolf shifter tonight. It's an easy win for her, and the third in a row that's been a cakewalk compared to her first. Either they're trying to lull her into false complacency, or they want to keep her on the roster long-term.

I frown and make a mental note to investigate the owners. They could be hiding a bloodthirsty vendetta against angels or strippers—I laugh at myself, shaking my head at my stupidity. As if Alistair hasn't already learned everything there is to know . . .

He's more likely to pay someone off to secure easier opponents for her than leave stones unturned, except I doubt he's dumb enough to do that. Celine would kick his ass. And my spying has made one thing crystal clear: Alistair is still in the doghouse—proof Celine is every bit as stubborn as I am.

Her fist plows into the wolf's shifted face, and his human body collapses.

I cheer along with everyone else while assessing the guy. His control is impressive. Shifting only his head and claws while leaving the rest of his body human isn't easy to do. Growing up surrounded by shifters taught me that. The control many of these Fringe fighters have . . . it makes me wonder why they ended up here to begin with.

Joshua should expand his recruitment—No. I stop myself. I'm not here for the enclave or Dad or Joshua. For once, I'm here for me. For Celine.

Someone drags the wolf shifter from the cage, and Celine blinks out at the crowd like she's surprised by their ferocious support. I smirk. For someone as confident as she is, she never expects praise, and she's having a hard time adjusting to how much they love her.

Celine scans the sea of spectators. Her eyes land on me and stop, sparking with irritation. I hold her glare but don't return it, letting an unhinged smile split my face. For a solid minute, she stares at me. Shivering, I soak in her attention, letting her anger burn to the marrow of my bones.

Fuck, she's hot when she's pissed.

The emcee nudges her warily, and Celine blinks. Surprised to find she lost time staring into my eyes? Gods, I hope so. Pivoting, she disappears into the cage wall without a second's hesitation.

Without the heat of her anger, I shiver.

"She'll beat your ass for that stunt, Casanell."

I turn my smile on Luca and clear my throat. "I'm not that lucky, and we both know it."

He rolls his hazel eyes. "Why haven't you turned us in?"

Letting my smile fall, I raise one eyebrow. "You know the answer to that question."

"Celine thinks it's psychological warfare."

"Devious." I snort a laugh. "Celine thinks I'm cooler than I am."

"Don't distract her during her fights," he says. "And watch out for Ali, he's really pissed—"

"I can speak for myself." Alistair appears at Luca's side, a furious glower on his face. His fingers flex around nothing, and I remember how they felt around my throat.

Something crazy takes over me, and I can't stop myself from messing with him. Leaning forward, I smooth the furrows in his forehead with my index finger. "You shouldn't frown so much," I tell him. "People will think you're bad in bed."

Alistair bats my hand away and hisses.

Luca laughs. "Okay, I'll bite. Why would they think that?"

Raising both eyebrows, I lick my lips as I look him up and down. "Imagine how it would feel to never get anyone off . . . wouldn't that make you frown?"

"I don't know." Luca grins. "I've never had that problem."

"Stop entertaining this," Alistair demands.

"Stop telling me what to do," Luca says mildly, tossing his arm around Ali's shoulders.

"Did you lose the winged himbo?" I glance behind them, but there's no burly angel in sight. He's been glued to Celine since I returned to Vegas, and I'm dying to know the story there.

"He's waiting for Celine."

"Good," I say. "Should we meet them there?"

Alistair grunts and vanishes into the crowd.

Luca runs his fingers through his hair, making the melted milk chocolate strands stand on end. It should be goofy, so why do I want to kiss him? "Be careful, Ciprian. It's not safe around here, especially not for you."

I nod and watch him weave through the spectators. His warning encourages me. It may be dangerous for a Casanell on the Fringes, but Luca called me by my first name. Like an inchworm crossing a six-lane highway, I'm making progress.

Since Celine's fight is over, there's no reason for me to hang around any longer. Whistling cheerfully, I push past drunk witches and rowdy shifters, reaching the exit with no problems.

The stars wink down at me, so bright that I can see them over the blinding city lights.

I kick a mangled aluminum can, dribbling the trash all the way to the spot where I street-parked my SUV, pleased to see it hasn't been stolen or keyed. I press the button to unlock it and squeeze the handle. Tonight went super well. After I get them used to seeing me around again—

My face smacks the roof of the car, nose first.

Someone wrenches my arm behind my back.

I try to break their hold but they're too strong. I scramble for my magic. I'm about to make whoever decided to touch me without permission run for the hills when I catch her scent and groan. "Hot wings, I thought you'd never find me."

Celine grabs my hair, yanks my head back, and drives my face into the roof of the car again. It barely hurts. She's being careful.

"Quit fucking with me," she hisses. "I can't waste time worrying about who's hiding behind every face when my dad could attack at any minute."

I frown. "Celine, I didn't mean to scare you, I just wanted to—"

"Play your stupid fucking mind games, I know."

"Make sure you didn't forget about me," I admit, cringing into the cool metal of the roof at how pathetic that sounds. Her grip on my hair loosens, and the warmth of her body disappears a heartbeat later.

I spin to face her, relieved to see she hasn't left yet. She's standing across from me, arms crossed tightly over her chest.

"I don't want to play," Celine says.

"Are you sure?" I ask quietly but without any bullshit. "Everyone deserves games sometimes. Shit gets too serious without them." *Let me make you laugh. Please.* Her face closes off, and she backs up a step. My stomach flips. Like always, I've said the wrong thing.

"Maybe that's true at the enclave," Celine says. "But the rest of us don't have that luxury."

She leaves me leaning against my car, heart pounding out of my chest.

I wait until she turns the corner and groan. "You were magnificent tonight," I whisper. "Please forgive me." Then I get into my car and drive back to my lonely apartment.

It's time to make a new plan.

FOURTEEN

ALISTAIR

It's times like this—when the sun forces me indoors like a rat in a trap—that I'm the angriest. Each twenty-four-hour stretch brings with it the same familiar torment. Unable to feel heat on my face during the day . . . Without Celine's touch, the night holds no comfort for me either. I get a few short hours in her orbit before she slips away from me under the cover of dawn, leaving me to brood in my apartment alone.

I thought if I gave her time to consider my apology and cool off, she would come around. But if her anger is cooling, it's also hardening—into an unbreakable crust, something I could spend a lifetime chiseling away at but never penetrate.

My angel is content pretending she never let me touch her. It's horrible. And it's not working for me anymore.

Tired of my own shitty company, I yank the refrigerator door open and select a bag of blood. Tossing the stopper on the counter,

I bring the nozzle to my mouth, suck, swallow, and immediately gag.

It tastes like a garbage bag stuffed with rotting meat smells after a day in the sun. Eyes watering, I spit the blood into the sink and watch it trickle down the stainless-steel walls and slowly circle the drain.

Cautiously, I sniff the bag, then freeze. *How strange.* There's no obvious stink. I've never found the flavor of cold blood gross before, but maybe my taste buds have decided to be fussy.

Resigning myself to the extra work, I get a ceramic cup from the cabinet, fill it, then put it in the microwave and wait. Forty-five seconds later, I give it a stir, then pop it back in for another fifteen.

Once it's done, the blood should be close enough to body temperature that I can close my eyes while I drink it and pretend my fangs are buried in Celine's throat while she rides my cock.

A snarl rips from my throat. My retinas burn with bloodlust, and my fingers curl around the counter. *Fuck.* I never should have indulged in that fantasy.

Thinking about Celine while I'm this thirsty is a recipe for disaster. It brings out the worst in me. Erasing all my carefully laid plans until I'm nothing more than a ruthless predator, willing to cut through anyone in my path to get what I want—even when the obstacle is beautiful, cunning, and strong.

I watch the plate in the microwave spin obsessively. The blood inside the mug bubbles once, twice, three times as it oscillates. The timer dings.

I give it a stir and take a careful sip.

It's like drinking hot trash.

Fury overtakes my disgust. Fuck my fussy taste buds, I'm thirsty. Plugging my nose, I chug the blood defiantly, dissatisfaction gnawing at me with every swallow.

I slam the mug down in the sink, and the handle snaps off.

Two drips roll down the inside of the ceramic. My stomach churns ominously. *Don't be sick. Don't be sick. Don't be sick.* It doesn't help. I have to use my vampire speed to make it to the toilet in time.

After I'm done, I drag myself to the sink, rinsing my mouth out with water. I've never thrown up blood before, not even right after I was turned . . . A flicker of unease makes my insides cramp, even though there's nothing left to eject.

Am I ill? Surely not. I never get sick. That bag must have been spoiled. I'll try again later—once my stomach quits attacking me.

After splashing my flushed face with cold water, I head to my office to fixate on the one thing I can control: my knowledge. With my artificial sunlamp on full blast, I scan what I've cataloged so far about the supernatural species living on the Fringes.

My upper lip curls. *It's not enough. Not nearly enough.*

I'm still in the dark on too many things: celestial magic, demonic strengths and weaknesses, and shifter limitations, to name a few. How many of us are there? How do the different types prefer to kill? How can I kill them?

Ciprian's identity would have been obvious to me if I'd known what to watch for.

The Fringe mentality of never asking questions is bullshit. I'm done obtaining information only for money; I want it for myself now so that I can never be tricked again. Call it paranoia or insurance—I don't give a damn; I *need* to know.

If that means I compile the most detailed dossier of supernatural abilities and traits in existence, that's fine by me. I've got time. My angel wants nothing to do with me.

My fingers fly over the keyboard as I add the details I've gathered on demons: nightmare, incubus, and ravoc. There are rumors of others, but these three types are the easiest to find information on because of their connection to the enclave. It's still thin. For such a visible family, the Casanells are good at scaring people silent.

The laptop I'm using is encrypted, and I've never accessed the internet with it before. It's not an efficient way to research, but it is secure, which is way more important. Letting this data fall into the wrong hands could put more lives at risk than my own. Lives I'm not willing to risk.

Air tickles the skin below my ear.

"I heard you've been asking about demons. I see it's true."

I slam the laptop shut and jump to my feet. The sunlamp flickers once, twice—then steadies, humming too loudly in the silence. Nausea forgotten, my blood pumps through my veins with enough force to make them bulge. I whip my head around. There's no one there. No one anywhere. Only me, alone as always . . . but I heard a voice. I'm certain I heard a voice.

Didn't I?

My palms begin to sweat.

My legs are oddly stiff and disconnected from my brain. Primed for action—I know they could move at a moment's notice, but I'm not sure the movement will follow my orders.

I force them to walk, anyway. *Get yourself together, Alistair. You're imagining things.*

Room by room, I check my apartment for intruders. There's no sign of anyone but me. No foreign scents. But the tingle on the back of my neck . . . my throbbing fangs. The less I find, the surer I am that someone is watching.

"Who's there?" I demand. My voice cuts through the heavy silence like a beam of sunlight through exposed vampire skin. It's horrible. *There's no hiding now*, my body tells me mournfully. *It knows we're here.*

Gods. Of course, it knows we're here. It—whatever it is—snuck up on us. Hiding was never the answer. My fingers curl, and a ghostly whisper crawls along the curve of my neck.

"My apologies," the voice titters, the timbre genderless and almost metallic. "I didn't mean to startle you."

I spin to face the general direction it came from. Near the couch, I think? My triumph at being right about the intruder evaporates as reality sinks in.

Someone is *in my home*. My heavily warded—maximum-bloody-security, doesn't even allow sunlight inside—home. Only three people even know this place exists.

"Show yourself," I snarl and bare my fangs, a clear warning to whoever had the unmitigated gall to break into my fucking place.

"Unfortunately, that's quite impossible," they say, a hint of melancholy joining the buzz of the words. "Speaking to you at all is quite difficult."

"No bullshit," I hiss. "Tell me who and what you are, or my next move will be finding a way to kill you. Painfully."

"Who I am: unimportant. What I am, given your research, is far more interesting. But the question you should be asking is where I live. I'll give you a hint: I'm not from around here, I can assure you of that."

Given your research. Any hope that this creature didn't see what I was working on dries up. A document on demonic abilities, focused on the three types known to be part of the enclave? That alone gives this stranger enough rope to hang me. I can't let them leave until I return the favor. Mutually assured destruction is the best I can hope for.

I raise one eyebrow and do my best to appear less hostile. "Where do you live?"

They laugh. "That's the spirit; I knew you'd come around. There wouldn't be such a thick file on you at the enclave if you weren't clever, Alistair Ashbourne."

That gets my attention, so I go out on a limb and guess. "You live at the compound?"

"Indeed," they hiss. "Quite clever, as I suspected."

I run through what I know about the supernaturals in residence within the compound walls. Shifters, demons, and most recently, fae. Shifters don't have magic like this. From what I know of fae, some have powerful glamour abilities, but they're not immaterial when they use them. A fae would need to break down the door to get in, invisible or not.

That leaves only one option.

"You're a demon, aren't you?"

"Precisely," they say. "I have valuable information for you about a development within the Casanell family, something I expect you to find most interesting given young Ciprian's interest in your lover . . ."

They leave the statement hanging. I stiffen. Are they threatening Celine? Ciprian swore he would keep our secrets, but I knew better than to believe him. And his father has spies everywhere. I need to play this carefully.

My back is against the wall.

"You're threatening me," I say stiffly. "Which isn't a good cornerstone for a trusting working relationship."

"Never. I'm simply offering you leverage," they say. "As a show of good faith, I'll tell you something about myself. I have no physical form and rely entirely on the magic of other demons to power my own. Even now, I'm beginning to fade. Bring Ciprian Casanell here—I'm quite incapable of harming him—and I'll charge my magic, prove I'm telling the truth, then we can discuss my other information."

Bring Ciprian here? I'd rather remove my own fangs with rusty pliers than invite that duplicitous asshole back into my home. He won't buy it either. Ciprian is a liar, but he's also perceptive.

I frown, wishing I had more to go on than the tonal shifts of a disembodied voice.

If this is a trap, why didn't the enclave simply knock the door down and let the sun do its dirty work? Sending an invisible demon to do the job is convoluted.

My hands fist at my sides. "I can't—"

"Please," they whisper. "I've much to tell you, but you must hurry."

They sound scared. Are they dying? What did they risk by breaking into my home? More importantly, if I don't bring Ciprian here, how will I get them to leave? My ridiculously expensive wards were useless in keeping them out, and the offer of leverage is tempting.

If I can protect Celine from the enclave, will she forgive me?

There are too many questions by far, and I'm aching to answer them all.

Your curiosity is a curse. Mum's words echo through my mind, sounding as much like a prophecy of doom in my memory today as they did when she said them to me growing up.

But curiosity is exhilarating to me. Terrifying too—like walking along a cliff in fog so thick you can taste it on your tongue. The uncertainty, not knowing where your foot will fall next, means there's always another secret to uncover.

"Bollocks," I mutter, scanning my living room once more for the source of the voice.

There's nothing, and the sense of being watched has faded too.

Are they dying? Or in some sort of stasis? I've never been able to resist a mystery. It's why I chose to be turned against Mum's wishes. She sees my decision to become like her as a betrayal, but I spent eighteen years of my life straddling the line—not human enough to be satisfied with the ordinary, and not supernatural enough to fit anywhere else.

Always alone. Achingly, endlessly alone.

Today, I face yet another choice. I can return to my flimsy demonic research and wait for the enclave to come for me and everyone I care about, or I can take a risk and save us all.

I'm dialing Ciprian's number before I even make the conscious decision to do so.

"I was surprised to hear from you," Ciprian says, smiling warily as I open my apartment door.

It's exactly one minute after sundown, and I can't help thinking he waited somewhere nearby for the last ray of golden, deadly light to fade before knocking. Courtesy or calculation? I can never tell with him.

Fingers twitching, I banish the glimmer of unease that runs through me. I owe Ciprian no loyalty. My life debt is paid. If I'm being shady to gain information from him, it's nothing compared to how he embedded himself in our lives. The fact that I'm still questioning his motives is a testament to the absolute mindfuck he did on me.

Besides, I won't pretend to accept his apology. While it's the cleanest way to trick him, the pinch in my belly when I imagine telling him he's forgiven, knowing I'll later rip that forgiveness away, feels cruel, even by Fringe standards.

"I have a new project I'm working on," I admit, keeping my excuse close to the truth.

Ciprian cocks his head, his white-blond hair purposefully tousled. In the weeks since his attack, he's completely healed. If I hadn't seen him beaten and bruised and smelled his dried blood beneath my fingernails for three days after the attack, I would never have believed he came so close to dying.

He looks me over too, a pinch appearing between his eyebrows as we lock eyes.

Making eye contact with Ciprian is like staring down a well: mesmerizing, weightless, and utterly disorienting. The inky depths swallow every particle of light. But if you brave the unsettling sensation for long enough, you'll notice there are different shades of black in his eyes, broken up by a charcoal ring around the pupil.

"A project . . ." Ciprian says. ". . . that you're telling me about? Yeah, right. Where are the hidden cameras? Is Luca going to pop out and turn me to stone once I make a shocked face?"

I roll my eyes. "Has anyone ever told you you're dramatic?"

He scoffs. "Only every day of my life. If you're hoping to call me something new, you'll have to be creative. I get around."

I walk to the kitchen and pull two glasses from the cabinet, considering the tone of his response. The subtle vein of self-deprecation—it's deeply embedded in his humor. He wields it like a shield, a way to keep people at arm's length. But what exactly is he trying to hide?

"You know what?" Ciprian asks, surprising me when he tugs on his hair and messes it up completely. "Scratch what I said. Yes, I've been called dramatic a lot, but I don't like it. It pisses me off."

I blink at him.

He knocks another strand of hair loose with his roving fingers. "You don't have to say anything. In fact, please don't. I'm just following the advice of someone I respect for once. Tell me about your project."

I hold my breath. This is the risky part, the gamble. For this to work, I have to show him some of my cards. "I want to know more about the strengths and weaknesses of the different supernaturals in our territory."

Ciprian pushes off the counter and stands upright, his posture rigid. "Are you trying to get yourself killed?" he demands. "If you poke around in legacy secrets, someone will make you a cliff note in their soon-to-be-erased-again history."

He's flustered, rattled even. This is interesting.

I take a step closer. "Will they?"

Ciprian laughs. "The question isn't what they'll do; it's what they won't do. Try asking a witch how she teleports. She'll yank your fangs out, grind them up, then use the dust in her sunscreen to punish you a second time when she goes to the beach. Or maybe you flirt with a fae at the bar. Chill, fun—a little tedious, sure—but not everyone is a sparkling conversationalist. Wrong! It's not chill, it's fucking frigid, because the motherfucker freezes you into an Alistair-shaped icicle for mentioning the color of his magical aura."

"Can you see a fae's magical aura?" I ask, surprised. I'm not sure why I hadn't considered Ciprian a useful source of supernatural knowledge before—he's heir to the enclave, he must know something.

"Don't ask that," Ciprian snaps. "Gods. I just told you not to ask that—Why the fuck are you smiling at me?"

"You're having a meltdown," I say drily.

"No," he hisses, pointing his finger at me until the blunt tip nearly grazes my cheek. "You'll be the one melting down after the fae gets his hands on you. I'll have to buy like three hundred and fifty hair dryers to defrost your ears enough to say I told you so."

"Hilarious." I pour him a glass of scotch and press it into his hand.

"It won't be." Ciprian scowls and tosses the amber liquor back, never flinching. "Ali, it's dangerous."

"So you've said. Explicitly."

He studies my face, those fathomless eyes roving over every ridge and dip. I'm confident in my ability to remain unreadable, but Ciprian looks at me so intently that I wonder if he sees something in the curve of my mouth or the rhythm of my pulse.

"You're going to tell me I'm being dramatic again," he finally says, the molten interest in his stare cooling a few degrees. Without moving or saying a word, I've disappointed him.

"I wouldn't dream of it," I purr.

I drink my own glass of scotch slowly, letting the flavors seep into my taste buds and chase away the lingering haze of my earlier sickness. Like a slap to the face, the liquor makes my heart race.

"But why?" Ciprian asks. His voice is soft and . . . vulnerable?

That can't be right. Gods, his reactions never make sense.

"Because it pisses you off," I say, holding his gaze and licking my lips. "You don't like to be called dramatic, remember?"

"Oh, I remember." Ciprian places his glass on the counter and steps toward me. "Don't fuck with me, Alistair. You can't choke me out one night, then invite me to your place and flirt with me like you forgive me the next. Unless you mean it . . . Get your revenge some other way."

His sincerity guts me. Rips me open so thoroughly, I expect to see my intestines spilling onto the kitchen tile between us. Damn him. Gods-fucking-damn-him. I have Ciprian exactly where I want him, and I can't close the distance and seal the deal. Not this way.

"I don't forgive you." He visibly retreats at my words. The life drains first from his eyes, then from the rest of his expression, eventually spreading to his posture too. He loses an inch of height as he slumps, and I steel myself to continue. "But I do want your help."

"Okay. I'll help you, but you have to promise me you'll be careful. Asking the wrong questions could get not only us killed, but Celine and Luca too."

It's dangerous. I know that, but the invisible demon has me cornered. For a second, I consider telling Ciprian the enclave has a rat. He might be grateful. He might deal with the problem and owe me another debt—but I've never revealed a source before, and his betrayal is too fresh. Godsdammit, there's no clean way out.

"They're not involved in this," I say, choosing to sound like a naïve idiot instead of an overconfident asshole.

"They're known associates of yours—don't be absurd. Everyone's seen you hanging onto her at the club."

"No one touches her," I snarl as boiling blood pounds the backs of my retinas. The idea of someone going after Celine ignites an irrational rage inside me. Gods above. This is why I needed to feed earlier. When I get like this, it's impossible to reason.

"Don't forget this anger," Ciprian says calmly, looking at my face with no sign of fear on his own. "You'll need it if this goes south."

I nod, and a ghostly presence stirs against my lower back. Is the demon reminding me they're here? In my apartment, with me at their mercy and Celine in their crosshairs? If they're trying to give me a sign, they need to work on their nonverbal communication because touching me while I'm this amped is a recipe for disaster.

"I won't tell you anything that could get someone hurt," Ciprian says, his eyes unfocused as he thinks my proposal over. "Only basic stuff I've noticed and the things you would have learned if you'd gone to Starfall Academy."

Bitterness chokes me. Mum thought supernatural learning was a waste of time. Once the deed was done, she said I had damned myself. To her, there's no point in educating a monster. She told me bits and pieces about the supernatural world. Immigrants in a realm native only to humans and witches, born vampires share Earth with all the creatures who decided to leave their home realms behind. Since no one else around the Fringes ever mentions attending an academy, I'm confident I'm not the only one stumbling around in the dark.

"I'm not trying to hurt anyone," I tell Ciprian, irritated by his insinuation. These are my people. The Fringes are my home. And I never hurt anyone unless they cross me first.

"Sure," Ciprian mutters. "But do you have complete control over everyone you sell information to?"

"Do you have complete control over the information you provide the enclave?" I hiss.

Ciprian releases a puff of air. "Obviously not, dude. Why do you think I keep half of what I hear to myself?" He shakes his head and tucks the wild strands of hair behind his ears. "I'll put some information together and bring it to you soon."

I imagine Ciprian compiling data haphazardly in his apartment and then dropping a stack of loose-leaf papers in an alley on his way here, and I grimace.

"I'd rather you worked on it here."

Ciprian holds my stare. "Am I a slow-burn captive?"

I raise one eyebrow, annoyed yet again by how often he takes me off guard.

I hate asking for clarification, but with Ciprian it's almost always necessary. He loves to make obscure references and pretend they're part of everyone's lexicon. Although, if I stay quiet long enough, he might explain without—

"It's like getting a wild animal used to a cage. You let them come and go at will. Until one day—*bam!*" He claps his hands. "You close the door, and they're stuck."

"If that was my plan, I wouldn't admit it to you," I say, rolling my eyes. "I'm more concerned about you getting too comfortable and refusing to leave."

"What do I get out of this anyway?" Ciprian asks.

"A good night's sleep for the duration of your stay on the Fringes." I rub the tips of my fingers together. "I never kill my informants."

"Bro." Ciprian claps me on the shoulder. "If all your deals go like this, your informants need to unionize. Pronto."

"Start work tomorrow at noon?" I ask, ignoring his joke.

He rounds the kitchen counter to leave, nodding over his

shoulder as he heads for the door. The tingling presence grazes my back again, softer this time . . . approval? I guess they've gotten everything they need.

"You're going to forgive me, Ali—I've got a good feeling about this."

The grin on his face is boyish. All charm and hopeful excitement.

I stay quiet, but my chest tightens. It's official now. I'm using Ciprian Casanell for information while hiding the truth from him. In one way, it's poetic justice. In another, hypocrisy. I tell myself I shouldn't feel guilty. I'm not sure I believe it.

The door closes firmly behind him, and I hurry to lock it. Ciprian may be right about earning my forgiveness, but it remains to be seen if repaying his omission with one of my own will sever the final thread of trust between us.

FIFTEEN

ALISTAIR

"Well done," the voice says. "Are you convinced now that I mean you no harm?" I have a hard time hiding my disbelief. The only thing I'm convinced of is that I'm talking to a snitch. And the longer they continue to invade my privacy, the less patience I have.

"What did you do to him?" I demand.

Ciprian didn't appear sick or hurt, but the invisible demon clearly feels better now, and magic is nothing if not a complex system of checks and balances.

"Again, you ask the wrong questions," they say. "Let's return to *what* I am: a mazzikin demon. Made entirely of magic; formless, we exist only by remaining in the presence of other demons, preferably powerful ones."

"You live at the compound—"

"Out of necessity and tradition, yes. My clan has been linked to the Casanell family for centuries. We siphon their magic to power ourselves and do a few simple household chores in exchange. An agreeable deal for the most part. As for what I did to him, young Casanell didn't notice when I siphoned from him at age two, and he certainly won't notice now. Do try to quell your absurd qualms."

Household chores, siphoning magic, their obvious defensiveness—if they're telling the truth, I'm starting to believe this demon can't do much physical damage. But keeping an invisible servant around is the perfect recipe for a ready-made spy that no one suspects.

"Your history lesson was fascinating, but I have no way of verifying it," I say, examining the cuff of my shirtsleeve. "I think it's time you told me why you're really here."

Their silence is absolute, interrupted only by the gentle drone of electricity and the puff of cool air exiting the ceiling vents. The mazzikin is trying to make me nervous and get me to backtrack. I'm far too experienced with silence for that to work.

I sit on the couch and casually prop one ankle on my opposite knee. With a steady pulse and nothing but time, I wait them out. I'm not the one who needs siphoned demonic energy to make myself heard, and I've already begun the good faith portion of this negotiation by bringing Ciprian here to be snacked on.

The mazzikin will come around, or they won't. The outcome can't concern me. My business remains successful because I refuse to scramble. Ever.

"There's a prize at the compound—a being more powerful than any born on Earth in hundreds of years. She dropped into the enclave's lap quite by accident, but they won't hesitate to make use of her."

My brow wrinkles. That's incredibly vague. "Use her how?"

"Money, power, control . . . the implications are endless," they whisper smugly.

"Uh-huh." I steeple my fingers and relax against the couch. "That's fascinating, but from where I stand, the enclave already has all those things. Why should I give a damn if they do some recruiting?"

"You're a fool," they hiss. "Have you seen many djinn walking your scum-encrusted streets? Her powers will ignite war. These lawless Fringe communities, where you do as you please and answer to no one, will disappear—turned to dust with a snap of her fingers."

I focus on keeping my breathing even and my face slack. The djinn report is interesting. It's worth investigating, but the mazzikin's heated speech made it clear they aren't here for equality and justice for all. "Why would you betray the Casanells?" I ask.

"My motivations aren't part of our bargain."

"I say they are." I push to my feet. "I'm happy to pay you for this information—half now and half when I verify it—but our dealings are done unless you tell me why you're really here."

My blood heats. This is the tipping point.

In the Fringes, I wouldn't ask. Any potential client wouldn't tell me anyway, and the deal would be lost, but this mazzikin says they've been part of the enclave their entire life. If that's true, they've been spoon-fed the enclave's talking points for decades. They must have a reason to justify their betrayal, and I want to know what it is.

"Harboring the djinn will destroy everything the demons have built here," they say grimly, quieter than before. "She's an outsider and powerful, but Dimitri Casanell doesn't see the target he paints on his back, only the potential: for riches and reconciliation with his son."

"Ciprian?" I ask.

"The family fool?" The mazzikin cackles. "He's a lost cause, and his father knows it. Ciprian will go nowhere and accomplish nothing; that's clear from his shameful fascination with the

Fringes. Callum has potential, but only if the djinn is dealt with."

Anger burns in my belly.

I'm not sure if it's my hunger or my irritation with this smug, bitter demon, but I want them gone. The information—if it pans out—could be the most valuable I've stumbled upon in years. What I don't know is the cost and who will be asked to pay it.

I raise one eyebrow and reach for my wallet. "I assume you prefer cash?"

I pace the length of my apartment, wearing out the floor as I consider the angles. A powerful djinn, drama among the Casanells, a file on me and my dealings, and interest in Celine?

How does Ciprian fit into all this?

His frantic concern for his unnamed friend flickers through my mind. More than a month ago, he sat here on my couch, pale with blood loss from saving my life, gripping his phone until his knuckles turned whiter than his face.

Could that friend be the djinn the mazzikin believes will tear the enclave apart? It's a flimsy theory, but I can't stop thinking about it. Call it gut instinct or paranoia, I need to know if this person is one and the same.

If I confront Ciprian about this and it goes poorly, the enclave will almost certainly have me killed. But if he is close to the djinn and I regain his trust . . . he could make an introduction.

What am I willing to risk to earn a wish? I know I'm playing a dangerous game, but I'm backed into a corner. I have no choice but to fight my way out.

The memory hits fast—I should have expected it. Because I've been in this situation many times before: wanting something no one will let me have.

"You ask too many questions, Alistair. It will be your ruin." Mum's lips are pinched. She's annoyed with me again, this time for talking to the gardener's children. But she doesn't understand. They move differently than she does, differently than anyone else on our estate—besides me—and I want to know why.

"You don't answer any of them," I protest.

Her eyes flash red. "Children are to be seen and not heard. Are your needs not met? Honestly, Alistair, one would think I deprive you."

My fingers curl into fists. I hate it when she talks to me like this.

What she says is wrong, I know that, but I don't know why. And if I don't know why, I can't win the argument. And if I can't win the argument, I won't get answers. I'll never know why her eyes turn red when she's angry, yet mine stay as blue as the trout pond when the lily pads split to reveal the crystal surface beneath.

Cautiously, I switch gears, adjusting my face until it's picture-perfect—like the paintings in the formal sitting room Mum loves so much. "Will you play outside with me tomorrow?" I ask.

"Unfortunately, my schedule simply won't allow for that, but I'm happy to have the front lawn lit for an evening game of croquet." It's as I suspected. She won't step foot outside until the sun retreats below the treetops.

The heavy curtains are always drawn tight in the residential wing. The gardener's children have a theory, and they were more than happy to tell me that our home and everyone in it is cursed to burn in the sun. I laughed in their faces, pushing my sleeve up to reveal the dusting of freckles on my skin courtesy of the summer rays.

The oldest, a boy called Samuel, smiled at me then. It was the smile I hate—the one that says someone knows more than I do. Samuel gestures to the rolling green hills and our stately stone estate. "Everyone here is cursed. Everyone but you," he says. "One day you'll be cursed too, unless they eat you first."

I frown, my heart beating too fast. I don't understand. Samuel isn't making any sense. Something nibbles at the back of my mind —like the mouse in the stables consuming the wedges of cheese I bring him when I'm at my loneliest.

"No one will eat me," I retort, fury gripping me.

"Not until you're bigger," Samuel says with a shrug. "Then they'll eat you for sure."

Before I can think through why I shouldn't, anger gets the best of me. My fist slams into Samuel's nose. He wails, presses his fingers to the injury, and makes a bubbling snort-like sound. My head feels light. I watch, transfixed, while blood—as red and shiny as the cherries from our finest tree—dribbles from his nostrils.

His sister Peg shoves me, and in my surprise, I fall on my bum. "I hate you," she screams. "I hope they eat you soon, do you hear me?"

A chill runs down my spine, but it has nothing to do with the superstitions Peg is spewing and everything to do with the shadow covering all three of us.

"Get on with you," the stable master snarls at the gardener's children.

They scurry away, never looking back, and I scoot toward the wall, hoping Ansel doesn't notice me. As always with Mum's servants, it's a pointless hope. His eyes dart to me. I blink and scramble to my feet.

"Forget what those urchins told you," Ansel says, his tone sending a shiver down my spine. His eyes are red and terrifying. I can't look away, even though I want to.

A commotion among the horses draws his attention, and I run directly into the sunlight outside the stable. Ansel doesn't follow, and deep in my belly, I know he won't. I keep running until the stitch in my side is impossible to ignore, and my face stings from the heat of the sun.

Cursing, I blink rapidly and replace the memory of the bright summer day with the reality of my dim, shuttered apartment. As a boy, secrets called to me, just as they call to me now.

I won't be able to let this go.

The aching burn in my throat spreads to include my mouth. I can taste my own thirst—a mixture of salt, bile, and desperation.

I glance at the sink, filled with one broken mug and a dozen opened pouches of blood. Inexplicably rancid, all of them, I've tried and failed to drink from every single one.

Shaking my head, I chuckle wryly.

I traded the sun's burn for another twice as insistent. Mum would call me a fool. Perhaps she would be right. One thing is clear to me: if I don't hold blood down soon, everyone around me will be in danger.

Starving vampires don't ask permission.

SIXTEEN

UNSPOKEN RULE OF THE FRINGES #502:
HABITS CAN BE DEADLY; MAKE LIFE-SAVING ONES INSTEAD.

CELINE

I spit blood into the bowl of the ceramic toilet and flush, watching the pink swirls disappear down the pipe. Brushing his teeth, Luca watches me from the corner of his eye.

"Spit it out," I sigh, knowing he's got something to say.

He shrugs and turns his charming grin my way, toothpaste bubbling from the corners of his lips. "Looks like you already did, baby."

I secure my hair in a loose bun on top of my head and turn the shower on. "It's only a bruised lung, Luca. Minor. The kind of injuries most *nish thatsha* wouldn't notice."

"Metal," he says, spitting into the sink, then rinsing his mouth out.

As I strip, my annoyance simmers. Since I've already stowed my wings in preparation for my shower, the itch between my shoulder blades is impossible to ignore.

Biting my lip to keep from picking a fight with Luca, I step into the shower. Steaming water rolls down my back. Rotating slowly, I keep the spray off my hair and let it crash against my chest instead.

Even the tiny drops of water hurt.

I took a blow last night that sent me crashing into the cage wall. My wings helped me get away before my opponent could snap me in half with his follow-up attack, but my entire body feels bruised.

Under the stream, I sag, breathing deeply through the pain. Every rise and fall of my chest squeezes another ache out of my body. *Be positive, Celine.*

I am getting better; I know that. I've won every fight so far, although there have been some close calls. Good for business, according to Resker—except I can't stop worrying that one of these days, I won't be fast enough . . .

The worst of it all is the anticipation. Peeking around every corner. Tossing and turning every night—haunted by memories of the past and fears for the future.

What is my father waiting for? Will his assassins strike once they see me hobbling around, bent over with pain? I'm sure he would love to prove all my efforts are futile before killing me. A double victory for him. A hopeless death for me.

The shower curtain rustles, and a rush of cold air hits my ass as Luca steps in behind me. I don't turn around, letting the water do its work and relax my tight muscles. With my eyes squeezed shut, I hear Luca lathering his hands before placing them on my shoulders.

He massages them, slowly increasing the pressure until I want to cry and scream with agony and relief. By the time Luca turns me to face him, I'm more string-limbed marionette than ferocious fighting angel. He kisses my forehead, my cheeks, the left corner of my mouth, and the swell of my right breast where the worst of the bruising is.

Tears burn behind my eyes. I refuse to let them fall.

"Would it be so bad to let yourself hurt, baby?" Luca asks. His lips move against my skin, softer than butterfly wings. "You're the toughest person I know; you don't have to prove anything to me."

I open my mouth to respond, to tell him why that's dangerous, but a hiccup comes out instead of my carefully workshopped argument.

Oh gods, I think I'm going to cry.

I cover my mouth and stare into Luca's warm hazel eyes in horror.

His expression doesn't change: compassion—without a whisper of judgment—and a sturdy support that makes me feel as if he would take care of me for as long as I need him to and never complain.

It's terrible.

"Some things are too heavy to carry alone," Luca whispers.

He kisses my forehead and leaves his mouth there. Tiny rivulets of water divert at every point where our bodies touch, their downward progress distorted by our connection.

Will my fate be like this water—changed because of Luca's support—or will his future be wrecked because of my love? It's the truth that plagues me most; one my magic is useless in uncovering.

A sob rips free from somewhere deep inside me, careening up my throat, then ricocheting out of my mouth violently.

It's guttural.

My shoulders shake.

This pain doesn't have a godsdamned thing to do with my bruised lung.

My wings shoot from my back. They wrap around me and Luca,

creating their own tears. Chilly drips run along the edges of the feathers and drop to the shower floor to mix with the hot water. The drain can't keep up with the influx of liquid, and tepid water swirls around our toes before it's sucked through the grate and carried away.

Gods, I'm crying hard enough to give Imani a submersion panic attack. Where did all these tears even come from?

"It hurts," I admit, the sound of my voice thick and unfamiliar to me.

"I know, baby," Luca says. "Let it out. Tell me what hurts."

Can I? This burden is mine to carry. I've held it alone for as long as I can remember. Even when Mom was alive, I couldn't unload on her. She couldn't, or wouldn't, leave him, and there was no point begging for something I couldn't have.

"The fights hurt," I say, starting in the shallow end to test things out.

"Of course they do. Your opponents are brutal."

"And Alistair." I hiccup. "He thinks I'm a slut." *And I miss him.* I'm not brave enough to say that part out loud, but Luca isn't dumb. He knew about my feelings for Alistair before I did.

I can still picture the feral expression on Alistair's face as he tore into me for stripping. I've been on guard against guys like him for years, but he acted different. I'm still having a hard time believing the things he said.

"You have to take your power back," Luca says. "Later, though. Keep venting, Celine. I'm here." His words trigger a flashback to Ciprian's rampage ramble, and the next sob out of my mouth is so ragged it hurts my bruised chest.

"C-Ciprian," I sputter, lifting my head to meet Luca's eyes through my blurry vision. "He was a liar. I gave him my trust and my fear, but he was part of the enclave all along."

Luca holds me tighter. "You feel betrayed."

I pause. Do I feel betrayed? I'm mad. Ciprian stomped all over my sense of justice, but for someone to betray you, they must first be a part of you—someone you've allowed to weave themselves into the fabric of who you are. If I allowed Ciprian that far beneath my skin . . . I'll have no choice but to cut him out and make myself bleed in the process.

Which is exactly what this feels like.

I heave in air. "Yeah, that seems right." It's a relief to admit it. As if I'm naming the dark cloud over my head for what it is and not what I'd prefer it to be. "Malach being here makes everything harder."

"Why?" Luca asks. His voice is curious but not demanding.

I consider the question. Malach hasn't given me a minute of trouble. His ambushes of the guys were diabolical, but now that he's stopped attempting impromptu 'judgment' attacks, there have been no issues.

The root of my unease goes deeper. It runs through me like a vine growing from my bones. Malach's presence hurts because of everything he reminds me of. My painful past. The realm I left behind. He deserves someone who will live in the celestial realm with him and give him a good life. And I will never go back.

Two truths, diametrically opposed and sharp as knives. They cut.

"He makes me remember the life I should have had," I say. "The life I don't want anymore. I see him making plans in his head that he has no idea how to hide, and I know I'll hurt him. And I hate that."

I broke my betrothal vows when I ran away from home, but that story isn't for Luca to hear. That pain belongs to Malach and me alone. Because on that day, I made myself a liar—and my magic nearly killed me for it. "When I see him, I remember it all."

Luca kisses my cheek and holds me until the water runs cold. My tears are all dried up, the ones from my eyes and my wings. Like a wrung-out dishrag, I'm limp and exhausted, but I feel lighter too.

I turn the water off, scared to face Luca, and stare at my feet.

As always, my toes are painted—emerald green with a glittery topcoat—but one is chipped. Fuck me, I'm just like my middle too.

But if I can cry all over him, I should be able to look at him afterward, right? Even if he judges me for it. *Don't be a coward, Celine.*

Bracing myself, I lift my chin and meet his hazel eyes.

His expression nearly knocks me on my ass . . . because the only thing I see there is love.

SEVENTEEN

TRADITIONAL *NISH THATSHA* BETROTHAL VOW:
MY FATE IS NO LONGER MINE TO COMMAND, BUT OURS TO
WEAVE. SHOULD I EVER SEVER THE THREAD BETWEEN US,
MAY IT STRANGLE EVERY FORTUNE I DARED TO
SHAPE WITHOUT YOU.

MALACH

I don't intend to listen in on Celine and Luca's conversation. My moral fiber prohibits intentional eavesdropping, but this apartment is small, we're due a visit to the young angels soon, and I'm simply attuned to her voice.

With my hand pressed to the bathroom door, I listen to her cry. Her tears claw at my soul, exactly as our celestial heritage intended. I'm *supposed* to rend realms from their orbits when she weeps. Anything to banish her sadness.

How Luca listens calmly, I cannot fathom. Curious, I send a band of magic through the crack beneath the door, whispering under my breath until my skin is crowded with runes.

Judgment: the radiant magic I was gifted with. It can be

finicky, but I've spent a lifetime honing it. Shifting through layers of bias and intent, known and unknown, I search the heart—not the organ distributing blood to their body, but the motivations that drive them.

Unseen and unfelt, my judgment finds Luca and surges eagerly inside.

There's anger—bright orange. Hot. Coiled in the corner of his chest, it burns inside him. *His basilisk?* Around the flame, there's a massive red orb, something I've caught glimpses of in others but never seen in such abundance before . . . devotion.

My hand curls against the smooth wood grain of the door. *It's beautiful.*

Luca is utterly and completely devoted to Celine. While there are spots of green around his heart—ambition—and black—bitterness—he's smothered them to mere pinpricks. Shoving them out of the way so he can offer her what she needs: comfort, compassion, and a safe place to unravel.

I was wrong to judge him in battle. While he *is* a lethal monster, Luca's intent shines brightest when he focuses on her. I rub the back of my neck as my mouth goes dry. Have I judged others unfairly before?

Retrieving my magic, I drop my hand from the door. What am I doing? They deserve privacy. I turn to leave, but Celine's next words stop me hard, as if I attempted an unlawful crossing of the echelons only to be rebuffed by the magic guarding the celestial pathways.

She hates the plans she sees in my eyes.

It hurts more than I expected. I-I can't bear it. Stumbling away from the door, I bump into the bedframe, and wince at the thud. The room seems smaller. The walls are closing in around me. While I judged Luca, they judged me and found me wanting.

Does Celine mean the things she's saying?

My magic quivers eagerly in the back of my mind. I could

send it out again, just for a moment—No! I swore I wouldn't. I held her hands in mine and vowed never to use my judgment against her. She deserves the chance to show me her truth.

I'm numb all over.

The celestial realm will always be where our story started. It doesn't have to be where it ends. Not entirely, at least. She used to know my every thought before I did, yet she's read my intentions entirely wrong.

How can I get her to know me again? Do I even know her?

I glance around the room. Her bed is flawlessly made. Each corner neatly tucked. Green pillows of a variety of shapes prop against the headboard.

I run my hand across the fabric of the one closest to me. The soft texture scrapes against my rough fingers—delicate and subtle: everything I'm not.

Celine could turn these pillows to feathers in seconds, yet she takes the time every day to arrange them on her bed. Order and beauty—these pillows make her feel happy and in control. Dual-purposed, I must show her I can be that way too, that life with me isn't limited to what her fears tell her.

Unfortunately, that means not breaking through the bathroom door to change her mind right now. Some truths must be proven over time.

Celine is my person, the one I swore to navigate life with, but she's forgotten how good we are together. I'll remind her that our connection isn't a mistake, because without her help . . . I'll be lost forever.

Pain pierces my temple, the headache threatening to blind me.

It's a visceral reminder of why I can't fail.

Celine thinks she severed our vows when she left, but they aren't broken, only bruised. Judging her intent rather than her actions, our combined magic knows she left to escape her father, not me. Until her heart rejects me, they will persist—tattered and worn, tethering us until time itself unspools and the stars forget our names. I will do the same.

"Tell me more about the orphans," Celine says.

I study her, surprised she's asking—especially now.

Walking by my side down the street, she shows no sign of her earlier tears besides a slight swelling of the skin around her eyes.

Beyond my initial explanation, Celine hasn't brought up life at home, except to ask how and when I believe her father might attack.

"They were marked by your father for assessment," I say. "He ordered they be collected and bound with silence to await his verdict about their place in society."

Celine grabs my arm, her fingers strong and determined as she pulls me to a halt. "Don't sugarcoat it, Malach. You wouldn't have dropped them here if you believed there was another way."

I stand a little taller, rolling my shoulders back. Her faith in me feels good. Warmer than the bold, garish star that gives life to this planet.

"Some orphans are never given an assignment . . ." I grit my teeth, remembering how horror consumed me when I learned of S'lach's plans. I was too late for dozens of my people. "His dedication to balance has reached unsettling heights. And with his radiant word—"

"Anyone with enough balls to speak against him or blow the whistle gets silenced. I know how he operates."

Celine scowls, her face twisted with anger. I flinch. It can't be easy to hear how her father's evil has spread. It used to be concentrated on her and her mother.

Gods, this conversation is difficult for a myriad of reasons.

"Why didn't the kids remember you, though?" Celine asks.

"You don't have magic that would make them forget being abducted, yanked through a gateway, and dropped in Sin City."

"I was surprised too at first," I admit. "But S'lach's stasis held absolutely until we came through the gateway. I left before they woke from it, watching from a distance to make sure they were okay."

Celine shakes her head, her upper lip curling at the corner. "Leaving me to provide an explanation to panicked angels with no idea where they'd landed. Convenient."

I look at my feet, the brown leather of my boots dulled by dust. I never meant to give Celine more than she could handle; I only wanted to get them to safety. And I knew she wouldn't fail them.

"Hey." She squeezes my arm. "That wasn't a criticism. You did good to get them out, especially knowing what he would do if he caught you defying his orders."

Behind layers of muscle and bone, my heart constricts painfully.

Her faith in me feels good, but her praise hurts.

Flapping wings echo off the pavement, and Celine's fingers drop from my arm to wrap around the hilt of the thin blade strapped to her thigh.

I hold my hand out when I recognize Lyklan, relieved we aren't under attack and pleased to see her reflexes remain sharp. "Lyklan works for me."

"Yeah, I figured that—he's going to cause a scene."

She glances at the townhouses lining both sides of the street. From my weeks of surveillance, I know this neighborhood is home to a variety of supernaturals, but I understand her worry. Celine doesn't want word getting out that the angel population has "motherfucking skyrocketed" as Luca so eloquently phrased it.

Lyklan lands and dips his chin respectfully, first to Celine and then to me.

It's the respect she's owed as a *nish thatsha* and my betrothed, but his adherence to tradition makes her uncomfortable. Standing stiffly at my side, Celine glances away from Lyklan in favor of scanning the street again. It's empty; however, my time here is proof that someone is always watching.

"You can be at ease, Lyklan," I say gently, hoping my tone strikes the proper chord. I want Celine to be comfortable around angels again, but the guardian in front of us has been loyal to my family for many years. I won't disrespect him.

"Of course." He smiles at Celine and tucks in his wings. "The indicators you asked me to set up near the gateway are functional. As you suspected, multiple celestial signatures have been detected breaching the plane between our realm and this one."

"He's coming for me," Celine whispers calmly, fingering the hilt of her blade once more. If I hadn't heard her crying in the shower hours ago, I would have no idea she feels even a shred of disquiet.

Lyklan meets her gaze, his own serious, and nods grimly. "All evidence points to S'lach."

re fidgeting."

ce myself to stop moving and rack my brain for a way to
e him to read the book after I leave. "There's a chapter on
mental magic," I say. I only know that because I skimmed
dex before giving it to him to be sure nothing was too
minating about the enclave families, but there's no reason to
him that.

The textbook is a good resource, but I'm not surprised it's not
mmon knowledge. If you left your home realm and moved here
s an adult, as many in the Fringes do, you wouldn't have an
pportunity to go to school and learn it.

"Gods, the witch section is one-third of the book," Alistair
exclaims.

I snort and pretend to jerk myself off. "Yeah, they're pretty
high on themselves. A witch probably wrote the book."

Alistair continues flipping through the pages. "I found the
experimental magic section," he murmurs, sitting up straighter on
the barstool. "It says that, in rare instances, magic users can
combine their gifts with other species to create new abilities."

Whoa. That's cool. Clearly, I wasn't in the class the day that
was covered. "Does it say how?" I ask.

Alistair shakes his head. "This book has no instructions of any
kind."

"I'm not surprised." I shrug. "It's an introductory textbook. It
wasn't assigned to a practical class." My memories of the academy
are foggy. It's been a few years, and I spent more time seducing or
pranking my classmates than learning.

There is one thing about it that strikes me as strange. "All the
applied classes were divided by species, though," I tell him. "I'm
not sure they ever give anyone the opportunity to try." Pushing to
my feet, I flip my frown to a smile. "Are you thinking what I'm
thinking?"

EIGHTEEN

CIPRIAN

"You brought me a textbook?"

"Yep." I toss the chunky hardback at Alistair, throwing in a
cheerful smile for good measure.

"It looks like it's never been opened."

I yawn. "I wasn't what you would describe as academically
inclined."

Alistair's apartment is as bland as I remember. Gray walls,
grayer furniture, even the flecks of color in his granite counter-
tops are—you guessed it—gray. Except for one streak of . . . what
is that? I squint at a flash of color near the sink and scrape my
thumbnail against it. *Blood.* I should have known.

Blood splatter in a vampire's kitchen is more predictable than
sun in the desert.

Alistair's apartment may be boring, but it's better than my car, which I spent the last twenty hours crammed inside while driving to get him the textbook he's so unimpressed with.

Stuffed in a chest with my embarrassing collection of snapback hats, the textbook had been collecting dust since the academy and I decided it was mutually beneficial we part ways.

As Alistair thumbs through the pages, I study him as thoroughly as the counter. He's twitchy today. Wired. The circles under his eyes are deep purple, and his cheekbones are sharper than normal, even in the gloom.

He looks like shit.

It could be his falling out with Celine, but my gut tells me it's more than that.

I open my mouth to ask, then shut it with a snap. Alistair won't answer my questions; he barely let me through the damn door. I'll learn more by watching.

"There's a lot of information in here." He sounds surprised, and I roll my eyes.

"Duh. It's a textbook. That's kind of the whole point."

"Is it accurate?"

"How would I know? I didn't read the damn thing."

Lips pursed, Alistair flips ahead in the book and clears his throat. "Nightmare demons are considered one of the most powerful types of demonic beings. Known for their heightened senses and fear-based magic, most influence the subconscious by targeting the mind during sleep. However, some nightmare lineages produce stronger abilities, creating immersive illusions that alter the perception and reality of one or more alert individuals."

I raise my eyebrows. "That's not bad, honestly."

"You're not a normal nightmare." Alistair spits the words like an accusation, his expression darkening.

I scoff. "Of course not."

"They don't list any weaknesses," page, then back again. "The information

"Again. Of course not. The academy from—"

"Rich assholes," Alistair interrupts.

I roll my eyes again. Alistair is doing fine for not dumb enough to point that out. "It's not o pulling the strings," I tell him. "Witches founded Sta modern covens are so enmeshed with the school th onto campus feels like getting dunked in an ice bath." remembering the gross sensation of the academy's magical protections.

Dad was livid when I got expelled, but it was worth his a to get out of there. I didn't get a good night's sleep the entire tin I lived at Starfall. Part of it was the unsettling prickle of witch magic, and the rest—well, let's just say it wasn't a popular place to be a Casanell either.

Alistair isn't paying attention to me anymore—he's completely focused on the book. I sigh and consider rifling through his fridge for a snack.

I don't know why he can't read it after I leave. This is boring.

"I'm happy to answer any questions you might have," I say, grimacing. I sound like a fucking customer service bot, overly eager to please and one angry customer interaction away from taking a bath with my toaster.

Alistair grunts.

I groan.

"What's wrong with you?" he demands.

Please, what's wrong with me? Has he looked in the mirror recently? *Don't bring it up. You'll piss him off.* I thrum my fingers against my thighs and say, "Nothing. Nothing at all."

Alistair's blue eyes leave the book to skim over my face. "I sincerely doubt it."

"We should try to combine our magic! Cook up something new."

"That's not the point—"

"Yeah, but it's more fun. Plus, you have hours to read and compile your files while the sun's up." I waggle my eyebrows as Alistair's nostrils flare.

"Fine," he mutters. "But only if we work on the dossier first."

"Yeah, yeah, let's do it." I crack my knuckles and rock back on my heels. Alistair is too sexy to be a hopeless nerd. This shouldn't take long at all.

———————

I've never been more wrong about anything in my life.

Alistair is the biggest nerd alive. His ability to focus for hours at a time is the scariest thing I've ever seen. He's barely moved, transferring information from the book to his laptop with fingers that move in a blur as they type.

He asks for my input occasionally, and I give it gladly. Desperately. Fuck, anything to alleviate the boredom. When I check my phone for the thirty-second time in half an hour, I can't stifle my sigh.

"If you're tired, we can attempt the magical combination some other time."

I snap my head up, preparing to steal his laptop—damn the consequences—when I catch the smirk on his face. The tips of his fangs poke over his lower lip, and I shake my head and mutter, "Bastard."

"I suppose I am," he says.

My eyes flit to his face, and I prepare to apologize, but there's no sign that I've offended him. There's even some color in his pale cheeks, as if Alistair is energized by digging through a mountain of boring information. *Yep, major nerd.*

"I'm assuming you can compel people?" I ask.

He nods.

"But you don't have any neighbors we could practice on?"

His answering glare is ferocious, and I grin.

"We need someone else then. Otherwise, we won't be able to tell if it works. You know who's the perfect test subject?"

"She doesn't want to be around either of us," Alistair snarls, scrubbing his hand over his face angrily.

"No. Not Celine. Gods, she would kick our asses for trying, and with the truth thing, she'd be too difficult to convince, anyway." I let my smile stretch across my whole face. "We need Luca. He's perfect."

Alistair cocks his head and nods shortly. "I'll see if he's free." He types a message on his phone, blue eyes studying me even as his fingers move across the screen. "You aren't supposed to know about Celine's magic."

I raise one eyebrow. "You forget I lived in that tiny apartment with all three of you for days, and you blurted it at the Fang. I know about Celine's magic and Luca's, although his was harder to figure out."

"He still pretends I don't know about that," Alistair says, giving me his full attention.

"And it should stay that way," I say seriously. "With omni shifters around, the last thing we need is a bunch of people able to use his powers without the benefit of his lifetime of restraint."

Gideon and his family are as ethical as they come, but they can't resist adding new animals to their shifting options. All it would take is for one of them to see Luca in his shifted form and they'd be able to transform into a basilisk whenever they want.

Alistair's phone buzzes, and he glances at it, his black eyebrows lifting high on his forehead. "Luca's coming over."

A rush of excitement hits me. I tell myself it has everything to do with the fact that we're about to test something cool and nothing to do with Luca. Lying again.

Within ten minutes, he knocks on the door. It's not a moment too soon.

Sullenly, Alistair stops arguing with me about the best way forward and retreats down the hall, away from the sun. I open the apartment door, pasting a cheerful grin on my face. "Welcome, lab rat."

Luca shakes his head and shoulders past me, his body grazing mine.

I shut the door behind him, and Alistair reappears in a rush of stale air that smells faintly of copper, salt, and disinfectant.

"What's this about?" Luca asks him. "Why did Casanell call me a lab rat?"

"You didn't explain?" I laugh.

Alistair sneers at me, flashing his fangs. I shudder and don't bother to hide it. He's hot, and I haven't forgotten how it felt to have his teeth buried inside me. "We're attempting to combine our magic. We need someone to test it on."

Luca adjusts the worn baseball cap on his head, glances between the two of us, and sighs. "I really am a test subject."

"We won't hurt you," I assure him.

"We don't even know if it will work," Alistair adds, a muscle in his jaw ticking.

Luca sighs again and drops onto the couch. "Have at it then." He glances at his phone. "I've got to head to the club in two hours."

"First, we should establish a baseline," Alistair says.

I mutter a halfhearted agreement. Of course, he wants to make it more boring.

Crouching gracefully in front of the couch, Ali's arms graze the inside of Luca's spread legs as he catches his eye. "Lay back," he whispers.

Luca's stare goes unfocused, and he sinks deeper into the couch. His entire body relaxes. And the contrast . . . Hovering over Luca, Alistair is coiled to strike—lean muscles bunched, his eyes red and searching.

Compulsion should be creepy, so why am I hard? I squirm, trying to subtly adjust myself without drawing attention.

Alistair blinks twice, and Luca jolts upright. His cheeks are flushed; the silver hoop is caught helplessly between his teeth. "Do you want me to try to keep you out?"

"Not yet," I say. "We should start easy and work our way up."

Luca nods. His pupils are blown, with only a sliver of hazel visible.

My stomach flips. This is the opposite of boring, and I'm more excited to show him my magic than I want to admit. That dazed expression on his face . . . the streaks of pink on his tan cheeks . . . I want to be the one putting them there.

I rack my brain for what to show him. He's a basilisk, so maybe a jungle? That's not an easy nightmare to pull off, but I want to impress him.

I close my eyes and take myself there.

Waxy leaves dripping dew, the spongy give of a forest floor covered in layers of decomposing plant matter, and the sensation that everything—from the lichen to the air itself—has a pulse.

Once my skin pebbles, I lock in and get to work.

First, I create a thick canopy of towering trees, snaked with vines, connected to the ground by fat, sturdy trunks. Wispy ferns. Mushrooms that look suspiciously like puddles of vomit. A flower —fire engine red—bigger and brighter than all the others. Creeping moss becomes a racetrack for two rival slugs caught in an epic grudge match.

I polish the vibe by peppering in a loud argument between two catty birds and a cunty chimpanzee—he threw a rock at the birds' nest, and everyone's sick of his shit—then sculpt a green-striped hammock to drop Luca in.

Chest heaving, I spritz the entire nightmare with wet and nod. *It'll do.* I pull back and search for Luca's mind. I find it right in front of me, active, alert, and pulsing with energy.

I drape the nightmare over his consciousness like a heavy linen tablecloth. His mind quivers with the tiniest shiver of resistance, and I tighten my magic, smoothing any visible wrinkles before he spots them.

Luca gasps, and I pull my focus out of the nightmare enough to watch him experience it. His hazel eyes are wide, his head on a swivel.

"Holy shit," he murmurs, his fingers grazing the bark of the tree I attached his hammock to. "It feels real."

I hold my head high and let his reaction soothe my ego. The past few weeks have been hell on my self-esteem. This is exactly what I needed.

"What are you showing him?" Alistair demands.

Instead of answering, I reach for his mind to pull him in and face my first resistance. If Luca's head is a beating heart, Alistair's is a blinding light. Trying to cover it feels impossible; light keeps getting through. I grit my teeth and push more magic into the nightmare until it's less tablecloth and more padded moving blanket.

When I successfully pull him in, Alistair goes completely still.

"This isn't a nightmare," he says.

I roll my eyes, more pissed than I should be by his reaction. "Not all nightmares are scary but if that's what you want . . ."

I split the illusion down the middle, leaving Luca to recline in a tropical paradise while I give Alistair's cranky ass what he's asking for. The vines around him morph into snakes. Green, mottled with yellow, I give one red bands—the exact color of his vamped-out eyes.

Each snake is different, but they share one common mission: get Alistair.

An anaconda the size of a food truck comes for him, wrapping around his body. He doesn't even flinch. If it weren't for the slight increase in his heart rate, I would think he escaped the nightmare. Alistair studies the snake closely, then grins into its gaping maw. "This is remarkable!"

Those three words feel amazing. All the rejection, being a constant disappointment. Suddenly, the hatred of the other supernaturals in the Fringes is a little easier to take.

I let myself smile, relieved neither of them can see me, then insert myself in the nightmare, banishing the snakes and merging the scenes again.

Shooting Luca a mischievous grin, I add a cocktail to his hand —the same orange one he made for me a lifetime ago at the club. His eyebrows disappear beneath the brim of his baseball cap, and he takes a sip before I can stop him.

"Oh fuck!" He gags. "Dude, this is shit."

"I know. Sorry!" I scrub my hand over my face. "I've never been able to simulate taste."

Luca shrugs and studies the glass in his hand. "I felt that go down my throat, but I didn't actually drink anything, did I?"

I shake my head. "My magic is inside your brain. If I stimulate the right places—which is mostly instinctual for me—you will smell, hear, and feel things as if they're real. It's what makes nightmare illusions different from something a fae or witch might do. They show you a picture. I create the picture with you in it."

"That must take a lot of energy," Alistair says.

I nod. This is an elaborate nightmare, but it's within my limits. I can weave simple illusions off and on for three to four hours or maintain complex ones for an hour without slipping. I'll feel like death afterward, but it wouldn't be the first time.

"I can't do it forever," I admit, giving him a nonspecific version of the truth.

I'll help Alistair with his project, but I'm not going to tell him my weaknesses. That would be idiotic. I'm not desperate enough for his attention to make myself vulnerable.

"Try the combo thing." Luca takes another sip of the orange drink, then spits it over the side of the hammock. "Still ass," he tells me cheerfully.

Alistair takes a few steps forward, standing in front of the hammock in the vision and the couch in reality. "Hand me that drink," he says. Like melted chocolate running down the sides of a fountain made of gold—it's the most decadent sound I've ever heard.

But Luca's fingers stay firmly wrapped around the drink. "Get your own," he teases.

Alistair sulks. "I can't connect to him. There's a barrier."

"It's probably my nightmare," I say. Thanks to his lighthouse mind, this nightmare is super thick. "You need to get through it without piercing or tearing it down."

There's a pause, then Alistair growls, "How the bloody hell am I supposed to do that?"

"Careful, Ali," I tease, grinning despite the headache creeping along the base of my skull. "Your scone-encrusted past is showing." I love it when he forgets to hide his British background, but I'll be damned if I ever let him know it.

He growls again, and I feel sharp pressure on the illusion. I roll my eyes. "You're bludgeoning it. That's the literal opposite of going around, dude."

Alistair tosses his hands up in both realities, creating a double vision effect when I look at him—as if he has twenty fingers instead of ten. It feels like being drunk, and I have to swallow a few times to banish the nausea.

"How am I supposed to go around something with no edges or corners? That makes no sense." He's infuriated with me—and I love it.

"I shouldn't be telling you this, but look for ripples," I say. "I'm always good but never perfect. They'll be there."

I sense his focus; the intense way he studies my nightmare, and shudder. His inspection is fucking intimate. Plenty of people at the compound have used my nightmares to practice their mental walls, but it's never felt like this before.

"I see one," Alistair whispers.

A warm, enticing trickle of his magic slithers against mine; it may as well be my bare skin. When Alistair's compulsion makes it inside my nightmare, I know immediately. The sensual magic is almost uncomfortably warm. It pulses with intensity just like him. It doesn't feel like he went around either . . . it feels like we've merged.

Alistair crouches in front of the hammock again and stares directly into Luca's eyes. "Can I have a sip?" he purrs. "Give me a taste. Please."

Luca's pupils dilate, and his hand shoots forward, offering Alistair the cocktail. Condensation runs down the side of the glass, and their fingers graze. As soon as Luca lets go, Alistair punches the air triumphantly, sloshing the orange drink everywhere.

"We did it," he shouts.

Heat hums low in my belly. Like the first sip of whiskey trickling down my throat after a long day, mixing my magic with Alistair's is addictive. Does he sense it? The intimacy?

He still hates you, idiot.

It's the reality check I need. Hands shaking, I let the nightmare crash around us, revealing the gray, boring apartment. The jungle isn't real; there are no ass-flavored cocktails, either—only a couch and three supernaturals with more problems than we can count.

"I've got to go to work," Luca says, his throat bobbing. "But great job with that. Both of you. It was . . . cool to experience."

The raspy tone of his voice makes me wonder how Luca felt being bathed in our magic. I want to ask him if it turned him on. If Alistair weren't here, maybe I would. But I'm the one on the outside, and I need to stop forgetting it.

NINETEEN

CELINE

Working the pole is more of a penance tonight than anything else. My body hurts. Each muscle screams at me to cut it some slack. Internally, I scream back, reminding them they only get to feel sore because they aren't rotting in a shallow grave.

Dad's killers are here. Like a breeze against my skin, I feel it. They're coming for me. I'll have to kill them all. Sore muscles or not.

My grip falters, and I drop a foot down the pole. A few guys clustered around the stage gasp, but I catch myself before I hit the ground. That draws a few scattered claps—good, they think I did it on purpose. That's better than everyone here knowing I'm too tired to work the pole.

My song ends, and I force myself to bend and pick up the

loose cash, groaning quietly. There's no way this is sexy. I feel about two hundred years old.

I hobble off stage, skirt the main floor, and drag myself directly to the bar.

Luca hands me a water bottle. I consider rolling it over my aching joints, but that would send a weak message. What I need is something to take the edge off. Leaning against the bar, I do my best to look natural.

"Tequila," I say, sipping the cool water slowly. "Can you pour me a double shot?"

Luca raises one eyebrow and checks me over from head to toe.

I wait for him to offer solutions I didn't ask for. He'll tell me to rest or suggest I skip my next set and do a floor routine instead . . . I'm so primed to argue that I wilt when he scoops ice into a cup—four cubes, exactly how I like it—and fills it to the brim with top-shelf tequila.

"I'm rattled," he tells me, glancing around to make sure no one is within earshot. "Can we watch a few episodes of that crazy island dating show when we get home?"

I haven't thought about that show in weeks, but the idea of collapsing on the couch with him and distracting myself from everything sounds so euphoric I moan.

"Is that a yes?" Luca asks, his crooked grin startling the butterflies in my stomach.

I toss my head back and down the tequila. An ice cube bumps my upper lip, cold and soothing—the perfect contrast to the burn of the liquor as it crashes down my throat.

"You've got yourself a date," I say, leaning over the bar to kiss him.

It's a spontaneous decision. Strippers typically don't kiss their boyfriends fifteen feet from the main stage. It isn't good marketing. I'm selling a fantasy, like Malach said, and if I remove the illusion of availability . . .

"Only a couple of people saw," Luca says, correctly reading my expression. "I'll come find you during my break."

He smirks, and the familiar playful expression melts some of my worry.

I love both sides of Luca—the one who respects my boundaries, and the one who accommodates nothing but the raspy screams he tears from me while he fucks me.

My libido lifts its head speculatively, and I hand off my empty glass and push it down. Now is not the time to get horny.

The music pounds around me, and I drag my tired feet down the hall toward the employees-only spaces. Inside the dressing room, the girls giggle as they change.

I smile, but duck into the storage room instead.

If I join them, they'll know something is wrong and ask questions. I can't tell them the truth for their own safety, and the pain of lying to them would drive me to my knees—my magic would make sure of that. Avoidance is my best option. I wish it didn't sting so much. Keeping my distance has shown me how important my friends at the Fang are to me.

Sighing, I close the door behind me and freeze. I'm not alone.

I cock one hip and raise my chin, ignoring how the extra weight on the ball of my left foot makes me want to lop it off and throw it at his fucking head. "You look like shit," I say, running my eyes over him.

I'm not just being bitchy; Alistair really does look terrible. His blue eyes are sunken, and his pale skin somehow skipped porcelain and went straight to corpse white.

"And you're beautiful, as always," he says, something wild flickering across his face.

I narrow my eyes. His voice sounds like he hasn't cleared his throat in a decade, but why do I even care? Alistair isn't my problem. He never was.

"There's no reason to flatter me," I say. "You got what you wanted. Do us both a favor and stop pretending."

Alistair sits down on a wooden crate, and I settle sullenly on the one across from him. I feel cheated by his appearance. He isn't struggling because of me——and I want him punished at my hands or no one's.

"We were good together," he says, his eyes raking over my legs.

I bite back everything I want to say. Alistair has no right to look at me as if he's starving. Not anymore. I've tolerated him showing up at my fights because I can't stop him and he introduced me to Resker, but he doesn't get to sneak around the Fang acting pitiful. The "we" he throws around so casually is broken. He did that all on his own.

I let my knees fall open—punishing and testing him at the same time. My inner thighs wail in relief, and I laugh out loud. "Of course we were good together," I say. "We're both hot and great in bed. Why wouldn't the sex be awesome?"

"It was more than that," Alistair snaps.

"Maybe to you . . ." I shrug, being careful to trail off before my magic can call me a liar. "For a dildo and a slut, we did exactly what we were designed to do: fuck and come."

Alistair winces, and I smile. Luca told me to take my power back. I doubt he meant this, but when you give vague advice, you should expect creative liberties to be taken. I'm sore and tired. If I want to see how far I can push Alistair to cheer myself up, I will.

I spread my legs wider and massage my right inner thigh.

Alistair grabs the edges of his crate and scoots closer. My green bodysuit is sheer. He can see right through it, and he's not pretending to look anywhere else.

My pulse jumps, and I fake a yawn as I drop my legs open fully. The fabric shifts against my pussy. It's irritating, confining, and I want someone—not Alistair—to tear it off me.

"You seem to be missing your dildo, angel," he whispers.

My eyes lift to his, and my body comes alive under his stare, every nerve singing with anticipation. The magnetism between us is unreal, and there's nothing I can do about it.

I want Alistair to beg to touch me.

I want him to crawl for me.

Maybe then I'll be able to forget what he said.

"Dildos wear out," I say, deliberately skating my thumb over the crotch of my bodysuit. My nerves light up, then sputter with disappointment when the erotic touch stops. Who am I teasing? Him or me?

Alistair's gaze collides with mine. The naked hunger . . .

"Please," he hisses, palming the outline of his hard cock.

I smile, soaking in his desperation. There's no better revenge than giving him a taste of what he threw away. Deliberately nonchalant, I lean back, my lower half liquefying under the heat of his stare.

"No biting. No kissing on the mouth. No being nice," I say, showing him the angry angel behind the sexy act. "If I allow you to fuck me again, you don't get to play pretend."

"But—"

"Take it or leave it, Alistair. You won't get another chance."

He drops to his knees on the concrete floor and inches toward me at a glacial pace. My leg muscles burn. I order them not to tremble under the strain of my wide stance.

Alistair runs his fingers up the inside of my knee, then digs his thumb into the aching muscle of my inner thigh.

I wince and recoil. He eases the pressure.

"You're sore," he says.

Angry that he noticed and angrier that I gave him a reaction, I scoff. "Do you like it when I flinch away from you?"

Alistair digs his thumb into my other thigh, working the muscle almost savagely. I manage to hide my reaction . . . barely.

But when he presses both thumbs in at the same time, a groan escapes my parted lips. Damn him.

"I like making you notice me—especially when you don't want to. I like leaving marks on you that you can't wash off or explain." He presses my legs wider, and I bite my lip. "And I like helping you push your limits."

"Be honest," I say. "You like breaking me down."

Alistair shakes his head; his stare fixed on my legs and says, "I like that you can't be broken." He slips his right hand over my pussy, dragging the damp fabric to the side and working two fingers inside me. "I like that you fight me every step of the way."

He releases the pressure on my left leg, ending the painful stretch. The relief is euphoric, and my hips rock greedily toward him, eager for more.

"I'll always fight you," I snarl, dropping my fingers to rub my clit.

For a second—just a second—I remember the last time I touched myself like this.

The skin of Alistair's belly was pink from the healing sword wound. He was pale and exhausted, and I wanted to make him forget the pain. I climbed on top of him and fucked him slow and quiet while wearing that stupid T-shirt he cut holes in to accommodate my wings. The same one still hiding in my bottom drawer. The same one I can't bring myself to throw away.

It scared the shit out of me then, but remembering now hurts.

Part of me wishes that had been the last time. That he was the one who stayed broken and soft, instead of transferring that vulnerability to me and using it to tear me apart.

Alistair watches me touch myself, transfixed by the sight, then slaps my wrist away. "Lean back on your hands," he orders.

I narrow my eyes and lean forward instead, daring him to boss me around again.

His eyes flash red, and the tips of his fangs peek past his lower lip as he smiles. "If you need me to stop or slow down, all you have to do is tell me."

"I won't," I assure him, my words clipped.

He shoves me flat on the crate, his hand pressing against my chest too quickly for my tired muscles to combat. I buckle. My back aches from the punches I took during fight night.

"Arch," Alistair demands, pressing his lips to my clit before I can kick him in the face.

His tongue lashes me, driving my arousal to a near-painful level in seconds. I'm right on the edge, two licks away from breaking when he stops. "Arch your fucking back, Celine, or I'll stop right now."

I ignore him and grind my pussy against his face.

He smiles against me—I can feel it—but his tongue stays stubbornly behind his lips. Dammit, I don't want to arch. My abs are the sorest muscles on my body. Leaning back while supporting my own weight will be excruciating.

"If you give me a little arch, angel, I'll fuck you so good you'll forget you're sore." Alistair punctuates the sentence with a soft kiss to my inner thigh, and the combination wrecks me.

Holding my breath, I brace my shoulders on the crate and arch my back. Pain shoots through every muscle in my abdomen until I'm trembling from the effort.

Alistair pushes my bodysuit to the side and curls his fingers inside me again, bringing his other hand up to support my lower back. "That's good," he whispers. "You're doing amazing, angel. Give me a little more."

Maybe if I were fighting and my life depended on it, I could make it happen, but my body still trusts Alistair. It doesn't think we're in danger, and all it wants to do is curl up in his arms and rest.

"Ali, I can't," I sputter, tears burning the backs of my eyes.

Immediately, the ceiling blurs, and I find myself lifted, spun, and dropped directly in his lap.

Limp, I barely notice the aches anymore. His brutal stretches have stirred up tension of a different kind.

I lick his neck and he trembles. Frantic, Alistair drops his pants to his ankles, frees his dick, and shoves me down on it until we both groan.

Gods, he feels fucking good inside me. Why did he have to ruin everything?

"Don't think," he begs. "Just let me fuck you."

I meet his gaze, telling him without words exactly who's fucking whom.

He grins, showing fang, and I contract my inner muscles around him and imagine strangling his erection the way I wanted to strangle his neck after he destroyed everything.

"Harder," I taunt. "If you want me to miss your cock, you have to do something with it worth missing."

Alistair's hands spread around my waist, his fingers digging into my sore abs as he picks up the pace. The friction, the ache, the dangerous ruby glint in his eyes—he's impossible to resist.

When he drops one thumb to my clit and rubs in tight, vicious circles, I explode around him. The orgasm is sharp and torn from me like the scream I barely manage to swallow. It fades quickly, leaving me desperate for more.

Alistair stands, driving us both into the wall with a muted thud. "Is this what you want, angel? An angry fuck? Something to confirm the lie you insist on believing—that I don't care?"

"Yes." I bury my hand in his hair and yank his head to my breasts. "That's exactly what I want."

"Fine!" He licks my nipple. "It's not my fault if someone comes running."

I don't get a chance to process his words because Alistair goes full vampire, his hips thrusting faster and faster and faster until they blur. Or maybe that's my vision.

Either way, Alistair fucks me so hard all I can do is take it. He's deep. Too deep.

I consider taking it all back, then bite my tongue. I'd rather walk sideways for a week than tell Alistair I can't handle him. Shit, I think I'd rather eat my own tongue than lose an inch of ground to him.

And yeah, it's a lot. He's relentless, but I like it rough. Once I accept the burn, the flames turn from pain to pleasure. The only thing that would make it better is if I could scream my lungs out. Or kiss him. To avoid both, I bite my lips until I taste blood. It trickles from the corner of my mouth, and Alistair stares, transfixed. His eyes track the single drop, and he redoubles his efforts.

"Angel," he moans. "You're torturing me."

The power rush goes straight to my head.

My breath escapes in frantic puffs, and I bring my finger up to collect the drop of blood. Before I can come up with a reason not to, I shove it in his mouth.

He sucks on it desperately, and his pace stutters as his tongue laves the digit.

The scrape of his fangs is a delicious warning. My breath hitches, skin pebbling from the phantom memory of his teeth sinking deep. I'm cursing my rules, even as I gasp, "No biting!"

Alistair growls. Adjusting his grip, he tilts my hips and sinks impossibly deeper.

I shatter. Every muscle in my body tenses, then relaxes, then tenses again—until each drop of pleasure I have to give is wrung from my body.

Sore muscles forgotten, Alistair's touch is no longer too much.

My pain is gone, exactly as he promised.

I slump against the wall as he thrusts three more times before coming with an agonized groan. Carefully, Alistair slides us to the floor.

"Did your knees buckle?" I ask. The sudden intimacy of being wrapped around him, his softening dick still buried inside me, is an unwelcome reality check.

"Don't tell anyone," he whispers, nuzzling my neck.

I try to pull away, but there's nowhere for me to go. This is too familiar. Dangerous.

Alistair reaches for the neckline of my bodysuit, but I brush his hands away and stumble to my feet. He doesn't get to fix my clothes anymore. That's the sweet bullshit that got us in trouble in the first place.

"That was hot," I say, keeping my voice cool.

I straighten my bodysuit and pretend my hands aren't shaking. A few black spots dot my vision, and I shake my head. It would have been a lot easier for me if I'd gone to the dressing room and let the girls interrogate me.

Alistair's shoulders sag. His blue-black hair is tangled from my fingers. And he looks . . . He looks like I hurt him.

My fingers twitch. I curl them into a fist.

Lifting my chin, I stretch to my full height and wait for him to say something. Anything. But he doesn't. The silence crawls along my skin, more pervasive than his talented fingers. I hate it. I'd rather he yelled at me again . . . Call me a whore for stripping. Anything but this quiet defeat.

My wings shoot from my back, only to droop and betray me. I stumble out of the storage room and slam the door before they can tell him what I refuse to say out loud: that I miss him, and I hate myself for it.

TWENTY

LUCA

I never thought I would have this.

Celine curled on the couch, her head on my shoulder. Every time she exhales, the hair behind my ear sways and tickles my neck. My basilisk is content. It's pleased to have her safe and close where it can keep an eye on her.

The TV casts vivid, saturated colors around the living room, bringing the tropical island vibe to our midnight desert hideaway. On the screen, palm trees sway in the breeze as the cast members smile and flirt their way into one dramatic situation after another.

Malach is fucking engrossed.

And it's killing me. I may not survive the effort it takes to keep from laughing my ass off. Brow furrowed, he watches the dating show with the gravity that human political correspondents reserve for a fucking congressional hearing.

Whenever one of the contestants says something illogical or ridiculous—which is almost always—he frowns, and I watch in real time as he puzzles out their possible meaning. More than once, I've caught his lips moving as he repeats a phrase.

Fuck me, I think he's trying to memorize them. I swear, if Malach wakes up talking like a reality-star diva tomorrow, I'm going to lose it.

"His intentions aren't honorable," Malach mutters, jerking his thumb toward the roided-up gym bro Celine and I love to hate. His name is Wolfe, something Celine and I always botch, which is laughable considering how weird it is.

"Agreed," I whisper. "And there's no way he's good in bed—in another episode he said he doesn't even eat." Which, incidentally, is the most heinous crime a bisexual can commit. Wolfe should be locked up for sheer audacity.

Malach drags his focus away from the screen and looks at me. "Eat? He must eat something to maintain that musculature."

I blink at him and wait for his poker face to crack, but it never does. His green eyes are impossibly earnest. Swallowing a groan, I brace myself. I have no choice but to explain. I can't allow Malach to keep wandering through life—in any realm—knowing nothing about head.

Do it for the greater good, Luca.

"Not food." I clear my throat. "I mean pussy. Or ass. Or pussy and ass."

Malach's eyes flicker to Celine. "I see," he says. "Eating is slang, and the act is pleasurable?"

I nod. "If it's done right. What do you call it in your realm?"

He frowns, a muscle in his jaw flexing. "We don't discuss intimacy casually or around others." Okay, that makes sense, but— A crazy suspicion enters my mind.

"Have you ever?" I ask, keeping my face as neutral as possible.

Malach and Celine were betrothed young. Neither of them has explained what that means, but he's rigid about rules . . .

"I have maintained my vows," Malach says simply and without shame. "However, I do not begrudge Celine the life lived while we were apart. She believed our paths would never cross again; I could not accept that."

My respect for him grows. To have waited for Celine all this time . . . gods, he must love her nearly as much as I do. I wonder if she knows he's a virgin. It's not my place to tell her. Malach is confiding in me. I won't betray his trust by spilling his personal business.

"Did she forgive the vampire?"

His subject change surprises me as much as his actual question. Malach skipped the club tonight, saying he needed to check in with his guards, so I'm not sure how he knows Alistair showed up at the Fang. Did he pop in and I missed him, or does he have his guys spying on us?

"Forgive isn't the word I would use," I mutter, remembering the fury on Celine's face when she stumbled from the storage room earlier.

I expected to get yelled at on the way home for not warning her that he was in there. Instead, she pressed her nose to the glass of my passenger window, brown eyes locked on the crescent moon like it might hold the answers to all her questions.

"I don't understand it," Malach admits, drawing my attention back to him.

The bright light from the TV casts his face in a series of harsh, chiseled lines. With his brow furrowed and his jaw clenched, Malach looks carved from stone, like he caught me on a bad day and paid the price.

I scrub my hand over my jaw, stubble scraping the skin of my palm. How can I explain toxic attraction to a virgin who's still getting the hang of the English language? Words fail me, and I finally shrug. "I wouldn't dare say it to either of them, but they don't understand it either, Malach."

"It hurts her," he says, his face twisting with anger.

I sigh. "It would hurt her worse to let him go."

Not that I think Alistair would allow that to happen without a fight. He watches Celine with a feral intensity that's more familiar to me than the unshakable dedication in Malach's eyes. An obsessed monster I understand—I walk around with its twin in my chest every day. It's exhausting. Some days I think it would have been better if my parents had allowed my basilisk to be bound instead of fleeing to Earth to prevent it.

"Do you miss home?" I ask before I think better of it, not sure what I'm even getting at. Celine doesn't talk about the celestial realm. I have almost no picture in my mind of the place she spent most of her life.

"That's a difficult question." Malach looks at the TV, his shoulders tensing. "Have you ever arrived somewhere and been overwhelmed? By the sights, the smells, the feeling that settles into your skin that you belong there?"

He doesn't expect an answer; he's setting the stage, painting a picture for me, but his description is as foreign to me as their realm.

I was born on Earth. Mom and Dad planned their escape from the monster realm as soon as they found out about me. I've spent almost thirty years moving between Fringe communities and hiding what I am . . . Many things catch my interest, but the sense of home he's describing—I doubt I'll ever experience it.

"When I hear the hum of the transportation pathways or see a child's face after their wings hold them up for the first time, that's home. Warm, comforting"—Malach clears his throat—"and overshadowed by the agony of watching my realm be cut to ribbons."

I make a noise to let him know I'm still listening. I asked, but I wish I could take it back. It's upsetting Malach to explain, and I've ruined the relaxation of our trash TV night.

"You asked me if I miss it, but I miss what it should be . . . what it could be. I'll miss the home we might have had until I draw my final breath." Malach looks at Celine as she sleeps, and his face softens. "Yet nothing compares to how I felt when she left. As if half my soul and all my heart were torn from my body. I thought I would never draw a full breath or sleep a restful night again."

"You helped her get out though," I say, remembering Celine's surprise when learning how she stumbled upon the illegal gateway to Earth. Malach worked behind the scenes, making sure she would find it while never knowing he was to thank for helping her escape.

"Yes, I did, and I would do it again. If she needed my lungs to breathe, I would cut them out for her too." Wincing, Malach rubs the heel of his hand against his chest. "I would sink to the depths of the sea to spare Celine pain. That is my duty and my honor because she is my home."

Fuck, that's poetic.

I focus on the TV, giving him space to process.

It's four o'clock in the morning. We should go to bed—Celine's obviously exhausted—but I'm reluctant to move. On the screen, Ashley M. spills her mimosa, dousing Breanna in a drink that in my professional opinion looks about 80 percent champagne and 20 percent orange juice.

No wonder there's constant drama on this show; they're always fucking—

Glass shatters in slow motion. I shoot to my feet. Celine is only a second behind me as the room-darkening shades ripple from the impact of gods know what.

I watch, transfixed, as a glowing ball rolls across the floor, silent and pulsing. It's beautiful and hypnotic—hard to look at and harder to look away from. The light throbs like a heart, shining brighter with every beat. It should cast shadows, but there's nothing.

I squint. My eyes water.

Then the orb begins to sing, a high-pitched, awful wail that echoes inside my bones.

"Fuck!" Celine covers one ear with her left hand and reaches for the orb with her right.

Malach shoves her out of the way. "Get down!" He grabs it himself, hissing, and throws it back out the window. A second later, a sound like a million bells ringing all at once deafens me. It's chased by a resonant hum and the grind of crunching metal.

I blink in confusion, my ears ringing.

A flash of red zips by me.

Celine yanks on the deadbolts with one hand and grabs Malach's massive sword with the other. Fuck. Fuck. FUCK. I stumble over to her, slapping the flat of my hand against the door to hold it shut.

"Baby, wait! We can't storm out there; we don't know what's going on. You were asleep thirty seconds ago!"

"They're going to escape," she hisses. "They threw a *koil'-nashra* through my window."

Malach lays his hand on her shoulder, then yanks it back, his face twisting with pain.

I smell blood, and my eyes bulge as I process the damage to his hand. "Shit, man, that doesn't look good." His palm is raw, the skin shriveled and uneven—like the first few layers were burned or ripped off.

"Listen to Luca," he rasps. "They're trying to lure us out."

Celine grits her teeth; her eyes caught on his ruined hand. "There's nothing stopping them from throwing more of those," she argues. "We're fish in a barrel."

"Wait a second," I interrupt. "They don't know what I am, right?"

Malach raises his eyebrows. "S'lach likely doesn't know anything about Celine's associates yet. He hasn't had time, and you hide your heritage well."

I jerk my head toward the shattered glass. "This is a shot in the dark."

"Yes," Celine says, her face pinched. "And it almost worked."

"But it didn't," I remind her, winking as I kiss her cheek. "You draw their attention, and I'll show them how to make a shot in the dark count."

"Don't joke," Celine mutters. "Walk me through exactly what you mean."

I point to the sword and keep my eyes on the broken window, still mostly concealed by the room-darkening shade. "You stick your head out the window and wave that sword around. Once they look at you, I'll pop out and turn them to stone."

"And if they throw another *koil'nashra*?"

I grin. "Then we'll find out how good you are at bat, baby."

Celine studies me with sharp eyes, her messy bun listing to one side. She adjusts her grip on the sword, kisses my lips, and makes for the window without another word.

I curse and blink rapidly to prepare my eyes. "Don't make eye contact with me," I whisper. "I mean it. Under no circumstances will either of you look at me."

"Duh," Celine says.

Malach dips his head, slow and grimly. It's the most serious nod I've ever seen in my life.

Walking to the window, I crouch to Celine's right, keeping my gaze focused on the floor. *Let's do this.* I tell my basilisk, embracing the cold, bristling feeling of its magic. *Our magic.*

Icy, sluggish tendrils creep into my eyes, coating my vision in a yellow, poisonous mist.

My eyesight isn't great as a basilisk, but it doesn't matter if I can make out my targets' pores. If they lock eyes with me even once, that blink will be their last.

It's petrification, and it's fucking permanent.

In nature, it takes thousands of years for bone to mineralize and millions more to become stone. That's if decay doesn't win out. But me? I don't need time. I don't need patience. I just need a motherfucker to give me one good look.

"I cannot see a thing," Malach grumbles behind Celine. He's cradling his injured hand against his body. Once the emergency is over, we're going to have a long talk about what the fuck that angry crystal ball of death was.

"Grab a blanket off the couch," I hiss at him. "In case another one gets through, so you don't lose the skin off your other hand." His heavy footsteps tell me he's following my advice, and I tap Celine's foot with my hand. "Ready when you are, baby."

She yanks the shade down and throws it behind us, the screws coming loose from the drywall with a crumbling pop. Through the yellow film over my eyes, I see smoke, a strangely round, SUV-sized ball of metal, and . . . a deserted street.

Celine leans out the window, hanging dangerously over the edge, and more glass snaps. "Careful," I say, grabbing the back of her sweatpants. The leverage isn't great, but maybe it will be enough to keep her from falling out the window.

Her wings are pinned tightly to leave room for me at her side, the blade-like feathers rubbing against each other with faint metallic whines.

Celine screams out the window. While I don't have a clue what she said, from the way Malach gasps, it wasn't polite. Until told otherwise, I'll assume she said something metal like, 'Face me and fry.'

A yellowish blob moves on the ground, and I squint, realizing it's *someone*, not something. "I see one," I whisper. "If you get them all to come out, I'll draw their attention."

A bead of sweat rolls down my back. Celine's body is radiating so much heat . . . It's all she can do not to light up like a candle.

She spews another furious sentence at top volume. A light turns on across the street, and I wince. There's no way her neighbors are sleeping through this. The entire street is supernatural, but we're breaking all kinds of Fringe rules.

I don't have time to worry about that, though. The blobs are mobilizing.

"They're coming," Celine says. "Five, no—six total."

"Got it!" My stomach does a backflip. I've never killed that many. Shit, I've never planned to kill anyone before either. Breathing deeply, I smell the burned skin of Malach's palm, and my resolve hardens. They made their beds, now they get to die in them.

Movement comes from several spots along the street. They're spread out, strategically spaced at the corners of the intersecting roads. *Blocking our exits.* Only one of them is close enough to have thrown the orb in the window.

"Change of plans," Celine mutters. "I love you."

Dread hits me like a truck. I try to get a better grip on her sweatpants, but I'm too late.

Celine dives through the window, flapping her wings hard. She hovers there, three or four feet above the window, bare feet dangling with Malach's sword raised high above her head.

"Tell me," she says, voice quivering with rage, "have you ever told a lie before?" She repeats the sentence in a celestial dialect, and her skin lights up like a glow stick—the truth rune etched across every visible inch.

My heart slams against my ribs. She's a target. Even if some of these guys are bad shots in the dark, she's lit herself up brighter than a godsdamned lightbulb.

"Baby, I don't think calling them on their shit right now is the best idea . . ."

"Stay back," Malach says, grabbing my shoulder with his good hand.

Golden magic shoots from Celine's chest in six pulsing bursts. My jaw drops as the beams transform into spears of light, zipping through the air toward each target.

The closest angel ignores the beam coming for him and hurls another glowing-death ball at Celine.

With the poise of a veteran batter, she swings the sword, driving the flat of the blade into the ball. The crack echoes— impossibly loud and terrible—like a mallet hitting a gong made of pissed off cats. It's all I can do not to cover my ears.

The angel who threw the orb tries to dive out of the way. He's too slow. Through my yellow-tinged vision, I watch the ball of light devour him whole. It expands rapidly, sucking him and a nearby trash can in before contracting to a pinprick of light and spitting out a round, lumpy mass. A round, lumpy mass dripping blood and guts.

I gulp, the chill behind my eyes spreading to cover my whole body. *Nothing could be worse, right?* The thought seems reasonable. Then Celine's truth beams hit the remaining five angels, and I realize I was wrong. Incredibly fucking wrong.

I'll never forget their screams.

The closest one—about ten feet from the base of our building —grabs his head as he wails. It's torment come to life.

Shit. Fuck. Gods. I'm going to be sick. *No, focus Luca. You have a job to do.*

Shaking my head, I block out the wailing and shout at him. Whether he hears me or glances at my corner of the window by accident, I'll never know. We lock eyes, and I end his life and suffering at the same time—immortalizing his final shriek in stone.

His death sets off a chain reaction. Two more angels look at me in shock, and I petrify them both, shuddering as my blood circulation becomes sluggish. It happens every time, a taste of my own medicine, and a reminder that all abilities have limits.

Two more angels remain, and one of them—fuck, he isn't wailing anymore.

Jaw clenched, he crawls along the pavement, fumbling to open a pouch strapped to his waist. Shivering, I grip the windowsill and try to catch his eye, but my angle's no good, and we've lost the element of surprise. I need a better vantage point.

Leaning out the window, I reach for Celine's foot. If she anchors me, I'll be able to surprise him during his next throw. My fingers graze her ankle, and I miss, lose my balance, and free fall toward the concrete.

Celine screams.

I wait for my life to flash before my eyes, but all I see is asphalt.

Then thick arms wrap around my waist like a vise. Hair in my eyes, stomach in my throat, Malach's wings flap wildly as he tries to support us both.

"Can you"—he pants—"get a shot off?"

I nod. "Line me up!"

Malach dives. My stomach leaves my body entirely. The dripping ball of trash and liquid-angel passes on my right, then I find myself face-to-face with the crawling angel.

I kill him. The chill spreads from the pocket of arteries behind my eyes to the patchwork of thicker veins in my limbs. I shiver, violently, the kind of full-body shudder that belongs on a snow-capped mountain and nowhere near Las Vegas.

My feet skim the ground, and I force my knees to bend. It's hard. Harder than it's ever been before. Fear grips me. Will I be stuck this way forever?

Malach groans and adjusts his grip on me. "One more," he

says. His voice is strained, his accent more pronounced as he supports our combined weight.

I blink lethargically and try to focus on the final angel as my eyes water. He isn't screaming anymore, and he's pieced together what I can do. Instead of looking at me, his gaze is fixed on the ground. He's digging ferociously in his bag. Gods. If he hurls one of those death balls at us from this range, we're fucked.

"Drop me on him," I demand.

Malach's arms tighten instead. I open my mouth to argue.

Then he throws me. Brittle and achy, I collide with the angel, grabbing his hair and forcing his head up. He tries to close his eyes, but he's too late.

I petrify him, and it feels like I'm petrifying myself. His stone face blurs, and I roll to the side, the pavement unbearably cold against my bare feet and arms.

Breath. Don't stop breathing. I beg my body to listen, focusing entirely on the grinding rise and fall of my chest. In. Out. In. Out. I'm not ready to die.

My throat spasms as I swallow, venom-laced saliva trickling down my esophagus. It's bitter, but unmistakably liquid. I'm not a statue; not yet at least. Relieved beyond belief, I force my arms and legs to move, wiggling them until the stiffness turns to pins and needles.

"Luca!" Celine drops to her knees at my side.

Her fingers are scorching against my face.

Satisfied that the cold burn behind my eyes is gone, I pry them open. Stars wink down at me, pure white and crisp, without the fuzzy yellow halo.

"I'm okay, baby," I murmur, squeezing her hand.

Black spots blot out the stars, and I can't hear her response over the deafening roar inside my head. *Spoke too soon.*

Celine's worried face is the last thing I see.

TWENTY-ONE

CELINE

Mouth open, Luca's head lolls to the side.

His skin is paler than I've ever seen it, chalky and lit only by my wings. They're flaming like a bonfire, and I can't fix it—I'm too furious.

Angels hurt him. And it's my fault.

"Luca will be fine," Malach says, maintaining a healthy distance from my flames. "You must control yourself, my truth."

I hear him. I do. But I can't calm down. It's too late for that.

Overheated, my hairline damp with sweat, a red tinge creeps along the edges of my vision. I'm not sure if it's from the flames or if I'm that mad. The longer I stare at Luca's slack face, the stronger the rage gets. It's the safest choice. If I stifle my anger, the emotions churning behind it might get free.

Air brushes my bunched thighs. *Someone is here—they'll take him from me.*

I spin and crouch protectively over Luca. *Kill them.*

Alistair narrows his eyes at my position and looks at Luca. "I hear his heart beating. Are there injuries I can't see?"

"He used a lot of magic," Malach says. "I think he's exhausted."

"You think"—my fingers curl—"but you don't know."

"Then move aside so I can get him off the street." Alistair passes dangerously close to my flaming right wing. I tuck it into my back automatically, even as I consider using it to incinerate his bossy judgment.

"Why are you here?" I snap. "If anyone sees you with—"

"*Everyone* has seen me with you, angel. In fact, three of my informants called to tell me there was a magical battle happening outside my girl's apartment."

I grind my teeth and face him, wincing as something sharp digs into my bare foot. It's probably a piece of metal spat out by the *koil'nashra*. I've never seen one in action before, but they certainly lived up to their name, which roughly translates to death coil.

Alistair's nostrils flare. He lunges at me, grinding to a halt when I hiss in warning. "You're bleeding," he says, his voice like glass dragging against steel.

"I'm fine," I echo Luca's earlier reassurance, relieved when I don't get dinged for it. At least my magic doesn't think I'm pussy enough to consider a cut foot grounds for a lie.

Luca stirs, and I hoist him into my arms, wincing as I survey the surrounding rubble. "This is a mess," I say.

Malach grunts and raises his hands. Moonlight catches on his wings, reflecting off the feathers and bathing the carnage in subtle shades of gray as he directs his magic at the shrapnel and stone.

A curtain shifts on the bottom floor of my building.

I swallow a curse as Alistair's words sink in. We fought a battle in the street outside my apartment complex. Six angels are dead, and with celestial magic flying everywhere, it was loud and impossible to ignore. My neighbors won't be able to pretend they didn't see or hear. They will talk about this, and there's nothing I can do to stop it.

Luca is heavy in my arms. I need to get him inside, but—I never finished unlocking the door. I glance up. My window has never seemed higher, and my wings are weak from years of disuse.

The final oozing hunk of metal disappears with a groan, whisked away by Malach's magic. He's at my side a second later, bumping Alistair out of the way.

"Allow me to carry him inside," he says.

Nodding, I transfer Luca to Malach's arms reluctantly, watching with a nauseous twist of envy and gratitude as they reach the window and disappear inside.

"You ignore my help and hand Luca over to that murderous lunatic?" Alistair advances on me. "Have you forgotten he tried to kill us both? He could be smothering him as we speak."

"Things have changed."

"Have they or is Luca's life less important than your pride?"

"Fuck you!" I shove his chest. "This has nothing to do with pride; you're the one I can't trust!" I shove him again, stumbling when my cut foot grazes the jagged edge of a pothole.

Alistair grabs my arms, his eyes flashing a wild, feral red as my flames flicker against the harsh planes of his face. I've never seen him this angry. I flinch away.

He makes a wounded sound low in his throat.

"Please," he begs. "Please, angel. Let me help."

My burning wings are inches from his arms. They could hurt him. My stomach churns, and the flames go out. Horrified, I try to back away, but Alistair doesn't let go. He walks with me, his gaze crimson and impossible to look away from.

"A-Ali," I stammer. My voice cracks, and I lick my lips. What is there to say? Everything's broken, and I don't know how to fix it. Not this time.

Alistair saves me the trouble. His lips drop to mine in a hungry kiss. My feet leave the ground, and air moves around us. I keep my eyes squeezed shut.

If I don't look . . . If I refuse to watch the life I built crash around me, maybe it won't.

A door slams. My ass hits something smooth and cold. I shiver, and my tongue grazes the tip of one of Alistair's fangs. A burst of salty copper coats my mouth, and my shoulder blades connect with the countertop.

Alistair's hands are rough—exactly how I prefer them—and I moan as my wings bump something that falls to the ground and shatters.

"Hot," a voice says. "And appropriately violent. Any chance you two can postpone the hate fuck for a few minutes, though? We're in a situation."

My eyes fly open.

Ciprian closes the door behind himself and locks it—securing all three deadbolts before he faces us. Alistair pulls away from me, horror and hunger flickering across his face before he smooths the expression into something blank.

"I'll kill you, Casanell," he says, his voice a ripple of pure menace.

"Of course." Ciprian rolls his eyes. "You can issue as many death threats as you want if we can fast forward to the part where I convince you I'm suitably intimidated. We've got bigger problems."

"There is no we," I remind him, wiping the back of my hand

over my lips. It does nothing to erase Alistair's taste from my mouth.

"I'm sorry, hot wings." Ciprian's black eyes snap to me. "I forgot to account for your pathological need to remind everyone you're an island who needs no one. Consider me put in my place, then kindly shut the fuck up and listen for once!"

"Don't talk to her like that," Alistair growls, his voice barely recognizable.

That terrible night at the Fang flashes through my head. Alistair yelling at me; Ciprian calling him out for it. They've swapped roles, and I'm still miserable.

Ciprian's eyes never leave mine, and I shiver. Alistair is dangerous—everyone knows that. Ignoring him is a simple way to communicate that you're just as dangerous. It's a hair's breadth away from an outright challenge.

"One of your neighbors reported you to the enclave," Ciprian says. "I'm supposed to take care of you now."

My blood chills, and I brace my hands on the counter.

This is the moment Ciprian's been waiting for. He'll punish me for Roscoe's death and the fiasco with the angels, and no one will question it. After all, we created a loud, dramatic incident. If a human heard or saw anything, the entire supernatural community would be at risk.

My heart sinks. We'll have to kill Ciprian and run. Then it will be a race to see who catches me first: my father's assassins or the enclave.

Blood drips from the ball of my foot to the tile floor, mocking me for how badly I've fucked up. Alistair's gaze snaps to the growing red puddle and stays there. I frown and unspool a paper towel, pressing it against the cut to help it clot.

Ciprian begins to pace. "So completely fucked," he mutters. "I knew they would be trouble, but this is godsdamned catastrophic. Dad's going to be an absolute cunt about it too."

He glances at the couch and freezes as he spots Luca. Guilt swamps me. I should have checked on him immediately, but instead I prioritized making out with Alistair. What is wrong with me? This is a dream. It's got to be. The worst kind—where I make all the wrong decisions. I'm going to wake up any minute.

"What the fuck did you do to him?" Ciprian looks at me in horror. "He's a basilisk, not a ghost. Did you get hungry?" He directs the last question at Alistair, who blinks and reluctantly tears his eyes away from the bloody tile.

"I just got here," Alistair says. He's so outraged, it would be funny under almost any other circumstances. "I haven't touched Luca."

"Well, someone should!" Ciprian tosses his hands in the air. "There's obviously something wrong with him."

Malach strides into the room, the first aid kit woefully small and inadequate in his huge hands. "I retrieved your box of healing."

Ciprian snorts and drops to his knees beside the couch. "Toss me Celine's box of healing, big guy." The euphemism breaks through my foggy thoughts like nothing else has, and I rush to the couch and press two fingers to Luca's neck.

His pulse is strong, but Ciprian is right: there's something wrong.

"My name is Malach."

"I know that."

"If you try to kill me while my back is turned, I'll let Alistair eat you," I threaten Ciprian, ignoring his exchange with Malach.

Ciprian snorts. "Don't threaten me with a good time, babe. You forget he's taken a bite out of me before, and I liked it. A lot."

Frozen near the counter, Alistair doesn't respond to Ciprian's joke.

I frown. Ciprian bends over Luca but shifts his gaze deliberately toward Alistair. "Something is up with him," he whispers. "Have you noticed?"

Have I noticed? I'm not sure. Alistair and I aren't on good terms. We're allies and fuck buddies at most. He wants things to go back to the way they were, and I . . . don't have the first clue how to forgive him.

If Ciprian sees a change, though . . .

No. He's a master manipulator. A Casanell, for gods' sake. He twists the truth as easily as he draws breath. Dammit, he's proved that to me multiple times, yet I keep falling for it. Even now, I'm leaning into him, close enough that my arm brushes his shoulder, listening to his concerns with my fucking brow furrowed.

I recoil and spot the singed section of carpet where the *koil'-nashra* landed. It was close . . . too close. And Ciprian said he's supposed to "take care of us." That certainly doesn't mean patching us up and paying for our therapy. There's too much happening, and I don't have a good grasp on any of it.

My wings tremble, the blades grinding against each other. If I could get a minute alone . . .

Delicate threads of golden magic wrap around the singed fibers of the carpet, slowly but surely erasing all signs of damage. I watch Malach repair the carpet until I can't see through the tears blurring my vision. A small piece of order restored; it's a life preserver when I need it most.

Fingers graze my cheek, and Luca blinks up at me groggily. "You look worried, baby," he whispers.

"You passed out," I tell him, tears spilling from the corners of my eyes. No—not now. Not with people watching. I have to be strong, strategize, and fix this.

Ciprian rocks back on his heels and sighs. "You look like shit."

Luca chuckles. "You should see the other guys."

"I heard all about them," Ciprian says drily. "If you didn't have

Mr. Clean's better-looking cousin erasing evidence, I would have seen them too. Front-row seat, like Celine's snitching neighbors."

Luca raises his eyebrows, then yawns. "Are you here to kill us or take us in?"

"I haven't decided yet." Ciprian sighs. The sound is heavy, as if he's carrying the weight of the world. I can't decide whether it pisses me off or makes me more stressed.

"Can it wait until morning?" Luca asks.

Ciprian snorts a laugh. "It is morning, dude."

As soon as he says it, I see the glow coming through the shattered window. Malach got rid of the broken glass, but his magic can't repair something that badly damaged. He fixed the carpet for me—to make me feel better—and I know it was difficult for him. He's always been better at removing messes than fixing them.

After a few seconds of blissful silence, everyone turns to Alistair.

Fists clenched, he's still staring at the kitchen tile. *What the hell is wrong with him?* Maybe Ciprian is right, and I've missed something.

"Alistair." I snap my fingers to get his attention. "Get to my room before you fry."

He blinks at me, his eyes crawling almost wistfully to the rays of sun stretching across the living room floor.

Ciprian jumps to his feet, rushing to the window and pressing the ruined shade over it. "Hurry up," he says.

When Alistair finally moves, it's slowly. I hold my breath as he walks around the counter, past the couch, and into the hallway. As soon as he's covered in shadow, air leaves my mouth in a whoosh.

"I can fix that," Malach says, dipping his head toward the ruined shade.

Ciprian moves out of the way so he can get started. "I'll stay on the couch," he says, glancing at me. "Get some sleep, Celine. We'll talk it through in five or six hours."

I nod. A strange numbness takes hold of me and makes it easier to think logically.

I can't be mad at Ciprian for this. It wasn't his fault that someone called the enclave to report what happened. The fact that he's conflicted enough to keep us in the loop tells me . . . something. I'm too tired to know exactly what, but I do know it would be stupid to antagonize him any more than I already have.

"Thanks." I force the word out through a jaw clenched too tight.

From the halfhearted curl of Ciprian's lips, he knows exactly how hard it was for me. "Don't pretend with me, hot wings; I know you still hate me. We can talk about this like adults once you've rested, but you don't have to force a lie. I prefer you as you are, pissed and all."

I pull Luca to his feet and drag him out of the room before I can do something absurd, like hug a fucking Casanell.

TWENTY-TWO

ALISTAIR

I grip the headboard to give my hands something to do.

Fire scalds my throat, and my fangs throb. I'm anxious and thirsty. So thirsty. My mouth is somehow too wet and too dry, and if I close my eyes, I can still taste Celine's blood on my tongue. I almost dropped to my knees and licked the tile like a starving dog.

Because that's exactly what I am, and there's nothing I can do about it.

The door closes, the snick of the latch bashing my eardrums. I shake my head to clear the ringing.

I want it. I need it. Her blood. It's here—no, *she's* here. But her blood calls to me; I can hear it pumping through her veins.

It would taste good.

Everything would stop hurting.

If I took a little . . . things couldn't get any worse, right?

Luca is too weak to stop me right now, and Celine wouldn't expect it—

Horror eclipses my hunger. My fingertips turn brittle and cold.

I'm losing it. Gods, I'm dangerous to them.

My heart throbs against my ribs, desperate to escape this cursed body. I don't blame it. I'm a bloody monster. A starving, bloody monster. And I'm terrified.

"What's wrong?" Luca asks.

His hand hovers over my back. I feel the heat and wait for the pressure of his touch, but it never comes. Loneliness and rejection join my thirst. Together, they gnaw me to the bone like a ravenous pack of wolves.

"Nothing," I say.

Celine clears her throat. "Don't lie to him, Alistair."

"I didn't—"

"Watch it," she warns.

In this moment, I hate her magic with every fiber of my being. The truth isn't always needed; some things should remain private. I don't want to crack myself open for their inspection—especially while I'm trapped here by the sun, longing only to fuck, drink, fuck, repeat until none of us can stand.

"I don't know," I seethe, spinning to face them. "Is that what you want to hear? I'm fucked all the way up, and every swallow is agony. What I do know is that it doesn't concern either of you!"

My mortifying explosion is met with complete silence.

Luca sits heavily on the bed, the box spring whining under his weight. "I can only speak for myself, Ali, but I'm concerned," he says, running his fingers through his messy hair.

"I'm not trying to violate your privacy," Celine whispers. Her face is free of expression, but her wingtips drag on the floor.

I'm pushing her further away.

Since the moment I cut holes in my T-shirt for her wings, I've done everything wrong. I might as well have cut those holes in myself—it hurts the same.

We're out of sync, our trust is strained, yet I want her more than my next breath.

My curiosity and the mortifyingly consistent aloneness that drove me to pursue her and Luca might get me killed. And the joke will be on me, because I'm still fucking alone.

"We can talk about something else," Luca says, dropping sideways against the mattress. He cuts his eyes to Celine and raises one eyebrow. "Like how you tossed the plan out the window—along with your whole body—and launched truth beams or something at those dicks. What the fuck was that, baby?"

Celine purses her lips. "I didn't throw out the plan; I improvised."

"I don't care about that part anymore. I've come to terms." He points at Celine. "You'll keep putting yourself in danger, and I'll keep aging at a premature rate until they bury me in ten to fifteen years from the long-term effects of some fatal stress syndrome."

Celine smiles . . . genuinely, and a chill runs down my spine. She's so beautiful it hurts. Crossing to the far side of the bed, she bends to smack a kiss on Luca's grinning mouth.

"I love you," she says. "I'm glad you're okay."

Her words sink into my heart like barbs, and I avert my gaze, wishing I were anywhere else. I'm happy for Luca, but envy has me in a chokehold. *Why can't I have this too?*

"I love you too," Luca says, yawning audibly. "But don't think I didn't notice you skipping over the truth beams. I want to hear about them, then I want to sleep until Ciprian drags us out of bed."

Celine winces and drops onto the bed, mirroring Luca's position. Her pale neck is inches from my leg. I stare transfixed, at the tiny throbbing pulse below her jaw.

"I don't use them often. The results are awful." She shudders.

"In layman's terms, my magic forces the collective pain of every lie they've ever told back on them, making them face the physical consequences of their lies. If someone doesn't lie often, they won't hurt much. But those angels worked for my dad, so I knew . . ."

"That they would go down like a ton of bricks," Luca says.

Celine sighs. "Something like that."

"I killed five people tonight." Luca closes his eyes and fists the covers.

Neither of us responds. He needs to say it out loud to share the weight, but he's not asking for absolution. Celine slides her hand over the mattress until she finds Luca's fingers, prying them loose and lacing them with hers.

"You both need to rest," I say.

Celine looks at me upside down, a tiny wrinkle appearing between her eyebrows. I fight the urge to squirm and barely win.

"Join us. For tonight," she says softly.

My heart skips a beat. I've shared a bed with them before, but not since everything fell apart. Celine isn't a pushover. If she wanted to make me sleep in the bathroom with the door closed until sundown, she would. This is an olive branch. It's time-sensitive and fragile, but it's movement. I'm more than desperate enough to take it.

I nod, not trusting my voice.

We get ready for bed, moving around each other with a rhythm that's almost as domestic as it is coordinated. I find myself anticipating when Luca will finish brushing his teeth and how long it will take Celine to massage moisturizer into her face.

No one says a word. Within ten minutes, Luca and I stand on opposite sides of the bed—me by the window, him by the bathroom.

"You're on my side," he grumbles, scrubbing a hand over his jaw.

I roll my eyes and swap places with him, but part of me knows

I did it on purpose. To see if he'd still insist on being nearest the window in case sunlight got through. For a minute, Luca's loyalty drives the wolves back. It's the exact reassurance I've always wanted and never had.

Stop it. You're nothing to him. Nothing to her either. Wanting something doesn't mean you get to have it. I swallow the bitter reminder—one I learned long before I had fangs—wishing I could spit it out like the last ten bags of blood I've failed to drink.

We settle in the same as we did weeks ago with Celine in the middle, but none of us are touching this time. After their breathing evens out, I let myself drift off, my throat stuffed with sizzling embers.

I wake to the most delicious smell. Warm, spicy, and sweet, I want to drown in it.

Inhaling deeply, I frown as someone shouts in the distance.

The words are unclear. I don't try to make sense of them. It's pointless . . . a complete waste of time. I'm on the edge of ecstasy, about to sink my fangs into something delicious. Earthy heat teases me, and I lick the throbbing pulse. It beats faster beneath my tongue, and I smile, savoring the moment. Anticipation makes the bite sweeter for both of us.

"Don't startle him. I don't think he's awake."

These words are clear, but they make no sense. Of course I'm awake. Who could sleep through this temptation?

"Alistair." The throat beneath my lips moves. "Ali, come on, wake up."

The voice is familiar and beautiful, but it's trembling. Who has frightened my angel?

"I think he's waking up." Luca sounds relieved. Wait. Why is Luca relieved?

I yank my head up, blinking to adjust my eyes to the darkness. "Alistair, it's okay," Celine says. "Everything's okay."

The lamp turns on, and I flinch away from the bright light, hissing as my body registers the boiling agony in my eyes and throat. "W-what?" I demand.

"Easy, Ali," Luca whispers. "Deep breaths."

"Not sure that's a great idea," Celine mutters.

"What happened?" I demand. The scorch in my throat hits a new, devastating level.

"You jumped Celine and started gnawing on her neck."

Revulsion consumes me as I see exactly what he means. Celine's skin is red and chafed, with the shadow of a bruise forming. I hear a choking sound and realize it's coming from me.

"You didn't break the skin," Celine says. Her voice is soft and gentle. She's trying to avoid spooking a wild animal. Caged by the sun, I'm the wild animal—a danger to her, exactly as I feared.

Leaning over Celine, his body tense, Luca positions himself as a shield between us.

He doesn't trust me anymore.

My eyes dart to the clock, then to the window. It's almost seven-thirty—the sun is setting. Twilight is painful, but I have no choice. I've got to get out of here.

Blindly, I sprint from the room.

Ciprian jumps up from the couch, his black eyes sharp as he gets between me and my way out. I snarl and shove past him, slamming the door in his startled face.

Then I'm running. Down the stairs, across the parking lot, into the nearest alley. I run without thought. Each step takes me deeper into the seedier parts of the Fringes. Heat from the fading sun presses against me, but I ignore it, running at random until the smell of freshly spilled blood yanks me in the opposite direction.

I follow it blindly, greedily sucking in the scent of wet copper.

It doesn't smell as good as Celine's neck, but there's a lot of it. As I get closer, I hear the unmistakable sound of fists pounding against flesh. Someone is taking a beating. I should turn around and head to my apartment, but . . . I can't.

For the first time since I was turned, my starving body overrules my brain. Internally, I scream, but I can't stop. Then I spot the source of the blood: three grimy supernaturals. I recognize two of them as members of the local shifter gang; a gang I've refused to work with in the past. They're despicable. Predators.

But my fangs are bigger.

I tear through the tallest one's neck before any of them see me. He dies easily and tastes terrible. I toss him aside and turn on the second. This one struggles. My fangs do more damage because of it. His blood tastes metallic—better than his friend's—but far from good. When he goes limp, I drop him to the pavement, glancing at the guy he was beating up.

Eyes glassy and unseeing, a knife protrudes from his chest. I cock my head to listen, but the only heart beating in this alley belongs to me. I growl softly. Their deaths weren't enough—I need more. I'm so thirsty. But . . . why? How?

Between the two gang members, I drank a gallon of blood, yet I'm thirstier than ever, and . . . My stomach roils. A brutal cramp folds me in half, and I fall to my knees.

Then I vomit fountains of blood.

Again and again and again and again. My body purges until the only thing left is bile. Fear and shock clear my bloodlust quicker than a slap to the face.

With one arm wrapped around my middle, I stumble to my feet, trying and failing to quiet my growing terror.

I'm starving. Dying of thirst. Slowly and painfully. I told myself the bagged blood was tainted. A bad batch. But this was fresh—straight from the vein, and I just painted the street with it. *Why can't I drink blood anymore? Am I damned like Mum thinks?*

Questions roll around my head a mile a minute as I stumble to my apartment.

I manage to text a cleaner to take care of the bodies. It will cost me, but I'm in no condition to deal with them myself.

I can't pretend any longer. Something is terribly wrong with me. Something I've never heard about happening to any vampire, turned or born.

Until I know what it is, I need to stay the fuck away from Celine and Luca.

The realization guts me. How can it be that now—when I need to fight by their sides the most—I'm a liability?

As soon as I lock my apartment behind me, I run to the toilet and throw up again.

My organs twist and writhe, and no matter what I do, I can't get any relief. The smell is nauseating. Stumbling to my feet, I splash water on my face, rinse my mouth out, and sag against the sink.

I need to keep them safe, but how? Information. It's always been my greatest weapon. There's nothing I can do about Celine's father, but the enclave . . .

The djinn. I can use her against them. For the first time since I woke with my fangs pressed to Celine's neck, I see the situation clearly.

Ciprian will hate me forever.

But for Celine, I'm willing to pay the price.

TWENTY-THREE

CELINE

The covers are bunched in my lap, my wings blanketing more of the bed than they are. I stare at Luca in shock. *What the fuck just happened?*

I woke to Alistair kissing my neck. Pulse racing, I was about to give in and kiss him back. Then I realized something was off. He wasn't kissing my neck; he was sucking on it. Scraping his teeth against the skin . . . everything but driving his fangs in.

"Are you okay?" Luca asks for the tenth time.

I shoot him an annoyed look. "I'm fine. Alistair wouldn't hurt me."

Luca scrubs his hand through his hair, chewing on his lip ring. "Normally, I would agree with you, but that wasn't the normal Alistair, baby."

I open my mouth to deny it, then close it again. He's right.

Alistair was lost to something. His thirst, maybe? Except he had every opportunity to bite me and didn't.

That must mean something.

"What did he say before bed?" I ask, remembering how we found him hunched over the headboard. "Something about every swallow being agony?" He shut us down, but we should have pushed harder.

Luca groans. "I don't remember exactly but it was something like that. He seemed strung out."

"He was off last week too," Ciprian says, popping his head into my room. He doesn't bother pretending he wasn't listening. "I thought he was just mad at me, but that doesn't make complete sense. Are you—"

"Don't ask if I'm okay." I sink into the pillows and consider pulling one over my face and screaming until I'm hoarse.

Luca glances between Ciprian and I, his brow furrowed. "When was the last time he drank from one of you?"

Ciprian shuffles his weight awkwardly. I squirm against the mattress.

Luca rolls his eyes. "Don't be such babies. I've watched him bite both of you and turn you into mindless, horny fuck monsters. There's no reason to be embarrassed, I'm trying to put together a timeline."

I sigh and glance at Ciprian's unusually pink cheeks. "Unless I missed something between you two, he drank from me last. It was right before we learned who you really were."

Luca raises his eyebrows. "That was weeks ago."

"But he drinks bagged blood all the time," I argue. "I've seen it at his place."

Luca shrugs. "I'm not saying it makes sense, but something has him rattled."

"He left his shoes behind." Ciprian points to the boots tucked beside the bedroom door. "Shoved past me barefoot and crazed."

"I'll call and check on him." Luca grabs his phone off the nightstand and walks into the bathroom.

My back itches. I'm alone with Ciprian, and we're both studiously ignoring the enclave-sized elephant in the room. Dark circles frame his darker eyes, the kind that come from more than one sleepless night.

"Stop looking at me like that," he says.

"How am I looking at you?" It's a bad idea to antagonize him, but I can't help myself.

"Like I'm about to grow a monster head." Ciprian points at the closed bathroom door. "That's your boyfriend's issue, not mine."

Snarky motherfucker. I sit up straight, my hands fisting in the blanket. "If you barge into my bedroom looking like shit, I'm going to look," I tell him. "Why did you let us sleep this long, anyway? What are you plotting?"

Ciprian closes his eyes and pinches the bridge of his nose. "I've been busy making all the paintings in your apartment crooked—what the fuck do you think? I've been racking my brain for the last twelve hours, trying to figure out how to keep you alive."

He advances on me, and for the first time since I met him, he looks more demon than human. Even with a bitter joke tossed in, Ciprian Casanell is being deadly serious. It scares me.

"I don't need your help," I insist, twitching as lie pain shoots through my nerves. My magic is hateful. It makes it nearly impossible to win an argument. "I won't let you kill me, Ciprian, and if you even think about laying a finger on Luca."

He groans. "Be so fucking real right now, because there's no way you don't know that I'm obsessed with you both. I think about laying a finger or ten on both of you fifteen times a day. That isn't the problem, hot wings, and it doesn't make this situation simpler either. You're in the biggest mess I've ever seen."

Ciprian's blunt words bring the full force of my guilt roaring to the surface. My wings tremble, and I force them into my body before they can reveal anything damning.

"It's my fault," I whisper, rolling my shoulders to help with the itch. "I never should have gotten involved with any of you; I knew the risk."

I'm not sure why I tell Ciprian what I'm thinking. He didn't even ask, I volunteered the information. Even knowing who he is, I want to confide in him. It's pathological.

"Do your magic," Ciprian says, planting his hands on his hips.

I blink at him, confused by his exasperated tone. "Why?"

"Because we have a hellish immediate future ahead of us, and I don't want to have to repeat myself after you inevitably call me a liar."

I activate my truth runes, too curious to bother arguing. He's better at it anyway, and I hate to lose. My magic is so near the surface I could probably tell if he was lying without the runes— like when I called Alistair out last night—but this way is foolproof.

Once my skin is crowded with golden marks, I look at Ciprian, raise my eyebrows, and gesture for him to get a move on.

He rolls his eyes. "Here's the truth, Celine: you're the best thing to ever happen to Luca. He's stupidly in love with you, and nothing will ever top the moment you let yourself feel the same for him. Alistair is losing control, and he hates it, but there's no reality where he regrets getting tangled in your orbit. And as for that himbo angel—"

"My name is Malach!"

"Yeah, I fucking know that," Ciprian shouts. "Where was I? Yes, Malach learned English for you, left his realm behind to protect you, and tried to off your fuck buddies. That's crazy fucking romantic, and you can't argue with that."

"It was judgment! And thank you."

Ciprian smirks. "Whatever. He's full of shit about that part. I'll bet you a thousand bucks he was trying to create space for his big ass in your bed by eliminating the competition."

Malach laughs out loud from down the hall, and my mouth drops open.

"Anyway, what I'm saying, Celine, is that no one—me included—regrets meeting you or getting caught in your mess. It's terrible and complicated, sure, but it's not your fault. Don't absorb the weight of inherited bullshit."

He softens, glancing at the window, then back at me before clearing his throat. "If you take anything positive away from our time together, let it be this: you can find solutions without also tricking yourself into thinking you're the problem."

Luca comes out of the bathroom. "I agree with most of that," he says.

I nod weakly, not sure how to respond. My magic detected no lies. It's going to take time for me to unpack everything Ciprian said, but I have the strangest urge to give him a hug.

"What did Alistair say?" I ask.

"He wouldn't answer. I called him half a dozen times. Didn't stop until he sent me a bullshit text saying he was fine."

"A text?" I frown. "Someone could have his phone."

Luca nods. "Which is why I demanded proof of life." He flips his phone around to show us a horribly lit selfie of Alistair. Eyes red from anger or the flash, he's shooting Luca the bird.

"Frame that one for the wall," Ciprian deadpans.

"So you could make it hang crooked? No thanks," I mutter, then narrow my eyes at Luca. "You were in the bathroom for a long time."

"Maybe I needed to take a shit."

"Did you?"

"No. I didn't want to interrupt this conversation. It sounded important." *There it is.*

Luca smiles at me, tiny lines fanning out from the corners of his eyes. I melt, then feel disgusted with myself. Luca is good looking. I've known that for years, so why am I turning into an angel with fluff for brains when he smiles at me?

I glance away to regroup, unsurprised that he's working his subtle brand of manipulation behind the scenes. Luca is far more likely to remain calm than Alistair or Ciprian, both of whom love to throw a fit, but he's damn good with people. I see it at the Fang all the time.

"What happens next? Are you going to bury us under your fancy Colorado compound or put all ten fingers to work?" Luca winks at Ciprian and wiggles his hands. "Wait. I need caffeine for this. Tell me over coffee."

Ciprian blushes, and they stare at each other with matching grins.

My stomach flutters. Pushing the covers back, I climb out of bed and let my wings out. They're feathers—for now—but it won't take much to summon the blades or flames if my emotions spike.

"Don't take this the wrong way, but you are an incredibly beautiful woman."

I snap my head up and find Ciprian's stormy stare focused on me. Not on my bare legs, or the curve of my ass hanging from the bottom of the oversized T-shirt, but on my face. A face I know is tired, stressed, swollen, and attached to a neck made splotchy by Alistair's sleep-gnawing.

"I can't tell if you're joking or not," I say. I mean to sound strong and confident. I don't. I sound edgy instead, like I've been pushed to the breaking point.

Ciprian's eyebrows pull together. A wave of something moves across his face too quick for me to read. "Trust me," he says.

I go to the bathroom and shut the door without responding.

I don't have the heart to tell him I can't.

Because I want to trust Ciprian, the stakes are simply too high.

I can't be weak or powerless again. I wasn't strong enough to save Mom from my father. I've accepted that, along with the grief and guilt that came along with it, but I will save myself and the messy family I've created here on Earth if it's the last thing I do.

"He won't take anyone from you again," I whisper, making the promise to my reflection and hoping I never see the day it makes me a liar.

TWENTY-FOUR

ENCLAVE EDICT #2:
IF A SUPERNATURAL IN OUR TERRITORY CREATES AN
INCIDENT, WE WILL ACT.

CIPRIAN

I take the cup of coffee Luca offers me and consider pouring it over my face. Second-degree burns? That's cool. I'll take anything to wake myself up. I'm not sure my skin has ever been tired before, but it is now. Combined with the grit no number of blinks can clear from my eyes, I want to crawl into bed and never leave.

There's no more avoiding this collision, though. Ever since Celine killed Roscoe and Dad sent me to Vegas, we've been barreling toward this moment: Fringes versus enclave, angel versus demon, stubborn bullshit versus stubborner bullshit.

It hit the fan last night, and it's still flying. I have to find the switch and turn the damn thing off—except it's more like a bomb than a fan—and if I cut the wrong wire, we all blow up.

The Fringes forge tight-lipped supernaturals, but someone snitched. To be honest, I can't blame them. Self-preservation is a powerful motivator. They wanted to cover their own ass and make it clear they weren't involved. I should follow their example, but I can't.

Celine is beautiful and smart. No one would argue against that, but I've met beautiful, smart women before. I love charisma and danger, and Luca is dripping with both. Risking my future for those traits, though? I don't think so. And Alistair? He's completely unhinged. I don't mind risk, and I go crazy for a surprise, but never at my own expense.

Face drooping, brain limping along at half speed, I do the math while I guzzle my coffee. Even when I factor in all the variables and carry the one, it doesn't add up.

I told Sarah they were important. My gut is telling me to help them, that they're worth it. And damned if I don't want to be their hero for once instead of a villain. Is that wrong?

Luca refills my mug and adds a splash of creamer to knock the edge off. I bring it carefully to my lips. The coffee flirts with the rim before I knock back a deep gulp.

"You're thinking hard," he says.

If anyone at the enclave said that to me, I would accuse them of mocking me, but Luca—as violent as he is—doesn't have much of a mean streak. At least not that he's shown me.

"This is a tricky situation," I tell him, sticking to the cold, hard truth.

"You're under pressure"—Luca sips from his own mug, his eyes going half-lidded with delight as the coffee hits his taste buds —"but are you in danger?"

He sounds like he would care if I was, and my heart flips. *Don't get your hopes up.*

"They won't physically hurt me, if that's what you mean," I say.

Luca hums and takes another sip. "There are more ways to be

harmed besides the physical, especially by the people closest to us."

"Don't I know it." I groan and let my tired eyes drift shut, wincing from the scrape of my eyelids. They might as well be sandpaper. "I'll have to go home. This can't be handled over the phone."

"And if we run?" Luca asks.

I open my eyes. "Then you'll be spitting on my gesture of friendship. I'm vouching for you, telling my dad you're not at fault—"

"We aren't," Luca snaps.

"Yeah, but half a dozen angels were killed in the street. People saw—lots of people saw—and this is after I already put my ass on the line by saying you weren't a threat."

"Why would you do that, Ciprian?"

It's a simple question; one I've already asked myself half a dozen times. "Fuck if I know," I say. "Please don't make me regret it."

He frowns. "I hear what you're saying, but you're asking for a lot too. You want us to go against all our instincts and trust you, yet you're obviously worried about pulling this off. Our experiences with the enclave don't point to fair decision-making, and you've already tricked us once."

"I didn't—" I stop myself and take a deep breath. "I tricked you, yes, but it wasn't done maliciously. I wanted you to be innocent."

"But we weren't," Celine says.

I turn my head, wincing as my neck cracks. Dressed in a crop top and skintight leggings, she's only five or six feet away, but she feels unreachable. Lips pursed, arms crossed, everything about her body language is closed off.

"But you weren't," I echo her words. "I've spoken to Joshua

Therion—the leader of the shifter contingent of the enclave. He's agreed to hear me out in person before deciding."

"Does he know about Roscoe?"

Telling her the truth is risky.

Lying might be worse.

I tighten my grip on the mug. Do I cut the blue wire or the red one? There's no pretending that Celine herself isn't a critical part of the bomb I'm defusing.

I open my mouth to dodge her question and—a trickle of her fear hits me.

It reminds me of the bathroom floor when she fed me her terror before telling me about Roscoe. In that moment, Celine trusted me with her secrets. She doesn't remember that feeling anymore, but I do. It was a punch to the gut and the most precious gift I'd ever been given.

For the memory of that alone, I owe her the truth.

"They know about Roscoe," I say grimly. "I made it crystal clear that Dad's favorite guard was killed by a gang of transient shifters over an illegal poker game."

My declaration is met with absolute silence.

I take another sip of coffee, hoping they don't notice the cup shaking.

"You told him—"

"What he needed to hear to move on," I interrupt her. "It's better this way, and not only for you."

A shadow falls over me, and I look up into the behemoth of an angel's face. Malach has a stare that follows you around the room. He nods at me, his expression stern and oddly arresting—a rococo painting behind bulletproof glass.

Gods, Mom would love to have a statue of him in the house. Something to scare everyone shitless before they meet her.

"As I said . . ." His voice is a low rumble. "I judged him worthy."

A choked laugh escapes me, and I spill hot coffee on my thumb. "I'm what?"

"Worthy," Malach repeats, his brow creasing as he looks at me. Is he second-guessing himself already?

"That's awesome," I say, taking the opportunity to escape the heavy tension of the conversation. "I'm glad someone around here finally caught on."

"Ciprian . . ." Celine's stare is penetrating. "I don't know what to say."

"You don't have to say anything." I cringe at the raspy sound of my own voice.

"When will you be back?" Celine sounds anxious, but I'm not naïve enough to think her worry has anything to do with my well-being. It's about her future in this territory and the escalating violence from her father. As it should be. She has enough to focus on, so why are her brown eyes still locked on me?

I shift my weight. "I'm not sure. I'll be in touch as soon as I can. But you all need to be careful. Lie low for a few days."

"We will." Celine's voice is subdued.

I dip my chin, hand Luca the rest of my coffee, and leave.

They don't try to stop me.

I'm ten miles down the road when my phone rings. *Alistair.* Worry for the surly vampire prickles my skin. He's in bad shape; he just won't admit it. I answer, half hoping he's ready to tell me what's wrong.

What he says instead turns my blood to ice.

I end the call, crushing the phone in my grip. The screen glitches, pink streaks slicing through the display.

I'm an idiot. I should have known Alistair wasn't coming around.

The dossier . . . merging our magic—it meant nothing to him. Ever since he learned my last name, he's been biding his time, waiting for a moment to cut me where it hurts the most. And now he's succeeded.

Somehow, he found out about Sheena, my only fucking friend. Sheena, who's been through more than enough at the hands of our world already. Sheena, the love of my brother's life and the weakness I'm least armed to protect.

Rage makes it hard to focus on the road.

For two hours, I drive as if I don't want to reach my destination in one piece. For the next seven and a half hours, I think harder than I ever have. I crush my panic, bury my anger, and fucking think until I have a plan that might work.

Alistair used Sheena against me, playing a card he never needed to use. I was already going to help Celine and Luca. By forcing my hand, he's torn my blinders off. I see him for who he is —a desperate, cold, angry, lonely monster.

I never should have pulled the sword from his gut.

TWENTY-FIVE

ALISTAIR

" . . . so I threatened him."

In the storage room at the Fang, Luca and Celine stare at me, unblinking. Their silence grates, even as their heartbeats merge with the thumping bass coming through the flimsy door.

I can't stop imagining what they would do if I sank my fangs into their necks.

"I don't understand," Luca finally says, scrubbing his palm over his face. "Ciprian said he had a plan, but you didn't believe him, so you decided to threaten his friend?"

I blink at him and growl. "My source said this djinn was the key to destroying the Casanells."

"Right," Celine adds. "Because losing a friend is awful."

My fingers twitch. They're watching me like a dangerous animal that's escaped its enclosure. It isn't fair. I wasn't even there when the street fight with the angels happened, and I'm putting all my energy and resources into helping.

"You're the one who always thought he was hiding a girl-friend," I remind her. "Think of this as insurance."

"I'm not saying I trust him, Alistair, but even I think it's reck-less to threaten him when he's literally on the way to do us a favor," Celine says. "He could change his mind, come back here with an army, and kill us all."

I scoff. "The enclave doesn't maintain a fighting force large enough to meet anyone's definition of an army."

Celine sighs. "I'm not arguing semantics with you."

"Then what are you arguing about, angel?"

"This reckless decision!" She throws her hands up, scowling at her cleavage as several moss green body jewels get dislodged. Luca bends to pick them up, making the curve of his neck vulner-able in the process. I gulp.

"You didn't even talk it over with us before you called him, and after the way you stormed off . . ." Celine doesn't finish the sentence, but we all know what she's talking about.

My shame demands I lash out so that I won't have to feel this way any longer. Stubbornly, I hold my tongue. Anger may be safer for me, but Celine doesn't like it.

She drops her chin, and her fingers twitch. With a muffled curse, she removes the remaining jewels from her belly and chest. They're too uneven for my angel.

Sighing, Luca grabs a bottle of whiskey from a crate, uncorks it, takes a healthy swig, then offers it to me. "What Celine is trying to say is, are you okay, Ali? You haven't seemed like yourself recently."

I'm tempted to ask him which out of character moment he's referring to. The horrible scene I made the night I discovered who Ciprian was? Or nearly biting Celine without her consent before sprinting barefoot through the Fringes?

Ever since I surrendered to my hopeless fascination with her, everything about my life has spiraled out of control. My temper is erratic at best. My self-control is hanging on with slippery fingers, and my bloodlust . . . well, Celine's heart has beaten one hundred fifty-seven times in the last three minutes, and I would kill anyone or anything to feel her pulse around my fangs.

I gulp the whiskey instead and taste nothing. The normal burn doesn't even register because my throat is already on fire. My vision tinges red. I take another sip, then swallow.

As an experiment, I tried eating a rare steak last night. It ended the evening with a flush, as has every drop of blood I've attempted to consume for weeks.

I'm dying. There's no denying it anymore.

Maybe I could accept death, but the monster inside me refuses to give up. It wants blood, and I'm becoming increasingly afraid of the lengths it will go to get it.

Will I lose myself to the bloodlust? Will I pierce every vein in the Fringes until I tap someone with blood I can keep down?

The idea is revolting. And it would destroy my business. My neighbors may trade information with a vampire who would tear their throat out if double-crossed, but they aren't likely to get within striking distance of one who's gone feral.

"I'll be fine," I say, forcing the words through my clenched teeth and praying to the gods that they're true.

Before Celine or Luca can push harder, I use my vampire speed to leave.

Neither of them follows me. I tell myself it's for the best.

———

"I'm responding to your blackmail," Ciprian says, his voice angry, even through the phone.

I bite my swollen tongue to stop myself from telling him I

wouldn't have used personal information against him if he hadn't played me for a fool.

"I'm listening," I say instead, then chug a glass of water. It tastes like ash and does nothing to mute the agony in my throat.

"If I were to set up a meeting for you, would you keep her identity a secret?"

My eyebrows lift. He's willing to introduce me to the djinn?

I expected death threats, but this . . . This is far more interesting.

"I take the confidentiality of my clients seriously, Casanell."

"Sure, you do." He makes a guttural sound in the back of his throat—a cross between a laugh and a scoff. "If she becomes a client of yours, I want your word you won't try to fuck her over."

"As I said, I do my utmost to deliver satisfactory results to everyone who makes a deal with me."

Ciprian laughs at that. The sound is ugly—nothing like his usual carefree amusement. "Because you didn't turn on me the second you got the chance, even while I was actively helping."

"You know why that happened," I say. "Celine and Luca—"

"Had nothing to fear from me," Ciprian interrupts. "I want you to swear to me you won't hurt Sheena. She's been through enough, and—" He chokes up, his voice fracturing before he clears his throat. "She deserves to have some positive interactions with this fucked-up supernatural shit show."

I frown, wishing I could see his face.

Ciprian is mad. He also sounds emotional, but that could be an act, an attempt to gain my sympathy before he pulls the wool over my eyes again. I can't forget how good he is at playing the game he pretends to hate.

"I swear I will treat her with respect," I say. "Providing she offers me the same in return."

For a full minute, the only response he gives me is heavy breathing.

Ciprian is thinking hard. This djinn, he truly cares about her. I'm convinced that part is no act. "I'll tell you when we're on our way," he finally says.

I scowl. "You've given me no assurances that the enclave won't attack Celine and Luca. Our deal isn't done."

"That was never part of the deal, Ali, because I was never going to sell them out. Celine told me what happened, and I believe her. You see enemies in every corner, even when there are none. You're fucking blinded by my last name."

"Excuse me for protecting my . . . ." I trail off. Helpless anger presses on my chest.

"Your what? Oh, that's right, she's not your girlfriend anymore, is she?"

I hiss, unable to hide my rage. "Perhaps I see enemies in every corner because I'm haunted by a nightmare."

"Yeah? Keep telling yourself that, dude. Whoever or whatever made you this way has nothing to do with me. I'll be in touch about the meeting."

He hangs up, robbing me of the last word, and I taste my own blood. Gods. It's been years since I accidentally tore my lips with my own fangs. I swallow, but the drip can't satisfy my thirst. Another glass of water, it is.

I stand and stumble. Black dots muddle my vision. The room spins, and . . .

———

I wake to the deep, sinking sensation of fear. My head is pounding.

Did I pass out? I roll to my side, my shoulder throbbing from the uncomfortable way it's wedged against the base of the couch. My forearm stings. I blink, confused.

Glass. Why is there broken glass on the floor? My empty cup.

It must have shattered when I collapsed. *When I collapsed.* This is even worse than I thought.

My stomach growls loudly, twisting in on itself with a cramp that squeezes the air from my lungs. This thirst. It isn't normal. I've found nothing to explain why it's happening to me, but I'm losing the ability to function. *You've got to call her.*

Mind rebelling, I stagger to my bedroom to plug in my phone. It's completely dead, giving me the length of time it will take to power on to talk myself in or out of calling my mum.

It's the middle of the night in England. I know she'll be up. Asking for her help, though . . . My stomach cramps again. The only thing I want to do less is drink another bag of tepid blood only to decorate my toilet bowl with it later.

The phone screen lights up. I unlock it and open my contacts. Scrolling through the names, I hover over hers, waiting for a better idea that never comes.

Turned vampires don't ask questions. They don't congregate in groups, and they don't compare notes—except with their maker. It's a maker's responsibility to care for their progeny, and they usually take it seriously. Unless, of course, they're a vampire who hates what they are . . .

"Bloody hell," I mutter, pressing on her name and bracing myself.

I listen to the ringing absently, half hoping she won't pick up.

"Alistair, to what do I owe this unexpected surprise?" Her voice sounds the same. Posh and cool. The disdain dripping from the words wouldn't be obvious to everyone, but I know her. The bitter anger that lurks beneath the surface when she thinks of me and my choices is as familiar to me as the back of my hand.

"I can't keep blood down," I say, coming right out with it. The sooner she refuses to tell me anything; the sooner I can explore other options. *But there are no other options.*

Her delicate intake of breath is the only sign she heard me at all. There's a clink of fine china, and I picture her setting her cup of tea down on the saucer. Gritting my teeth, I wait. And wait. And wait.

"Mum?"

"What have you done?" Her cold indifference is gone, replaced with the white-hot fury I've only seen on the rare occasions she allowed her vampiric nature to surface.

"What do you mean?" I ask. "Why do you assume I've done something?"

"Answer my question, Alistair, have you bitten a lover?"

I freeze. A strange tingling sensation runs down the back of my neck. Mum sounds . . . scared.

"I-I have," I admit, swallowing around the growing lump in my boiling throat. "Only a couple of times, though. It wasn't a big—"

"You've doomed yourself," she hisses. "More comprehensively than I ever expected. First, you insisted on becoming a monster, now you've created a blood circle. Tell me, Alistair, is your marked safe? You must always keep them in your sight."

"Slow down, Mum, you're not making sense. What's a blood circle?"

"A blood circle is what happens when foolish vampires bite for pleasure. The bite can be harmless, but when deep attachment or emotion is present, a blood circle forms."

"And what happens then?"

"You will be linked to that person—your marked—and only able to consume their blood. Any attempts to seek sustenance elsewhere will fail."

My heart begins to race. "Is this why I've been struggling to control myself? My anger—"

"Will only grow worse. If you fail to feed regularly from your marked, you'll lose all control, then desiccate."

"How long does it last?" I demand, grasping for options,

anything to redirect the creepy, hopeless way she's talking to me. "If I wait long enough, it will wear off, right?"

"It won't wear off, son. A blood circle is broken only by death, yours or theirs; it doesn't matter which comes first, you die either way."

Mum laughs, but there's no humor in the sound.

Oddly enough, it reminds me of my phone call with Ciprian. As soon as his snarky face pops into my head, my heart skips a beat. I bit him too. The night I was stabbed. That blood saved my life, but if Mum is right, it shouldn't have. I had already formed the blood circle with Celine at that point.

"I bit someone else," I tell her. "After the first person, but not during sex." I wince, not wanting to have this intimate conversation with her. "That blood was fine."

"Blood circles are not limited to one marked. In rare circumstances, vampires have reported adding to their sources, but only if they're able to form a genuine attachment. The circle thrives on emotion, yours and theirs." She says the words as if they disgust her to her core, as if she doesn't think I am capable of—or deserve —such feeling.

"Why?" I demand, my hand trembling around the phone. "Why didn't you tell me this? As my maker, it was your responsibility to explain, yet you refused."

"Vampires shouldn't exist," she snaps. "You gave me no choice but to turn you, therefore I kept the grotesque knowledge my maker told me to myself. It was what you deserved for forcing my hand."

Her need for revenge overshadowed any maternal feeling she had for me. Familiar anger and sadness war inside my chest, even as my mind races.

"Why tell me now?" I ask, my voice flat and emotionless.

"Because you're beyond redemption," she says. "As I always feared, your insatiable curiosity will be your downfall. It's too late to save you, but you might as well understand the full consequences of your careless actions."

"What about your careless actions, Mum? If you had told me like you were supposed to—" I bite my tongue. Arguing with her won't help. It never has.

Another ceramic clink, this time louder.

"If I had warned you of the blood circle. Explained the taboo of it along with the danger and risk of binding yourself to the whims of another, your contrary need to experience everything would have drawn you forward like a moth to a flame. In leaving you in the dark, I bought you a longer lifespan. You should thank me."

I breathe through my bitterness and her familiar disdain for me. Maybe she's right. If she'd told me about the blood circle, I might have wanted to experience it, but by hiding it from me, she set me up to fail.

"How can I thank someone who never wanted me to succeed in the first place?" I demand, making no attempt to be polite. Why bother if she already thinks I'm a monster?

Through the phone, I hear a dish break and smile cruelly.

I picture her tossing her cup at the wall in rage, blue eyes flashing to red as tea drips onto the ancient, polished hardwood.

"You mistake me, Alistair. All my life, I have longed for nothing more than to repay the indignity of my creation by raising a child who would live a long, healthy, human life. You robbed yourself of that life, and you'll rob yourself of its devilish echo too."

My fingers tighten around my phone until they ache.

"I chose my life, Mum, complications and all. This blood circle may be dangerous, but I'll navigate it on my own as I always have. You may wish me damned, yet I won't fall easily. I'll survive this —I swear it—but I won't call you again."

I hang up before she can respond, then rack my brain, wondering how the bloody hell I'll keep my promise.

TWENTY-SIX

UNSPOKEN RULE OF THE FRINGES #402:
KICK ASS.

CELINE

Malach brings the sword down in a slicing arc, and I parry, clashing my blade against his. The recoil is intense, rattling from the tips of my fingers to my armpit.

"Is that all you've got?" I taunt.

Smirking, I charge and dip into a deep lunge, snapping my wings to the sides to halt my momentum. It works perfectly. Malach doesn't have time to account for my changing angle. I flip my blade and hit him with the flat edge instead of spilling his intestines on the gym floor.

He dips his chin, a half-smile curling his mouth up at the corner. "It's returning to you, as I knew it would."

My cheeks flush, and it has nothing to do with the exercise.

Malach's praise sounds lukewarm, but sword work isn't the only section of my memory getting a refresher . . . I forgot how much his quiet respect means to me.

"Nai khirith, mash n'tel," I say, dipping my chin and lifting my sword in salute.

Malach's green eyes brighten when I address him in our native *thatsha* tongue—like I gave him a precious gift. It wasn't even a conscious decision. The traditional combat exchange just slipped out.

Luca strides over and kisses my sweaty cheek. "What does that mean, baby?"

I blink a few times, struggling to come up with a direct translation. It's been so long since I let myself think in my language.

"Nai khirith means my thanks," Malach murmurs. "The second part is harder to explain. It's an expression, I suppose."

"Like an idiom?" Luca asks.

I nod. "Translated literally, *mash n'tel* means 'peace protects,' but it's more charge or blessing than statement—like 'may peace guard and keep you.' That's the sentiment, at least. It's traditional between sparring partners in our echelon."

Luca smiles. "That's beautiful. Wishing for peace for your loved ones while preparing to fight by their side."

A chill runs down my spine. I guess he's right. There's an irony in the salute that's inescapable once you think about it. *Hope for peace; prepare for war.*

"Language is interesting," I admit.

I glance at Malach, but his green eyes are clouded.

The itch between my shoulder blades hits me hard. I wiggle my wings, but it doesn't help. Without a word, Luca's fingers search for the spot, gently scratching until I relax.

"We need to talk about Alistair, baby," he says gently.

My wings sag, and I sigh. "Something is wrong with him; I know that, but if he doesn't want to tell us, I don't see what we can do about it."

Luca nibbles his lip ring. "That's the Fringes talking. Not you."

I frown. "Alistair is as Fringe-coded as it gets, Luca. He doesn't want us digging around in his business." The electric sting in my fingertips tells me I'm not nearly as confident in my words as I want to be.

"He's spiraling, or circling the drain, or something," Luca insists. "His face was gray last night, Celine. Fucking gray. That's not normal."

I picture the sunken, sickly pallor of Alistair's skin and shiver. Combined with the lurching way he ran off . . . Dammit, Luca's right.

"What do you think?" I ask Malach.

He's been mostly keeping his opinions to himself. It's a relief, but also wildly unlike him. Malach wields judgment as effectively as his sword, and he's never been shy about it. Either I'm not the only one who's changed during our years apart or he's holding back.

"Nai varash di-snai, khirel . . ." Malach says.

I stiffen as yet another box I keep carefully locked flies open and yanks me inside, ripping me out of the Vegas gym and pulling me back in time.

We're young, Malach and I—hardly mature enough to be making promises to each other. Dressed all in gold, expensive silk caresses my skin as I face him on the raised dais. My hands shake and his throat bobs. His nerves calm me down. I feel myself smile and watch my lips curl—somehow inside and outside my body at the same time as I relive our betrothal day.

"Nai varash di-snai, khirel, tallom shmai. Ifek di varash turns'-tel, di jharim karash'tel." Malach's voice cracks halfway through the vow, and it's perfect. He's perfect. A tear rolls down my cheek, and hope—its wings made of folded steel—wraps around my heart.

A better life with Malach . . . In that moment, I believed and longed for it with everything I had.

Heart pounding, I turn away from the past and focus on the

present. The salty smell of sweat in the gym. The burn in my biceps from an hour of sparring. And a pair of familiar green eyes. Those I won't forget, even if I live ten lifetimes.

"My word belongs to you, beloved . . ." I murmur the vow and continue past where Malach left off. "As fully as it breathes life inside my soul. May the day I use it against you also be the day it carves my beating heart from my chest."

The memory scrapes me raw.

It's better to forget. Remembering hurts.

"Why, Malach?" It's all I can think to say. Why remind me? Why come here? Why cling to the past when it's tearing us apart?

Malach breaks eye contact abruptly, and it throws me off balance. When he drops his sword to the mat and rushes out of the gym, I want to follow him. Beg him not to go. Yell at him for making me remember. But my feet won't move.

"People keep storming away from me," I say. "I'm not sure I can stand to know why. Not on top of everything else."

Instead of responding, Luca threads his fingers with mine and squeezes. Warmth radiates from his palm to mine, a quiet comfort that anchors me even as the storm rages inside me. Gods. *What would I do without him?*

"I don't think you're cold-blooded at all, Luca Saratelli." Turning my head, I kiss him softly. Our lips meet like puzzle pieces slotting together, and I sigh as I pull away.

"He's adapting well, all things considered," Luca says.

I smile. "Not cold-blooded at all," I repeat.

Luca's soft heart challenges me. He sees things differently than I do. Where I expect the worst and assign motives to every interaction, Luca prefers to wait and see, keeping a neutral point of view until proven otherwise.

I tuck my head into the hollow beneath his chin. Another perfect fit. "Who should we prioritize? Alistair, Ciprian, or Malach?"

"I prioritize you," Luca says firmly. "From there . . ." He blows out a heavy breath that rustles a strand of hair against my cheek. "Alistair, I think. This is Ciprian's chance to come through for us. Malach needs a moment to breathe, but Alistair . . . My gut tells me he's in over his head."

I nod and check the time. We need to be at the club in two hours, which doesn't give us enough time to ambush a surly vampire. "If he doesn't come to the Fang tonight, we'll go to him," I say.

I collect Malach's fallen sword, wrapping it with mine in a piece of sturdy fabric. While there are a handful of acceptable reasons a modern human might carry a sword around, none of them match my aesthetic.

"I'll take those if you want," Luca says.

Smiling, I hand them over. It's not impossible to carry them on my bike, but it isn't easy. His car is a much better choice. Luca holds the door of the gym open, kissing me again before heading for his car. "See you at home, baby."

My heart flips. Luca sees my apartment as home. Our home. It should terrify me. It doesn't.

Alistair doesn't show at the club.

So, a little after three o'clock in the morning, we go to him.

The light above the door is off, and if Alistair has something on inside the apartment, it's not visible through his industrial-grade window shades. I've never minded the dark—Vegas rarely sleeps—but I'm oddly nervous as Luca does his signature two-thump knock.

We wait but hear nothing. No movement, no rumble from the TV. "Maybe he's not home," I say, but my stomach is churning and my back itches ferociously. *Something is wrong.*

Luca presses his nose to the seam of the door and inhales deeply. "I smell blood."

"He's a vampire, Luca." I try to keep the worry out of my tone and fail miserably.

"And vomit." Luca sniffs again. "Definitely vomit."

That makes me frown. Alistair isn't a particularly heavy drinker, so why is he throwing up? "Should I break the door down?" I ask, lifting my foot.

Before I can bash it to splinters, it swings open with an ominous whine. I drop my foot, doing my best to hide the fact that I was about to kick the damn thing off its hinges to get to my . . . whatever the fuck he is to me.

Hunched in on himself, his face is hidden by lank strands of hair and the penetrating darkness. A shadow of himself, Alistair barely looks alive. It chills me to the bone.

"What the fuck, Ali?" I demand, surging forward to catch him as he collapses.

My momentum carries us both over the threshold, and Luca follows, shutting the door behind us. Alistair clings to me, and I half drag him to the living room couch.

It's not overpowering, but now that I'm inside, I pick up the stale, sour scent Luca mentioned. It smells like sickness, but I didn't know vampires got sick.

"What's wrong?" I ask, my nerves humming as I imagine a million different worst-case scenarios. Did my father have him poisoned? Did one of his clients give him a rare disease?

"Careful, Celine," Luca says warily.

I frown. Can't he see Alistair is about as strong as a kitten? I try to look at him, but I'm unable to pull back. Alistair is latched on, his nose pressed to the curve of my neck. Nuzzling, no . . . He's searching for my vein.

Not as weak as he appears, I guess, but not as strong as me

either. Forcefully, I detach him from my neck and shove him against the arm of the couch.

Eyes shining like rubies, Alistair snarls and lunges for me.

He's painfully slow. Carefully, I brace my hand against his throat and hold him at arm's length, narrowing my eyes as I study him. Alistair snaps his teeth at me, his fangs hanging half an inch past his lower lip.

I lick my lips and glance at Luca. "This isn't normal."

"Get ahold of yourself, Ali!" Luca approaches carefully. He doesn't try to take over, and I don't need him to, but I am relieved to have backup if I need it. I would never hurt Alistair. This creature, though . . . I don't think it's him. It's thirst wearing Alistair's face.

I gasp as my eyes adjust fully to the dark. "His skin!"

Wispy gray veins decorate his pale skin like cracks. His eyes are sunken in, and the half-moons carved beneath them are vividly purple. I shiver even though I'm actively trying not to freak out.

"Ali, can you hear us?" Luca asks.

Alistair's eyes flicker from red to blue to red again, before slowly returning to blue. He stops struggling in my grip, sagging suddenly.

"Go," he begs. "Both of you go."

"Fuck that," I say. "Tell us what's wrong."

"Thirsty," he mutters.

"I got that part." I try to sound teasing, but my voice comes out raspy instead. I'm more unnerved by Alistair's gauntness than his aggression.

"I can't keep blood down," he says.

Luca runs to the fridge and sniffs the bags he finds there. "They smell fine. I can heat one up for you right now."

"It won't help." My skin pebbles. Alistair sounds defeated. Completely hopeless.

"Do you need me to go pick some up for you?" Luca asks. "I've got a few packs at the Fang."

I shake my head as my heart begins to race. This is taking too long. Alistair needs blood, and he needs blood now.

When Alistair opens his mouth to answer Luca, I shove my wrist between his lips.

He's consumed my blood multiple times and had no problems. We don't have time to argue about fucking expiration dates. My blood is fresh, and I'm stronger than he is. This is the best solution.

Since I was prepared for the sting of the bite, I'm able to hide any reaction to his fangs piercing my skin. For now, at least.

"For fuck's sake, baby." Luca slams the refrigerator door and rushes over to us. "This might be a bad idea. We don't know what's going on."

I roll my eyes. It was a great idea. He would see that if he weren't panicking. Already, Alistair looks better. The gray spiderweb veins are gone, and his skin is perking up like a plant growing toward the sun.

Moaning low in his throat, Alistair tugs me into his lap, and I let him. I'll lecture myself about it later, but I need to feel his heartbeat against mine.

"Angel." He breathes the word against the skin of my wrist, licking the puncture wounds, then kissing my fingers one by one.

I frown. "You need to take more. There's no way that was enough."

"I won't take more from you," he says, wincing. "Not tonight, at least. You need your strength."

"And you don't?" I demand.

Luca unbuttons his lightweight flannel shirt, determination burning in his hazel eyes. "She's right, Ali. That was scary. If you won't keep drinking from Celine, drink from me."

Alistair glances at him, his eyebrows climbing high on his face before his gaze dips to Luca's muscled, tan throat. "Are you sure?"

"Would I offer if I weren't?" Luca bites his lip. "Fuck, just do it already."

Alistair pulls Luca down on the couch and presses him into the leather cushions. Then he climbs on top of him, straddling his waist and dragging his lips up the side of Luca's neck. I expect him to lunge, snap his fangs, and drive them into Luca's skin.

But Alistair is back in control now . . .

"Last chance to back out," he purrs.

"Not a chance. And I want the sexy one." The words have barely left Luca's lips when Alistair kisses down his neck and slowly sinks his fangs into the taut skin.

The moan that leaves Luca's mouth is indecent.

I can't look away. I don't even want to blink.

Alistair's hands tenderly cradle Luca's jaw before one drops to the waist of his jeans.

"Do you want him to touch you, Luca?" I ask, smiling as his eyes snap open to reveal a hint of horizontally slit pupils.

"Fuck yeah, I do," he says.

Alistair's fingers toy with the button. Luca rolls his hips; a sexy grunt escapes his mouth. My breath catches in my throat, but Ali refuses to rush. By the time he finally slips the button loose and draws the zipper down, I'm more impatient than Luca.

I lean against the opposite arm of the couch, watching, transfixed, as Alistair's fingers dip into Luca's boxer briefs. He pulls his cock out and gives it a rough stroke, then runs his thumb over Luca's piercing.

"I think he wants to play with that one like you do the hoop in your lip," I say.

Luca's moan is loud in the quiet of the apartment.

Tired of watching, I bend at the waist and swallow him to the hilt, pulling back only to grin at him. "A little something for the friction."

Luca curses. He's losing it, and I don't blame him.

I know exactly what it's like to be at the mercy of Alistair's bite. As every single pleasure receptor on your body fires at once. So good you're terrified he'll stop and terrified by what you might do if he doesn't.

Alistair strokes Luca fast and hard, running his thumb over the head of his cock every few strokes. I love the aggressive way they handle each other—knuckles whited out, their Adam's apples bobbing.

Arousal rolls through me, hot and demanding. Luca buries his fingers in Alistair's hair, arching his neck against his mouth as he comes with a sexy, delicious groan.

Alistair's thumb makes one final swipe, spreading cum over the tip of Luca's cock. "Shower," he says, slurring the word until he sounds drunk.

I nod, climbing to my feet and steadying myself on the arm of the couch. I didn't realize Alistair took enough blood to make me woozy. I should be thanking him for his self-control.

When we get to the bathroom, I wipe all expression off my face.

It's a mess. And that's a kind way to put it.

Luca seems almost as blissed-out as Alistair, so I guide them to the shower. Once they're in, with steam curling around the curtain, I dig around under the sink for cleaning supplies and get to work. In five minutes, the toilet is sparkling clean, and the sour smell is gone—replaced by the fresh scent of lemon.

My neck prickles. I look over my shoulder to find Luca and Alistair watching me from a gap in the shower curtain. Alistair's chin rests on Luca's shoulder. I shiver. I feel their eyes like a physical touch.

"It's clean, baby," Luca says.

"Let us touch you."

I raise one eyebrow as if I'm thinking it over, but I've already made my decision.

I was scared tonight. I may not understand what's between us, and we may not be back to normal yet, but I care about Alistair, and I need to touch him.

Holding eye contact, I strip slowly.

Inch by inch, I peel my shirt over my head and toy with the front clasp of my bra. It drops to the floor. My cotton shorts fall next. Bracing my palms on the lip of the sink, I perch on the edge and spread my legs.

The only things between me and them are steam and a scrap of red lace.

TWENTY-SEVEN

LUCA

I'm buzzing. This is better than any high. As if my orgasm just happened, is still happening, and is about to happen all at once. Even the drops of water from Alistair's shower feel better than normal. Warm, wet trails licking my skin.

Ali curls against my back. I can feel his heart beating. If Celine comes within arm's length—I'll have everything I want.

She wants to torment me first, though. That's Alistair's fault, obviously, but I'm caught in the crossfire. Her red underwear begs me to tear it off with my teeth. If I don't get my hands on her in the next thirty seconds, I may scream.

As he watches her, Alistair vibrates with tension. Grinning, I grind against his erection. If I'm going to get teased, I might as well make things harder for Ali while I'm at it.

Smirk firmly in place, Celine laps his desperation up, licking her lips.

It's too much for me.

"Baby," I beg. "Please, come here." I don't give a shit if I sound needy. I need her, don't I? I wasted years hiding my feelings, and I won't make that mistake again.

Celine dips her fingers beneath the red lace slowly and rolls her bottom lip between her teeth. When she lets it pop free, it's plump and pink, begging for me to devour.

"Why should I?" she asks. I groan as she slips one finger inside herself. "Do you think you could do a better job?"

That's a loaded question. It's her body. It gives her constant feedback. I have to read her reactions to know if I'm doing it right. Honestly, I need to think about that for a—

"Yes," Alistair hisses. "We can steal the breath from your lungs and drag so many orgasms from you, you'll lose count. You'll beg for our cocks before the water runs cold."

My eyes flutter closed. Fucking *fuck*. Why do they have to make everything a competition? And why does it make me hard every time?

Celine yawns. Deliberately. The challenge in her brown eyes is impossible to miss.

"Boring," she taunts. "Predictable too. I'm not sure you're worth the steps it would take to get over there."

"I would worship you," I whisper, trying to sweeten the deal before Alistair fucks everything up by being a competitive bastard. "You can put me on my knees for as long as it takes, baby." I'm not a submissive guy by nature—but I like to think I'm a quick learner, and if Celine wants to be in charge, only an idiot would try to boss her—

"Come here now," Alistair demands.

I elbow him in the gut, hoping he takes the hint.

He has no idea how to grovel. It's shocking. Maybe the transition to vampire destroyed his common sense. Or maybe it's the blood loss . . . I don't give a shit, but if he runs Celine off, he's going to have to deal with the massive erection digging into my lower back on his own.

"You're doing it wrong," I say.

"If she would come closer, everything I do to her will feel bloody perfect."

Celine leans against the mirror and slips her fingers out of her underwear. "You know, I'm not sure I'm in the mood anymore."

The heat behind me vanishes as Alistair climbs dripping from the shower and grinds to a stop in front of her. Soaked, his black hair curls at the ends. Water runs along the muscles of his back, quickly creating a puddle on the floor.

"Would you have me on my knees, angel? Or would you rather I beg?"

They stare each other down, and I hold my breath. So stubborn. So sexy. At this point, I have no idea who will break first.

Celine lifts her chin defiantly and drags the finger she was using to play with herself up Alistair's chest. "I want you to watch Luca have every inch of me—quietly and without complaint, knowing there's no relief ahead for you."

I shiver. Her voice is cold except for the slight hitch at the end, which tells me she's not nearly as unaffected as she pretends to be.

Alistair's shoulders tense. "Angel, I'm sorry for what I said that night. I never meant it, not even for one second. I swear it on my life."

"Prove it."

The steam in the bathroom swirls angrily around us, as if it senses the boiling tension too.

I want to comfort them both, but they have to fix this on their own in a way that makes sense to them. Celine is fierce. She's far from emotionless, though. Alistair hurt her pride when he cut her down at the Fang in front of everyone, and this . . . gods, this is her way of showing him how it felt.

Slowly—like it's killing him—Alistair nods and backs away from her, one inch at a time, until he's hunched against the wall, defeated. Water rolls down his chest. His cock is fully erect, and I wince. I can't believe he's going to try.

Celine pulls her thong off and offers the lace to him.

He snatches the red fabric from her, nostrils flaring.

"Can he get back in the shower to watch, baby?" I ask, feeling bad for the guy. "It's cold out there."

Celine nods as she steps into the shower with me, but Ali shakes his head. "I'll stay away until she wants me with her."

Gods, they're killing me with the loaded statements.

I pull Celine into my chest and drop my lips to hers. She melts against me. She needs this kiss, this hug, this reminder that I'm not going anywhere—and I have no problem giving her all the reassurance she needs.

Her mouth is soft and sweet, the opposite of the tense standoff I witnessed. When her bottom lip quivers against mine, I kiss her harder. *Your secrets are safe with me, baby.*

Bending over, I hook my forearms under her ass and lift her, teasing the head of my cock against her wet pussy. The urge to thrust inside her is hard to ignore, but we have a show to put on, I have a role to play, and Alistair has a lesson to learn.

I scoot to the side until he can see exactly what he's missing. Slowly, with my eyes locked on Celine's, I push inside her and gasp. She feels amazing. Every time I think I'll get over how good it feels to be with her, she surprises me all over again.

I wedge her tight against the shower wall.

Slow and steady, I ease in and out. My body, riled by Alistair's bite, has other ideas. Ideas that involve using the shower wall as leverage to fuck her hard and fast.

My breath comes in hungry rasps, and I grind my pelvis against hers on every thrust.

Alistair's jealous fury adds to the intensity, his predatory stare making the skin on my neck pebble around his bite mark.

When Celine gasps my name, I lose it.

Bringing one hand to her pussy, I rub her clit. Her fingers squeeze my shoulders, gripping me almost frantically.

As she grazes my collarbone with her thumb, I groan and say, "You can break it again if you want."

Celine frowns with lips swollen from my kisses. "I never want to hurt you. Never."

Her wet hair is a darker shade of red as it hangs over her shoulders and tangles around us both. When her chin falls, I drop my mouth to her neck. "If you worry about a couple of broken bones, you'll make me look soft, baby."

She rolls her eyes, but the sadness disappears.

A strangled grunt reminds me that Alistair is still exiled, watching from his cold, lonely corner. I glance over my shoulder, and my breath catches.

Head pressed against the wall. Blood-red eyes locked on us. Alistair's jaw is clenched painfully tight. My eyes trail over his naked body, admiring the veins in his forearm as they throb, then tracing the lines of muscle and bone down to his white-knuckled grip on Celine's red thong.

Alistair shivers, but the heat in his stare . . . it makes me shiver too.

"He's sorry, baby," I blurt. "Look how fucking sorry he is."

Celine's breath stutters, and her lungs expand against my chest.

I'm not trying to rub his face in anything—fuck, I hope Ali knows that. I just want us to be okay again. I want to fall asleep knowing we're watching each other's backs. I want to wake up and check the windows for sun sneaking around the shades.

When Alistair inevitably gets prickly over the reminder of what he can't do, I want to remind him how good the night feels so he forgets how much he misses the sun.

"Get in here, Ali," Celine says.

Alistair joins us so quickly the curtain flutters and cold air stings my bare ass.

I pull Celine away from the shower wall and jerk my chin toward the now vacant spot. Alistair slides into the space, and I grin. He can be my leverage. I ease Celine back against his chest, kissing her deeply.

"Little help?" I let Celine slide an inch down my waist. "It's slippery in here."

Alistair shoots me a wild look, then laces his fingers with mine under Celine's thighs.

Dropping my mouth to her nipple, I lick and nibble at the tip, increasing the pressure until she makes my favorite sounds. When she bites her lip, I pull it free with my teeth. "Don't," I beg. "I want to hear you."

Dragging my lips back to the curve of her breast, I hear the smile in her voice as she orders me to keep going. All demand. Celine knows what she wants, and it's my pleasure to give it to her.

"Right there?" I sputter, adjusting my angle until I hear her gasp.

Her answering wail makes the burn in my quads worth it, and when she stiffens in our arms, it's all I can do not to follow her over the edge.

Alistair's fingers shake against mine. His eyes flit from Celine's neck to my lips to the place where we're all stacked together, warm water trailing over muscles and curves. It's messy and a little clumsy, but I can't get enough.

The coil inside me snaps, and I fuck into Celine mindlessly, losing my rhythm as my orgasm crashes over me. Knees trembling, my vision whites out. Blindly, my lips find hers, and I only pull away to bury my face in her neck when I run out of air.

Don't drop her. Don't drop her. Don't drop her. I repeat the command to my malfunctioning brain, grateful for Alistair's helping hands.

"Holy fuck," I moan as sensation returns to my body.

Pulling my head back, I look at Celine. Her eyes are glazed. Her perfect tits are a rosy, splotchy pink—from the hot water and my stubble. Lips puffy from my kisses, she rests her head in the crook of Alistair's neck and smiles. My stomach twists. *She's beautiful.*

"Thank you," Celine whispers.

I blink, unsure if my inside thoughts got loose or if she's thanking me for the fuck. My exhausted dick twitches at the thought. I focus on Alistair next.

Water rolls down his cheekbones as he blocks Celine's face from the direct spray. His eyes—blue and shiny—are clear for the first time in weeks. He's staring at Celine like she's the answer to every question he's ever had.

I shudder. Ali notices and aims his possessive gaze my way.

I'm aware of every place we're touching—from the brush of my foot against his to our fingers grazing around Celine's thighs. It's fucking intimate.

I wait for Alistair to break eye contact, but he doesn't.

It settles the hungry, restless itch inside me.

Maybe we're sturdy enough to come through the other side of this—if not unchanged, at least stronger. No matter what happens, if they're with me I'll have no complaints.

My basilisk and I are in complete agreement over that.

TWENTY-EIGHT

ALISTAIR

The bass at the club pumps in time with my excitement. I feel incredible. For the first time in weeks, my body is flush with blood. I'm practically buzzing with it.

Ciprian is bringing the djinn to meet me. Or he says he is. I'm not sure I believe it.

We agreed to meet in the storage room at the Fang, so here I am waiting, pacing around crates of liquor and wearing a groove in the dusty concrete floor.

Then he knocks.

I take a deep breath and wipe my face of all expression. Overeagerness is the quickest way to turn a good deal into a bad one. Flipping the flimsy lock, I throw the door open and use my vampire speed to move to the back corner.

Ciprian steps in first. He's followed by the fae who recently joined the enclave—Idris, according to my sources—and a big guy I've never seen before. The djinn is here, I can smell her, but she's hiding behind the others.

I barely resist rolling my eyes. Spoiled princess, acting like she needs guards to visit the Fringes. While it may be true, it's also insulting . . . and conspicuous.

Although Ciprian's black eye—courtesy of a run-in he had earlier with Imani—probably isn't doing much to convince the djinn we're civilized.

Luca texted me earlier, saying Ciprian had shown up at the club looking for Celine and run into her best friend instead. Assuming he was here to take Celine in, Imani told him to go to hell and socked him in the eye.

I wish I could have seen it, but I have more important wishes to focus on right now.

I paint a mocking smile on my face. "So you came back," I say to Ciprian. "I'm honestly surprised." It's hard to keep my smirk in place as I take in the cold fury hidden beneath his blank expression.

"I said I would." Ciprian plants his feet wide and crosses his arms, keeping the door at his back as if he doesn't trust me to stand behind him. "Alistair, this is—"

"I only care about the djinn," I interrupt, gritting my teeth. His body language is pissing me off. It's going to give the djinn and her entourage the idea that I can't be trusted, which is bloody rich coming from him.

Someone huffs and pushes past the fae.

I blink a few times as I look at the bite-sized woman in front of me. It's no wonder I couldn't see her. She's a full head shorter than Celine, brow furrowed, lips pursed, and wary . . . incredibly wary. Unlike my angel, she doesn't strike me as the kind of woman who hopes to stumble into a fist fight.

"I'm Sheena," she says. "Who are you?" Her voice is low and

melodic—thank the gods. I expected something squeaky and grating. Still, a supernatural of her size can't be as powerful as the mazzikin implied.

I swallow a sigh, bow at the waist, and look her over again while I'm at it. Perhaps there's more to her than meets the eye. "Alistair, at your service, love," I purr. Even if she's a fraud, I need to be sure. *Charm it is.*

"My eyes are up here, Alistair." Sheena points at them, and they flash purple. I freeze. My research revealed dozens of supernatural eye colors, hundreds if you count shade variation. But only one supernatural species has purple eyes.

My mouth goes dry. "So, it's true," I breathe, turning to Ciprian, genuinely shocked. Is he in love with her? Is she truly as powerful as the mazzikin believes? My head buzzes with unanswered questions. But I've got to stay calm. In control. This is my meeting.

"Honestly," I say, trying to sound bored. "I assumed it was another lie like every other word out of your mouth." I'm clinging to my composure by a thread, but I need to test them.

"Don't talk to him like that," Sheena snaps. To emphasize her point, she steps away from her other two protectors to stand at his side. Interesting. Very interesting.

"You don't think he's a consummate liar, love?" I cock my head. This is the perfect opportunity to figure out the nature of their relationship and what he's told her about me.

"I think context matters," she says, a defiant note in her voice as she glances at Ciprian. "You act like you've never lied before. Never had responsibilities back your personal desires into a corner. Never been charged with protecting someone else no matter what it cost you."

Ciprian's eyes fall from my face to his feet, as if he's embarrassed she's lecturing me on his behalf. I smile. "And would you lie to protect?"

There's a collective inhale around the stuffy storage room, and I lean into the tension, delighted. The others know my question is loaded. They also know better than to tip her off. If Sheena lies to me about lying . . . this whole meeting will be a wash.

When she lifts her chin and stares me down, there's no hint of softness or indecision on her face. "Without fucking flinching," Sheena says. "I would lie with a smile on my face, and I wouldn't lose a wink of sleep after."

I raise my eyebrows and let the moment linger to see if she'll break, but Sheena doesn't flinch. *Perhaps she would fit in on the Fringes, after all.*

The mazzikin wants her dead. They think she's a harbinger of doom or something. I think she's the best opportunity I've encountered in years.

I grin and reveal my fangs. "It's a pleasure to meet you, love."

"It's Sheena, actually." She reaches out to shake my hand. *How human of her.*

I take it, pulling her fingers to my mouth and grazing my fangs over her knuckles. She tastes like soap and nerves. Not my flavor at all. The big guy growls and everyone else freezes, as if they're waiting to see if I dare break her skin.

"She's loyal to you. I'll give you that," I tell Ciprian. "Let's hope for her sake you don't live to let her down."

It's a barb—less delicate than my last—but I want to get a rise out of him. I disliked the way he talked to me on the phone. As if I was the one who crossed the line by using Sheena against him when he started it by sneaking into our lives under false pretenses.

"What can you tell me about Lysander and his plans?" Sheena asks, drawing my attention away from Ciprian by bringing up the real reason for our meeting.

Lysander, one of the many people hunting her, is giving the enclave trouble. They've been unable to locate him, which tells me he's likely hired or coerced a witch into concealing his location. Ciprian wants me to poke around on Sheena's behalf, demanding I do some digging before he would agree to this meeting.

What I've found so far is sickening and painfully thin. Lysander leads a dodgy gang of sadistic shifters. They never stay in the same place for long, everyone is happy to see them go, and no one likes to see them coming.

Everyone will be better off if the enclave disposes of them.

"Not much yet," I admit. Sheena's face falls, and I rush to continue before she can decide I'm useless. "But I'm happy to find out everything you need to know. For the right price."

"We are prepared to pay," Idris says. I hide a shiver. His voice sounds like ice brought to life . . . and people say I'm creepy.

"I'm sure you are, fae, but I'm not interested in your money," I say firmly.

This is it: the moment the deal will fall apart or become reality.

Darting to Sheena's side, I drop my head to whisper in her ear. "I want five days of your time—of my choosing—and two wishes. In exchange, I'll share everything I can find about the movement of Lysander's gang."

Asking for wishes is obvious, but requesting her time is a gamble. If I can show Sheena life on the Fringes and draw attention to the struggles the enclave turns a blind eye to, maybe she can force change from within. Or at least she'll think twice before lending her power to further the enclave's agenda.

"Three days and one wish," she whispers back, too quiet for anyone but me to hear.

I blink, then grin, my heart beating faster as the others lose their shit.

The fae grabs Sheena's arm, but the bigger guy gets to me first, shoving me with the force of a small car. I go with the motion; my grin locked firmly in place. Last night, that push would have flattened me. Thank the gods for Celine and Luca.

I inhale and raise my eyebrows as I catch a whiff of the big guy's scent. It's mostly human, and I'm surprised I didn't notice it sooner.

"You brought a pet, love?" I tease. "Did you think to soften me up with a snack?"

"Touch him even once and you'll find out exactly how far I'll go to protect what's mine," Sheena snarls. Her green eyes bleed to purple, and a strand of her dark hair begins to float.

Can't she tell I was kidding?

I'm not a rabid animal foaming at the mouth. I apologize, as genuinely as I can, and dip my head to show my respect for her unconventional choices. If she wants to waste her time on a human, that's her business, not mine.

"Do we have a deal?" I ask.

"Almost." Sheena tosses the human a warning look. "I'll grant your wish on one condition."

Idris's cold stare snaps to my face. He's not thrilled that I asked for a wish, but there was no reality where I took this risk without attempting to secure a wish of my own. And it's the perfect way to find out if she's even half as powerful as the mazzikin thinks she is.

"Lies, truth—all your secretive games aside—you must agree not to tell anyone," Sheena says. Internally, I roll my eyes. Confidentiality is a pre-understood part of the deal. She doesn't need to negotiate to secure the core tenet of my business model.

"Deal," I say, my heart pumping with excitement.

Don't get your hopes up, Ali. It won't work. There's no way she's strong enough. If there's even a chance, I've got to try. I've spent so long in the dark . . .

"I wish to move undamaged in the sun, feel its warmth on my face, and live freely without the curse of the vampire, burdened only by the secret origin of this gift, which I can never reveal to anyone."

I make the wish with more confidence than I feel. The sun curse is an immovable force . . . If I believed Sheena was capable, I might have asked her to break the blood circle, but if she tried and failed, everyone in this room would know about it.

There's a part of me that doesn't want to lose the connection, and—*gods above!*

Sheena's feet leave the dirty floor. Her head rolls back as blinding purple light shoots from her hovering body into mine. At first, it's uncomfortably warm, then it begins to burn—exactly like when the sun reaches me.

I fall to my knees, grunting from the pain of my boiling skin. I can't believe it. The tiny woman with the stubborn chin is actually attempting to lift one of nature's most ancient curses.

Please gods . . . if you're listening, give her the strength.

The burning moves from my skin to my eyes, then my organs, invading my body layer by layer until I'm certain that acid has replaced my blood.

I lock my jaw to keep from screaming. Through vision blurred with tears, I see blood drip from Sheena's nose. Ciprian tugs on her legs frantically, his black eyes panicked as her spine curves unnaturally. His mouth moves. I think he's shouting, but I can't hear anything over the roaring in my ears.

The three of them circle her floating body, and I blink my melting eyes rapidly, trying to get a better look at what's happening. *Is my wish killing her?* That was never my intent. I open my mouth to take it back, but no words come out.

One by one they touch her. My pain gets worse each time. Ciprian's body gives off black smoke, and Sheena breathes it in. The burning penetrates my bones. My fangs slice up the inside of my mouth, and I taste blood on my tongue.

As they collapse, fear and hope war inside me. I'm not sure if

Sheena siphoned magic from the others or if I hallucinated it, but I feel lighter, freer, better—

The burning stops so suddenly it's as if I imagined it. If it weren't for the lingering ache in my joints and the four crumpled supernaturals on the concrete floor, I would think I dreamed the whole thing.

I crawl to Ciprian's side and press my trembling fingers to his neck. His pulse is strong. I sag in relief and check the others, finding them in a similar position. By the time I reach the fae, his glacial blue eyes are open.

"You're awake. That's good," I say cautiously, hiding my shock as hope swallows me whole. No one can know what happened here. I swore not to tell in my wish, and I have no intention of figuring out what would happen to me if I violated magic as powerful as Sheena's.

"I'm going to need help to get them out of here."

The sun beams on my face, and my eyes sting. This time it's not from heat, or bloodlust, or thirst, or magic—it's pure emotion. I can't believe Sheena managed it.

Any minute now, my skin will blister as my blood boils in my veins. I'll fall to the oil and piss-stained street, eyes melting in their sockets as they face the force of the sun's wrath for the final time. The warm, glorious light will fade, and I'll be back where I belong: in the bloody, endless, impenetrable dark.

But it doesn't happen.

I don't die.

Everything is bright.

I'm exhausted—haven't slept a wink—but I can't stop walking. If I go to my apartment to rest, I might wake up and realize it's all a dream. That a djinn didn't lift my sun curse and give me what no vampire, turned or born, has ever been gifted: life in the light.

So I keep walking. Shirt unbuttoned to the waist; I put one foot in front of the other. Each step is better than the last.

Near the Strip, I pass tired, hungover human tourists still wearing their wrinkled clothes from the night before. Sequined, jewel-toned dresses catch rays of sunlight and shoot chaotic, squirming fractals of color against a Grecian-inspired building.

An older man wipes his glasses on his shirt, then fumbles in his pocket for a cigarette.

When I leave the tourists behind and pass an apartment complex, I watch a small, scruffy dog with a crooked tail and a bright pink bow piss on a scaly succulent. It's visibly suffering from the injustice of countless lifted legs.

The dog looks at me and growls, then takes two steps back. I smile at her. She pees again, the stream lit by magnificent, glorious daylight. When her owner glances up from her phone to see why her baby is riled, I hide my fangs and wink.

The woman's eyes dart over my exposed chest, and she blushes. I marvel at the clarity of my vision—the bloom in her cheeks as capillaries burst to the surface, a tide of blood rolling beneath her skin.

I dip my chin as she drags the dog away and keep walking.

When my stomach growls, I buy an ice cream cone from a corner store near a park, then eat it sitting on a bench with my face upturned. I have the spot to myself. It's the only one in full sun. Every other bench is crowded with sweaty people searching for shade and a break from the heat.

Gods. I think Sheena really did it. I think my sun curse is gone.

This changes everything.

I stuff the end of the cone in my mouth and keep walking.

I end up outside Celine's apartment. My hand hovers over the door. I want to share this moment. With her. With Luca. Ciprian's face runs through my mind, and I push it out. His friend gave me this gift; not him.

The door opens without me knocking, putting me face-to-face with Luca. He blinks in surprise before grabbing two fistfuls of my shirt and yanking me inside.

"What the fuck are you doing?"

"I'm fine—"

"Honest to fuck, Alistair, you're freaking me out. Forty-eight hours ago, you looked half dead. Now, I find you skulking around during the heat of the day. You might as well stick your head in the oven—"

"Luca, I'm fine," I assure him. His eyes are wild, and a secondary warmth rolls over me. This one has nothing to do with the sun.

Celine runs down the hall, wings tucked, her brown eyes wide as she looks from me to Luca and back again. "What's going on? I heard yelling, are you hurt?"

"I don't know!" Luca waves his hands at me. "I found him outside, and the UV index is insane today." Since when does he monitor the UV index? Overgrown lizard that he is, Luca loves the sun, and it loves him right back.

"Take a breath and look at me," I say. "Am I burned?"

Luca takes his time staring, narrowing his eyes as he notices what I'm having a hard time coming to terms with myself. Unblemished skin. "I don't believe it," he mutters.

Celine grabs my arm and tows me into the kitchen. Under the faint hum of the fluorescent lights, she studies me, her frown growing by the second. "How?" she asks.

Before I can come up with an answer, she yanks on my shirt. The two buttons I left fastened come loose, ricocheting off her cabinets with muted pings. My shirt falls to the tile forgotten, then all I can feel are Celine's fingers caressing me.

"How?" she repeats. She sounds dazed. I can't blame her. I also can't tell her the truth.

I drag in a shaky breath. "I can't tell you."

"Bullshit," Luca argues.

I reach for his face, hoping to reassure him, but he bats my hand away and shoves the hair hanging in my eyes behind my ear. "You're fine," he says. "I can see that, but how long were you in the sun?"

"Hours," I admit. A lump bobs in my throat.

"Did you buy a spell?"

I shake my head.

"How long will it last?" Celine's voice is tight, choked with emotion.

I shrug. "Forever, I hope."

The last part is hard to admit. Hope makes me vulnerable. But I want to tell them everything. How the blood dripped from Sheena's nose to the floor. The pain, my disbelief, how her men and Ciprian shared their magic to give her the power to lift the sun curse.

"This has something to do with your meeting last night," Luca guesses. "The one you asked to have in the storage room with Ciprian. We never saw you leave." Because the fae's glamours are incredibly powerful.

My silence was a part of the wish. If they guess the truth, will I be cursed again for breaking my word? I stiffen. Maybe coming here was a bad idea.

"Stop asking him questions," Celine says. "His heart is racing." Her palm rests warm and heavy against my chest, and I realize too late that she isn't examining me anymore and has transitioned to monitoring my vitals instead.

"Okay." Luca releases a ragged sigh. "Fuck, as long as you're okay. You scared me to death, Ali."

Something in me snaps.

I pull them both into me, one on each side, and slump in their arms. The exhaustion of my sleepless night hits me as the elation fades, leaving me with nothing but the soul-crushing weight of relief.

A tear rolls down my cheek. Another chases after it. And before I can put a stop to it, a sob escapes. *Gods, this is humiliating.* I'm supposed to be strong. Powerful. The one you go to when you're out of options. I can't cry in front of them. They'll be disgusted.

Luca's hand moves to my hair, and he guides my head to the crease between his neck and shoulder. "You're safe, Ali," he murmurs in his rough baritone. "Let it out."

As if my body were waiting for permission, I fall apart. My shoulders shake, fat tears rolling down my cheeks to be soaked up by Luca's shirt.

Celine's arms tighten around my waist, and her wings graze my back as she wraps them around all three of us. They're soft and fluffy now, but if someone tries to hurt us, they would turn to knives in a flash.

With blinding clarity, I realize the truth I've ignored: I'm not curious about Celine and Luca or obsessed with collecting them —I just need them. Fighting by my side in every battle life throws at us and celebrating every win.

And I almost destroyed it.

Even after the horrible things I've said and done, Celine and Luca care enough to make sure I'm safe—safe enough to let my guard down.

Suddenly, I see the future clearly: everything we could be if I stopped getting in my own way. And it's as beautiful as the bloody sun.

TWENTY-NINE

**UNSENT CORRESPONDENCE, TRANSLATED TO ENGLISH,
AND ADDRESSED ONLY TO MY TRUTH:
I HAVE JUDGED THOUSANDS, BUT YOU ARE
THE ONLY ONE I KNEEL TO.**

MALACH

Alone in the spare room, I listen to Celine and Luca comfort Alistair, an ache throbbing behind my skull.

The vampire doesn't mean her harm, but my magic remains unsure about him. There are many colors inside Alistair, mostly shades of gray, and they're constantly in flux. I've never met someone with motives so wholly changeable. Either he stands for nothing, or he hasn't found anything worth taking a stand for.

He bears monitoring.

I sink onto the bed and massage my temples.

This burden is heavy.

Celine dances and fights.

I watch and wait.

Dread is my constant companion. Checking every corner, suspicious of every shadow—my mind clouds and aches. I fear what comes next. What it could do to her. To me. To us.

So we train. And Celine progresses, reaching her goals, and then setting new ones.

It's the only satisfaction I get, besides knowing she's safe. As one day stretches into the next, and she remains alive and strong, I count my blessings.

The sun rises; I give thanks. It sets; I brace for the worst.

Celine watches me from the stage, a sturdy divot marring the skin between her eyes. I force a smile, but her frown only grows.

"Are you okay?"

I spin around on what I've begun to consider my regular barstool, surprised to see Celine's friend Imani looking at me with concern. Since I revealed myself weeks ago, we haven't spoken. Her intent toward Celine is deep purple—pure loyalty.

"I am in perfect health," I say, dipping my chin respectfully.

Imani laughs, and the sound is oddly mesmerizing. "There are plenty of ways to be in perfect health and nowhere near okay. Ask anyone in here."

I study the faces around me. Flushed with liquor, most of them smile and trade laughs with their companions. I'm tempted to judge them and find out if Imani is right about their hidden pain. Given how easily she spotted mine, I decide to save my energy.

"Celine said you learned English for her," Imani says, hopping onto the stool beside me.

Luca passes her a bottle of water, then rushes to the other side of the bar where customers clamor for his attention. A drop of sweat beads on his temple, a near-perfect reflection of the condensation rolling down the glass in his hand.

Too late, I remember Imani asked me a question and I look at her.

She sips her water and smiles at me.

"I gave it my best. English, I mean." I frown as the simple words come out thicker than they sounded in my head, like my tongue is swollen. I'm an outsider, and my accent makes it impossible for me or anyone else to forget. "I've never been good with language."

Imani raises her eyebrows. "Really? That shocks me, honestly." Taking another sip of water, she shudders. "It took me five years of listening to be brave enough to say more than ten words out loud. I've heard some Earth languages are easier, but English is a bitch."

"You struggled?" I look at her more closely. She doesn't give the impression of someone who encounters much difficulty.

"Hell yeah," she says. "Celine makes fun of me for them now, but those word of the day things really helped me grow my vocabulary." She pulls her phone from a pocket in her shiny green shorts, then shows me the screen. I move my lips slowly, mouthing the unfamiliar syllables.

"Try it out loud," Imani suggests. "This is a weird one."

"P-pereg—" I clench my fist as the end of the word gets tangled in my mouth.

"Peregrinate," she says. "That one's hard."

"Wandering from place to place," I read the definition she's typed to the side carefully, my fingers uncurling as I realize she's not judging me.

"Some would call that an adventure," Imani says, screwing the cap back on her water bottle. She's barely touched it. Combined with her dry tone, I'm positive she doesn't agree.

"What would you call it?" I ask, feeling lighter than when I sat down. Less burdened. If possible, I want Celine's kind friend to walk away from this conversation feeling the same.

"You first," Imani says. "If you think hard about what a new word means to you specifically, you'll be more likely to remember it."

I raise my eyebrows. That's a clever idea. Perhaps if I had employed the same rationale in my earlier language studies, I wouldn't have found them so tedious.

"It sounds lonely." I admit.

"Missing home is a universal experience . . . except when it isn't." Imani turns to look at Celine—she's finishing her dance on stage—and forces a weak smile. "Some of us are jealous of those with the ability to miss home."

If Imani is trying to warn me not to get my hopes up about returning to the celestial realm with Celine, she's wasting her time. I gave up on that dream many years ago.

"That water won't drink itself, Imani," Luca says, appearing in front of us again and pushing his messy brown hair out of his face.

"You're a nag," she mutters, unscrewing the lid and chugging until the bottle is empty. She tosses it to Luca, and he smiles.

"What were you two talking about? Looked interesting."

I raise my eyebrows. Is Luca checking on me?

"Peregrinate, pros and cons," Imani says. "Go."

Luca's smile turns upside down at once. "Only cons, the seeds are weird looking—like alien eggs—and there are way too many of them."

I stare at him blankly. That . . . doesn't match the definition I read at all.

Imani throws her head back and laughs. "Oh gods, Luca. Peregrinate, not pomegranate."

He shrugs. "Sounds the same. I stand by what I said."

Imani laughs again, the sound carrying around the room. Twenty pairs of eyes stop what they're doing to stare at her with glassy eyes, her siren song enough to draw their attention even when she's not trying.

"I needed that," she groans. "Even more than the water, so thanks."

Luca shakes his head and salutes her good-naturedly before tossing the water bottle in the trash and returning to the growing line.

Imani glances at me, then down at her phone. "One second."

I shift on my stool, hoping she plans to let me in on the joke without making me admit I didn't get it. After typing for a while, she shows me a picture of a strange fruit.

"This is a pomegranate. Gods bless it, he's kind of right about the seeds."

"Do these grow around here?" I ask.

She shrugs. "I have no idea. We'd have to percgrinate and hope we stumble upon a pomegranate while we're at it."

I mutter both words under my breath, and she smiles. "Like I said, impressive. Keep your chin up, Malach, it gets easier." I'm not sure if she means living here, the language, or all of it, but I nod anyway because I feel better already.

THIRTY

ENCLAVE MEMO (INTERNAL)

Gather up as many fighters as possible.
Lysander's gang must be stopped.

CIPRIAN

My hands grip the steering wheel as leafy, tapered trees make way for patchy shrubs and tumbleweeds. Heat waffles off the road, making the yellow lines dance beneath the late summer sun.

Is it possible to be pulled in half without anyone laying a hand on you?

I've been away from Vegas for three weeks.

Three weeks of wishing I could come back. Three weeks wondering where I stand with Celine and Luca. And three weeks of flashbacks to the backroom at the Fang where Sheena performed a fucking miracle.

While there's some suspicion surrounding the deal I brokered between Sheena and Alistair, almost everyone is optimistic. They don't dare say anything else—at least not loudly—because Sheena is done with their shit.

My best friend has started throwing her weight around, taking her own future in her hands, and flashing those angry purple eyes at anyone who crosses her. I'm proud of her, but the seed of worry I've had since we met has grown into a colossal redwood tree.

It feels a lot like fear, and I'm not the only one caught in it.

Fear is contagious. It's panic in a herd of wildebeests or a flock of plump, napping quail—all it needs is one inciting spark to ignite a frenzy. My magic reserves are charged to the max because of it. Knowing why makes my strength bittersweet, as if I won a race after someone I care for tripped on the final lap.

Parking my car, I grab my bag and unlock my apartment. After a few weeks away, the unit smells even mustier than usual.

I'm not supposed to be here. Dad doesn't want me on the front lines of the enclave's war with Lysander's gang, and he doesn't want me in Vegas either.

I took a play out of Sheena's book and came anyway.

This is my life, and what Dad doesn't know can't hurt him.

The winged roach has been busy adding to its herd . . . flock? I don't give a shit what they call their family unit; I just want them out. I kick the bed and jump back when three of the monsters scurry out from under it.

Skin crawling, I retreat to rinse off in the shower before heading to the club.

As I open the door and pass through the tickle of the ward, I smile at the familiarity. It's good to be—*what the fuck?* I freeze.

I've spent more than enough time at the Naked Fang by now to know its quirks. From the cracked vinyl in the corner booth to the symphony of drums, catcalls, and clinking ice—the Fang usually feels like wearing a cozy sweatshirt at the end of a long day.

But someone replaced it with fishnets and leather and didn't bother to warn me.

Cages hang from the ceiling, with a handful of dancers

performing inside them. Brandy, I recognize. The other two women aren't familiar. Questions flood my head, like: who hung these cages? And do they have an up-to-date construction license? If they aren't hooked to load-bearing beams, Celine could get hurt.

Fuck me, I want to speak to the manager about this.

I turn to the bar for answers, but the woman behind it is definitely not Luca. She doesn't even have a lip ring. I hiss, wondering for a second if I wandered into the wrong supernatural strip club by accident.

"Lost, demon?" Celine's voice is beautifully familiar.

I face her, pointing first at the cages, then at the strange bartender. "What the fuck?"

Celine shrugs. "Sal decided to make some changes."

"Did Luca get fired?"

Celine adjusts the sheer green slip she's wearing and scoffs. "Hardly, Sal's cheap ass finally broke down and agreed to hire some help. I think he was worried we were both going to jump ship and start working at the Mouth of Hell or something. Lyss is cool."

I narrow my eyes at the woman behind the bar. She looks vaguely familiar, but I can't place her, and it's driving me crazy. "What the fuck is she?"

"Keep your voice down!"

"Sorry," I mutter. It's still early, and the club isn't crowded. We won't be overheard unless someone is deliberately snooping. "At least the hottest woman alive still works here or I would have thought I was lost."

Celine shakes her head at me, grabbing my hand and pulling me to the corner booth. I slide in next to her. The tear in the vinyl is still there, and I relax. Celine, on the other hand, is squirming against the seat like the roaches followed me in. "I-I wanted to . . ."

"Spit it out, hot wings," I say. Her lack of confidence is worse than the other changes at the Fang. "I'm the same guy I always was."

"Thank you," she says. "For handling, you know . . ." Her lips curl into a wry smile, and I shake my head. This awkwardness between us sucks. I prefer her pissed.

"There's no need to thank me," I say. "The enclave is supposed to stand for justice. I'm sorry we've failed so often around here that no one believes that."

Celine studies my face as if she's trying to figure out what my game is.

I sag against the booth. Maybe coming here was a bad idea. I might have been better off bunking down with the roach colony and hoping they accepted me as one of their own.

"Are you—" Celine cuts herself off again, and I groan.

"Is this a pity talk?" I ask. "Because if it is, I'd rather skip it." I raise one eyebrow and try to look sarcastic while fighting the urge to drop my head into my hands.

"Fuck you!" Celine shoves her shoulder against mine. "I'm trying to check on you, and you're making it impossible."

I raise both eyebrows. "Is that what that was? Really?"

"Fuck you!"

"You already said that," I tease, then draw in a deep breath. "Shit, maybe you're doing a better job than I thought. Somehow, I feel better."

"You're impossible." Celine nudges my shoulder with hers again, and I nudge back. Her arms are wrapped in muscle, and when the stage lights spin our way, they land on a bruise she hasn't quite managed to hide.

"When's your next fight?"

She follows my gaze and sighs. "Can't believe I missed one. I'll be back in the ring tomorrow."

"Still kicking ass?"

"Of course." She grins, and it's about a dozen times more natural than the start of our conversation. "Do you—" She clears her throat. "Do you want to come?"

I pinch my thigh under the booth to keep from punching the air like an eighties rom-com protagonist. "Yeah, I'd love to."

A blush climbs Celine's cheeks, visible even in the dim club lighting.

I'm trying to remember if I've ever seen her this flustered when Luca squeezes into the booth on my other side. He sets two drinks in front of me. One is a shot—tequila, maybe—and the other is an elaborate cocktail with alternating layers of red and pink. The rim is lined with sliced strawberries.

"One to knock the road off"—Luca points at the shot glass—"and another to sip until you smile." He scrubs his fingers through his hair, his leg warm and solid against mine under the booth. I gulp. *Does he realize how fucking cute he is?*

I down the shot to hide the fact that, drink or not, he always makes me want to smile, then sip the fruity concoction, smacking my lips as the taste hits my tongue. It's tarter than I expect, and I take another sip before letting the smile loose.

"You're pure magic." I shoot him a flirty wink. Maybe if I can make him squirm again for old time's sake, I won't feel out of place in the club anymore.

Except Luca doesn't squirm. He faces me and leans in close, his distracting lip ring grazing the shell of my ear. "Do you really think so?"

On my other side, Celine laughs. "Is this the way all those conversations at the bar went between the two of you?"

"Why?" Luca aims his scruffy smolder at her. "Is it turning you on, baby?"

Now it's her turn to squirm.

I take another sip of my drink, enjoying being trapped between their heat. "Get a load of the confidence on this guy," I say to Celine. "All it took was getting fired as head bartender, and he's flirting right and left."

"I didn't get fired," Luca drawls. "But that reminds me. Don't order anything but beer from Lyss yet. Her skills lie in other areas."

"Than bartending?" I glance at the brunette behind the bar and snort when the head from the beer she's pouring overflows the glass and runs down her fingers. "Why hire her?"

"She'll get better," Celine hisses. "It's only her second night, and her boss is too busy flirting to train her properly."

"That's true." Luca shrugs, grinning mischievously at Celine. "But for someone with eight legs, she's damn clumsy."

I squint at the bar, as if that will help me see through the solid wood. "How many legs did you say? Is she a fucking—"

"Spider shifter."

"Arachne," Celine says, annoyance in her voice.

I groan. "I can't get away from bugs."

"Lyss is a shifter, not a bug, and she could kick your ass with her eyes closed."

I hide my smile, not wanting to get on Celine's bad list. She's clearly adopted this monster with no bartending skills and decided to defend her from all attacks—even good-natured ones. "She sounds like someone else I know," I say.

Celine slides out of the booth and plants her hands on her hips. She tries to look stern, but her lips are twitching.

I point at the corner of her mouth. "It's showing around the edges, hot wings."

She growls and spins to leave, but not before I see a flash of her teeth as she smiles.

Like the first night I saw her, Celine's confidence makes her impossible to ignore. So much has happened since then, but she hasn't lost the unshakable certainty in who she is. I thank the gods for that and sit up straighter, hoping some of her energy will rub off on me.

"How are things with . . ." I make a bizarre gesture with a strawberry slice, then pop it into my mouth to hide my embarrassment. It's a half-baked attempt to encompass the entirety of the shitshow, but Luca gets what I'm trying to say.

"Nothing since the attack," he says, flexing his hands on top of the table. "I can't help feeling like he's charging up for something big, though."

"Or waiting for your guard to drop," I mutter.

"Exactly." Luca winces. "Alistair has been gone more than he's here—night and day. Do you happen to know anything about that?"

I frown. Part of me thought Alistair would tell them—confidentiality clause be damned. "I might be able to shed some light on that," I say. "Let me check with someone first, though."

Luca nods, and his hazel eyes rake over my face.

"What?" I ask. "Do I have strawberry seeds in my teeth?" I take a sip of my drink to cover my nerves.

"You look good, Ciprian," Luca says. "Like you haven't had a good night's sleep in a few weeks, but it works for you."

I blink, fighting the sudden urge to slump against him and find out if he's as solid as he seems. I resist the urge. "Things are hard at home," I admit.

Luca sits up straighter in the booth and braces one elbow on the table. "Are you in danger?"

"Worse," I sigh. "People I love are."

"Fuck, man, I'm sorry." He glances down the hall in the direction Celine disappeared. "So you're here on enclave business. I guess I thought . . ."

"What did you think?" I don't bother to correct his assumption and clear my throat. It's bone dry, despite the two drinks I've polished off.

"Nothing." Luca pats my thigh before he stands. "I thought you might be back for unfinished personal business. It's good to see you, Ciprian." He ambles away, disappearing behind the bar before I can think of a damn thing to say in response.

The Mouth of Hell is packed. Like, half a dozen people might be crushed to death before the night is over, packed.

Shoulder to shoulder, Luca, Malach, and I push toward the cage. My ribcage is black and blue by the time we make it there. I rub my side and wince. "And I thought the fight was going to happen up there."

"If we'd gotten here earlier, it would have been easier," Luca says. "But Celine is a headliner now."

"Make some noise for Tusker," the emcee roars.

I snort. "Is he for real with that?" I caught some of Celine's early matches, but I never paid much attention to the other fighters.

"Oh yeah," Luca says. "You'll love this."

Malach nods at me, his green eyes dripping with sincerity. They're both right. Watching Tusker fight the startled witch is hilarious. The shifter has a flair for showmanship. I don't know if I want to laugh or cheer when he ends the match by kicking his opponent in the balls with a hoof-sized pig foot.

"What is he?" I mutter.

"Unicorn pig," Luca grunts. "Sounds dumb, but those tusks are no joke."

Malach laughs as Tusker shifts into a hog the size of a small car and does a victory lap. The cage rattles noisily as he circles the fallen witch. The crowd goes wild.

"If they start oinking for him, I'm out!" I yell to make myself heard over the raucous cheers, stiffening when Alistair appears at my side.

"Wait until you hear what they chant for Celine," he says.

"Funny." I slant a glance at Luca, then address Alistair. "I didn't know you were coming."

Luca chews on his lip ring and avoids eye contact with both of us. The shady fucker insinuated Alistair would be out of town tonight. Is he trying to Parent Trap us? If so, it won't work. Alistair took things too far when he involved Sheena, and I can't let it go.

"I never miss her fights," Alistair says simply. "You look tired, Casanell."

"And you look tan," I drawl. "It doesn't suit you."

Malach bends to whisper in Luca's ear, his rumbly accent carrying easily over the crowd. "Do either of them ever say what they mean?"

Luca grins and raises his voice to a obnoxious level. "I think it's their version of foreplay, but I'm too scared to ask."

Malach nods as if that makes perfect sense, and I roll my eyes. How cozy of them to share a joke together at our expense. I wait for Alistair to lose his shit, but he pretends he can't hear them and focuses on the cage.

The lights shift—red at the base of the ring, orange in the middle, and blinking neon yellow at the top. Fire for my hot wings. It's clever.

A sense of anticipation settles over the crowd, and someone starts a chant. It spreads fast until the entire warehouse is screaming, "Make me sin," at top volume. Luca shakes his head, a muscle in Alistair's jaw ticks, and I throw my head back and laugh.

"That's perfect for her," I shout.

"But inaccurate," Malach says, a muscle in his jaw ticking. "Sin is a foolish human construct." Clearly, he's been brushing up on the human lore about angels . . .

"Demon propaganda is annoying, too," I say. "Do I look like I have horns and a tail?" Malach examines me, then shakes his head earnestly.

"Here she comes!" Luca points to a glowing red circle at the top of the cage. I squint, and my mouth falls open as Celine drops into the ring, her wings engulfed in flames. Probably thinking about Alistair . . .

Lips painted red, Celine's makeup is sharp enough to cut. I groan as I notice the scraps of leather she's wearing. They fit her like a second skin, showing off miles of muscles and curves. She's upgraded her fighting attire since the last time I was here, and I am super into it.

Unfortunately, I'm not the only one.

"Gods, I would fuck that smug look right off her face." The guy behind us chuckles and drunkenly elbows his buddy. "She'd tap out before I even got started."

Alistair stiffens at my side, but I've already latched onto the loser's mind, draping my magic over every inch of his consciousness. His lesson will be quick and memorable.

I change nothing about his surroundings except for the cage—which I detach from the ceiling and move to hover directly over him before dropping it.

He falls to the dirty concrete floor, covering his face with his hands and twitching as he screams. People stare. Someone yells at him to shut up or get out. Drunk and dumb, he doesn't deserve my best work, but terror I can give him.

I layer in the crack of splintering wood, a blanket of crushing darkness, and a spray of green sparks to simulate failing enchantments. He's now experiencing an accurate simulation of what might happen if the witch magic protecting the cage really failed.

Finally, to give him the full experience of being crushed to death, I add a few bone-snapping sounds. And since a true artist never forgets practical effects, I shove my foot back and kick him in the face. *That should do it.*

A gentle, calloused touch on my face brings me out of the haze between nightmare and reality. I blink rapidly as Luca drops his fingers from my cheek and grins. I may not have horns or a tail, but the angles of my face do sharpen when I use my magic.

Most people don't get the chance to notice.

The asshole's friends drag him away, and we watch along with the rest of the nearby spectators. He's still raving like a lunatic when I feel Celine's eyes on me.

I meet her gaze, then shudder. Because she's looking at me like she did in the bathroom, except this time there are no tears staining her face. For a second, everything slows down, and we're the only two people who exist.

Eventually, Celine breaks away, pivoting to hype up the crowd on the other side of the ring. I feel the absence of her attention as if someone stole my coat on the coldest day of the year.

Her opponent enters the cage in a cloud of puce-colored smoke. I snort, because that's one witch trick I'm more than familiar with. It sucks for this witch that their magic is such a gross color, because it's more sickly than cool.

They shake hands. The bell rings. The fight begins.

It's brutal.

After a few testing strikes, the witch goes on the offensive, hurling spikes of magic at Celine. Bobbing and weaving, she dodges them all. I'm exhausted just watching.

This is a stamina contest. The winner will be the one with more in the tank. When the witch's chest starts rising and falling in frantic, staccato beats, I smile. Besides a light sheen of sweat, Celine shows no signs of fatigue. It's only a matter of time.

Sure enough, the magical blasts get slower, and Celine doesn't waste a single opportunity. A jab here, an uppercut there. When she leaps six feet in the air, I hold my breath, watching mesmerized as she drives her fist into the witch's skull like a hammer.

Lights out.

I go crazy right along with the crowd.

Celine circles the cage and waves to her fans, but I'm fixated on the drip of sweat rolling down her neck. It trickles over the curve of her breast before disappearing into her leather crop top. I lick my lips and groan.

"Let's go," Luca says.

Nodding like a puppet on a string, I let him lead me through the crowd with one finger hooked in my belt loop. It's sweet. And considerate. And I'm too into Luca's attention to tell him I can keep up fine on my own.

The crowd thins as the four of us duck down a narrow hallway.

A metal door swings open, and Celine comes out with a few other fighters, including Tusker. He sees us coming first and wipes a drop of blood from his nose before tossing his arm over her shoulder.

"Your roster is here, Verity."

"Shut up." Celine shakes her head but doesn't bother to knock the fucker's hand off.

Glistening with sweat, her hairline is a darker red than the tips of her intricate braid. I force my eyes away from her to glare at the pig boy. "What was your stage name again?"

Luca groans and tosses an elbow at me that I dodge, but I'm still too worked up by the jerk in the crowd to care about his warning. If I want to be a prick to the sweaty oaf manhandling Celine, I will. He's lucky I don't drag him into a nightmare too.

Snapping my fingers, I raise my eyebrows. "Wait, I remember! Is it Ham Slam?"

Tusker's eyes widen. "No, it's—"

"Oinkzilla," I exclaim, cutting him off.

He spits blood on the ground, then runs his tongue over his teeth before smiling at me and putting a pair of blunted, oversized incisors on display. "That's not it either, man."

"You're right," I groan. "I can't believe I got it wrong again. That's my bad, Mr. Hogfather, sir."

"Ciprian," Celine hisses, her brown eyes sparking with annoyance.

I don't give a shit.

He's still touching her shoulder.

Tusker sees where I'm looking and wisely drops his hand before offering it to me. "I'm Dominic, but where the fuck were you when I was trying to come up with a good stage name?" He points at Celine. "This one was no help at all."

Dammit all to the monster realm and back. He's fucking nice.

Reluctantly, I settle for shaking his hand instead of breaking it.

With a distinctly troublemaking grin, Dominic waves and walks away, whistling cheerfully. As soon as he's out of sight, Celine advances on me. "Ciprian Casanell, I swear to the gods."

"You invited me," I remind her, backing away with my hands up. "And I'm glad you did. You were magnificent, hot wings!"

"Did I see you drag some random dude into a nightmare?"

I raise my eyebrows. "I'm not sure. Did you?"

"I saw nothing unusual, angel," Alistair says, holding a serious expression without breaking. Luca can't manage it. After making a strange choking sound, he covers his mouth with his hand to hide his grin.

Malach steps to Celine's side and begins meticulously removing the leather wraps from her hands. She shakes her head at me, then looks at him, her expression softening. "What about you? Did you miss it, too?"

Malach kisses her knuckles and grins. "As I told you, my truth. The demon is worthy."

Luca groans and I laugh. I'm really starting to like this guy.

THIRTY-ONE

UNSPOKEN RULE OF THE FRINGES #512:
IF YOU LET SOMEONE PAST YOUR GUARD,
EXPECT TO GET HIT.

CELINE

Ciprian fried that heckler's brain. For me. As if casually sending a grown man to the fetal position without bothering to turn around is no big deal. That kind of power is dangerous. Sure. Whatever. I'm more concerned about how fucking hot I found it.

He followed it up by directing petty taunts at Dom.

Childish? Yes. Stupid? Definitely. But with his black eyes flashing, and his lips pressed in a thin, angry line, he was so transparently jealous that my addled brain decided to be flattered.

Jealous Ciprian is delicious.

I've obviously taken too many hits to the head, because Luca, Alistair, and Malach backing his ridiculous behavior made it even hotter.

Desire rolls low in my belly, joining the leftover adrenaline from the fight. It makes me want to do something reckless, like tease all four of them until they beg for me on their hands and knees.

Pull yourself together, Celine. You should be too tired to be this horny.

"Movie night?" Luca asks. His question inspires a stunned silence and implies that we're in the habit of watching movies together as a group . . . which we certainly fucking aren't.

"I'm free," Alistair says, his tone innocent. I don't need to look at him to know he's watching me hungrily while waiting for my reaction.

What are they up to? And can I sit on the couch and watch a movie with them? It's too normal. Too relaxing. Even if I only pretend for one night, there will be a cost. My equilibrium. My dignity. If I allow a timeout, I could lose focus.

"If you don't want me there—"

I hold my hand up. "Don't put words in my mouth, Ciprian."

For once he shuts up, but now I wish he hadn't because I have no one to argue with. I need to think. Shit, they're all watching me . . . waiting.

I'm too warm. I should be cooling down, but the heat . . . Paired with the itch, I'm crawling out of my skin. I need to get out of here.

Shoving past Ciprian, I head for the door.

Luca calls my name, but I don't stop. I need air, and I need it now. If I get fresh oxygen to my brain, maybe I won't feel like the fate of the world rests on my ability to make this one simple decision.

The metal of the doorknob is blessedly cool against my fingers. The valley air is not. Arid and static, it settles around me more heavily than a coat. Frantic for an outlet, I throw my head back and scream at the night sky. Cold and unblinking, the dense canopy of stars draws me in.

They don't give a shit if I crack to pieces.

I would curse them all if I had the time.

Marching down the street, I crack my knuckles, distracted by the buzz of dozens of conflicting thoughts. Chaotic. Fractured. Disorganized. I miss who I was before I gave in to my attraction to these monsters. *Liar.* I wince. *You miss who you were before your father found you.*

It's a truth I'm not ready to face.

Ciprian plants himself in my path. Holding both of my motor-cycle helmets, he stretches one out to me, his expression carefully blank. "Want to find a bridge to throw me from? I promise to be terrified."

It's outrageous. And perfect.

His joke disrupts my spiral, puncturing the airtight bubble around my lungs. For the first time since Luca suggested movie night, oxygen floods my brain.

I take the helmet from Ciprian and grab his hand, glancing at the others over his shoulder. "Meet us at my apartment."

They don't respond, but I'm not worried. They'll be there, and by the time Ciprian and I join them, I'll be myself again. I've got to be.

Silently, Ciprian climbs on my bike behind me, his face hidden behind the helmet. His hands settle on my hips, sending bolts of awareness along my skin.

I rev the engine.

Release the clutch.

Then we're off, leaving a trail of burning rubber behind us.

I consider riding along Boulder Highway, but I don't want to deal with traffic lights. Instead, I head north toward one of the few remaining stretches of Old 91 that's still open to drivers. Made mostly obsolete by I-15, the highway was all but abandoned decades before I stumbled through the celestial gateway to make a new life for myself.

I lose myself in the ride, chasing the weightless feeling that reminds me of the freedom of flight. Pushing my bike to her limits, I careen around the curves and punch the throttle on the straights until we leave the city behind, and the desert swallows us whole.

True to his word, Ciprian lets me drive exactly how I want. The tightening of his thighs around mine is the only sign that he's nervous. If I lose control, we'll be little more than a smear on the cracked pavement—but it's worth it. Gods, is it worth it.

A coyote howls in the distance, and goosebumps creep up the back of my neck. I lean sharply to avoid a crater-sized pothole, and my heart skips a beat. Ciprian must be freaking . . . hard as a rock. My core clenches, and arousal hits me fast. The vibration of the bike adds to the sharp, needy ache between my legs.

The jealousy, the fight, the hot promise of his body against mine. It's too much.

I let off the throttle, pull off the road, and slam on the brakes beside a craggy formation of rocks. Once a popular scenic desert vista, this turnout is little more than a crumbling slice of pavement left to break down under the unforgiving summer sun.

It's perfect.

Dropping the kickstand, I spin on the seat, draping my legs over Ciprian's.

I'm panting, but I need to see his face. I need to know if he's turned on by the fear or by me.

I yank our helmets off and drop them both on the ground.

As merciless as gravity, I tumble into the inky depths of his eyes and groan. My gaze drops to his mouth. Ciprian's bottom lip is puffier than usual, like he spent the ride tormenting it with his teeth.

"Don't get any ideas," I whisper.

He cradles my cheeks, his fingers trembling. "It's way too late for that."

I kiss him with all the pent-up emotions I've been fighting

since I learned who he was. It's not a gentle kiss, but it's exactly what I need. *I know what I want now.*

I sigh into his mouth. My decisiveness is back with a vengeance. If I'm going to fall, I'm going to do it thoroughly. And if Ciprian's lips end the night swollen, it will be because of me.

His thumbs move against my cheeks, and he groans, the kiss a hot and messy tangle of teeth and tongues. I taste salt—there's no escaping the heat, even at night—and scoot further into his lap.

Ciprian yanks his lips away from mine to nibble on my earlobe. "You mad at me, Celine?"

I fist a handful of his hair and pull his mouth back to mine. "Fucking furious."

"Yeah?"

I bite his bottom lip. "Yeah."

"Can I get you off? Please?" His eyes are wild, and I shudder at the longing in his voice.

"I like it when you beg, Ciprian Casanell."

"And I like it when you say my name," he says, gasping. "If begging is what it takes to make that happen, I'll get on my hands and knees."

As appealing as that idea is, there are way too many spiky things around here to make him go through with it. The image of Ciprian crawling to me is enough. For now.

My gaze drifts to his lips. His shoulders. His heaving chest. "Is something wrong . . . Ciprian?" I pull his shirt over his head, then press my palm to his chest to better experience his heart pounding for me. "You seem worked up."

"I'm thirsty." He licks his lips and drags his eyes down my body until they land on my tiny leather shorts. "So thirsty," he repeats.

His words go straight to my pussy. I roll my hips toward him in invitation, stretching the shorts to their limit. I'm not sure I'll survive the night without knowing what the youngest enclave heir can do with his silver tongue.

A demon possessed, Ciprian reaches for me, pausing with his fingers an inch away to look up and whisper, "Please."

There's no coming back from this, but I can't think of a single reason to stop.

"Touch me," I say, not caring that I sound as far gone for him as he does for me.

Ciprian cups my pussy, groaning as his palm connects with the buttery leather of the shorts. "You're so warm."

"I'm curious how you plan to get them off." I rock against his hand, trapping his fingers between my body and the seat of my bike. "They're super tight."

His onyx eyes roll over me with obvious delight. "You leave that to me."

Yanking his hand away, he grabs my hips and lifts me. I find myself suspended as Ciprian latches onto my zipper with his teeth, pulls it down, and begs me to put my legs on his shoulders.

Calves propped against his neck, I brace my upper back beneath the handlebars and hold my body taut as he works the shorts over my hips and ass. Our position is precarious. Laughable even. But I'm hyper-aware of every sensation—and soaked. I can't wait for him to find out how much.

Then my shorts are all the way down, pressed against Ciprian's chin like a leather scarf. He sucks in a deep breath before lifting my ankles, one after the other, and removing the shorts.

I expect him to toss them on the ground. When he uses my belly as a tabletop and folds them neatly before tucking them under his leg, my jaw drops. Neat. Meticulous. And so fucking sexy. A trickle of arousal runs down my thigh.

Ciprian notices, pulling his bottom lip between his teeth. "Is that for me?"

If he sounded cocky, I might put him in his place, but—fuck me—he asked like a prayer—every syllable dripping with filthy, erotic hope. I want to keep the game up and tease us both more, but if he doesn't touch me soon, I'll be the one begging.

"Find out," I growl, rocking my hips toward his face.

I expect him to devour me immediately and brace for a rough touch—but Ciprian surprises me yet again. Pulling me away from the handlebars, he kisses his way up my legs as he reels me in. By the time his nose bumps the crease of my right thigh, I'm squirming.

The moonlight shines on Ciprian's hair, making it gleam like silver between my pale legs. When he finally licks me, I come hard from the first wet glide of his tongue. My pussy clenches around nothing, aching and empty.

Ciprian groans as if he's the one getting off, and his fingers dig into my ass cheeks as he plunges his tongue inside me. The ache goes away for a second, then comes back twice as strong.

"Another," I demand.

Ciprian whispers a response against my pussy, but since he doesn't bother coming up for air, I can't hear anything but an indecent wet noise.

His tongue returns to my clit, and I gasp into the night.

Lick by lick, Ciprian takes me apart, until I hear myself pleading for relief—a chaotic mix of *please*, *yes*, and *right fucking there* torn from my lips like they're the only words I can remember besides his name.

He whispers against my clit again, and the drag of his chapped lips over the most sensitive place on my body throws me over the edge. Toes curling in my leather boots, my thighs clamp around his head, and I worry that I don't have a lock on my strength and might crush him.

I wail, my head thrashing into the bike's horn.

Ciprian grunts—proof of life I can barely hear over the

roaring in my ears—and for a few weightless moments, I float, hovering outside of my body and gravity itself. Even with my wings trapped inside me, he's managed to make me fly.

Headlights on the horizon bring me crashing back to Earth.

Without a word, Ciprian helps me sit up, using his discarded shirt to shield me as the car passes. Then he looks at me and beams. A wide, genuine smile, with more teeth than practiced charm.

My heart stutters, and I distract myself by digging around in the bike's top case for the pair of cotton shorts I keep stuffed there in case of emergencies.

Ciprian puts the folded leather shorts in the compartment, but he seems reluctant to give them up. That's when I remember: this is the second time I've crawled on top of him, come hard enough to alter my blood pressure, and left him hanging.

"I didn't . . ." I wave my hand clumsily in the direction of his crotch. It's too dark to see much, which I'm thankful for, because I'm blushing for absolutely no reason except the fact that I've never sounded less sexy.

Ciprian laughs and scrubs his hand over his tangled blond hair. "I came when you did."

I blink at him. "The second time?"

He releases a heavy breath and shakes his head.

I'm officially confused. Is he trying to say he came as soon as he tasted me? Because that is by far the most ludicrous, far-fetched, flattering lie anyone has ever told me.

"There's no way," I blurt, annoyed that he would fib for no reason.

"Well, I'm not proud of it, that's for sure," Ciprian says.

"You're messing with me."

He shakes his head, studies my face, then groans like he's in pain. "I can't believe—you know what? I don't give a fuck. I'll prove it."

Swinging one leg over my bike, he stands and unzips his jeans, dropping them below his ass and dipping his hand into his boxer briefs. With jerky movements, he pulls his fingers free and holds them out for me to inspect.

They're dripping cum.

I giggle, not because it's funny, but because I'm shocked.

Ciprian closes his eyes, the night sky showing me a handsome face that's growing redder by the second. *You're ruining it, Celine.* The thought snaps me back to reality.

I grab his wrist and pull it to my lips, sucking his fingers into my mouth one at a time. His eyes snap open, and he watches, mesmerized, until I'm done.

Finishing with a kiss to his cheek, I give him a moment to reset his brain while I retrieve our discarded helmets and reflect on all that's happened between us.

I think about who he is and everything he hid from me. The murder investigation. His real identity. The things I shared and the things he concealed.

Next, I consider how he saved Alistair's life, lied to his family about Roscoe to protect me, and helped cover up the battle outside my apartment.

When I add in the fact that he came in his pants from the taste of me alone, the sting of our turbulent history doesn't hurt as much as it used to. Ciprian Casanell isn't bad or good—he's everything in between, and gods help me, I'm falling for him.

"Hold on tight. We're missing movie night," I say, cranking my bike. He chuckles and sags against me, radiating pleased exhaustion from every pore. "Oh, and Ciprian?"

"Yeah, hot wings?"

I smile under the safety of my helmet and raise my voice to be heard over the roar of the engine. "You taste good too."

THIRTY-TWO

LUCA

Celine and Ciprian slink into the apartment an hour and a half behind us, windblown, frazzled, and reeking of sex.

It's all I can do to hide my grin.

Alistair's head snaps to the entryway, his eyes flash red, and the arm of Celine's couch groans from the brutal press of his fingers.

I know that possessive expression intimately, but he may as well forget it.

The way I see it, we've reached a critical fork in the road.

By treating this relationship like a race, we've played it all wrong. The sabotage and the lies—they're all bullshit. The only thing we've done by creating a demolition derby out of reaching Celine's heart is ensure no one reaches the finish line unbruised.

She needs us all. We're far better off working together. And the sooner Alistair accepts that, the better it will be for everyone.

I don't expect it to be easy, but the dazed, dreamy look on Ciprian's face tells me it's worth the effort. On paper, we have almost nothing in common. He's a rich, powerful demon from a connected family, and I'm a scruffy bartender from the worst realm in existence. But at our core, we're both hers; I'm sure of that.

I am curious where—on a motorcycle in a crowded city famous for its nightlife—they managed to find a place to fuck.

"I need to rinse off," Celine says, her voice forcefully breezy. She hangs her keys on the hook by the door and refuses to look at the rest of us. I snort. She spins to face me, planting her hands on her hips. "Because of the sweaty fight."

"If you say so," I joke, enjoying making the two of them squirm for a change.

"Do you have something to say to me, Luca Saratelli?"

"No," Ciprian cuts in. "No, he doesn't. Do you?"

"I guess not." I shrug. "Better take Casanell with you, though. He looks super *sweaty* too, and I'm tired of waiting to start the damn movie."

"Great idea," Celine purrs, grabbing Ciprian's hand and towing him after her.

I wait for the door to close behind them before addressing the seething vampire in the room. "Chill out, Ali."

"I'm fine," he grunts.

"Mmhmm. Is that why you're about to tear the arm off the couch, or did it do something to you when I wasn't paying attention?"

"How can you be so calm?" he hisses, looking first at me, then at the chair where Malach is sitting. "And you, her bloody fiancé—"

"Betrothed," Malach corrects him calmly.

"Whatever!" Alistair narrows his red eyes.

"You weren't jealous before." I scratch the stubble on my chin. "Why now? What's different?" I know the answer, but Alistair needs to get there himself before he can get a grip.

"Nothing," he spits. "Absolutely nothing, except the fact that I want to tear his throat out and drain him dry for touching her."

"Okay, that's graphic but honest—I can work with that. Let's run through some hypotheticals. What if it were me in the shower with Ciprian?"

Alistair growls ferociously, and the sound wakes my basilisk. Once it recognizes who issued the potential threat, it coils contentedly in my chest.

"What if it was Celine and me in the shower, and Ciprian was six feet under or fucking around in Colorado or something?" I ask. Alistair's fingers twitch against the arm of the couch, and I chuckle. "Still sucks, doesn't it? Sounds like you can't blame this on Ciprian, can you?"

"Get to the point," Alistair snarls.

Malach mutters something that's clearly angel speak, then looks directly at Ali. "You are a possessive individual," he says patiently, as if he's explaining something obvious to a child who won't listen. "The common factor is not who lays with whom; it's merely that none of the ones you consider yours are currently laying with you."

He pushes to his feet and strolls to the kitchen like he didn't blow Alistair's entire mind. I choke on my laugh, then watch Malach suspiciously as he opens the fridge. The big guy is deadly with a blade, and he's even more dangerous in the kitchen. I don't trust him near a bowl of chips, much less an actual meal.

"What are you doing?" I call out, getting up from the couch and patting Alistair on the shoulder as I pass. He's blinking at the TV in shock, like he never once considered that he was the source of his own rampant jealousy. Poor guy.

"Making a drink," Malach says.

I clap him on the back. "I don't mind doing that."

He grins. "I hoped you would say that."

I gather my mixers as an ugly suspicion grows in my head. "Hey, Malach. In your study of English, did you ever run across the expression 'weaponized incompetence?'"

He considers that, laughs out loud, then winks at me. "Never."

That son of a bitch! Shaking my head, I focus on the drinks and hide my smile.

I have to get creative with Alistair's Blood Tide, since Celine doesn't keep all the ingredients I stock at the Fang, but I get close. Glancing at the back of Ali's head, I drag a knife across the top of my forearm, then twist to let the blood drip into his drink. The first drop has barely fallen when he pins me against the cabinets.

"What happened?" he demands. "Did you cut yourself?" I was expecting the sting of fangs in my neck or arm, but his frantic concern takes me off guard.

"Yeah"—I clear my throat—"on purpose, and you're wasting it."

Gently, I reach around him to continue transferring blood from my vein to his drink. Once it's the color I want, I hold my arm over a spare glass and add a few shots of blood to it. If we're watching a movie, he'll want a refill.

Satisfied, I present the faintly throbbing cut to him. "Do you mind?"

Without taking his eyes off me, Alistair licks my arm to close the wound. I shiver and open my mouth to tell him to quit hovering. I don't get the chance.

Ali drops his head to kiss me, groaning against my lips.

I can taste his bewilderment. He licks into my mouth, then drops his lips to my neck, devouring the spot beneath my ear like he's never tasted anything better. The possessive glide of his tongue is sexy, and I'm obsessed with the way it feels to be the focus of his intensity.

Running my thumb over his throat, I pull back and grin. "Better?"

He nods, still sullen as fuck, so I kiss him again before pushing him out of my way to finish the drinks. A glass of merlot for Celine, a fruity vodka-based monstrosity for Ciprian, Alistair's freshly sourced Blood Tide, and two domestic beers for Malach and I.

The overgrown angel adores beer, and I've grown used to ending the day with the twin clinks of our bottle caps hitting the kitchen counter.

"You're wonderful, Luca." Celine breezes into the kitchen with swollen lips, her skin pink from the hot shower. Even scrubbed clean, she smells amazing.

I kiss her, then hand Ciprian his drink.

He takes one sip, glances at me, snorts, and leans in to poke the side of my neck, eyes dancing with mischief. "He did it again."

Groaning, I roll my eyes. "Godsdammit, Ali—I told you before, no hickeys."

"What if I said it was an accident?" Alistair's answering grin is confident and unapologetic. Seeing the tips of his fangs hanging over his lower lip makes me shiver.

Celine snorts. "Then I'd be forced to call you a liar." She picks my arm up to examine the healing cut and raises her eyebrows. "Although I'm not surprised."

"Why?" I ask. "Are you saying you'll be tempted to give me a hickey every time I hurt myself? Should I start wearing turtle-necks around you all?" I fake a dramatic shudder.

"If you sliced yourself up to make me my favorite drink, I'd want to leave my mark on you too." Celine winks at me, then takes a deep sip of her wine and heads for the couch.

Ciprian follows her, but Alistair doesn't take his eyes off me.

He's standing between the fridge and the counter, blocking my exit. To get past, I'll have to move him.

Excitement rolls through me. Alistair's attention hangs like a drunken dare between us, the kind of reckless enthusiasm you eventually outgrow, until one day it's so far beyond reach you can barely remember the feeling.

"You're standing in my way," I say, my voice coming out raspier than intended.

"Am I?" Alistair pulls the corner of his bottom lip into his mouth. I've never seen him do that before—Wait . . . He's mirroring me. I release my lip ring and grin. *Bring it on, Ali.*

I shift to the right. He does too.

Then the left.

Finally, I approach him head-on, crowding him until our chests bump.

"Do I have to make you move?" I ask.

Pink stains the blue of his eyes—he likes that idea as much as I do.

Alistair dips his head until his lips hover directly over the mark he left on my neck. "I'll move on one condition," he purrs. "You promise not to deliberately spill your blood for me unless it's dripping down my fangs."

Every word is possessive.

I should hate it. He's basically claiming me as a source, but it's hot. I'm getting off on challenging the monster behind his eyes. The blood-sucking creature inside Alistair is exactly the kind of danger I'm into. The opposite of a cold beer at the end of a long day, but just as dependable in its own way.

Alistair wants me and my blood badly, and I like knowing that. I like it a whole lot. Surging forward, I bite his neck and suck. Not hard enough to break his skin, but hard enough to leave behind the angry, pink indent of my teeth.

"Sounds good," I say, flipping the charged conversation on its head and brushing past while he's still reeling. His erection grazes my thigh, and I swallow my grin.

Movie night was a great fucking idea.

It takes only twenty minutes for me to change my mind.

Every breath I take is dripping with sexual tension. From the way Celine curls into my side—looking relaxed but feeling anything but—to how Alistair spreads his long legs wide and manages to crowd everyone's personal space.

"I don't understand," Malach mutters. "This is supposed to be comedic, yes?"

I drop my head against the back of the couch. "Yeah. It's funny."

"You're not laughing," he says. *That's because there's nothing amusing about having a neglected erection.*

"It's not that funny," Ciprian says.

I sigh. "We can pick a different movie."

Celine yawns. "It's too late for that. I'm tired."

I grab the remote and press pause, cutting the laugh track off mid-chuckle. Alistair stands, stretches to his full height, and heads for the door with barely a grunt, stopping at the last minute to remind me to lock up after him.

I grumble under my breath. As if I would forget something that important.

Ciprian stands and curses. "My car isn't here."

"I can give you a ride." Alistair's offer surprises us all. Whether he's trying to be helpful or doesn't want Celine to let Ciprian stay over is anyone's guess, but the angry tension between the two of them is so real, I think I could reach out and grab it.

A muscle in Ciprian's jaw ticks. "I guess that's better than a rideshare." He walks to the door, stops, and pivots. Two steps bring him back to the couch, and he bends directly over me to put his face level with Celine's. "Thank you for inviting me to the fight."

He kisses her gently, using both hands to cradle her face. With Celine tucked under my arm, I feel her sharp inhale as his lips move against hers. The last drop of blood faithfully circulating my body makes a frantic beeline for my cock, and I stifle a groan as Celine slumps against me, boneless.

"Let's go, Casanell," Alistair snaps.

Celine pulls back and glares at Ali. "Don't kill him."

Alistair raises his eyebrows. "I wouldn't dream of it, angel."

I laugh at him, shaking my head. "I don't know why you're mad, Ali. I'm the one who made the drinks and picked the movie no one liked, and I haven't had a goodnight kiss."

With absolute chaos dancing in his black eyes, Ciprian bends over again, aiming for me.

I lift my chin. Before Ciprian's lips can touch mine, Alistair darts across the room and shoves him bodily onto the floor.

"Holy shit, Ali—"

I don't get a chance to finish my thought before he's kissing me instead. Angry and demanding, my bottom lip splits from the force, and I groan. As soon as Alistair tastes my blood, the kiss turns feral, ending as abruptly as it started when he backs away and drags the back of his hand over his mouth.

"Now you have," he tells me. "Be in the car in thirty seconds, Casanell, or walk home."

Then he's gone, moving so fast the air blurs.

I adjust myself as discreetly as possible while Ciprian gets up from the floor. "Next time," he tells me with a wink, clapping Malach on the shoulder as he follows Alistair out the door.

Celine shakes her head and yawns, securing the deadbolts behind them.

Malach looks at me, then at the TV, then back at me again and smiles. "That was a lot funnier than the movie you picked."

I chuckle, because he's fucking right.

THIRTY-THREE

Unspoken rule of the Fringes #74:
Silence often speaks loudest.
Don't forget to listen.

ALISTAIR

I glance at the passenger seat from the corner of my eye as my fingers squeeze the life out of my steering wheel. Luca's blood lingers on my tongue, spicy and electric, but the uncomfortable silence in the car suffocates my lingering pleasure.

Casanell is angry. It's clear from the tight angle of his jaw and the focused way he watches the neighborhood career past his window. This part of town is nothing special, just brick and mortar in various states of decay. Since I've experienced what he's capable of creating with his own imagination and magic, I know these buildings have nothing new to offer him.

His silence doesn't sit right with me. It's out of place, belonging to someone far less . . . everything than Ciprian Casanell. His anger with me feels wrong too.

"Pushing you down was uncalled for," I say, forcing the words through clenched teeth.

Ciprian scoffs. "I'm not mad about that, asshole."

I consider that uncomfortable statement and decide to ignore it and change the subject instead. "The dossier is coming along," I tell him. "I've compiled more than a thousand pages of data so far."

A grunt is the only response I get.

He's refusing to play along. From a consummate pretender, it's especially annoying.

To punish him or myself or the bloody both of us at once, I slow the car to a crawl. Fifteen miles per hour. Twelve. Eight. How slowly can I go before he mentions it?

I drum my fingers against the wheel, my agitation growing.

Ciprian talks to everyone else, making jokes and saying any number of things he doesn't mean. He'll say anything to smooth a conversation along, yet ten minutes in the car with me isn't worth the effort it takes to be civil?

He reaches for the handle. "I can fucking walk."

Hissing, I lock the doors, punch the gas, and take the next left. Unfortunately for Ciprian, it's in the opposite direction of where he left his car.

Turning his head slowly, he looks at me. "What is this, Alistair?"

I open my mouth only to close it again, because I don't know why I'm fucking doing this. It's pointless and petty, but I can't stop. "I've gathered a lot of information for Sheena—"

"Shut up," Ciprian snarls. "You don't get to talk about her. Sheena nearly died for that stupid tan you're sporting. She may consider you a friend now, but I haven't forgotten that you were willing to use her safety as a bargaining chip. I won't. Not ever."

There it is—the loyalty I once suspected he didn't have. A curious craving stirs in me, the same way it did when I first observed Luca and Celine's obvious care for one another. Why can't I have it? Is it cursed fate or my own missteps?

I clear my throat, the burn I lived with for weeks nonexistent after my Luca-flavored cocktails. "I did that for Celine," I bite back. "But I never would have hurt Sheena."

"You wouldn't hurt her yourself, that would be too honest." Ciprian laughs. Like pellets of ice bombarding my skin, there's no humor in it. "You would just out her as a djinn to someone who would do the job for you. You never have to get your hands dirty that way . . . right, Ali?"

Ciprian's slumped form floods my mind, his face swollen beyond recognition from the beating he took. A beating I saved him from. "Are we talking about Sheena or you?"

Instead of falling for the bait, he looks out the window again. I might think he didn't care if it wasn't for the bone-white gleam of his knuckles against the handle of the passenger door.

"This may be a foreign concept to you, Alistair, but one day you'll have people whose pain hurts you more than your own."

I'd rather he punch me in the face. Of all the sanctimonious, hypocritical things he could say to me . . . Wrenching the steering wheel to the right, I head toward the Mouth of Hell, fed up with his bullshit.

"You're in love with Sheena. Admit it," I hiss.

Ciprian glances at me and scoffs. "I pity you, honestly."

"Don't," I snarl, incensed—why does it feel like I'm the one losing this argument?

"Have you ever had a real friend?" he demands. "Or would that be a waste of your valuable time?"

The scent of him. His blood pumping through his veins . . . Even well-fed, I'm teetering on the edge of my control. How could I add Ciprian to my blood circle? Why would the gods be so cruel? We aren't compatible by any definition of the word.

I slam on the brakes and breathe through my mouth, the sleek lines of his expensive SUV glowing yellow from my headlights. Gritting my teeth, I unlock the doors, wishing he were miles away.

He won't stay. Why did he bother coming back at all?

Ciprian climbs angrily from my car, his fingers curled around the metal edge of the door as he braces to slam it in my face. Like two pieces of flint colliding, our eyes lock, creating a spark that burns bright, then falls forgotten to the cracked pavement.

It's pointless. There's nothing left to burn. Our bridge is ash beneath our feet.

"I have friends, Casanell," I say softly. "You're just not one of them."

He closes the door carefully—as if we didn't say terrible things to each other.

My hands shake.

I got the last word and claimed the moral high ground, so why does it feel like I lost something I couldn't afford to lose?

———————

It's funny how life doesn't stop moving when nothing makes sense.

Weeks pass. I bury myself in research. Without the sun to hold me back, I'm limitless. My mind runs thousands of simulations and hypotheticals, but I'm strangely disconnected from it all.

I drink from Celine and Luca regularly. Their blood fuels me, even while I hide the reality of the blood circle from them. Every time I try to come clean, something holds me back. I'm at their mercy, and it's bad enough that I know it. If they know it too . . . I couldn't bear to drink from them if pity fueled the exchange.

After encountering Ciprian at the club twice, I stop going. Every time I see his smiling face, I hear the mazzikin's voice whispering in my ear and wonder if I made a mistake. My mind refuses to rest.

It gets worse every time I meet with Sheena. She's nothing like I expected. With no experience in our worlds—enclave or Fringes —she sees everything as new.

As I show her the realities of the Fringes—playing a bleeding-heart Robin Hood archetype I've never aspired to be—I feel hope. Naïve, embarrassingly so, but she gave me the sun. Is it far-fetched to believe she could mend the cracks of our society that many supernaturals spend their entire lives crushed between?

I understand why Ciprian protects her.

Only a monster would have leveraged her safety against him. As the damned, blood-sucking, creature of darkness that I am, I fit the mold perfectly.

Damn me, I want to help her. Beyond the original scope of our deal. So I dig, researching night and day, deploying all my existing contacts, developing new ones, and lurking in the shadows of every seedy room within a hundred miles.

Until I find it. A smoking gun in the form of an invitation.

My chance to pay Sheena back for lifting my sun curse.

If I deliver this intel, maybe I can forget what I destroyed to secure this deal.

Except Sheena doesn't answer her phone. My palms prickle as I dial again. No answer. Sunlight illuminates the motes of dust in the air as I glance at my open window. This can't wait. Groaning in my empty apartment, I scroll to Ciprian's contact.

ALISTAIR

Where are you?

He reacts to my message with a question mark, not bothering to reply.

Pacing, I type so quickly my fingers blur. This is no time to let pride get in the way.

Lysander is coming. To Vegas. I can't get in touch with Sheena.

My phone rings a second later, Ciprian's name dominating the screen. I swipe to answer. At least he's able to overlook his grudge for long enough to have a conversation.

"Are you sure?" he demands, all business.

"I am." I explain the invitation, nearly stumbling over my words in my hurry to get them out. An auction here in Vegas, with the worst of the worst in attendance. The product for sale? Supernatural women abducted by Lysander's gang.

He's going to use this event to fund his war on the enclave and gain allies while he's at it. But if Sheena shows up and takes him down while he's exposed, no one in this territory will have to worry about his predatory schemes ever again. And my deal with the enclave will be done.

"I'm on my way to your place," Ciprian says. A door slams in the background, and I frown. I can't have him here in my personal space, not after everything that's happened.

"I'll meet you," I say. "Where are you?"

There's a pause. A heavy breath. "I'm at the Fang." Then Ciprian hangs up.

I run the two miles to the club.

Ciprian is sitting at the bar, the stage lights painting purple highlights in his blond hair. His head snaps up as soon as I come in. "She's in an enclave meeting, that's why she's not answering the phone. My brother won't pick up either."

I grunt, watching as he calls Sheena repeatedly—like a complete lunatic—until she answers. His face twists, and he grabs me by the wrist and tows me into the storage room to get away from the club noise.

After that, it's deceptively simple. Ciprian explains the

urgent timing—tonight, while I respond to the invitation and secure a table for Sheena. Trepidation ripples through me as I see some of the names on the attendance list. Dangerous supernaturals—the most powerful players in the world—all coming to Vegas.

I don't want Celine or Luca anywhere near this.

Absently, I hear Ciprian end the call.

He looks at me, black eyes sharp. "I'm your plus one."

I frown. "That wasn't part of the plan—"

"Fuck that," Ciprian snaps. "I'm your plus one, and if you try to fight me on this, Ali, I swear to the gods . . ." His use of my nickname takes me off guard.

I find myself nodding like an idiot. "As backup only," I insist. "This isn't our fight."

A muscle in his cheek twitches. He disagrees. I brace to throw down. I can provide dozens of facts to support my argument. If he would listen to me for five minutes and stifle his urge to be a reckless—

The door opens.

Luca tosses us a friendly smile, whistling as he rifles through the crates of liquor. He pulls a bottle out, reads the label, then puts it back. Strolling to another box, he repeats the process. The silence stretches, made worse by his tuneless whistling, as Ciprian and I wait for him to leave.

"Fuck, dude," Ciprian finally blurts. "Can I help you find it?"

The whistling cuts off, and Luca raises his eyebrows. "Am I in your way? I'm sorry about that, it's just—oh yeah, this is my workplace. How could I be in your way?"

"You aren't," I say dryly. "You have, however, already checked that crate."

Luca slaps his thighs, mischief all over his face. "Now that you mention it, I think I have what I need behind the bar. Silly me."

"Nosy ass," Ciprian mutters even as his lips twitch into a

reluctant smile. "I can't come to Celine's fight tonight. Will you tell her I'm sorry?"

"Why don't you tell me yourself?" Celine walks in and shuts the door behind her with a determined thud. "Do you have a date?"

"Unfortunately, I do." Ciprian grabs her hand and kisses her knuckles as he looks her up and down. "But you are infinitely hotter."

Celine frowns, then wipes the expression from her face. "Anyone I know?" She does her best to sound bored, but lukewarm feelings aren't her strength. Fiery anger and chilling sadness? She's got those down. But pretending she doesn't give a damn who Casanell is seeing tonight? Yeah, no one's buying that.

"It's Alistair," Ciprian says, shrugging as he kisses her cheek. "The stubborn bastard finally wore me down." *Oh, for fuck's sake.*

Celine smirks and shoots Luca a triumphant look. "Pay up."

He shakes his head. "This doesn't count, baby. They're hiding something."

"Not well enough," I say. "Our secrets are being uncovered much more easily than the elusive bottle of liquor you're hunting." I do my best to sound aloof, but my heart is racing. "We will meet up with you after the fight, angel."

Celine nods, but her eyes are narrow as she searches my face.

"Where's Malach?" Ciprian asks. "I haven't seen him here all afternoon."

"Someone on his team reported movement near the gateway, so he's out hunting assassins," Celine says, her brow furrowing. "It's been oddly quiet since the last attack."

A prickle of unease curls in my gut and spreads. If there's movement by the gateway to the celestial realm . . . I don't like the idea of leaving her side. But I promised Ciprian. Torn, I look at Luca, and he nods, yellow briefly consuming the hazel of his eyes.

I can't be in two places at once, but Luca will do whatever it takes to keep her safe.

For tonight, that will have to be enough.

A voice in my head whispers that I could lose them all.

I tell it to shut the fuck up.

Celine eyes me and sighs. "I know it's not my business. I didn't pry about the sun curse, and I've kept my mouth shut about your frantic research. You two can obviously do whatever you want—you don't need my permission—but I feel sick right now."

She wraps one arm around her stomach. "Can you at least tell me that you plan to be careful? I *need* you both to be okay. I-I won't be able to fight tonight unless I'm sure."

My teeth grind. Her uncertainty—I hate it. If it was up to me, I would tell her everything. I'm tired of the secrets and lies. They're wrapped around me like a damn noose.

"Alistair is helping my best friend," Ciprian says softly. "The one I told you about. She's the one who lifted his sun curse. Sheena's been in trouble for a long time, but if tonight goes as planned, she'll be safe again and his deal with the enclave will be done."

Celine raises her eyebrows. "But will you two be safe?"

"We won't be on the front lines," Ciprian says. "I'm Sheena's backup while she acts as bait, and Alistair is her ticket in the door."

"It doesn't sound as simple as you're making it out to be," Luca says.

"Come on, have a little faith in us!" Ciprian smiles, but it's missing his usual charm. "It will be a piece of cake."

My stomach flips.

I wish I felt that confident. Unfortunately, I'm out of wishes.

THIRTY-FOUR

UNSENT CORRESPONDENCE, TRANSLATED TO ENGLISH, AND ADDRESSED ONLY TO MY TRUTH: MY MAGIC FELT LIKE DAMNATION, BOILING ME FROM THE INSIDE OUT. IT HAD NEVER FELT THAT WAY BEFORE—NOT ONCE SINCE THE DAY I RECEIVED MY RADIANT GIFT.

MALACH

The motel smells of stale cigarette smoke and something evil called ocean breeze.

When I found these lodgings—months ago now—I spent hours hunting the source of the sickly sweet scent, only discovering the jagged piece of cardboard after sticking my head beneath the bed. I still regret the decision. I've seen sword wounds less horrifying than that one glimpse beneath the sagging mattress.

My team deserves better, but this location is too good to give up.

Lyklan eyes me gravely as he delivers his report. "At least two dozen celestial signatures came through the registered gateway."

So many? Through the monitored portal? My muscles tense. S'lach is making a move, and he doesn't care who knows it. *It's too soon. We're not ready.* I cradle my head, the pain a spike through my skull.

"Are you well, Malach?" Lyklan asks.

He reaches for me, freezes, then drops his hand. I pretend not to notice the slip. My guardians won't touch me unless I'm gravely wounded. In the celestial realm, even offering would be considered an offense. Earth manners are infecting us all.

"Only a headache," I say, pushing the pain from my mind. "Celine has a fight tonight."

Lyklan rubs his hand over his chin, considering that. "The venue is public—"

"But she'll be exposed on the way there and back," I finish his thought.

"And her method of transportation . . ." He winces.

Yes, Celine's bike is dangerous—but after watching her ride, I can't ask her to give it up. Especially since I've experienced the loss of flight myself since revealing myself to her. The longing is acute, and I've only spent a few weeks with my feet on the ground. She's lived this way for years.

"I'll suggest Luca drive her tonight."

Celine won't argue with that. She may be understandably protective of her independence, but she's too intelligent to quibble over temporary safety precautions.

I salute Lyklan and leave the motel, convinced that he's as prepared to mitigate this threat as possible. He and his team will patrol the Fringes, keeping their eyes peeled for unknown angels and eliminating them if necessary.

It's a tall order. They've been patrolling nonstop for weeks. They wear their fatigue like armor; new creases clinging to the corners of their eyes and mouths.

Since the ambush at Celine's apartment, they've killed ten assassins.

My hand twitches involuntarily, phantom echoes of my injury.

Every time I almost tell Celine about the continued attacks, something holds me back. Perhaps it's the smile on her face when she looks at Luca, or the satisfaction in her eyes when she wins a fight and donates her winnings to the orphaned angels. No matter what it is, I cannot bear to worry her, so I haven't.

Instead, I see killers in every reflection.

The skin on my hand has grown back, but I still feel pain from the *koil'nashra*. One second of contact consumed layers of tissue. We cannot hope to win against weapons like that. If S'lach decides to wipe the Fringes from the map . . . I shudder. He's more than capable of it. Especially if he grows frustrated by repeated failure.

Disquiet hums in my gut as I enter the Naked Fang and bump into Ciprian.

He smiles at me, the expression cracking around the edges. When Alistair silently follows him out, I shake my head. Their situation lacks any semblance of order. It's a mess, and I fear it will remain that way until one of them decides to clean up after themselves.

I won't hold my breath.

The supernaturals in this realm are callous. Stubborn to a fault, they fight everything, no matter how big or small. It's as if they've never known peace or ease. Luca bends when necessary, but perhaps he's like me: willing to twist anything but his tether to Celine.

Imani smiles as I settle on the stool next to her. "We're doing slang today, big guy."

She's made a habit of this. Whenever things at the club are slow, she joins me at the bar to talk about words. At first, I feared she was creating a buffer to keep me away from Celine, but now I look forward to our conversations.

"Slang," I repeat. "Including idioms, colloquialisms, and turns of phrase? Can we defeat such a broad topic in one sitting?"

Imani shakes her head. "Oh no, buddy. That would take years, and by the time we finished, all the popular ones would have changed. Like all of us, slang has a fleeting life expectancy. Today, we're talking about one word and one word only: ass."

I raise my eyebrows, glancing unintentionally toward the stage as Celine drops into a deep squat and grinds to the beat of the music. "I believe I already know the meaning of that word," I say, blood rushing to my cheeks.

"Uh-huh, sure you do. There are about fifty bajillion ways to use it, though."

"I see."

"Not yet, you don't"—she clears her throat—"but you will. Let's start with the big three: asshole, dumbass, and smartass. The first one is a self-explanatory insult. The second two seem like opposites but aren't. Any guesses?"

I consider them. "I presume a dumbass is an unintelligent individual."

Imani nods.

"But smartass isn't the more intelligent counterpart?"

"Nope, a smartass is someone sarcastic, like this grungy bartender." She points at Luca as he approaches. "Next there's asshat, asswipe, and half-assed. The first two are insults, but the last one—"

"—is when someone does something shittily, like Imani pretending to care about her health while simultaneously refusing to drink enough water to keep a camel hydrated." Luca drops the bottle in front of her as she rolls her eyes.

I smile at their aggressive teasing. "I'm sensing a theme."

Imani glares at the water bottle, her lips twisting with disgust. "You think you are, but they're not all derogatory. Kickass is positive."

"What's your favorite?" I ask Luca.

"Probably fuckass." He smirks. "It can mean whatever you want, depending on your tone."

I cringe and shake my head. Relativism in linguistics is the enemy of clear communication. It should be avoided at all costs.

Celine leans between us, resting her elbows on the bar. "What's the topic today?"

I devour her with my eyes—the only acceptable way to get my fill. Everything about her is striking, from her flaming wings to her fiery hair. Even her shape—muscular and soft, angular and smooth—defies reason while demanding notice. I want her to notice me, too.

"Ass fucks," I say calmly, hiding my smile as Celine gasps. In the process of taking her first sip from the dreaded bottle, Imani snorts water from her nose and stares at me with shock that quickly morphs to glee.

"That"—Imani bumps her fist against mine—"was badass."

It was stupid and crass—much like the movie we tried to watch with Ciprian and Alistair—but I'm proud of myself for surprising Celine. I don't get the chance often.

Luca offers me a beer. I shake my head. I need to be sharp; we all do.

Celine notices and stops laughing. "What's wrong?" she asks.

Imani hops down from her stool. "That's my cue." She pats me on the back. "Until next time, Malach."

I nod at her, then fill the others in on Lyklan's report.

"We can take Luca's car," Celine says, her hand grazing my arm absently. It's an involuntary gesture, but the strip of skin she touched feels more alive.

"Would it be better to skip tonight?" Luca asks, his hazel eyes searching my face.

"I don't think it makes a tremendous difference," I admit. "The apartment is stocked with weapons, but it's not the most defensible location, and they already know where it is."

"The prize money for this fight is a big deal," Celine whispers. "If I win tonight, we could afford security upgrades."

"What does your gut tell you, baby?" Luca asks. "Would he send assassins to the fight?"

Celine's forehead wrinkles. "I don't think so. It's not his style —too public."

"So, we're careful but not locked down," Luca says, glancing away as someone waves him over for a drink. I nod, and he grimaces apologetically before moving to serve the customer.

Celine's hand settles on my lower back, warm and reassuring. "If I haven't said it before, Malach, I'm grateful that you're here. Risking your life. Far from home . . . I know it's not easy."

Can't she see the truth? Standing at her side is easier than breathing. Celine walks away before I can tell her there's nowhere in this universe I'd rather be.

THIRTY-FIVE

UNSPOKEN RULE OF THE FRINGES #31:
EXPECT PAIN.

CELINE

I slide into my padded wraps, flexing my knuckles against the jelly-lined fabric. Black and designed to look like leather, they're more a part of my outfit than actual protection. With opponents who attack with magic or fangs, getting out of the way is usually a better strategy than trying to block.

My itch is acting up tonight.

"You good?" Lyss asks, standing on her tiptoes to reach her locker.

Hiding a smile, I reach over her and grab the black tank top she's trying and failing to get down. "We need to get you a stool."

Lyss gasps, snatching the shirt from me and clutching it to her chest. "And ruin my street cred? You wouldn't dare."

"Please." Dom winces while awkwardly attempting to wrap gauze around his ribs. "If you keep poking holes in everyone you fight, I don't think anyone will say shit about a boost."

Lyss pulls the tank top over her head, her voice muffled by the fabric. "How's your spleen?"

Dom shrugs. "Which one, bitch? You tore it in half. Math logic says I have two now."

"Math logic," I snort. "Otherwise known as my favorite subject in school."

Dom tosses a playful punch at my shoulder. Their fight last week was grisly. Like, Resker called a pause afterward so someone could mop up the blood, grisly. I can't believe Dom is planning to get back in the cage already.

"Is it safe for you to shift before it's fully healed?" I ask him, curious about how that will affect the process.

"Trying to uncover my secrets, Verity?"

I roll my eyes but move to his side to help him secure his bandage. He grunts his thanks, and a handful of Ciprian's silly nicknames for him run through my head.

"Never," I tease. "I wouldn't dare risk the wrath of the Hogfather."

He groans, and my lips twitch.

"Resker still won't let you change it?"

"She said I had my chance, wasted it, and I'll be Tusker until I die."

That sounds like a threat. Grateful that I'm standing behind him, I grin as I imagine Dom trailing after the terrifying woman and begging to change his stage name. I bet her entire body became a scowl.

"She could change her mind." I toss in the conditional to avoid an outright lie and pat him on the back.

Dom cranes his neck, hope transforming his square features into an almost boyish expression. "You think so?"

I nod, accepting the punishing sting of the nonverbal lie. There's no chance in the many fucked-up realms that Resker would walk back a decision. That would make her look weak, at least in her mind, but I can't tell Dom that . . . the poor guy has two spleens.

Lyss peeks under Dom's gauze and sighs with relief. "It's not infected. That's good."

Dom and I exchange a glance. "Did you poke me with poisonous toes, eight legs?"

She shakes her head, then buries her head in my empty locker . . . the only one she can reach. I raise my eyebrows. Lyss is a terrible liar. Poisoned legs would explain why I had such a hard time healing from her attack during our audition fight. Good to know.

I survey the locker room, taking it in. Most of the fighters are focused on themselves, with only a few clustered in groups like ours. To my surprise, Dom and Lyss were determined to befriend me. Even more surprising, I don't hate it.

"Double-check the board," Resker shouts, poking her head through the door and smacking the flat of her hand against the wall to make sure she has everyone's attention. "The first fight starts in five."

The energy in the room swells with a contagious combination of adrenaline, excitement, and fear. Add in the hodgepodge of supernatural essences mixed with sweat and blood, and breathing through your nose is a risk.

"Good luck," I tell Lyss and Dom.

They're both fighting early, but my name is last on the lineup next to 'special guest.' That tells me absolutely nothing except that I should be ready for anything. Casually, I scrape my itching back against the ribbed locker vents and hope no one notices.

"Make me sin!"

"Make me sin!"

"Make me sin!"

"Make me sin!"

My heart beats in time with the chanting crowd, and I focus on regulating my breathing as I duck through the tunnel.

Left foot. Inhale. "Make"—Right foot. Exhale—"Me"—I grind to a halt as the itch spreads from my spine to my fingertips— "Sin." Air catches in my throat.

Something is wrong. Very wrong.

I glance behind me, but besides the light from the locker room, I can't see much. *No way but forward, Celine.* I force myself to keep moving toward the cage. If something bad is waiting for me out there, I'll face it head-on with my eyes wide open.

"We've got a show for you tonight, folks. Verity—your favorite fighting angel—will take on a very special guest . . . the one, the only . . . Secooooond Cominnnnng!"

I reach the end of the tunnel and drop to the floor of the cage, ignoring the screaming fans and skipping my normal hype lap. Resker will be pissed, but something about the special guest's fighter name is setting off all the alarm bells in my head. Who the fuck is this asshole?

The side entrance opens to thick, black smoke. It swirls around a pair of sturdy shit-kicking boots planted in a wide stance. As I drag my eyes up the body they're attached to, I curse the damn smoke. I can't get a good look.

The fighter takes three slow, measured steps forward.

His face appears under the lights, hulking and familiar.

I freeze, hands clenching and unclenching at my sides. *It can't be.* I ground him to bits and buried him and his shit across multiple dumpsters. There's absolutely no fucking way that Roscoe Daemyn—enclave enforcer, bad tipper, and all-around son of a bitch—is facing off against me in the ring right now.

There's roaring in my ears. I can't tell if it's the crowd or the tsunami of blood crashing around in my head as it tries to reconcile what I know to be true with what my eyes are telling me.

The roaring changes to ringing—no, fuck, that's the actual bell.

The fight is starting.

I lift my hands into a relaxed, guarded position. Second Coming matches the move. Exactly. Hands curled and hovering loosely in front of his chest. It's a common guard, but something tells me it's not a coincidence.

I lift my right pinky to test him.

Raising one thick, bushy eyebrow, he lifts his middle finger instead.

The crowd eats it up, no spoon required.

My anger comes as a relief, mercifully chasing away the shaky fear that swamped me when I saw his face. I don't know who or what Second Coming really is. They can't be Roscoe, though. They're someone else—something worse, wearing his punchable face like a mask.

I circle cautiously. Someone is trying to play god with my past. This reappearance is going to stir up rumors and put Ciprian at risk for covering up Roscoe's death.

His fist slams into my jaw without warning, and I see stars. Instinctively, I retreat, protecting my face with my forearms as my vision jitters in and out of focus. He's strong. Ravoc demon strong, according to Ciprian's demonic explainer, but he's not angel strong.

I let the pain focus me and remind myself that I'm undefeated for a reason.

This is my fight to lose.

Advancing, I throw a punch, then duck as he throws the move back at me. Jab, cross, two right hooks while driving my back foot into the cage floor for extra power—a sweep with my right leg—feint, an uppercut at half-strength.

Twisting in the air as a distraction, I hurl my left elbow toward his face.

The sequence is flawless, creative, and lightning fast; and I know without Malach having to tell me it's also some of the best fighting I've ever done.

There's only one problem: none of my hits land.

Second Coming counters every single one, moving with none of the clumsy, lumbering strength I remember from Roscoe's assault. It's another confirmation that I'm dealing with something new, something other.

His next move breaks my rhythm, and I barely manage to dodge the haymaker in time. His knuckles graze the side of my braid, barely missing my face. I counter, hoping the power of the punch left him off balance. It didn't. He leaps over my sweeping leg like he's jumping rope on the playground.

Stumped and a little shaken, I run through my standard moves to see how he reacts. He mirrors each one, reacting only a fraction of a second behind me each time. It's like facing a bigger, uglier version of myself, and I'm fucking over it.

This is the Fringes; it's time to fight dirty.

I throw a knockout punch with my left fist while aiming a dropkick at his balls. Even though I know it's coming, I barely duck his mirrored hook in time.

Our feet collide with an agonizing crack, and pain radiates from the ball of my foot to my knee. I absorb the shock and shift my weight to my other leg. It fucking hurts. I'm not sure if it's broken, but something isn't right.

Roscoe's lookalike face ripples before locking on the angry expression I remember from the Fang. He shows no sign of pain, but he took the same impact I did—it must have done something. *Please have done something.*

Gingerly, I try putting weight on my injured foot. Pain shoots up from the heel before settling at a mid-level throb. Okay, that's fine. I can do this. I can still beat him. I just can't wear him out by running circles around him.

The itch, barely noticeable over my pain and adrenaline, skyrockets as Second Coming strikes again. Dropping into a squat, I release my wings and use my good foot to power my launch. That should get me airborne and give me time to—

Fingers, meaty and made to crush, close around my ankle. *Shit.*

He hurls me to the floor of the cage, and I block everything out. The pain, the crowd, my body's instinct to panic—they're not going to help me survive this fight.

Creative. Be creative, Celine. Malach's voice echoes inside my head, but I'm out of ideas. Second Coming anticipates my every move.

As if they sense my despair, my wings curl around me and take over. Transforming into flaming knives, they slash at fake Roscoe's body from his ankle to his forehead. Blood gushes from the cuts. It sizzles and boils as it encounters my fire.

Roscoe's face, now singed and sliced to ribbons, wobbles and warps, revealing an oddly smooth surface beneath his skin. A shell? A mask? Polished bone? I can't tell, and it doesn't matter. There are only two acceptable outcomes: knock him out or force him to tap.

I can't kill him in front of a crowd, not while he's wearing the face of someone who would still be alive if it weren't for me. Even if I could make it out to be an accident, word would get back to the enclave, and we'd all be fucked.

Tensing my abs, I kip up to press my advantage and slam my fist into his nose. He stumbles; I hit him again. His head rocks to the right. I throw another punch, this time to his temple; he staggers and drops to his knees.

Winding up for the knockout blow, I charge, forgetting for one agonizing second about my bad foot. It buckles, and suddenly we're eye to eye.

His pupils are mere pinpricks. *Finish him.*

I brace to deliver the final blow, and his face warps into Alistair's, black hair framing piercing blue eyes. So familiar, they see right through me. He holds his shaking hands up, begging me not to hit him.

Trembling with unease, I slam my fist into his forehead.

Alistair would never beg.

Second Coming falls to the cage floor, his body becoming leaner as he slumps onto his side. His face . . . gods, it's not a face at all. Smooth, indistinguishable, and without features—he's faceless. The harder I stare, the more wrong it feels.

I hear the emcee call my name and climb to my feet unsteadily, doing my best to hide the excruciating pain I'm in as I wave to the crowd. *Tough it out; you've had worse.*

Resker's hired muscle—the stubby one and the one with the boring, forgettable everything—enter through the right tunnel. They gather Second Coming between them and drag him out, taking the answers to all my questions with them.

More than exhausted, I duck into my tunnel and limp toward the locker room. The pain in my heel is blinding. I may have to break down and ask Alistair for a healing potion. I already know I won't be able to stay off my feet long enough for it to heal on its own.

A shadow blocks the light at the end of the tunnel, and I stiffen until I recognize his shape. Luca rushes to me, wrapping his arm around my waist to support my weight. "We've got to go, baby. Malach is getting the car."

His voice vibrates with tension.

I grind to a halt, my wings scraping the edges of the tunnel.

"You're afraid," I say, dread creeping along my spine. I've never heard his voice like this. Not when he was ambushed by

Malach's guys or when we were attacked at my apartment. If Luca is scared . . .

I gasp. "Did something happen to Alistair or Ciprian?"

Luca cocks his head, his eyes glowing yellow and metallic in the gloomy tunnel. I see my own wide eyes reflected in his. "Ali is fine, I think. I haven't heard from him, but"—he sucks in a raspy breath—"you just fought a fucking veydra."

"I don't know what that is," I say. "Is that why he looked like Roscoe?"

Luca groans. "The veydran are bad news. Mimics, mirrors— whatever you want to call them—they're death in disguise. When they lock on a target, they don't rest until they're dead."

"And I'm his target?" I demand. "Why? How do you know this?"

"They're the boogeymen of my home realm," he whispers, urging me to keep moving.

We step out of the tunnel into the deserted locker room. I sag against him, relieved that the other fighters have gone home.

"What can they do?" I whisper, replaying all the crazy things that happened during the fight. They didn't seem real, but living on the Fringes has taught me that the universe is crowded and nothing is impossible.

"They're shifters, but they don't have an animal or monster form, only what they can copy from others. Thankfully, there aren't many of them left." Luca runs his fingers through his hair, making it stand on end. "But that's not important right now! You've got to come with me!"

With the noise of the crowd muffled by the heavy metal door, I slide my hands to both of his cheeks. "Breathe, Luca," I say. "I beat him; he's not all-powerful."

"But he could be anyone. Hiding behind any face you recognize."

I stiffen, studying the familiar lines of Luca's face. His lip ring is exactly right, but he's not chewing on it . . . The itch consumes my entire body.

"How many times do you knock?" I whisper.

"What?" He blinks at me. "Celine, we've got to go!"

I drop my hands from his cheeks like I've been burned. "When you come see me, how many times do you knock?"

The confusion on his face is exactly right, from the crinkling of the skin around his eyes to the number of lines that pop up on his forehead. But he doesn't answer.

"It's not a hard question, Luca . . . or should I say Second Coming?"

He drops the confused act and grins, the expression wholly unfamiliar and horrifying on Luca's face. "Good girl," he purrs, breathing deeply through his nose. "So beautiful, so challenging."

Someone pounds on the metal door. "Baby!"

I shove fake Luca. He barely moves. "What the fuck do you want?"

"To deliver a message," he says.

From the corner of my eye, I watch the door dent from the force of Luca's beating. Did Resker lock me in here with this asshole? Keeping my focus on the threat in front of me, I lift my chin defiantly. "You're wasting my time."

He cracks his neck. Seeing the strange mannerism on my boyfriend's body sends a shiver of revulsion through me, but I hold my ground.

"You're brutal—just as he said you would be," he murmurs. "I didn't believe him. After all, most parents have a way of not seeing their children clearly."

I retreat two steps involuntarily. If my father sent him . . .

My enemy studies my retreat with unveiled interest, and I curse myself for letting the instinctual reaction slip past my guard. His face ripples, silver lines ticking across his skin until Luca's face is wiped away and replaced by my worst nightmare.

Cruel brown eyes. A hard stare. The copy is perfect, but it lacks the true menace my father oozes. Calm . . . until he isn't. I remind myself this isn't him. If it were, I would tear his head from his body and mount it on a cactus for the vultures to devour.

I force my lips to curl into an amused smirk.

"Damn, he's getting old." The taunt is barely true enough to get away with. There are new streaks of silver in my father's hair. Otherwise, he's unchanged.

"You fear him," the stranger wearing my father's face says. It's not a question.

I shake my head and laugh, letting bitterness coat the sound. "I loathe him."

"Yet, the resemblance . . ." He points to himself, then me.

"Don't even think about finishing that sentence," I warn him. "Deliver your message and get lost."

If I could kill this veydra, I would, but I'm wounded, exhausted, and dealing with too many unknowns—like how he recovered so quickly from the beating I gave him.

"S'lach wants you to enjoy your freedom."

"Done," I snap. "Anything else?"

"He says to tell you he'll see you soon."

"Cryptic message received," I snarl, advancing on him as fury overcomes my fear and my bladed wings begin to smoke. "If I ever catch sight of him again, I'll force my sword down his throat and make him pay for his evil deeds in blood. You can tell him I won't be silenced; not now and not ever."

Nodding, the messenger smiles and backs into the tunnel in even, measured steps, revealing a flicker of strange facial bands before he's swallowed by the darkness. "Until we meet again," he whispers.

His ghostly words echo, and I shiver violently as the door to the locker room is blown from its hinges.

THIRTY-SIX

CELINE

Luca catalogs my injuries, frantically running his hands over me. His knuckles are swollen and bloodied—it's the first thing I notice when he careens into the locker room. The second thing: yellow eyes, wilder than I've ever seen them.

The hair on the back of my neck stands on end, and I stare at my feet. *Chill out. This is the real Luca.* Even with the reminder, it's hard to shake the gross violation of being tricked. Second Coming, or whoever he is, toyed with me, wore Luca's face, and helped me limp from the tunnel . . . just because he could.

"I'm okay," I say firmly, pressing a kiss to his trembling palm. "I swear it."

"That was a veydra in the ring with you." Luca's voice is more hiss than speech.

Sickening déjà vu rolls over me. I don't want to have this conversation again. "I know."

"How?"

I flinch. The answer isn't going to make Luca calmer. It's best to get it over with, though—get all the bad out on the table so we can sort it all at once. Slowly and without inflection, I tell him what happened, including what Second Coming said to me while wearing Luca's face . . . and my father's.

"Motherfucking shuck. He was taunting you," Luca snarls.

I roll my shoulders, working through the kinks with a wince. Hearing him confirm my suspicions makes them easier to process.

"I'll kill him," he promises.

I risk lifting my gaze to his chest. "*We* will kill him."

Slipping my eyes closed, I raise my chin for a kiss. Luca's mouth crashes into mine, his tongue slipping urgently inside. I can taste his fear on my behalf. Pulling back, I frown. "How many times do you knock?"

"Two, why?"

His answer is a knife to a balloon—and I slump in his arms as the lingering panic and adrenaline evacuate my body all at once. "He didn't know the answer," I say. "That's how I knew he wasn't you."

"That was smart, baby," Luca says. "Veydran can't read minds —they're chameleons without consciences. We'll have to start verifying each other's identities, at least until he's taken care of."

"You called him a shuck. What does that mean?"

Luca grinds his teeth. "It's what he is—a soulless, faceless husk, stealing from others with no true identity of his own."

"Really?" I ask. That sounds strange . . . beyond creepy. I've never heard of creatures like that before, not in the celestial realm or the Fringes. I shift my weight and grimace. The pain in my heel is getting harder to ignore.

"That's the rumor at least," Luca mutters. "Veydran run the

monster realm. They're basically wardens, keeping anyone from escaping. They're evil—"

"I believe you," I say, squeezing his bruised hand gently. Luca talks about the veydra the way I used to vent about my father to— I gasp. "Where's Malach?"

Luca scowls. "He got called away by his right-hand guy, some sort of disturbance."

The itch spreads along my spine. Malach can take care of himself, but he's not a god.

"We need to find him," I say, yanking the wraps off my hands and tossing them in the direction of my locker. "Second Coming or whoever he is knew his name. If he sneaks up on him while wearing one of our faces . . ."

Luca curses. "You're right. He said he would meet us at the apartment."

"Then we'll go there first." I take one experimental step on my injured foot, and the blood drains from my face. "We need to get him a phone," I moan, doing my best to hide the pain.

"And you need a healing potion." Luca steadies me with one hand while fishing in his pocket for a glass vial of murky, sewage-colored liquid. "Alistair sent me with one. Just in case."

"Is it awful that I'm relieved and disgusted?" I plug my nose and down the chunky goo, denying my gag reflex through pure force of will. This one tastes even worse than the others. "My tab is going to be expensive to close."

Luca rolls his eyes, and I'm relieved to see they've returned to their familiar whiskey-soaked hazel. "There's no world in which he lets you pay him back. You know that, right?"

"I'm good for the money," I argue, groaning as the witch goop does its job and painfully mends my heel.

I test my weight and only cringe a little. It won't be fun, but I can walk on it without limping if I keep up a steady internal monologue made up entirely of curses. Steeling myself, I make for the door, gripping Luca's hand firmly in mine.

"We have one stop to make before we go home."

I shove through the door to Resker's office without knocking. It smacks against the wall and sends a puff of aging drywall dust into the air.

"Hello, Verity," Resker says calmly, reclining in her chair and steepling her fingers together. If she's surprised by my violent entrance, she doesn't show it. "You seem upset."

"Did my father pay you to have me killed?" I demand, refusing to waste time on bullshit. The blades of my wings are stained a deep red from the blood of the veydra.

Resker's eyebrows arch gracefully, drawing attention to the scar on her face. "If he did, I would owe him a refund, wouldn't I?"

"Don't fuck with me," I snarl. "You let a veydra into the ring with me—no warning, nothing—a veydra hired to kill me."

Resker pushes back from her desk and stands, stretching to her full height. "And I'll tell you, exactly as I told the face-shifting menace, I don't allow intentional deaths at the Mouth of Hell; only accidents."

"But you love a good show," I hiss. "Anything to entertain the crowd, right?"

She laughs. "This is the Vegas Fringes, Celine; we're all playing to win here."

"My life isn't a game, Resker."

"That's where you're wrong, angel. For people like us, survival is the only game that matters." She opens the drawer by her hip and pulls out a fat wad of cash held together by a thick, waxy rubber band. "Congrats on your win."

I take the money. It's crisp, smooth, and utterly benign against my palm, so why do I feel like each bill is dripping with blood?

Tonight proved I can't trust Resker, but I already knew that. Her bottom line will always come out on top. I'm not dead, and I got paid—so in her mind, we're square. But I won't forget this. And from the cool way she's staring at me across the desk, she won't either.

"By allowing him to fight here, you let him get his claws into the Fringes. Our Fringes." I point through the door. "Every person out there is less safe now that he's seen them."

"Wake up, Celine," Resker snaps, finally losing her calm. "They're never fucking safe, and neither are we."

I leave without a backward glance.

———————

Malach isn't home.

And I'm not handling it well.

"Where is he?" I snap at a helpless Luca. "Surely he shouldn't still be gone."

"I don't know, baby." Luca sets me carefully on the couch. He refused to let me walk up the stairs, insisting the potion needed time to work. Since I wanted his arms around me, I barely argued. My calm is in the past, though—I'm about to lose my shit.

"Something is wrong," I tell him. "I can feel it."

"I'll check in with Alistair," Luca says. "We need to warn him about the veydra, anyway."

New worry blooms in my belly. Alistair and Ciprian have enough on their hands tonight without adding this to the mix. Unfortunately, it can't wait. We need to tell them.

Fingers shaking, I pull up Ciprian's contact.

> I know you're busy. I wanted to tell you to be extra careful.

> Gods, that sounds stupid.

> Just watch your back, Casanell.

> And don't trust any familiar faces without proof of who they are first. There's a face shifter in the Fringes.

I groan, dropping my head against the couch.

Sending someone a string of crazy, popcorn texts is a textbook red flag. He's going to get the wrong idea and think I'm obsessed with him or something.

So what if I let Ciprian Casanell eat me out? He's nothing to me. *Liar.* He's something—if only a bad decision—but the thought of him being hurt sends my protective instincts into overdrive. Shit, I'm spread too thin to guard them all.

We're in too many locations, and until—

I groan as a bone snaps into place in my heel. Bracing myself, I rotate my ankle. When I manage that without pain, I press my heel against the ground gently. The agony is gone, as if it was never there to begin with. Springing to my feet, I rock on the balls of my feet.

"Feel better?" Luca asks.

I nod. "Luca . . ."

"You want to go look for Malach. I know, baby, I'm worried too." And he sounds it. I'm surprised at how quickly Malach became a normal part of my life on the Fringes. He shouldn't make sense here.

I open my mouth to respond, and something heavy smacks against my front door. It's followed immediately by a deep moan. *Malach.* I'm wrenching the deadbolts open one after the other before I can even think about why it might be a bad idea.

The door swings open.

Malach collapses at my feet, his face drenched in blood and sweat.

"*Schmi,*" he whispers, so softly I barely hear his cry for help. His thick lashes flutter and droop, cutting off my view of his green eyes—beautiful, even while glassy with pain.

My heart clenches.

Hinging at the hips, I drag him over the threshold and into the apartment.

Luca presses his fingers to Malach's neck. "His pulse is steady." Relief hits me so hard that I see spots. "Breathe, Celine. You can't help him if you pass out."

He's right. Freaking out during a crisis makes me worse than useless, and I refuse to be a liability. "Are you hiding any more of those healing potions?" I ask.

Luca's lips press into a flat line. "I gave you the only one."

My wings flutter. I want to lop my foot off for betraying me.

With trembling fingers, I unbutton the top of Malach's shirt. The skin beneath is covered in angry bruising. Gods, he looks like someone ran him over with a truck! I take a closer look and gasp as I recognize the familiar patterns.

"These are radiant magic blasts," I say, focusing on the facts to keep myself calm. It's hard to tell unless you know what to watch for, but the bruising is in a loose spiral pattern. "Only another *nish thatsha* could have done this damage."

"Will it kill him?" Luca runs his finger over a purple mark around Malach's bruised collarbone.

My heart stutters, and I shake my head. "He's too strong to die from this. It was meant to make him vulnerable . . ."

Luca's pupils stretch to horizontal slits. He jumps to his feet and slams the door, locking all three deadbolts. "He's out cold. If they were trying to soften him up, they might come here next."

Hot, angry resolve settles low in my gut.

Silently, I pick Malach up and carry him to the couch. Brushing the hair back from his forehead, I press a kiss to his cheek, aiming for the only spot not splattered with blood. Next, I grab my sword and sit on the arm of the couch, facing the door.

This is my fault, but I'm going to fix it.

"Let them fucking come."

THIRTY-SEVEN

ENCLAVE MEMO (INTERNAL)
We will strike the desert base in mass during the
auction. Send everyone. This is our only
window.

CIPRIAN

Sheena kicks her chair over. It clatters against the polished floor
of the venue, drawing gasps and murmurs from hundreds of
auction attendees. I grip my thighs under the table, forcing myself
not to drag her somewhere the evil, yellow-eyed monster can't see
her anymore.

"Your obsession is showing, Lysander," Sheena shouts. "If it's
me you want, come and get me!" *Fuck. No. That's not the plan.*

I told Celine and Luca we wouldn't be on the front lines of this
mess, but Lysander is using the women he abducted to force
Sheena's hand. The second he spotted her, tucked at the table
with Alistair and me, he's only cared about one thing: getting his
hands on her. This is going to get ugly—

The lights flicker out.

People start screaming and shoving. Gods. It's turning into a riot.

Someone wishes for light, and Sheena grants it, bathing the crowded venue in an artificial glow. A table of burly shifters—from somewhere in eastern Europe, if their accents are real—starts barking orders. They want to grab the abducted women and run off.

I can't let that stand. I'm enclave . . . I've got to protect them.

I push to my feet, but Alistair grabs my upper arm. "Don't even think about it," he says.

"I can't stand aside," I snarl, yanking my arm free.

But I'm too late—Sheena is already on it. Granting another wish, she sends the tables and chairs after the auction guests, using the furniture to herd them into a giant metal cage created by her purple magic.

I run around our table and high-five her, using the opportunity to check on her too. A drop of sweat rolls down from her hairline, but her eyes are bright and confident.

"Can you two handle this?" Sheena asks, pointing to the rapidly filling cage as she looks at Alistair and me.

"Duh." I wink at her. "Be careful, Sheena." I head for the cage, stuffed full of dozens of power-hungry supernaturals, and my blood heats. They deserve to be punished. They deserve to feel as helpless as the women they came here to buy.

I yank them all into a collective nightmare and show them dozens of cat-sized rats scurrying into the cage with them. Pink eyes, fleshy yeast-colored tails, and long yellow teeth. The rats are hungry, and the auction attendees are dinner. *Bon appétit, motherfuckers.*

I smile as they scream and trip over each other to get away from the nightmare.

"Ciprian, cut that out!" Sheena says.

I sigh and let the nightmare drop, watching with satisfaction as one of the guys who ordered his goons to grab the chained-up women cradles his broken arm. "You're no fun," I complain.

"Let's combine our magic," Alistair says.

I look at him in surprise. His blue eyes are bright and eager. My magic buzzes, and the excitement drowns out my annoyance with him. "Let's do it!"

It's easier this time. Pulling them into a nightmare, I force their attention to Alistair. He slides beneath the illusion like a knife through butter and compels them to sleep. One by one, they collapse on the floor. I smile widely at him, then wipe the expression off my face when I remember why I shouldn't.

Shouting breaks my concentration.

We leave the nightmare, blinking free of the illusion as Lysander reappears under the dome. Eyes wild with madness, his features contort, fur sprouting on his face in patches. He snatches up a hostage, presses his fangs to her throat, and dares Sheena to find out if her magic is faster than his teeth.

It isn't. I know it. She knows it. And, fucking hell, Lysander does too.

I feel like I'm trapped underwater as Sheena rolls her shoulders back and takes the first step forward. I shout for her to stop. Alistair reaches for her too, but she brushes past him. My fingers curl, helplessness sinking in as she descends the stairs and gives herself over to a monster.

———

"Give me the keys, or I'll show you a nightmare you'll never forget." I reach for Alistair, but he dances out of my reach, carefully guarding the pocket of his suit coat. Adrenaline and terror rip through me, coupled with rage. He has no right to keep me here. My best friend was taken, and I need to go after her.

"Just give her a chance, Casanell," Alistair says. "She's more than capable!"

"Fuck you!" I grab his shirt with both hands and shake him. "That asshole took her, and we just stood here and let it happen."

She's wired. I know that. She has a hidden camera with a tracker enabled. Eyes will be on her the whole time, but this was not the plan. She's facing him alone, and I hate that.

"You underestimate her strength. She can do this."

I open my mouth to yell at him again. If I have to wrestle his ass on the ground to get my keys back, I will. He doesn't care about Sheena. She's a bargaining chip to him, not the first real friend he ever made. If someone took me, she wouldn't rest until I was safe, and Alistair is stopping me from doing the same.

A portal crackles to life.

Idris steps through with someone draped over his shoulders. The fae is bloodied from the battle. He demands answers. I feel worse than awful when I have to tell him we lost Sheena.

His blue eyes ice over.

Then everything goes from bad to worse.

Idris lays the body—my brother—on a wine-stained table-cloth. The thready sound of Callum's heartbeat is barely there. He needs a miracle. He needs Sheena, but she's not fucking here. Panic unlike anything I've ever felt before consumes me, rolling from the top of my head to the tips of my toes. My face warps, my magic overflowing as my own fear spills out.

No part of me feels human anymore. I face Alistair as the demon I am.

"Give. Me. Your. Fucking. Keys."

Time passes in heartbeats.

Mine. My brother's. Alistair's.

Gideon comes through the portal. The battle is won. He wraps his arms around me. In a voice choked with tears, he tells me Dad didn't make it. I don't understand what he means. My dad . . . Dimitri Casanell . . . is dead? Killed by Lysander's gang of mangy wolves? It's impossible. But Gideon sounds serious, squeezing me until my bones ache.

I feel myself shutting down.

Guarding Callum, I let no one near him. It's all I can do.

Half feral, half numb, I listen to updates, feel Alistair's eyes on me, and wait.

Sheena returns, limping and frantic, and a piece of worry falls away only to be replaced by the crushing weight of my sadness. She heals Callum, but it's too late for Dad.

What did I do to help any of them? Not a damn thing. Some parlor tricks with Alistair to compel the captive auction guests into compliance. I was so proud when we combined our magic to subdue them. Now though . . . I know it was worthless . . . just like me.

The roaring in my ears is loud.

Everyone takes a portal back to the compound. I should go. Mom. Callum. The funeral.

My hands start to shake. It's embarrassing, a childish sign of fear. Is this grief? Have I ever felt grief before? Would I recognize it if I did?

Fingers link with mine, warm and strong. Mine stop shaking.

I breathe desperately. If I can get enough oxygen to my brain, I'll be able to think again. Think around this, find the positives— the funny parts. A strangled noise leaves my throat. It sounds nothing like laughter. Dad will never laugh again.

I yank my hand free from whoever is holding me back, step into the swirling lights, and let the portal carry me away.

THIRTY-EIGHT

ALISTAIR

Ciprian stumbles through the portal and doesn't look back, his shoulders sagging beneath the weight of his pain.

My heart twists, and for one heart-stopping second, I almost follow him.

Tonight went nothing like I had hoped. I now carry a burden I never asked for: the knowledge of how Ciprian looks while broken. His face crumpling as he dropped the mask, consumed by terror for his brother, worry about Sheena, then anguish when he learned of his father's death.

I couldn't stop those things from happening, I know that, but if I had kept my intel secret, would his father still be alive?

I hated Dimitri Casanell, but Ciprian loved him. And now he's broken. I saw it happen, felt his fingers tremble against mine . . . I won't be able to go back to the way things were.

Turning my back on the fading lavender sparks, I study the

crowd in the makeshift cell. Ciprian and I combined our magic to make them comply. Thanks in part to my compulsion, dozens of the worst supernaturals in the world are sleeping like babies as enclave personnel collect them for transportation to the compound in Colorado.

One of the demons processing the prisoners glances at me with suspicion. With Ciprian gone, I don't belong here anymore, and he knows it. I melt into the shadows and duck out the back before he can decide to confront me.

Outside the venue, the hot summer night rolls over me.

My skin is too tight. Prickly. But it's not the heat. Someone is watching.

Ordering myself to remain calm, I study my surroundings. It's bitterly dark. This part of town has more bankrupt event venues than streetlights. Ambitious humans once hoped to turn this block into a gold mine, but they cut costs, and it shows. The left-over buildings—most abandoned—are like shiny coins made of plastic and spray-painted gold. Scrape them with your fingernail and it won't take long to uncover the shit beneath the surface.

A flash of red catches my eye. My heart flips. I step closer—it looks like Celine's hair—then grind to a stop.

This redhead isn't Celine; it's a man, and there's enough moonlight shining on him to show me he's huge.

The stranger grins and winks at me before wiping something from his cheek.

A gust of wind kicks up, and I smell blood. His or someone else's? Gods, what am I thinking? The stairs of the venue are slick with blood, and I'm certain I've never seen this guy before. He can't be familiar; I'm imagining things. I'm rattled by what happened with Ciprian.

We're in the Fringes, though. I can't let anyone get away with staring at me this way.

I advance on the stranger. He retreats into the dark alley as my phone vibrates. Sighing, I stop and pull it from my pocket. There are a handful of missed calls from Luca and a confusing text telling me not to trust my eyes. With one final glance at the empty alley, I shake my head and leave the strange man to the shadows.

I drive to Celine's place on autopilot, my mind a mess of thoughts and memories I'd rather not have. The despair on Ciprian's face . . . I wouldn't blame him if he decided to leave Vegas behind forever. He's an enclave heir, for fuck's sake . . . and with his father dead, there will be a power vacuum to fill.

He doesn't belong here anyway.

I may never see him again.

Groaning, I push Ciprian from my mind, park my car, and get out. Immediately, the scent of fresh blood sinks into my nose. *Malach.* I've smelled his blood before—on the apartment windowsill and after he was burned during the angel attack—but this is worse. Much worse.

I'm running before I can consider the risk, taking the stairs three at a time. If Malach is hurt—the giant war machine that he is—then Celine and Luca . . .

No, don't go there, Ali.

The door is streaked with blood. It looks solid enough, but they came in through the window last time. Did I even glance at it as I was driving up? Would I have noticed if something was wrong? My distraction is a problem. I used to notice everything.

Heart racing a million miles an hour, I snarl and brace myself to break the door down.

"Who's there?" Luca demands, and I hear scuffling.

I groan, planting my hands on my knees as I catch my breath. "It's me. Let me in."

I wait for the door to open, but it doesn't. Instead, I hear only whispers.

"Tell me what you're allergic to," Luca says. His voice is wary.

"Tomatoes . . . Are you okay?"

I sag with relief as the door opens to Luca's grim face. I step inside, and he closes the door behind me quickly, locking it in jerky, efficient movements. Celine is slumped on the arm of the couch, a sword clasped in her fingers. She's guarding an unconscious Malach.

"Tell me what happened," I say as gently as I can.

"Dad sent a new assassin." She scrubs her free hand through her hair, wincing when her nails catch on her disheveled braids. It's one of the few times I've ever seen her with a hair out of place. Her beautiful, striking, red—

My stomach churns. "Angel, I wouldn't ask you this if it weren't important, but can you tell me what your father looks like?"

"Godsdammit!" Celine's fingers clench around the hilt of the sword as she snaps to attention. "You saw him, didn't you?"

I nod slowly. "I think so." *That's why he seemed familiar.*

Luca frowns. "I don't get it. How would you know?"

"Because I look just like him," Celine snarls. "Hair, eyes, even my fucking nose." She thumps the bridge angrily, a furious scowl contorting her pretty face.

"He was watching me," I tell her. "From the shadows outside the auction . . ."

She pushes off the arm of the couch, dropping the sword to reach for me. "Did he try to hurt you?"

I shake my head. "He smiled. And winked."

"Creepy shuck," Luca mutters.

I tilt my head as they exchange glances. "What aren't you saying?"

"I don't think you saw my actual father," Celine admits. "I think you saw the veydra he hired to come after me. It wore his face earlier . . . after we fought at the Mouth of Hell."

"Wait, wait, wait." I hold up a hand. "Your father's new assassin is a face shifter who signed up to fight you in the cage?"

She grinds her teeth. "He got a kick out of fucking with me too."

I look at Luca. "That's why you asked about my allergy. You were worried he was pretending to be me."

He bobs his head. "We'll need to verify identity every time we've been apart. It's annoying, but it's the only way to make sure he doesn't sneak into Celine's bed and kill us all when we least expect it."

On the couch, Malach groans.

"What happened to him?" I push the infuriating image of an assassin sneaking into Celine's bed from my mind.

"We don't know—" Celine's voice cracks. "He collapsed by the door an hour ago."

"I'm out of healing potions," I say. "But I can contact the witch who sells them to me. She guarantees delivery within twenty-four hours."

"Thanks, but he'll be mostly healed by then." Sighing, Celine pushes the hair out of Malach's eyes, then faces me. "Where's Ciprian?"

My mum thinks nothing remains of me but the monster. She's wrong. I'm sure of that because I've been dreading this question with every drop of humanity left in my body.

"He took a portal back to the compound," I say. The sentence comes out flat, like it means nothing to me, even as the truth tears me apart.

"What?" Luca takes two steps toward me. "Why? Is he okay?"

I loosen the knot of my tie, yanking at it until I can catch my breath. "No. No, he isn't. Dimitri Casanell was killed tonight."

Stunned silence greets the announcement.

Thanks to Ciprian, they know about my agreement with Sheena. It's a silver lining. I have no idea how I would explain if I had to keep everything a secret.

Celine's wings droop. "Is Sheena okay?"

I nod, relieved to deliver some good news.

Luca strides to the kitchen, drags a bottle of whiskey from the cabinet, and offers it to me silently. I unscrew the lid and let the liquor blaze a burning path down my throat.

Celine holds out her hand, and I pass her the bottle. She takes a sip. Her brown eyes are glassy with unshed tears when she hands the whiskey off to Luca. "Do you think he'll come back?"

She could mean the veydra, but I know she doesn't. My angel, the woman who carved her name into every inch of my heart, is far too strong to cry over an enemy. And Ciprian Casanell is not our enemy. I fear he never was.

Regret burns me, twice as hot as the liquor. I've been too angry and confused to accept what was happening in front of me. I pushed Ciprian away, forced his hand, then stood silently to the side as he lost someone he couldn't replace.

If he doesn't come back, it won't be Celine's fault, it will be mine.

THIRTY-NINE

CELINE

The veydra's rippling features play on repeat in my head. Like a slot machine cycling through symbols—except there's no luck involved. It lands on my father's face every time.

I wonder if I'll ever sleep well again. A shiver rocks me. I pull the blanket up and tuck it under my chin. There's no relief, though, because this cold has nothing to do with my body and everything to do with my past.

The memory overwhelms me before I can wall it off.

"You humiliated me in front of the other *thatsha*."

"I'm sorry, Father." I hang my head and curse my wings.

As soon as the meeting devolved into an argument, they turned to blades. Raised voices, the heavy anger of the other rulers . . . My wings knew what came next. Malach angled his body in front of me, trying to hide my wings from my father and his friends, but he wasn't big enough, and the clinking gave me away.

"You lack the discipline to rule."

Anger simmers in my belly, but my terror keeps it banked. If he knew how mad I was . . . It isn't worth imagining what he would do. I clench my hands, dulling my overflowing emotions by digging my nails into my palm until the pain drowns everything else out.

Father's cold eyes, the rigid tension in his jaw . . . There's nothing I can say to fix this.

Defeated, my shoulders dip. I'm old enough now to know my wings are his excuse. He's going to hurt me no matter what because the council meeting didn't go his way. The injustice makes me reckless.

"I don't want to rule," I say quietly, the tiniest hint of fervor infecting my tone.

Father's head tilts, an odd light in his gaze. "Wait for me in the training room, Celine. If you can defeat me, I'll forgive your childish act of rebellion. If not . . ." He lets the consequences hang in the air between us along with a flimsy strand of hope. It's a false hope. I'm twelve years old. There's no reality in which I defeat him in combat.

Determination sinks its teeth into me anyway, and I swear to the gods alive and dead that I'll try my hardest. And maybe, just maybe, I'll be able to give him a taste of the pain he loves to inflict on others.

Luca touches my back. It's enough, thank the gods—who I'm now convinced were never alive to begin with—to pull me out of the memory. "Are you okay, baby?" he asks.

Smile, I order my face. *Reassure him*. But like my wings all those years ago, my face has a mind of its own. It crumples, and Luca is ready—his strong arms curling around me, narrowly avoiding the sharp edges of my wings.

"I want it to be over," I whisper. "Seeing his face again . . . I hate him, Luca."

He's silent as he considers what I said, then hums under his breath. "If you want him gone and for this to be over; we'll have to stop playing defense."

I frown. Is that what we're doing?

Alistair is keeping watch in the living room while we rest. Bracing for the next attack. Hiding, no, cowering in this apartment. Damn me, he's right—everything I've done is defense. I spent two decades reacting to my father's attacks, and here I am doing it all over again.

This isn't the independence I wanted; it's a cheap copy.

"He won't come here," I say, sitting up in bed. "In order to kill him, I would have to take the fight to the celestial realm."

"So, we hunt his ass down," Luca says. "Then we come home and live life on our own terms. No more looking over our shoulders."

He kisses my cheek, and I study his face. The stubble, the dark circles beneath his eyes—even exhausted, he's stunning. My stomach twists. It isn't fair of me to ask this of him. He's been through too much because of me already.

"I swore I'd never go back."

"Technically, you aren't." Luca shrugs, and I raise my eyebrows. "No, think about it, Celine. You aren't going back; you're just poking your head in for long enough to deal with your dad. It's a necessary evil." *Or a false equivalence.*

"That's bullshit logic," I tell him. "And it sounds like a good way to get someone killed."

"Exactly." Luca grins. "Your dad. It's way past time for someone to kill him."

"But the veydra—"

"Sucks too, we can kill him while we're at it." Luca's pupils twitch, the shift barely visible in the dim light of my room.

"Malach will get his hopes up," I say.

"Malach is a big boy—huge, actually. He'll be okay, baby. All I'm hearing are excuses."

I shove him into the pillows. "I don't make excuses; I'm making you face the facts."

"I'd rather you faced your fears," Luca says. "They're as important as the facts."

Is he right? Am I focusing on the wrong things?

"I'll think about it," I whisper, pushing the covers off and climbing out of bed. I duck into my closet to grab a sweatshirt to ward off my chill.

Luca grunts. "Where are you going?"

"I can't sleep," I admit. "I'll take over the watch and send Alistair in to rest."

"Let me—"

"No," I insist. "You need to get some sleep, and I'm losing my mind. If I get tired, I'll wake you." I leave before he can find a better argument, stepping into the living room and rubbing the grit from my eyes.

Malach sleeps fitfully on the couch. His massive body makes the piece of furniture look small. Alistair's eyes flit from the door to me. I feel them on my body, seeing. . . fuck, who knows what Alistair sees. Too much. Always too much.

"I can take over the watch," I say, clearing my throat.

He blinks at me and pushes to his feet, abandoning the chair. It's not where it usually is—placed at the perfect angle to see the TV while remaining aesthetically oriented with the couch. He's turned it to get a better view of the door and window at the same time.

It ruins my living room setup, but I can't bring myself to care.

Silently, Alistair crosses the room until he looms over me, his clear blue eyes drilling into mine. Whatever he sees on my face must tell him my mind is made up, because for once he doesn't argue with me.

"It's been quiet so far," he says.

I nod and glance back at the couch.

"Malach hasn't woken."

"I should move him to the spare room," I say.

Alistair frowns. "No, this is better. If there's an attack, he's easier to protect here."

I raise one eyebrow. "Do you have a soft spot for him, Ali? After everything?"

Alistair looks away, pursing his lips. "I don't want to be the way I've always been," he whispers. "Rigid and unforgiving." Every word drips with guilt. He's being too hard on himself . . .

"It's not your fault Ciprian left," I say.

"Maybe not." Alistair's lips quirk into a wry smile. "But whether he comes back or not is a different story, isn't it, angel?"

I glance away. "Forgiveness isn't easy for some of us."

"Tell me," he says, "if there's hope for me to change. I don't mind if it's hard, but if it's impossible . . ." His voice is rough and desperate.

Something tells me we're not talking about Malach or Ciprian anymore, but I can't get into this right now. I break free from his tortured eyes and take the coward's way out.

"I'll wake you if there's trouble. Go and get some rest."

Alistair disappears down the hallway without a word, and my back itches more with every step he takes. I drop into the misplaced chair and sigh. I may be making messes right and left with decisions and communication, but if anyone tries to get through the door—no matter what face they're wearing—I'll end them.

FORTY

MALACH

The ache leaves no part of me untouched. Concentrated in my heart, it throbs with each beat. At first, that's all I know. Then I shift, and the fabric of Celine's couch grazes my arm.

I made it back to her. Barely, from the feel of it, but after everything that happened, it's a miracle that I managed it at all.

"Take it easy," Celine says. She's moving around. I hear her footsteps in the kitchen. Her scent grows stronger as she walks over to me. "Try to drink this, Malach."

The sound of her voice is such a relief. It overpowers the ache and gives me the strength to open my eyes and sit up. Her hair is tangled, and there are dark circles beneath her eyes. But she's alive. She's alive and here with me, holding a glass of water in one hand and a sword in the other.

"Are you okay?" I ask. The question comes out cracked and garbled.

"You're stealing my lines . . ." Celine looks me over, and I scramble to button my shirt, thankful that no one took it off while I was unconscious. "You're the one who crawled to the door and passed out."

I swallow painfully. My mouth is dry and tacky at the same time.

"Drink the water, please." Celine raises the glass to my lips, and I sip greedily. It burns my throat before easing some of the agony. "You were attacked?"

I nod, glancing up and wincing from the bright light over Celine's shoulder. Pressing the glass into my hand, she crosses to the kitchen to flip the switch.

"We were overwhelmed," I mutter and frown. The details are unclear—even in my mind.

"Your team?"

My heart shudders. I try to remember specifics, but everything is blurry. Clanging steel, flying magic—the worry that we wouldn't survive. Then nothing.

"Scattered or dead," I say slowly.

The words are simple, yet uttering them is excruciating—and it has nothing to do with my sore throat. Besides, "Celine is gone," no three words have ever hurt more. But my voice is cold, without inflection. *She will think you a monster.*

Celine drops to her knees by the couch, takes my glass, sets it to the side, then holds her hand out and waits. To salute. The lump in my throat threatens to choke me as I wrap my thumb around hers. The silent tribute to my lost guardians nearly snaps my control.

She understands. *Of course she does.* My eyes flutter closed as Celine presses her forehead to mine, our locked hands crushed between our pounding hearts.

"I'm sorry, Malach."

"The *nish* suffer," I whisper, weariness pulling at me.

Celine pulls away from me, her jaw tight. "Then they should fight back."

"As you are?" I don't mean to say it—wouldn't have, if not for the pain.

Celine absorbs my cruelty and goes impossibly still. "We can search for survivors once you're back on your feet," she says, retreating from me and the conversation. Suddenly, I'm desperate to stop her from pulling away.

"If you cannot face him in your mind, my truth, how will you face him in person?"

"Briefly," she snaps, "when I remove his face with my blade, so no one ever has to see it again."

She settles in the crooked chair and glues her eyes to the locked door.

I let the subject drop and watch the window.

Three days pass. Each one more confusing than the last. There's no sign of survivors or bodies—no sign of a fight at all.

Try as I might, I can't remember the specifics of what happened, only flashes of violence. My body heals, but the pounding in my skull won't go away.

Luca and Alistair suspect I sustained a head injury early in the fight. My brain has healed, but it can't return memories never captured. With my guardians gone, there's no one to fill in the blanks. My guardians. I brought them here only to lose them.

Celine plants her hands on her hips, eyes narrowed, but thankfully not on me. "I'm going," she says.

"It's too dangerous." Luca scrubs his hand over his face.

"It's way more dangerous here," she argues. "And he shouldn't be alone right now."

"He hasn't answered a single one of your messages—mine either—and he's certainly not alone. Even if your father doesn't think to look for you in Colorado, waltzing into the fucking compound without an invitation to visit the enclave is insane."

Celine studies Luca's flushed face calmly, then stands on her tiptoes to kiss his cheek. "I didn't ask your permission, Luca. I told you as a courtesy."

"I'll deny your time-off request," he grunts.

Celine rolls her eyes. "Nice try. I'll see you tomorrow."

"I'll come too then," Luca says, scrambling after her.

"No. One of us has to go to work, or people will talk. Besides, I'm not planning to knock. I'm just going to . . ."

"Hover like a fucking creep?"

"If that's how you want to describe it." Celine secures a back-pack to the front of her chest, tugging the waist strap low—almost to her hips.

I frown. "You haven't flown such a great distance in years."

"That's exactly why I should," Celine says, smiling at me cheerfully. "I'll be back tomorrow. Don't wait up."

"You waited for Alistair to leave on purpose," Luca groans.

Celine's eyes flash with anger before she hides them behind a pair of oversized sunglasses. "I don't need Alistair's permission to attend a funeral. He's the one who told me about the arrangements."

"That you weren't invited to," Luca reminds her.

"I'm going, Luca. Try to accept it." Celine kisses him on the jaw, waves at me, and walks out the door, shutting it firmly behind her.

Luca curses, yanking on the strands of his hair until they stand on end. "Only she would decide to crash a fucking funeral."

"It will strengthen her wings." I shrug. "I've been worried about atrophy."

"Gods, you two suck," he growls, throwing his hands up. "Not everything is about being as strong as possible. Rest, happiness—those things are important too."

I nod. He's correct about that, but we both know she's not preparing to fly several hundred miles to improve her fitness. "She's worried about him," I say.

Luca has no response to that.

FORTY-ONE

CIPRIAN

Surgeons have the decency to knock you out before cutting you
open, but the Casanell family has always preferred brute force.

Take Mom and Callum, for example. They just punched
through my chest and manually removed layers of years-old scar
tissue from my beating heart—all while sobbing buckets on my
nicest shirt.

Cathartic, sure, but I could have used an anesthetic first.

I leave the gardens in search of a drink. Whiskey maybe, or a
basic gin and tonic in honor of the old man? Who am I kidding?
I'm going to drink both. I have at least two or three more days of
blind drunkenness left before someone stages an intervention.

My eyes drift to the peak behind the compound, and I freeze.
Celine stands at the crest of the hill, her white wings blending in

with the clouds, red hair glowing in the light of the sun. I'm not even drunk yet, and already I'm seeing things.

Before I make the decision to go to her, my feet are moving, through the gate, around the towering stone walls, up the hill. Faster and faster, I climb until my breath comes in pants. Then I'm standing in front of her, blinking slowly to ensure I'm not hallucinating.

"No ripples in sight." I raise my eyebrows. "You must be real."

Celine came. I don't know what to think about that.

She runs a hand over her head. The gesture is uncharacteristically self-conscious.

I've never seen her this disheveled. Her hair is pulled back in a tight ponytail. Wisps have fallen loose to frame the sides of her face. Her cheeks are too pink—chapped, I think—but her brown eyes are bright, and they're looking at me like I matter.

"Are you okay?" she asks, her gaze flickering around me to the compound below us.

A choked sound leaves my throat. "Good enough, I guess."

"Ciprian . . ." Celine pulls her bottom lip into her mouth, a habit she picked up from Luca. "I'm sorry about your dad."

I nod, stop, then shake my head. "Are you really, though? How?" My father had flaws. I know that. Pretending he didn't won't change anything or make his death easier to accept.

Celine sighs. "I'm sorry that you're hurting. I'm sorry that you lost someone who mattered to you. I'm fucking—"

"Sorry," I whisper. "Thanks for that."

Tears well up in my eyes, and I brush them away angrily.

Celine takes one halting step forward, then another. She stops in front of me, and her body warms mine. We're as close to physically touching as possible, so why do we still feel a million miles apart?

"Y-you're here?" My question comes out pathetically jumbled, and I briefly consider tossing myself off the mountain and leaving Callum to carry on the family legacy alone.

Celine's arms wrap around me, followed by her wings. I sag against her, burying my face in her neck. Her hold is strong and determined. Cocooned by her wings, I'm protected from everything.

"You don't have to be okay, Ciprian," she whispers. "Not now. Not with me."

The words shred what's left of my composure.

Tears race down my cheeks, each one falling faster than the last. I breathe through my nose desperately. Even the air smells like Celine, and I want more of it.

"I'm sorry I didn't come to the funeral," she says. "I was a little late; it's been a long time since I flew that far and—"

"You flew here?" I pull back until I can see her face. "Is that safe?"

Celine groans. "Do you all have a secret group chat where you coordinate your reactions in advance?"

I roll my eyes. "Excuse us for being concerned that you flew from Nevada to Colorado. I didn't know you were a human jet; I've never even seen you lift off."

The corner of Celine's mouth tilts into a crooked smile. Her appearance makes perfect sense now. Gods, she flew hundreds of miles, and the only signs are a few pieces of dangling hair and some windburn. She's magnificent.

"You didn't answer my texts," she whispers, ducking her chin. It's the second nervous gesture I've seen from her since she got here.

It throws me off balance.

"I didn't know how," I admit.

She stands up straighter, drops her wings from around me, and takes a step back. "That's okay, I figured that. I only wanted to —fuck!" She groans, and I realize that Celine—the most self-assured person I've ever met and the only one without swollen, leaky eyes or a stuffy nose—is embarrassed.

It's the strangest thing I've ever seen . . . and I have nightmare powers. Speechless and kind of fascinated, I watch her unravel.

"I wanted to make sure you were okay," she sputters. "I didn't like the idea that you were going through something horrible alone. I've been there, and I wouldn't wish that on anyone, so I flew out here to make sure you had someone in your corner. I thought I would figure out what to say to you on the way, but I couldn't—still can't—find the right words."

She points wildly at the compound, wings trembling. "First, the big castle-prison loomed in the distance, and then I saw all of you grouped around the grave, and I panicked. I don't belong here, Ciprian. And I don't even know if you want me here, but I couldn't leave without making sure you were—"

I cup her face and kiss her.

Her being here . . . . Messy, vulnerable, and out of control: it means everything.

Our kiss tastes like summer and wind, with the faint chemical edge of her sunscreen mixing with the salt of my tears. Celine sighs into my mouth, her lips relaxing as my tongue slips in to tangle with hers.

Her hands wander up my neck and into my hair until her nails graze my scalp. Goosebumps explode along my arms and lower back. The wind blows, and her downy feathers flutter against my skin. I lose myself in the moment and hope I never find my way out.

When Celine pulls back, I have to stop myself from clinging to her.

She runs the tip of her tongue over her lower lip and clears her throat. "Anyway, I wanted to make sure you were okay, which I've done, I guess. Umm, I've got a long flight back. I should probably get going."

My eyes flick to the backpack on the ground a few feet away. "Aren't you tired?"

"I'll be fine." She smiles, but I don't miss the wince when she rolls her shoulders.

"Please stay," I say. "Luca will kick my ass if I let you fly sleepy."

"This is private time for your family; I don't want to intrude."

I laugh. "I'm good at sneaking around. You won't have to see them." Grabbing her bag, I back away slowly, prepared to hold her stuff hostage if I need to.

"Ciprian, I don't know about this . . ."

"Which settles it," I argue. "If you weren't exhausted, you wouldn't even consider it."

"What if someone arrests me?"

"For what?" I raise my eyebrows. "You've been cleared of charges, and you're my guest."

When she frowns and sighs, I know I've got her and take off. She follows me a second later, and it's all I can do not to sprint down the hill. With the sun crowding the horizon and Celine coming home with me, I'm reckless and painfully alive.

Since I'm not ready for her to see how creepy the Hall of Nightmares is, I head for the shifter wing. Joshua and Sarah keep a room for me there, and I've never been more grateful.

Wrapping a nightmare around us both, I tiptoe through the front door and down the hall to the Therion family's personal apartment. Carefully, I ease the door open, my heart pounding with excitement when it creaks like I knew it would.

I'm almost disappointed when we make it to my room without running into anyone. Then I get nervous. Shutting the door behind us, I hand Celine her backpack.

She shakes her head. "Very impressive, Casanell."

"Thanks."

"I meant the house," she jokes.

I clap my hand over my heart, glad that I decided to bring her here and not to the demon wing. Joshua and Sarah enjoy a cozy, lived-in space. Mom, on the other hand . . .

"Is this the room you grew up in?" Celine glances around, taking in the small sitting area, attached bathroom, and the big bed against the wall.

I run my fingers through my hair, suddenly nervous. "Actually, no. This is the shifter wing, but Sarah set this room up for me when I was little."

"Too hard to walk next door to your own?" Celine raises one eyebrow.

"Something like that." I stare at my feet, unsure if I want to get into all this.

Celine lifts my chin gently and says, "You don't have to feel weird about it." She gestures around the room. "I come from money too, and I promise you: if I'd had an escape hatch to a getaway room as a kid, I would've taken it most nights."

Sighing, I lean into her touch. "Yeah. I guess that's what we did—my brother and I." She glances at a picture on the wall and raises one eyebrow. I nod. "The enclave heirs at their finest."

It's of Callum, Gideon, and me. Arms tossed around each other, we're young and happy. My smile's so big it looks like I'm advertising my missing front tooth. With curls poking out in all directions, Gideon towers over us, his long limbs awkward and gangly.

Callum's body is angled partially in front of mine; his eyes focused on something behind the camera. I've wondered repeatedly over the years what he saw, because his stance is protective—my big brother putting himself between me and anything that might hurt me.

Sarah blew this picture up and hung it in here because she loves it. I've thought about taking it down a million times, but I can't stand to disappoint her and . . . part of me loves it too.

The feathers of Celine's wings quiver, and I rip my focus away from the past.

Jaw clenched, her eyes are glassy and far away. A trickle of fear hits me, and I frown. That night on the bathroom floor, Celine's fear was the strongest I'd ever felt. She shouldn't have to fight her memories alone.

"For a while I wished for a sibling," she whispers. "At first, I thought adding a better offspring to the mix would make him happy. Make me less of a disappointment."

"It was only when I got older that I realized it wouldn't have fixed him. That was when I started wanting a sibling for selfish reasons—so they could deflect his attention away from me. As it got worse, though . . . Gods, I prayed every night for no one new to be born into our home. Having someone else I couldn't protect became my worst nightmare."

Celine blinks, then forces a smile. "I'm sorry, Ciprian. You lost your dad, and here I am complaining about mine."

"Don't apologize," I blurt. It sounds harsh, but I hate how small her voice is. Imagining Celine, young and without protection, fearing the imagined burden of protecting someone even more helpless . . . It guts me.

"I don't like to talk about it," she whispers. Her wings dip until the tips drag against the thick rug.

"You don't have to," I assure her. "But if you ever want or need to, I'm here."

"Rampage ramble?"

"Exactly." I point at the bathroom, sensing her need to be alone and collect herself. "If you want to shower, I can go find us something to eat."

Celine nods and then winces, pointing to the small backpack. "I only brought water and snacks."

"No worries, I'll grab you a shirt." My heart thumps in my

chest—the dumbass has no chill—but I'm stupidly excited to see Celine in my clothes.

She disappears into the bathroom, and I wait for the water to turn on before rifling through my closet, testing the softness of each T-shirt by rubbing it against my face. I've been crying so damn much, my skin is extra sensitive. When I find one that doesn't irritate me, I'm thrilled.

I snort when I recognize it. Green and faded, the raised Starfall Academy logo is flaking around the edges. I think I kept it out of spite after I was expelled. It doesn't take much to tear two holes in the back, and I get a petty rush of satisfaction by defiling something related to those hallowed halls.

Satisfied with the shirt, I sneak to the kitchen and make some sandwiches. Thankfully, everyone else is still gone, and I'm able to swipe half a dozen of Sarah's chocolate chip cookies too.

I don't usually eat in my room. Crumbs in the bed are barbaric—I'm not a baboon—but for Celine, I'm willing to make an exception.

After I close the bedroom door behind me, I find her sitting on the bed, working through the tangles in her hair with my brush. The Starfall shirt hangs midway down her thighs. Air catches in my throat. She smells like my soap, my shampoo, my conditioner, my fucking moisturizer too, and I can't get enough. Desperate for more, I suck in the first full breath I've managed since Dad died. Celine smells like she's mine.

"You okay?" She lets the brush fall to her lap.

I place the food on the table. Take one step toward her. Two. Three.

Her eyes track my movements, flashing with heat.

Then we're stealing each other's air. All I can smell is her mixed with me. I'm suffocating in it, but I never want to stop.

Celine says my name, her fingers tracing my cheeks.

My heart thuds painfully against my ribs. "Can I tell you a

secret?" I whisper, dropping my forehead against hers. She nods, and my eyes drift closed. "I think I'm a little broken."

She strokes my hair, so softly I might be imagining it, and says, "It's okay to be broken sometimes."

"Can you . . . for tonight at least, can you hold me together?" My voice cracks, but I don't get a chance to feel embarrassed because Celine's arms tighten around me.

"Look at me, Ciprian." My eyes flutter open to find golden runes dotting her bare arms, neck, and face. A shiver rolls through me as her magic grazes mine intimately. "I've got you. I swear it."

Everything quiets inside me. Pain, regret, longing; they're all silenced by Celine's sincerity. Because she means it—at least for tonight, she means it—and that's enough.

Her lips meet mine, full and a little chapped.

I shudder. *She made herself messy for me . . .* "I want you," I gasp into her neck.

"You have me." Celine pulls the faded shirt over her head, and I drink her in. Every curve, every dip. No one has ever looked this good.

I want to lick every inch of her, but her self-assurance is what's driving me wild. I want to live inside of that confidence. Consume it. Make it mine. Forever.

"You're overdressed, Casanell," she purrs.

I crawl toward her on the bed, unbuttoning my shirt as I go. Starting at her ankle, I drag my nose and lips up her leg, inhaling the smell of skin drenched with me. When I reach the crease of her thigh, she grabs my hair and stops me.

"Not now," she says. "We've wasted enough time, don't you think?"

The stubborn heat in her eyes makes me chuckle, and I give her a long lick despite the tension on my scalp. "Take that back, hot wings." Another lick. "Time spent between your legs is never wasted. I'd happily die here."

"You can drown yourself later," she moans. "I want all of you."

I freeze. She's talking about my dick, I know that, but the choice of words hits me hard. Has anyone ever wanted all of me before? Pieces, sure, but I've spent a lifetime being too much. It makes me as impatient as she is.

Clumsily, I rip my pants off and toss them off the bed.

Next, I grab her and position her exactly as I want, kissing her grinning lips, then leaning back to survey my work.

Wet hair spread across my spare pillow; her legs cradle mine.

Nearly satisfied, I grab the pillow I usually sleep on and slide it under her hips. With any luck, she'll soak it, and I can spend all night reliving this moment every time I breathe.

My fingers wrap around my length, tugging roughly as I take her in. Celine is a fantasy brought to life. I could jerk myself raw just looking at her.

"It's big," she whispers, dropping her fingers to touch herself.

I search her face for any signs of worry. "I won't hurt you."

Celine smirks. "Don't make promises I don't want you to keep."

Groaning, I guide my cock to her pussy, running the head over her clit until we're both trembling.

"Ciprian, please." Celine reaches down, wrapping her fingers around my cock and notching it against her opening. All it will take is one thrust, and I'll be inside her like I've dreamed about for months.

But no matter what she says, I refuse to hurt her.

I push in an inch and stop, rubbing her clit until her muscles relax around me.

Celine moans, tensing again as I work another inch in. She's soaked, but it's still a tight fit—impossibly tight. "You're doing amazing. So good." I stroke her thigh. "You can take a little more, can't you?"

Celine slides her legs wider and nods.

I watch, dazed, as she hooks her heels around the edges of the bed and stretches into a full split. My cock twitches—it's only a quarter of the way in—but Celine has locked herself open for me, anyway, trusting me with her body.

I close my eyes, try to get a grip, then rip them open. *Don't be a coward.* Just because I've never seen anything this hot in my life doesn't mean I'm going to shoot my load early again. I can handle this. *Please fucking handle this.*

I push in another inch, Celine moans.

Sweat beads on my temples.

Gently, I work her clit and rock my hips, keeping my eyes locked on her face to read each shift in her expression. I want this to be great for her. Incredible even. Something she never stops thinking about. If I don't ruin her tonight, I'm fucked, because she's already ruined me.

Celine's orgasm takes us both by surprise, and I lose an inch of ground as her pussy contracts. I work her through the climax, soaking up every gasp and sigh. I'm living for this effort. I don't care if it takes all night.

"You're amazing," I groan. "Feels so good."

"More," she whines, her head thrashing against the pillow. With her legs spread, she's got very little control, but Celine still tries to force me deeper.

Heat boiling in my belly, I give her what she wants—harder this time, until I'm more than halfway inside her. Her voice catches on a choked moan. "Yes, that's it! *More.* Fuck me, Ciprian. *Please.*"

All reason leaves me.

My hips snap forward, burying me balls-deep in her warm, wet heat.

She comes again, strangling my cock in the process. I refuse to slip out, holding still, stuffed all the way inside her as pleasure devours me one bite at a time.

I see stars. Then her legs are wrapping around my waist, heels digging into my lower back, lips crashing against mine. I kiss her desperately, pleasure and tension colliding inside me. "Am I hurting you?" I demand.

"Yes," she gasps. "And it's amazing, don't stop."

"Okay, I won't. I promise." Stroke after stroke, I drive her into the bed without mercy. The pillow slides out from under her hips. I toss it out of the way and tilt her until I have the angle I want, slipping impossibly deeper.

She screams. Her head knocks against the headboard. I slide my hand behind her, a barrier to keep her from hitting it again.

Then I fuck Celine like I want her to be as broken as I am.

Except she's too strong for that.

She takes every stroke, her nails digging vicious half-moons into my shoulders even as her lips give me the sweetest kisses.

Exactly as she promised, Celine holds me together while I take her apart.

By the time my orgasm crashes over me, I've lost count of how many times I've driven her over the edge. Our bodies are slick with sweat, her hips are bruised from my fingers, and my bed smells like the perfect combination of both of us.

Celine is here. For me. For now, that's all that matters.

Lying on my stomach between Celine's spread legs, with my head pillowed on her stomach, I wake when the door swings open and bangs against the wall.

"I need to know you're okay, Ciprian. You can't wallow alone.

If we're going to be fucking sad, we can be fucking sad together—oh fuck."

I crane my neck in time to see Callum's mouth drop open.

Sheena chases him into the room, hand outstretched. "Come back here," she hisses. "I told you not to barge in."

Celine looks at them calmly, like two lunatics didn't just burst into the room. "Good morning," she says, yawning.

I drag my arm up to cover her bare chest and shoot my brother a death glare. He hasn't moved an inch.

Sheena giggles. "It's great to officially meet you. We're incredibly sorry about this. Callum was crazy worried about Ciprian and—"

"You're exaggerating," Cal mutters, shifting his weight uncomfortably as his olive-toned cheeks turn pink. "I'm sorry to intrude."

"Sheena and Callum, meet Celine," I say proudly. "She was also crazy worried about Ciprian and flew all the way here to make sure he was okay."

"Eww. Don't talk about yourself in third person," Celine says.

Sheena nods. "It's creepy."

I frown, not loving how they immediately ganged up on me. "This isn't bestie behavior," I tell Sheena. "Read the handbook."

"My bad, I'll get right on that." She grabs Callum's arm. "Since we know you're okay now, we'll get out of your—"

"Where's squirt? Is he depressed?"

I groan loudly at the booming voice and brace myself for the storm that's coming.

Sheena tries to head him off, I'll give her that, but it's kind of like asking a blade of grass to stop a tornado. Gideon scoops her up with one arm and keeps right on coming. "It's okay, baby. I won't stay long; I want to make sure he's hanging in there."

I look at Celine and sigh. "I'm really sorry about this."

When Gideon spots us, he whistles loud enough to damage my eardrums.

I shoot him a glare. Celine's going to kill me for this. I'll never get to touch her again and—Her giggle steals the fury from my panic, and I'm so relieved she finds this funny instead of offensive that I slump against her stomach and disassociate.

If I don't look at them, they'll leave. Right?

"We would love to join you for breakfast," Celine says.

Wait, what? I've clearly missed something. Lifting my head, I glance between them all, unsure how they've managed to trap me. Callum still hasn't moved. I'm pretty sure the sight of me in bed with someone cracked his brain. Honestly, it's insulting.

Locking eyes with Sheena, I widen mine. Gods bless her, she takes the hint and forcefully manhandles Callum from the room. "We'll meet you in the kitchen," she grunts breathlessly, using her full bodyweight to shove Gideon's big ass through the door. "Sarah and Joshua are having breakfast with your mom."

I nod, relieved and disappointed that I won't get to introduce Celine to the rest of my family. When the door closes behind them, I shake my head and groan.

Celine laughs. "I've never seen you that scared. Also, your brother is—"

"Don't say it," I beg. "Please don't say anything about how my brother, an incubus demon, is—"

"Almost as hot as you," she teases.

I kiss her then, pressing her deep into the mattress until she gets tired of pretending to be weaker than me and pins me beneath her. I rock my hips, and Celine grins. "Hold that thought. We have to get ready for breakfast."

I groan and sulk and argue and whine, but she refuses to take pity on me.

The only comfort available to me comes from planning my

revenge on Callum and Gideon. Sheena, I'll spare, but those two assholes are going down.

FORTY-TWO

UNSPOKEN RULE OF THE FRINGES #89:
NEVER GET TOO COMFORTABLE.

CELINE

After a whirlwind breakfast with Sheena and her guys, Ciprian and I spend the rest of the day in bed. When the sun sets, though, I know it's time for me to go home.

"Idris will make a portal for you," Ciprian says, looking up from his phone.

I raise my eyebrows. "Are you sure he doesn't mind?"

Ciprian snorts. "He always minds, but that never stops anyone from asking."

After the wing goes quiet, we sneak out, hand in hand. I'm pretty sure the Therions know I'm here by now, but they haven't bothered us, and the risk of getting caught is exciting.

Bathed in darkness, we meet the fae by the fountain in the courtyard.

"Thank you," I whisper. "I appreciate this."

Idris sighs. "At least someone does."

He raises his hands, and purple sparks light the air. Within seconds, I find myself stepping into the swirling magic with a smile on my face. Sheena has her hands full, but I'm surprised by how much I liked them all. I'm even more surprised when I feel Ciprian follow me into the portal.

The twist in my belly coalesces until my entire body is being squeezed through a tube. A second later, the portal ejects us, and I stumble into an alley I recognize. It's only a few blocks from the Fang.

Ciprian pops out next to me and raises his eyebrows. "This must be where Idris sent Sheena for her meetings with Alistair."

I consider Sheena and her guys. I'm not sure how they define the relationship, but it's clearly a relationship. Even while exhausted from everything they've gone through, they move like a unit, seeming happy to be together.

"Do you have questions?" Ciprian asks. There's a twinkle next to the shadow in his black eyes that I'm relieved to see making a return.

"Are they all together?"

Ciprian cringes. "I don't ask for details, but Sheena is with them all, and my brother and Gideon are sickeningly in love." I'm not fooled by his grossed-out expression. Ciprian is thrilled for Callum, no matter what he says.

"Your brother watches you," I point out.

"He's always waiting for me to fuck up," Ciprian says. "Or he used to be, at least."

I tilt my head, unconvinced. I lived for two decades with someone who was always waiting for me to fuck up. Callum's behavior struck me more as the watchful stare of the little boy in the picture on the wall—someone prepared to rain down hell on anyone who threatened their little brother. But what do I know about it? I'm an only child.

"He'll kill me if I hurt you," I say with a shrug.

Ciprian's head snaps up. "Callum wouldn't do anything to hurt you, I promise—"

"Whoa, chill out! It's not a bad thing, Ciprian." I pat him on the shoulder.

"You said my brother would kill you if you hurt me. How is that not a bad thing?"

I smile. "Because I don't plan to hurt you."

In a flash, the panicked, defensive expression on his face warps into something infinitely hotter. Blond hair ruffled from the portal; his expensive black joggers molded to his ass . . . Ciprian looks like trouble. And I want it.

He crowds me against the wall, eyeing me as if I'm wearing lingerie and a full face of makeup instead of barefaced and swimming in his oversized T-shirt and yesterday's jeans.

"I don't plan to hurt you either," he whispers.

I grab his face and pull it down to mine. Ciprian kisses me with everything he's got. It's pure seduction. He's entirely focused on giving me a kiss that exceeds my wildest dreams.

"Ciprian," I moan into his mouth.

He wraps his arms around me, pulling our bodies together as he says, "I love it when you say my name." When he holds me like this, I believe everything will be okay.

"Why did you come back with me?" I ask.

"Because you're planning to execute a recon mission in a hostile realm."

I caught him up to speed today while we hid away in his bed, needing to talk through everything and get my head on straight. Ciprian listened quietly when I told him I had decided to sneak back to gather information, but he never told me he wanted to go with me.

"I wasn't trying to manipulate you into coming," I say, the cursed itch digging into my shoulders. "This is my risk, and it should be mine alone."

Ciprian rolls his eyes. "The others aren't going to let you go alone, and they don't exactly blend in. You need my nightmares, hot wings, and I'm volunteering, no manipulation needed."

A muscle in my jaw ticks; I hate it when he makes sense. "I'm in charge," I tell him. "You'll have to listen to me. No cowboy shit."

"Cowboy shit? Me?" He jabs his thumb into his chest. "You've got the wrong guy. I love powerful women, and I'm more than happy to let you boss me around."

"As long as I don't ignore you."

Ciprian shudders dramatically. "Anything but that."

Smiling despite my worry, I grab his hand, and we walk to my place quietly. I'm acutely aware of how good his fingers feel against mine. Somehow, this infectious demon has crawled under my skin and embedded himself there, and I don't want him to leave.

When I unlock my apartment, I find all three of them waiting for me. Still, silent, and evenly spaced across my furniture, I can't help chuckling. "You all look like you've been petrified."

"Which reality star from our favorite show has a shriveled ballsack?" Luca asks, crossing his arms over his chest. I stare at him, confused, then realize he's trying to verify my identity with an *are-you-really-a-veydra* question.

"Probably most of them." I shrug and rack my brain for the guy's name. It's something dumb, I know that, but I can't remember what it is.

"Celine."

"I know, Luca, I know, but I can't remember his damn name." I groan at him. "Is it Bear?"

He shakes his head. "It's Wolfe, baby—but I'll take it."

Luca stands and crosses the room to kiss me. He turns to Ciprian next, surprising us both when he yanks him into a hug. "I'm sorry, man."

Ciprian grunts in response, but leans into the hug, his arms tightening around Luca's waist once his shock wears off.

"How did your wings hold up, my truth?"

Malach walks to my side and runs his fingers over my back, paying special attention to the spots where my wings are currently stowed. Shivering beneath his touch, I shoot him a look. But there's nothing sensual in his green eyes. As usual, Malach is studying me analytically, as if I'm a puzzle he's putting together in his head. It's infuriating.

"They're fine." I tilt my chin up and clear my throat. "I've decided to return to the celestial realm. Temporarily. I need to figure out what my father is up to."

"I knew you wouldn't let him win." Malach murmurs the words in our *thatsha* dialect, only switching to English to say, "When do we leave?"

"After we go over the plan. Several times." Alistair rises from the couch. His blue eyes dart to Ciprian then away, and the tension between them makes me squirm. They give off so much heat, especially when they refuse to look at each other.

"Food first," Luca says. "I'll order some pizzas, then we can hear what Celine's thinking."

I nod, doing my best to remain confident as all four of them focus on me.

Gods. This is happening.

I'm going home.

———

Grim determination fills me as we drive into the desert.

Squashed in the backseat between Luca and Ciprian, I refuse to panic.

We've gone over the plan. Several times, per Alistair's demands, and all of them refused to be left behind. It's reckless to bring them near my father, I know that, but if they're with me, I can at least try to protect them. All night, I tossed and turned, imagining the faceless assassin killing them while I was gone.

The illegal gateway I arrived through is camouflaged and located a few miles outside of Vegas. It can only be activated by someone with celestial magic, and as we get closer, I can't help remembering the last time I was here.

Scared, heartbroken, hopeful . . . My new life started that day, but it wasn't easy.

Luca squeezes my knee, and I realize I've been bouncing it up and down, my nerves finding an outlet while I was distracted.

"It's just ahead," Malach says to Alistair, directing him toward a large formation of rocks.

Alistair grunts and parks in the shadow of the largest boulder. He borrowed this Jeep from someone who owed him a favor. Since we're almost ten miles off-road and deep in the desert, I highly doubt anyone will spot it while we're gone.

Even with the doors closed, the celestial magic hums against my skin. It calls to me, and from the goosebumps on Malach's neck, he feels it too.

"Remember." I clear my throat. "Keep a hand on Malach or me at all times. The gateway doesn't work like the portals you're used to. It will only recognize our signatures and let you pass if you're with us. I don't want someone to get cut in half."

"Or be spat into the eternal beyond," Malach adds.

"Please don't explain where or what that is," Ciprian mutters. "I'll be glued to your ass, hot wings. I promise."

We get out of the Jeep, slide into our backpacks, then shut the doors. I watch the gateway shimmer, its delicate runic patterns clustered in the shape of a wheel against the rough rock face.

This is it. We're really doing this.

I roll my shoulders back. Luca laces his fingers with mine, and Ciprian wraps his arms around my waist, scooting flush against my ass. Alistair steps into my chest, dipping his thumbs beneath the waist of jeans.

I shiver and tell myself it's because of the enormity of what we're about to do.

With my free hand, I reach for the portal to activate it, then pause.

Malach is standing to the side, and it doesn't feel right. Going with my gut, I lace our fingers together. "You unlock it," I whisper before shifting into our language. "I don't think I can do this without you."

His beautiful green eyes dig into the side of my face.

They see too much. They always have.

"I'm by your side now, forever, and always. As long as my heart beats, you'll never be alone." Malach's vow is a punch to my gut, but before I can react, he slams his palm into the shimmering edge of the gateway.

It begins to purr.

Unlike the fae portal Ciprian and I used to get to Vegas, the gate is thirty feet tall and wide enough for a dozen people to walk through at the same time. It's a massive piece of magically engineered technology, and the most highly protected mode of transportation in our realm.

The purring gets louder, more of a whine now.

Hot, angry wind gusts around us, tossing my hair in everyone's face.

Then the gate sucks us in.

One second, we're standing in the desert while the sun beats down on us, and the next our feet are skidding along the dusty, cracked earth. A heartbeat later, I'm weightless, and all five of us are hurtling through space.

"Don't let go," I shout, the force of the wind doing its best to rip them away from me.

Lights flash—every color imaginable—some I haven't seen

since I left my home realm. I squeeze my eyes shut.

The whining turns to a wail, then a shrill scream, eerie and horrifying.

Luca grunts in my ear, his grip on my hand tightening. It's too loud, too rough. I imagine blood dripping from my ears, and I'm not sure if it's happening or all in my imagination.

It ends as suddenly as it began.

Like a rubber band snapping against an exposed wrist, the metallic screech cuts off abruptly. The wind rustling my hair is freezing cold. It makes no sense to me. The celestial realm is temperature controlled.

I open my eyes and look around, but there are no golden walkways. No bloodline-activated transportation tubes between the echelons. No background buzz of celestial lights.

Instead, we're standing in a brutal wilderness.

Craggy, jagged peaks shoot out of the crumbling ground like spikes erupting from the core of the planet itself. In the sky all around, there's a strange floating barrier made of glowing rubble. It reminds me of the cage at the Mouth of Hell—the one woven with dozens of enchantments.

Trembling from the cold, I look at Malach in horror. Something went terribly wrong, and the gateway we came through is nowhere in sight.

"This isn't how I imagined it," Ciprian says, chafing his hands against his arms.

Panic stirs in my veins, and I push it back desperately. I don't know what happened, but this is my fault. I led them here. I have to be strong.

Gritting my teeth, I face them and whisper, "This isn't the celestial realm."

Then Luca drops to his knees and screams.

EPILOGUE

LUCA

My basilisk hisses as fire tears through my body.

Celine's words were unnecessary. At least for me. My body knew where we were the second my feet touched the ground. Fear, primal and wretched, singes my nerve endings.

S-s-shift. Every muscle in my body shakes with the effort of holding back. I hit the ground, barely feeling the sting on my knees. *P-protect them. Now. Shift.*

The monster inside me is adamant, making all its earlier attempts to wrench control from me look like child's play. Venom fills my mouth, pooling against my taste buds as my fangs tear through my gums, bigger than they've even been before.

"Get back," I shout, cowering away from the unrecognizable sound of my own voice.

Celine shouts my name and reaches for me. She's afraid but I can't comfort her.

I'm losing control. Here, with all of them around me, my basilisk is forcing a full shift for the first time in my entire fucking life. I can't stop it. Twenty-nine years of resisting the monster, and it's removing my fragile illusion of control with one painful explosion of muscle and bone.

My spine cracks. The pain is worse than anything I've ever experienced.

My arms are next, absorbed into my body. I fall to my back—twitching—and stare at the sky. Any clouds I might see are blocked by the spiky bubble that surrounds the realm.

No arms. No legs anymore either. They're gone.

Yellow. Everything is yellow.

I'm not cold anymore. The chilly air feels nice along my scales, and I blink, a strange, hungry excitement bubbling to life in my belly.

For the first time in my life, my monster isn't curled up there.

We've switched places. My body belongs to the basilisk now, and Luca the man is confined to the small space in our gut.

Enraged and terrified, I scream to be set free. I'm a danger to everyone I care about, and I know exactly where we are. Every nerve in my body is shouting at me, telling me we're home.

This is the motherfucking monster realm.

AUTHOR'S NOTE

That escalated quickly. Brace yourself for monsters and mayhem.

Fear No Evil is available now.

If you enjoyed Shadow of Death, please consider leaving a rating
or review. These make such a difference for indie authors, and I
love hearing from you!

**Stay up to date by signing up for my newsletter or scanning
the QR code below with your phone's camera.**

ACKNOWLEDGMENTS

Shadow of Death was the hardest book I've written.

Even now, as I'm sitting here reflecting, my shoulders are around my ears. This book is where everything I've been working on in the Legacy Universe overlaps—and I badly wanted it to feel like a magically woven tapestry and not a NASCAR crash.

Only you will be able to tell me if I succeeded or not.

Since it was difficult to write, I'm even more thankful for everyone who was part of the process.

Mom, with the hype.

My sister, with the angst.

And my husband, who wielded the knife that poked more holes in this story than a slice of Swiss cheese. It pissed me off at the time, but I'm so thankful, because there are fewer holes now. Thanks for that, pumpkin.

To my editor, EJ Lounsbury—whose attention to detail makes every part of this book better, from the magic to the semicolons—you're a godsend!

And, as always, I couldn't do this without my beta reader team: Lisa, Gabe, Madeleine, Alyssa, Sara, Bruce, and Krista. You make my books better, but without your encouragement, I wouldn't be able to write at all.

Finally, for my readers: *Radiant Legacy* is halfway from my brain to yours—let's hope the back half of the transfer is everything we hope it can be. 🤍

ABOUT THE AUTHOR

 ALANA KAY is a romance author with a soft spot for imperfect heroes, tough heroines, and steamy love stories. She made her debut into paranormal romance in 2024 with her novel *The Last Wish* (Lost Legacy Book One) and completed the trilogy in February 2025. Alana Kay fell for romance novels in the early aughts after sneaking bodice rippers from her mom's dog-eared collection of paperbacks. A big believer in happy endings, she likes her love scenes on page, her adventures nonstop, and her magic off the rails. When she's not typing feverishly, she's either snuggling with her dog, cats, or husband in sunny Los Angeles or impulsively signing up for a sporting event she's not nearly athletic enough to commit to.

Author of the completed *Lost Legacy* series. Her in-progress *Radiant Legacy* series concludes with its fourth and final book, *Eternal Light*, releasing in 2026.

For updates, follow @AlanaKayAuthor on social media or head over to AlanaKayAuthor.com.

ALSO BY ALANA KAY

LEGACY UNIVERSE

LOST LEGACY

The Last Wish

The Last Dream

The Last Djinn

RADIANT LEGACY

Darkest Valley

Shadow of Death

Fear No Evil

Eternal Light
(June 2026)